The Palace of Eternal Youth
by Hong Sheng

The Peony Pavilion
by Tang Xianzu

The Peach Blossom Fan
by Kong Shangren

Adaptation by Chen Meilin

Better Link Press

Copyright © 2008 Shanghai Press and Publishing Development Company

This book is edited and designed by the Editorial Committee of *Cultural China* series

Managing Directors: Wang Youbu, Xu Naiqing

Editorial Director: Wu Ying

Editors: Yang Xinci, Mina Tenison

Adaptation by Chen Meilin

Translation by Huang Shang and Liu Tong, Kuang Peihua and Cao Shan, Kuang Peihua, Ren Lingjuan and He Fei

Interior and Cover Design: Yuan Yinchang, Xia Wei

ISBN: 978-1-60220-210-8

Address any comments about *Love Stories and Tragedies from Chinese Classic Operas (II)* to:

Better Link Press

99 Park Ave

New York, NY 10016

USA

or

Shanghai Press and Publishing Development Company

F 7 Donghu Road, Shanghai, China (200031)

Email: comments_betterlinkpress@hotmail.com

Computer typeset by Yuan Yinchang Design Studio, Shanghai

Printed in China by Shanghai Donnelley Printing Co. Ltd.

1   2   3   4   5   6   7   8   9   10

The Palace of Eternal Youth

About the Original Work

*T*HE PALACE OF *Eternal Youth* is an opera written by Hong Sheng, a native of Qiantang in Zhejiang (Hangzhou today). Hong Sheng was born in 1645, two years after the downfall of the Ming Dynasty. He died in 1704, the 43th year of the Kangxi period in the Qing Dynasty.

His family was wealthy and Hong Sheng was able to receive a good education. He composed poems when he was a child and entered the Imperial College in 1668. The following year he returned to his native place, Hangzhou. It is not known why he parted from his parents and lived in poverty, but in 1674, he returned to the capital and stayed for ten years, selling his writing to make a living. He went back to Hangzhou in 1691 and became even more destitute. He later traveled far and wide and died in Wu Town, Zhejiang in 1704 after falling into a river.

The downfall of the Ming Dynasty and his family circumstances had great impact on his life and work. This could be seen in the following lines, "A nation in mourning and a family in misfortune left me sleepless the whole night." To Hong Sheng, a nation in mourning meant the occupation of his hometown by the Qing troops. The fact that his famous tutors, Mao Xianshu and Lu Fanchao, died rather than take official posts in the Qing Dynasty, greatly influenced his work. The family in misfortune might have referred to the conflict between him and his parents, the death of his daughter, or the plight of his father, who was banished to

Xinjiang after a false accusation.

Hong Sheng was married at the age of 20 to a woman from an official family who was born one day after him. One year on the seventh night of the seventh moon, the couple enjoyed the moonlight together and Hong Sheng wrote a poem for the occasion entitled *The Seventh Night of the Seventh Moon*. A year later, his wife followed her father and returned to the capital. Immediately, Hong Sheng wrote a poem called *To My Wife*. It contains the following lines: "A hundred sorrows come to me in one day, and to whom shall I tell of my concern?" The sorrow of this separation made a strong impression on his writing.

Hong Sheng was first known for his poems and remained a very productive poet. One commentator, his grandfather on the maternal side, thought his poems tended to be gloomy and sad, but also noted something stately about them. Another commentator praised him for his unrestrained and uninhibited styles. He is mainly known for his operas, of which he wrote over 40. Only two, *The Palace of Eternal Youth* and *The Four Fair Women*, still exist. Of the two, *The Palace of Eternal Youth* is more representative of his work.

A friend of Hong Sheng wrote in a postscript to *The Collection of Tianlai* that Hong Sheng put more effort into *The Palace of Eternal Youth* than his 40 other operas. This was true; he spent a dozen years on it and re-wrote it twice. The first draft, called *The Aloe Pavilion*, was completed about 1673-1675. A second draft, *The Rainbow Garment Dance*, was written in Beijing. But the opera was not finished until 1688 when it became *The Palace of Eternal Youth*. It won immediate popularity and created a sensation in the literary world. It was so celebrated that in the summer of 1704, Zhang Yunyi, Provincial Commander-in-Chief, and Cao Yin, Head of Silk Manufacturing for the Imperial Palace in Southern China, took turns staging the opera.

The story of Li Longji and Yang Yuhuan is based on an old theme. It was used by Bai Juyi in *The Everlasting Sorrow*, a poem written in the Tang Dynasty, and the theme also appears in *Tales of the Everlasting Sorrow*, a prose poem written by Chen Hong. It is also found in more than ten literary works dating back to the

Song, Yuan and Ming dynasties, of which *Rain on Plane Trees* was considered to be the best. Hong Sheng's two later versions reflect his impressions of the earlier works and his own treatment of the motifs. In the preface he wrote that his aim was to exalt the love between men and women. It contains such lines as, "Since ancient times, who have remained true to love? As long as they were firm, they would finally unite," and "To borrow the story of Taizhen is to describe love." In the chapter on the lover's reunion, he used lines from *The Rainbow Garment Dance*, "Those who are close will understand it, and love will last forever." Hong Sheng's work is ostensibly about the love between Li Longji and Yang Yuhuan, but introduces other powerful themes. It comments indirectly on the social and political life of the time and touches on issues such as the misery caused by the excesses of those in power. In this respect it breaks the mold of the stories based entirely on brilliant men and beautiful women and gives a deeper resonance to the opera.

The love between Li Longji and Yang Yuhuan is more than the love between an emperor and his imperial concubine; it is a concept of love that ordinary citizens aspired to, as promoted in the novels written in the Song and Yuan dynasties. The desire to stay a husband and wife even after death, with the help of the Heavenly Emperor, has parallels in the story of Du Liniang and Liu Mengmei in the opera *The Peony Pavilion*, written by Tang Xianzu in the Yuan Dynasty.

But the story of Li Longji and Yang Yuhuan still retains elements of the traditional love stories of the Chinese emperor: Excesses and over-indulgence in pleasures lead to tragedy. Privileged by his relationship with the emperor, Yang Yuhuan's brother takes bribes, dominates the government, and squanders the people's money. People live in dire poverty but have no choice but to please Yang Yuhuan, as demonstrated in the lychee tribute episode that results in the destruction of the peasant's crops. These episodes inevitably draw to a tragic ending. The author's meaning is clear, but he was constrained by the conventions of the time, and thus arranged for a happy ending -- a reunion in heaven after Yang Yuhuan repents her sins. This is not convincing and is out of keeping with the rest of the opera.

Even with such shortcomings, *The Palace of Eternal Youth* is still an artistic achievement and a literary work of high ideals. Since it first appeared, the opera has been staged in many parts of the country. Extracts from "The Pledge," "The Secret Vow," "The Alarm," "Mawei Station," "Hearing the Bell and Mourning Before the Image" are part of the classical repertoire today. The complete opera has been translated into English, French, Russian and Japanese and is cherished all over the world by those who love opera.

We hope that our adaptation will introduce new readers to the beauty of Hong Sheng's timeless classical drama.

CHAPTER ONE

Taking an Imperial Concubine and Making a Pledge of Love

URING THE TANG Dynasty (618-907 AD), which lasted many hundred years, there were several emperors who showed determination and dedication in building up the nation. After the "Enlightened Administration of Taizong Li Shimin" there was the "Enlightened Administration of Xuanzong Li Longji", both of whom have been highly commended by historians. Li Longji, third son of Li Dan, at first had the title Prince of Linzi conferred on him and later was installed as the Prince of Ping for meritorious acts. After Li Dan ascended the throne, Li Longji became the Crown Prince and in the first year of Xiantian period (712), he succeeded to the throne and changed the title of emperor's reign to Kaiyuan.

When he first came to the throne, Li Longji was cautious and attentive and followed the advice of high officials. The cabinet ministers, who included Yao Chong, Song Jing, Zhang Yue, and Han Xiu, were loyal and upright and helped him handle state affairs. For a time, the country was prosperous, people were rich, prices were stable and the country was at peace. Swords and spears were stored in arsenals and no one violated laws. Peace, order and prosperity reigned for almost 30 years.

The title of the emperor's reign was changed to Tianbao during the 29th year of Kaiyuan, and Li Longji continued to rule for another fifteen years. During the later period, however, ranking officials who had served in the years of Kaiyuan had become old or had retired and the emperor, who had worked hard earlier on in his life to bring peace and prosperity to the country, now spent his leisure indulging in women and music. This led to the rebellion of An Lushan and Shi Siming and the loss of almost all of the Tang Dynasty's political power.

Since ancient days, emperors were said to have had an enormous harem of 72 imperial concubines, but Li Longji had "three thousand beauties" in his inner court. At first, he was fond of Jiang Caiping, or Lady Plum Blossom, but afterwards his eyes were on Yang Yuhuan, a native of Hongnong District whose her father held a government post in Sichuan. She had been a concubine of Li Mao, son of Li Longji, so she was in fact his daughter-in-law. Although Li Longji took a fancy to her, he was unable to make her an imperial concubine straight away. He made her a Daoist priest in the court and granted her the name Taizhen before moving her to the inner court. It is said that when she was born she had a jade bracelet on her arm bearing the words Taizhen; thus she was given the name Yuhuan (Yuhuan means a jade bracelet in Chinese) and her pet name was Taizhen.

In the fourth year of the Tianbao period (745), Yang Yuhuan was made an imperial concubine. Li Longji ordered that she be honored with a bath in the Huaqing Pool and sent two maids, Yongxin and Niannu, to attend to her and help her put on new clothes before she was presented to the palace. The emperor sat waiting impatiently in a side palace and ordered Gao Lishi, a eunuch, to send for her.

Gao Lishi went out the palace gate and said in a loud voice, "His Majesty orders Lady Yang to the palace." Yang Yuhuan was anxious to receive the order and was waiting at the palace gate. Though nervous she walked slowly and gracefully into the palace where she knelt before the emperor. In a sweet voice she said, "Your slave Yang Yuhuan is here. Long live the emperor."

On seeing a favorite concubine kneeling on the ground, a eunuch thought he knew what was on the mind of the emperor and said, "You may rise." How could Yang Yuhuan fail to respect the dignity of an emperor and rise in front of him? Still kneeling, she murmured, "I come from a humble family and I am poor and plain. I was fortunate enough to be chosen as a palace maid and was given a title, but I am afraid that I can never prove myself worthy of this high honor."

When Li Longji saw that she was humble, he could not restrain himself and praised her, "You come from an illustrious family, and you are as beautiful as you are virtuous. I am happy to have you as an imperial concubine."

"Long live the emperor! Long, long live the emperor!" That was all Yang Yuhuan could utter to show her gratitude.

Gao Lishi used the opportunity to say, "You may rise." Yang Yuhuan rose slowly only on his order because she knew that unlike the other eunuchs he was the emperor's confidant and had been appointed General of the Imperial Cavalry; he enjoyed greater power than any other minister.

Li Longji gave an order, "Let the feast begin." A group of eunuchs passed the order on and in no time, a feast was ready, accompanied by music. The emperor and Yang Yuhuan advanced to the table, the emperor to the host's seat with Yang beside him. Yang Yuhuan offered the emperor wine and Li Longji gestured to the palace maids to give her wine on his behalf. After drinking a few cups, they were relaxed and chatted to each other.

Li Longji said, "I gave orders for a nationwide search for lovely girls but failed to find the loveliest. Today I have a truly matchless beauty. You were given to me by the gods in heaven and should be the leader of the three thousand beauties in the inner palace. Therefore, I confer on you the title Guifei (Imperial Concubine)."

Yang Yuhuan was clever and used the moment to express her devotion, saying, "I am overwhelmed by your praise, for I do not deserve such an honor. I am plain and clumsy and am afraid that I could never properly serve at your side. Your sudden favor has raised me to the skies. I can only learn from outstanding imperial concubines of the past, such as Feng Si and Ban Ji, while waiting faithfully on my lord."

Feng Si was an imperial concubine of Emperor Yuan of the Han Dynasty. One day, when a bear suddenly broke out its enclosure, Feng Si immediately shielded the emperor with her own body to stop its attack. The other imperial concubine, Ban Ji, was a female official at the time of Emperor Cheng of the Han Dynasty. The emperor once wanted to ride in same cart as her, but she refused, saying that an emperor should be with his ministers instead of favoring an individual woman. Li Longji knew these stories by heart, but he was glad to hear what the newly appointed imperial concubine said. They flirted and drank together. The palace maids joined in the fun and said that from now on Lady Yang would be the happiest woman. She would be like Lady Swallow who won the love of Emperor Cheng of the Han Dynasty. They wished the emperor and Lady Yang a long life and eternal love. The palace attendants did not wish to be left out and followed the maids' example by wishing that the love between His Majesty and Lady Yang would endure as long as the earth. Li Longji and Yang Yuhuan were happy to hear these sweet words and honeyed phrases and they continued to drink cup after cup together. Their spirits were high.

Gao Lishi said to them, "The moon has risen. Would Your Majesty like to have the table removed and take a rest?"

Li Longji did not wish to rest and said, "The moonlight is bright. I shall watch the moon from the courtyard with Lady Yang." A young eunuch quietly repeated this to musicians and a while later, soft and lovely music floated in from afar.

Li Longji went down a few marble steps and led Yang Yuhuan by the hand to the courtyard. He turned her slightly to gaze at her under the moon and saw a ravishing beauty, more delightful than all the flowers in the garden. Stepping back half a pace, he looked at her figure that appeared under the close fitting garment; he was very pleased. No longer able to wait he said, "Light the lanterns and lead us to the west palace."

Surrounded by eunuchs and maids, the procession immediately went towards the west palace where Gao Lishi reported, "May it please Your Majesty, we have reached the west palace." Li Longji told the eunuchs to withdraw and just the maids were left to wait on them while they changed their clothes. After a while, the maids withdrew and the two of them were left in the sleeping palace.

Touching her shoulders, Li Longji said, "Our love begins this evening. Let us love each other as long as we live." He withdrew from his sleeve a double golden hairpin with two carved phoenixes and a jewel box wrapped in a piece of silk with a love knot on it. To pledge their love the emperor gave them to Lady Yang. Li Longji wished that they would be like the phoenixes on the pin, always flying together, and like the love-knot on the box, two hearts as one. Lady Yang said gratefully, "Thank my lord for your gifts. May our love be as close and as firm as this hairpin and the jewel box, may the phoenixes never be parted, and may the box never be divided." Hand in hand, they went to bed. From that day on, Li Longji indulged in pleasure day and night, and neglected state affairs all the more.

After Yang Yuhuan won favor with the emperor, all her relatives received high honors. Her cousin Yang Guozhong, through repeated promotion, became the prime minister with powers second only to the emperor. Afterwards he accepted bribes, took private property by force, lived luxuriously and indulged himself in pleasures.

At that time, there was a military officer, An Lushan, who was a native of Liucheng, Yingzhou. His mother's second husband was a Tartar tribal chieftain called An Yanyan, so An became his surname. An Lushan had joined the army when he was young. Afterwards he enlisted under the Youzhou Military Governor Zhang Shougui, who approved of his uncommon appearance, adopted him and appointed him a frontier lieutenant. He was sent to fight the Khitan tribesmen who defeated him and forced him to flee. An Lushan had lost because he was a braggart who boasted of his courage and had made a reckless advance. His failure warranted execution, but Military Governor Zhang did not carry this out; instead he sent him to the capital to be court-martialed. This gave An Lushan a chance to approach powerful officials and offer bribes.

An Lushan was experienced in bribery and knew how to win the support of people who worked for high officials. He had a sworn brother named Zhang Qian who was a steward in the Prime Minister Yang Guozhong's house and had done good service there. Yang now had power and could do whatever he wanted; the way for An Lushan to seek his help was through Zhang Qian.

As the saying goes, "A servant of a prime minister is equal to an official of 7th rank." Zhang Qian was also devious and had been entrusted by An Lushan to give a large sum of money to the guards asking them to be lenient on him. He sent gold, silver and treasures to the house of the prime minister. Yang Guozhong accepted the gifts with a smile and said that he would see An Lushan in his mansion.

An Lushan was elated as the reply indicated that there was a chance that his execution would be stayed and he headed there at once. On the way, he thought about what had happened to him in the last few years. Fate and other people were to blame; a dignified man like him had been tripped up by trifles. He was like a dragon who could ruffle the sea but he had fallen into a ditch and had been treated like a turtle. However, he felt fortunate to have bought off the prime minister with a large sum, otherwise he would have died. While he was thinking about these things, he reached his destination. Zhang Qian greeted him at the door, "So you have come, Brother An. His Grace has accepted all the gifts, which is a good omen. He is now waiting to see you in the hall."

"Many thanks for your great help."

"Don't stand on ceremony. We are sworn brothers. Would you please wait in my office?"

Yang Guozhong was sitting in the hall. He had accepted the handsome gifts from An and wanted to do something to exempt him from a death sentence. It was an easy thing for a prime minister to do as there was always an element of luck in war and to be defeated was excusable. Also he could say that he saved An because he wanted to save a useful officer for the state. This thought put him at ease as it made his acceptance of the bribe and his disregard of official policy.

He had made up his mind when Zhang Qian appeared again and reported, "An Lushan is waiting outside."

"Bring him in."

"I will, Your Grace." Zhang Qian went out and beckoned to An from the door of his office. An Lushan had been sitting sullenly on a bench and stood up at once to follow Zhang to the hall.

From the hall, An Lushan saw the prime minister sitting on the host's chair. He knew he was in trouble and his behavior was exemplary. He at once knelt down and advanced on his knees to face Yang Guozhong. He kowtowed and said, "The wretched An Lushan salutes Your Grace."

"Rise," said Yang.

"I dare not, since I deserve to be sentenced to death."

Assuming the airs of a prime minister, Yang Guozhong said, "Zhang Qian has told me why you are here. Give me your own account of the offense."

Still kneeling, An Lushan replied, "I beg to inform Your Grace that I, the wretched, was ordered to attack the Khitan tribesmen..." Yang Guozhong was sitting and could not clearly hear what was said. He said, "Rise and speak." Only then did An Lushan stand up. His head hung down and he pressed his hands against his body. He continued, "Relying on strength and boldness, I, the wretched, charged with my men, but the tribesmen made a sudden attack at night and surrounded our camp. Although we resisted as best we could, we ran out of arrows."

"How did you escape?"

"I rode a horse and fought my way out with a sword. I hoped to be pardoned for my past service and did not expect to face a court martial." An went down on his knees again and kowtowed, saying, "Your Grace, please be generous and have mercy on me."

Although Yang Guozhong had accepted the presents and was prepared to help, he would not let An off lightly. He said haughtily, "To lose an army and bring humiliation to the country is a serious matter and you should be punished according to law. Though I handle state affairs, I cannot make a decision without authorization. I fear I can do nothing for you."

This frightened An Lushan and he cried out, "I can live a second life only with the help of Your Grace." Granting a favor was exercising power and it pleased Yang Guozhong to see him panic. He gave a strange laugh and said, "I have a little power, the emperor will follow what I say. There are certain formalities which are hard to explain and which I cannot tell you about."

An Lushan was astute and understood the meaning implied in the words; he saw a chance of life. He continued kowtowing and said, "My life is in your hands."

"Very well. Tomorrow when I go to court, I shall see what can I do. If it is possible, I shall save your live."

An did not stop kowtowing and said gratefully, "I own Your Grace such gratitude that I can only repay you by serving as your dog or horse. As you are busy, most humbly I take my leave." Yang Guozhong asked Zhang Qian to show him out.

When one receives presents from others one should do something in return. Sitting alone in the hall Yang Guozhong thought, "This An Lushan is a junior officer who was at the frontier and has never distinguished himself. He should now be sentenced to death for his offences. If I try to save him, the emperor will suspect that something is wrong." He stretched his hand and took down the memorial to the throne sent by Governor Zhang and read it carefully. As he read it a plan formed in his mind and he said, "Ah, I have it! The memorial to the throne mentioned that An's knowledge of six barbarian languages and his military skill qualified him for the post of a frontier general." He could make something out of this. He decided not to be involved himself, but to drop a hint to the Ministry of War to propose to the emperor that An be summoned to court to be tested by His Majesty himself. If this worked, An's life could be saved. After he had made this decision, he returned to the inner hall.

Naturally, the Minister of War acted on the Prime Minister's suggestion; he knew what Yang Guozhong wanted and did not need a detailed explanation. He presented a memorial to the throne. As was expected, Li Longji gave his assent, and furthermore asked Yang Guozhong to give the test on his behalf. In the meanwhile, the emperor whiled away the time with Lady Yang in the inner court.

CHAPTER TWO

A Spring Outing in the River Bend

AFTER LI LONGJI made Yang Yuhuan an imperial concubine, he lavished all his love on her. They feasted and spent day and night together. Yang Yuhuan on her part did all she could to please the emperor and keep his love. However, she became physically tired and when the emperor attended to state affairs she rested. One drowsy day in mid-spring Yang Yuhuan fell into a deep sleep.

The palace was still, the smoke of incense curled up; outside Chinese crabapples blossomed and orioles sang. Yongxin and Niannu, the two maids, stood outside the gate, talking quietly from fear of waking up Lady Yang.

The sound of music and singing in the neighboring courtyard suddenly woke Yang Yuhuan, who asked, "Where does the music and singing come from?"

Yongxin and Niannu hurried in and kowtowed, saying, "There was a gathering in the neighboring courtyard, and the noise unexpectedly woke Your Ladyship. It is now about noon. Would Your Ladyship like to get up? All is ready for Your Ladyship's make-up."

Yang Yuhuan stood up listlessly and walked slowly to the mirror; Yongxin and Niannu helped her sit down. Looking in the mirror, she combed her black hair. Yongxin handed her a hairpin saying, "Your Ladyship please use the hairpin." She presented the rouge and said, "And here is the rouge, my lady." Then she asked Her Ladyship to pencil her eyebrows.

After Yang Yuhuan had made up her face, she was still a little tired and stood up slowly moving her waist as if to shake off fatigue. Niannu suddenly cried out, "Ah! You have forgotten the flowers, my lady." She picked up two cherry blossoms that had just been sent from the palace and pinned them lightly on the hair to either side of Yang Yuhuan's head. The maids stepped back half a pace and looked at Lady Yang. They were moved by her beauty and said, "Your countenance looks so delicate that one fears a breeze outside the window may harm it." The two helped her take off her sleeping gown, then dressed her in an apricot colored silk dress, a Hunan embroidered skirt and embroidered slippers. Her form was matchless. When she looked in the mirror, she could not help loving herself.

After Yang Yuhuan had spent much time dressing up and admiring herself, she had nothing to do; she yawned sleepily and stretched herself. Yongxin and Niannu had nothing to do either and said, "My lady, since you're so tired, why not sleep some more?"

"Yes, I will. I am still tired and think I'll rest a little longer. You two draw the bed curtains for me." She went to bed, lay on her side and was soon fast asleep.

The two maids left the room and sat outside the gate, chatting. Yongxin said, "Has the emperor not come because he has gone to see Lady Plum Blossom?"

"Sister, don't you know? Lady Plum Blossom has been forced to move to the Shangyang Pavilion."

"Surely not!"

"Sister Yongxin, recently the emperor has been so devoted to Lady Yang that he often comes here and doesn't even bring his attendants. We must take care and wait on them."

Let us ignore the chattering of the two maids. After Li Longji had made Yang Yuhuan his concubine, he took such delight in his new mistress that he wanted to be with her day and night. That day, after attending the morning imperial court session, he hurried on his own to the west palace. The two maids were at the gate. He walked over quietly. As he approached, the maids greeted him saying in a low voice, "Long live the emperor! Our Lady has just gone to sleep."

Li Longji, the romantic emperor whose heart was ruled by the fair sex, waved his hand and hushed them saying, "Don't wake her." He walked lightly to the bed and quietly parted the curtains; Lady Yang's body gave off a warm aroma. He looked at her and was overjoyed; she was like a piece of warm jade lying beneath the light silken bedcover. He stood there lost in thought.

Yongxin and Niannu were dumfounded by this and said, "With such gallantry it is no wonder that he has become the king of lovers!"

Maybe the gaze of Li Longji made Yang Yuhuan react and roused her from her deep sleep. She woke suddenly but still looked drowsy and asked in a frightened voice, "Who is it that dares to part the curtains?"

Still taken by her beauty, Li Longji murmured, "Even though she has just woken up and half her powder has been rubbed off, her lipstick gone and her hair in disorder, she is still a celestial beauty!"

Yongxin and Niannu saw that Her Ladyship was awake and went to help her get up. Yang Yuhuan opened her eyes, gave the emperor a listless look then closed them again. She got up, but was too weary to stand and sat down.

Full of sympathy, Li Longji saw that the two maids wanted to help her get up. He went forward to help them, saying in a low voice, "You're so sleepy you'd better have a rest." Aware that it was the emperor Yang Yuhuan leaned over his shoulder and murmured, "Long live and long, long live…"

"On this sunny spring morning it would be pleasant to stroll outside. Why do you sleep at noon?" Li Longji asked.

Yang Yuhuan blushed at this and whispered, "Last night I was favored by Your Majesty. You honored me so much that today I am weary and when I tried to dress, I fell asleep again. That is why I failed to welcome Your Majesty just now."

Hearing this Li Longji laughed and said, "So this is my fault!"

Yang Yuhuan blushed and remained silent. Li Longji said softly, "My love, you still look drowsy. Let us go to the front palace to pass a pleasant hour." Yang Yuhuan nodded. Li Longji took her hand and the two left the west palace for the front palace.

It goes without saying that a group of eunuchs and attendants in the front palace waited on the emperor and Lady Yang, who had tea and snacks in a hall.

While they were talking to each other Yang Guozhong sought an audience. Eunuch Gao Lishi entered the hall and said, "Long live the emperor! In accordance with Your Majesty's orders the prime minister has given An Lushan a test. He is now waiting outside the palace to make his report."

"Let him in."

Yang Guozhong entered the hall and kowtowed to the emperor, saying, "Long live the emperor! Long live Lady Yang!" After being ordered to stand up, he said, "I have tested An Lushan and beg to report that I find him a worthy fellow, skilled in six tribal languages as well as archery and horsemanship."

Li Longji was glad to hear it and said, "Yesterday I read General Zhang's memorial which said that this An Lushan knew six tribal tongues and all the arts of war so he had been made a frontier general. But he has been defeated in war and should be executed. That is why I sent you to test him. Since General Zhang's statement is true, you can tell An that his mistakes are pardoned and order him to appear in court tomorrow morning. I shall appoint him to a post in the capital and see how he conducts himself."

"It shall be done, sire." Yang Guozhong was, of course, happy with the result and he could now give a satisfactory reply to An. But he did not anticipate that An's presence in the capital would cause him trouble in the future.

After Yang Guozhong had gone, the eunuch Gao Lishi said, "Sire, the peonies at the Aloe Pavilion are in full bloom. Would Your Majesty and Her Ladyship care to see them?"

Li Longji was glad to hear this and said, "With such a lady and rare flowers, you must send Li Bai, member of the Imperial Academy, to the pavilion to compose a new poem for me."

Gao Lishi left to summon Li Bai. Li Longji rose from his seat and helped Yang Yuhuan to her feet, saying, "My love, let us go to see the flowers."

It was no mere accident that Gao Lishi, a personal attendant, held a post of first rank. Scheming and guessing the emperor's moods from his words and looks had allowed him to cater to the emperor's whims. He enjoyed the emperor's confidence and had won repeated promotions to achieve prominence in officialdom.

Gao Lishi was well aware that the emperor was infatuated with Lady Yang and did his best to please him. He thought that the emperor and Lady Yang were just having a good time and would surely tire of each other in the long run. People in the capital went on an outing during the Spring Outing, which fell on the third day of the third lunar month and he might persuade the emperor and Lady Yang to go as well. There were many scenic spots such as the River Bend Pond, Yichun Garden, Ziyun Tower, Furong Garden, Apricot Garden, and Ci'en Temple in the southeastern part of the city; the emperor and Lady Yang would surely like them. Later they would remember how he had contributed. He made up his mind and suggested to the emperor this outing.

Li Longji happily accepted his suggestion. It would please Lady Yang but Li Longji had other reasons for accepting. After Yang Yuhuan became the favorite concubine, her cousin Yang Guozhong, now brother-in-law of the emperor, had been repeatedly promoted until he held the post of prime minister, with only the emperor over him and millions answerable to him. Yang Yuhuan's three sisters had been made Duchess Qin, Duchess Han, and Duchess Guo respectively. As an emperor, Li Longji could not simply call on them when he liked and the suggestion of a spring outing gave him a chance to meet the three ladies. He ordered Gao Lishi to go to the prime minister's house at once to tell him and the three duchesses to accompany them on the outing.

Gao Lishi rode out at once heading for the house of the prime minister and then to the houses of the three duchesses. His galloping horse aroused the interest of the people in the city who guessed that the emperor and Lady Yang would be going on an outing accompanied by the prime minister and the three duchesses. Yang Yuhuan was a beauty and government officials and ordinary people knew it. Her three sisters were also renowned for their comeliness. But one was in the court and the others lived in mansions. Who could see them? The speculation that they were going on an outing and visiting River Bend created a sensation in the capital. All the people, men and women, old and young, ugly and beautiful, turned out to watch the matchless beauties.

It was acceptable to make a show for the people but the act would allow one scoundrel to sow the seeds of trouble. The scoundrel was none other than An Lushan. He had lost his army and should have been put to death, but his life had been saved because of the large bribe he offered to the prime minister Yang Guozhong. Afterwards, he had been given a post in the capital. He was a malicious person and his intentions were evil. He lived in the capital and saw that Yang Guozhong had used his position as brother- in-law to the emperor to behave arrogantly to the people. Although government officials of all ranks said nothing, they found him unsatisfactory; even the emperor sometimes disliked him, but he curbed his anger because he doted on Lady Yang. An understood the subtle relationship between the two. He also thought of how he had been humiliated the other day when he sought Yang's help; he wanted revenge. Because of this An tried hard to please the emperor in the hope that he could bring about the downfall of Yang Guozhong and avenge himself.

When Li Longji was with them, Yang Guozhong became more arrogant and An Lushan more cautious. In time Li Longji thought that An was loyal and started to give him more important assignments. This upset Yang Guozhong who was jealous, but An Lushan naturally disregarded his feelings.

An Lushan was born with a big belly. One day, when he was with Li Longji in a side hall, the emperor pointed to his belly and asked playfully, "What is inside? Why is it so big?"

Shrewdly, An Lushan replied, "Your Majesty, there is nothing inside except my loyal heart." His answer pleased Li Longji who favored him more and decided to make him a prince. An learned that on that day the emperor would be taking Lady Yang and the three duchesses for an outing. He longed to have a glimpse and changed into civilian clothes, mounted a horse and galloped along the banks of the River Bend in search of them.

After a while, a procession of carriages and horses approached. There was a smell of sweet perfume and the three duchesses appeared. Duchess Han wore an embroidered dress that contrasted with the white one worn by Duchess Guo and the red one of Duchess Qin. They were surrounded by a group of attendants and maids. Men and women thronged the road, vying with each other to catch a glimpse. An Lushan also saw the procession. He held the reins tightly and suddenly charged the carriages. The servants of the Yang family immediately stopped the horse shouting, "Halt there! The prime minister is here! Who are you? How dare you charge past?"

An made no reply, but gazed around trying to spot the beautiful duchesses in the assembly of carriages and horses. He saw that they were matchless beauties and stared at them. While admiring them, he felt envious of the emperor and murmured, "Ah, emperor of Tang, emperor of Tang! You have not only Lady Yang, but her sisters too! You are the most fortunate of men! You have all the beauties in the country and only by this means can you become the Son of Heaven!" As it was a rare opportunity to see the duchesses, An disregarded the shouts of the servants and spurred his horse on to take a second look. The Yang family servants blocked his way and shouted at him. Prime Minister Yang was putting on airs as he rode slowly at the back of the procession. Hearing the commotion, he whipped his horse to a gallop and met An Lushan face to face. Instead of greeting the prime minister, An turned his horse and left swiftly by a side way.

The family servants were very angry and said to Yang Guozhong, "We do not know the fellow who has just fled. He just rode towards us on a horse and no one could stop him!"

"Ah, it was An Lushan. Why did he run away when he saw me?" Yang Guozhong had not yet given much thought to An's insolence but the full force of it came home to him and he said to the servants, "Where are the three duchesses carriages?"

"In the front."

Yang Guozhong was suddenly enraged and said, "Aya, that fellow

An Lushan is rude! How dare he look down upon the imperial relatives. He charged at them openly and rudely. The scoundrel." He spoke sharply to his family servants. "Go at once and protect the carriages of the three duchesses. Use your gilded whips to lash anyone who comes near. No idlers or people not connected with them are allowed to approach the carriages."

This order was too late to stop An Lushan having a peep, but the men and women pressing forward were whipped. Instead of seeing the duchesses, they were now trying to hide and had to hold their breath until the carriages and horses of the Yang family had passed. They ended up behind the carriages and horses calling out to each other as they walked in small groups on the grass.

Someone suddenly cried, "Ah, there is a hairpin!" A young woman picked up the ornament dropped from a carriage and held it happily in her hand. Several young women surrounded her and wanted to see the hairpin. "Ah, there is a ruby on it." Just then, someone else called out. "Let's keep on searching, there might be something good!" The girls dispersed, searching in the grass. Someone found a slipper, someone else an inlaid box and another girl, a silk hanky. Each searcher found something and they said to each other how rich and extravagant the imperial relatives were.

The carriage procession with the three duchesses went fast and drew away from the crowds that had surrounded it. Family servants went ahead and bowed before their carriages to say that they had arrived at River Bend.

Duchess Han asked, "Where is His Grace, the prime minister?"

"His Grace has gone to Wangchun Palace, where His Majesty is now."

The three duchesses alighted at the same time and before them was a beautiful scene. Water wound between banks covered in red flowers and green grass. There were slender willow tendrils and young cattails; it was spring everywhere. A young eunuch approached and said, "By His Majesty's orders, Duchess of Han and Duchess of Qin will feast in the second pavilion, while Duchess of Guo is to ride to Wangchun Palace to feast with Lady Yang." The duchesses knelt down and said, "Long live the emperor!" They rose.

The eunuch urged Duchess Guo to go at once which made her uneasy and she said, "Why should I hurry! How can I leave my sisters here?"

Tactfully, duchesses Han and Qin said, "You are summoned to the palace thanks to your natural charm. You can appear before the emperor with your face unpainted. Go ahead, don't keep the emperor waiting."

THE PALACE OF ETERNAL YOUTH

CHAPTER THREE

Humiliated Because of Jealousy

NO ONE WOULD have anticipated that the pleasure tour arranged by Li Longji would have ended in discord. They had been in high spirits the day that he and Yang Yuhuan had gone to River Bend. But after just one night Yang Yuhuan came back alone while the emperor returned the second day.

Although Gao Lishi was a confidant of the emperor, he did not know much about the harems of the inner palace. He saw that the emperor was very angry and he spoke to the palace maid, Yongxin, "Can you tell me why the emperor has stopped going to Lady Yang's chamber?"

"Ah, Your Grace, don't you know? The two have quarreled and neither will give way."

"What did they quarrel about?"

"It was over an extra flower on the two-headed lotus flower." Yongxin did not explain further. Gao Lishi understood that there was a third person, but he did not know who it was. Yongxin refused to name the person and said with a smile, "Your Grace, you're so clever; if you guess, you will certainly solve the puzzle."

"How should I know! Sister Yongxin, please tell me."

Gao Lishi repeatedly pressed her for an answer and Yongxin told him the whole story. She said, "Well, it was Lady Yang who started the trouble."

Bewildered, Gao Lishi said, "How?"

"Her Ladyship often tells the emperor that Duchess Guo is a great beauty with good figure. This made the emperor summon her to the feast in Wangchun Palace. After a few cups, the two shared erotic feelings and they made love in secret. That was how it happened."

When he heard this, Gao Lishi clasped his hands and laughed, saying, "Aya. I suspected as much. But why then should Lady Yang be angry?"

Yongxin, a woman, knew more about love than Gao Lishi, a eunuch, and explained, "Lady Yang was afraid that someone might take her place in the emperor's affections. That is why she was angry and spoke rudely. But Duchess Guo is clever and left, saying nothing. The emperor was very angry because Lady Yang did not press Duchess Guo to stay and he has not come to the west palace today. Lady Yang is there, crying."

"I think Lady Yang carries matters too far. She is too self-willed and intolerant. The other day she insisted that Lady Plum Blossom move to the east wing of the Shangyang Pavilion and now she cannot even tolerate Duchess Guo, her own sister. She lacks sisterly feelings."

Yongxin was aware that they should not discuss the matter further and said, "Your Grace, let's drop the subject. There is one thing though. Usually the emperor never leaves Lady Yang's side and now he is staying away from her. What can we do?"

"What can we do? We can only wait and see…" At that moment someone from the inner court announced, "His Majesty sends for His Grace Gao." Gao at once went into the inner court.

Duchess Guo was also upset after she returned from the tour of River Bend; she stayed alone at home, reflecting. She had married into the Pei family, but her husband had died and left her a young widow. Nevertheless, she was careful and seldom went out for pleasure. Her sister had become the favorite of the emperor and she was now a duchess; she had to go on the outing because the emperor required her presence. Simply dressed and with no powder on her face, she went. She had not anticipated that, discreet as she was, she would not be able to escape the lascivious attentions of Li Longji. He had singled her out to force his attentions onto her in the Wangchun Pavilion.

During the feast, after a few cups Li Longji had become captivated by Duchess Guo's beauty and took her to bed; she had resisted but he took no notice. They spent the night together, but Li Longji was not satisfied and wanted her to stay at the palace. Duchess Guo thought that her sister was his favorite so she repeatedly declined his importuning and returned home. Her sister Yuhuan was angry and certainly did not ask her to stay; as for Li Longji, he failed to find a pretext to keep her from going. She went home. The affair had enraged her sister, aroused gossips and afterwards she had been most unhappy pitying herself over her sad lot. But her sister, Duchess Han, knew nothing of this and had only heard that she had fallen ill after returning from Wangchun Pavilion, so she visited her accompanied by maids.

"Duchess Han has arrived," an attendant of the Guo Mansion announced.

"Show her in at once," replied Duchess Guo.

Duchess Han entered the inner room slowly. The two sisters greeted each other, sat down and tea was served. Duchess Han said, "Sister, congratulations!"

"Why should I be congratulated?"

"The other day only you were honored. This beautiful flower has blossomed at the side of the emperor."

Duchess Guo blushed. "Sister, do not say so. I was summoned to Wangchun Pavilion just to attend the emperor during the feast. His Majesty holds us in equal favor, there is no difference."

"Aya, although you say so, a feast outside and a feast inside the palace are quite different. Sister, do not pretend. Among the thousands of flowers, you were picked by the emperor!" Duchess Guo felt unable to defend herself and she lowered her head without saying anything. Duchess Han noticed this and at once changed the subject. "How was Sister Yuhuan when you saw her at the palace?"

"Recently, Sister Yuhuan has been in high favor and the emperor cannot leave her for a moment."

"How much does the emperor love her?"

"I just know that they are together all day, but outsiders should not know how much they love each other."

Duchess Han pressed her. "Didn't you get any idea?"

Duchess Guo had to reply. "The only thing that is certain is that Sister Yuhuan has become even more quick tempered than she was before. She found fault in others and insisted on having her way."

"That has always been the case. Sister, you should give her some advice."

"No one can and no one wants to," Duchess Guo unwittingly complained.

"She was proud of her gifts and accomplishments and has had a bad temper ever since she was a child. As sisters, we should not gossip behind her back. Now that she is a favorite in court, she will certainly have her own way. No one can compare with her."

These remarks of Duchess Han unintentionally touched a nerve and Duchess Guo said loudly, "Who has competed with her to be favorite? There is nothing I can say about the temper she was born with, but I can say that the emperor is unpredictable!"

Duchess Guo's answer was revealing and Duchess Han stood up and murmured, "Ai, there must be some reasons behind what this sister from the Pei family says. She hides something while revealing something else and does not give a straight answer. I only hope that nothing will happen."

Just then an attendant rushed in and said, "I have something to report, Madame, an unfortunate thing has happened!"

"What is it? What's there to be alarmed about? Say it slowly." Duchess Han was alarmed while Duchess Guo, although not surprised, stood up.

"Her Ladyship has offended the emperor. The emperor was in a rage and ordered His Grace Gao to take her back to the prime minister's house."

Duchess Han was frightened and said, "Ya! Can it be true?"

"I said her temper would get her into trouble. Now it has happened."

"Even so, we are sisters, and this relates to our honor or humiliation. I think we should go to see her."

"You are right," Duchess Guo was unable to sit down. The two sisters rode to the prime minister's house in a carriage. On the way Duchess Han panicked as she spoke about it and Duchess Guo said, "Sister, won't Lady Plum Blossom find Sister Yuhuan's situation amusing?"

Without realizing what she was saying Duchess Han replied, "It is worse than Lady Plum Blossom, for though she has been cold-shouldered, she remains in the court."

Duchess Guo fully agreed and said, "Yes, our sister's situation is really worse than that of Lady Plum Blossom."

As the saying goes, "In nature sudden storms spring up and men's fortunes may change overnight." After his cousin had been made an imperial concubine, Yang Guozhong had been promoted many times and now he enjoyed great power as brother-in-law of the emperor and prime minister. But who could have told him when he got up that morning that he would learn that Her Ladyship had offended the emperor had been dismissed from the palace. He trembled at the news and did not know what to do. This shows the truth of the saying that "when you sit at home, a disaster descends from heaven."

Now we will set aside Yang Guozhong's fright and the coming visit of the two duchesses and turn to how Gao Lishi brought Lady Yang home.

As personal attendant of the emperor, Gao Lishi was able to gauge his thoughts extremely well. Although the emperor had sent Her Ladyship home in a fit of anger, like other emperors, he would long for his former lover later on when he had had enough of other women. Thus, as he advised Her Ladyship not to cry on the way, he was planning how to make the emperor change his mind. They arrived very soon at the prime minister's house. Yang Guozhong was already standing outside the gate with a group of men and women attendants and servants waiting to welcome them.

Gao Lishi got down from the carriage and Yang Guozhong who dared not neglect Gao when things were going well was especially attentive today. He bowed deeply; Gao Lishi waved his hand. Yang Guozhong turned and knelt before the carriage of the imperial concubine, saying, "Your subject Yang Guozhong welcomes Your Ladyship." Without waiting for orders, maids and servants pushed forward to help Yang Yuhuan out of the carriage.

Yang Guozhong turned to speak to Gao Lishi, but Gao did not consider himself to be an outsider and neglected the formality. He said, "Prime minister, show Her Ladyship in and I would like to have a word with you."

Yang Guozhong immediately ordered attendants and maids to take Her Ladyship to the house for a rest. Again he bowed deeply to Gao Lishi and said politely, "Please be seated. I wonder how this happened?"

"Generally speaking, Her Ladyship has been the most favored since she entered the palace. No one knew what happened yesterday. Her Ladyship offended His Majesty and suddenly they were estranged. Don't be offended if I speak bluntly. Her Ladyship is inclined to be arrogant because she is a favorite and she cannot tolerate the other ladies."

Yang Guozhong knew all about his cousin's temper and accepted the truth of what Eunuch Gao said. But the most important thing now was to reverse the situation and he asked Gao directly, "Your Grace Gao, what can be done now that she is dismissed?"

"Prime minister, you'd better go to the palace to apologize for her, see how things are, and watch for an opportunity."

"Your Grace, I shall depend on you to put in a good word for me to the emperor."

Gao Lishi replied with confidence, "Sure. Something should be done to help Her Ladyship return to the palace." Then he left and Yang Guozhong went with him to the palace to apologize.

Yang Yuhuan's banishment from the palace had filled her with alarm and she was sad. When Meixiang, a maid, took her to the back hall, she just sat silently at a table, grief stricken, her face covered in tears. She thought that at the palace she had been the emperor's favorite; she could trust him and their happy union would last for a hundred years. Who would have thought that she would have been sent home when the emperor was angry? Once she had left the palace, she felt that she was as far from it as earth is from the ninth heaven. She recalled the moon in the palace; it would not see her shadow there any more. Now that she was outside the palace she was like a flower that had dropped off a branch, she could not return. Her future looked bleak and she wept in self- pity.

Meixiang did her best to soothe her and Lady Yang gradually calmed down. She took out the clothes that she had brought back, but the sweet smell of imperial scent made her sad. The emperor had given in to her every whim and had been with her day and night. How he had loved her! Now they were separated because he wished to be with her sister as well. Could she return to the palace? She wished that the emperor would change his mind and said to Meixiang, "Girl, where can I see the palace from here?"

"Look northwest from the Yushu Pavilion at the front, my lady, and you can see the palace wall."

"Come with me to the pavilion." Yang Yuhuan stood up at once and Meixiang led the way. Once inside the pavilion, the maid pointed northwest and said, "Your Ladyship, can you see the yellow glazed tiles over there? That is the inner court of the palace."

When she looked to where the maid pointed, Yang Yuhuan saw the court, felt sad again and murmured, "Oh, heaven, I gaze at the palace from the pavilion, it is so near and yet the mist separates me from it. I was there yesterday. Now though I am still young, the emperor loves me no more. How can I make the emperor remember our former love and recall me?"

As if in response to her longing, Meixiang spotted something and said, "There in the distance I can see a eunuch on horseback. He may be coming to call you back, my lady."

Yang Yuhuan also saw the eunuch and hoped that instead of bad news he would bring good luck. As there was no time for her to ponder over it, she hurriedly descended the steps.

Gao Lishi had arrived when she entered the front hall and he knelt before her, saying, "Gao Lishi kowtows to Your Ladyship."

"Gao Lishi, what brings you back here?" Yang Yuhuan asked anxiously.

"Just now when I reported your return to His Majesty, he asked me to tell him what had happened here in detail as if he regretted what had taken place. Now he is sitting alone in the palace, sighing. He must be longing for you, so I came to report this to

Your Ladyship."

"Oh no, how could he be thinking of me?"

Gao Lishi assured her it was so and said, "I am stupid. Forgive me if I advise you, madame. Do not be too stubborn. The emperor is actually thinking of you. Have you anything that you could give me to take to His Majesty when I get the opportunity? You never know, it might soften his heart."

Yang Yuhuan thought this was reasonable. She had been obstinate and said anxiously, "Gao Lishi, what can I send to the emperor?"

Gao Lishi could think of nothing and made no reply. Yang Yuhuan thought, "What would soften his heart?" Besides herself, all that she had was gifts from the emperor. How could she string together on a golden thread her tears, which dropped like pearls? Ah, yes! She could send a lock of the glossy hair that once lay near his head on the pillow. That might move his heart.

"Girl, bring me the mirror and the scissors." Lady Yang let down her hair but could not help shedding tears, crying out, "Hair, hair, you have been with me all my youth. How can I cut you off? To show that my heart is faithful I have to give you up!" She wept and cut her hair with a trembling hand then held up the lock and said, "His Majesty, your servant has only this lock of hair and she hopes it will reunite us."

She stood up and gave the lock of hair to Gao Lishi, saying, "Gao Lishi, take it and give it to the emperor. Tell him that I deserve ten thousand deaths as I shall never see his face again in this life. I present him with this lock of hair as a token of my love."

Gao Lishi took the lock of hair with both hands and placed it on his shoulder. He said, "My lady, please don't worry. Your servant will leave you now. By this lock of silken hair, your servant will do his utmost to make the emperor change his mind so that you will be reunited with him until your hair turns gray."

After Gao Lishi left, Yang Yuhuan felt tired and sat down. She did not know what fate held in store for her and she shed tears in silence.

While she was weeping, Duchess Han and Duchess Guo arrived at the prime minister's house.

On the way there the two sisters had been very worried. They feared that, after Her Ladyship was dismissed from the palace, their cousin Yang Guozhong would lose power. It would be a big blow to the Yang family. They knew that they were powerless, and their only hope was that the emperor would recall Yuhuan. Attendants greeted them when they arrived and they asked, "Where is Her Ladyship?"

Meixiang reported their arrival immediately, "My lady, duchesses Han and Guo are here." Yang Yuhuan wept and did not reply; the duchesses walked in by themselves.

Duchess Han consoled her sister, "Your Ladyship, don't be distressed." She shed tears in sympathy but Duchess Guo took pleasure in Yang Yuhuan's misfortune and said, "That day in the Wangchun Pavilion, the emperor was very fond of you. How could this have happened?" Yang Yuhuan lowered her head and said nothing and she continued, "I thought that the love between the emperor and you would last a thousand years and however badly you behaved he would never take offence."

Duchess Han detected a hidden meaning in her words and at once stopped her. "Sister of the Pei family, you're too talkative. Her Ladyship, why is the emperor offended? What is the reason?" Yang Yuhuan said nothing.

Duchess Han did not mind her silence, but Duchess Guo could not stand it and said, "Your Ladyship, excuse me for speaking frankly, but being too much in favor can only lead to trouble. You must know that the emperor's love is like autumn leaves..."

Duchess Han immediately cut her short and said to Yang Yuhuan, "We have come to show our concern. Why do you pretend not to hear us?"

Yang Yuhuan had to reply, "It is my fate to be discarded by the emperor and I am grateful that my sisters show such concern. You can shower me with thousands of words but I shall try to keep my sorrows to myself." After she said this, she paid them no more attention and went into the other room.

"Sister! See how she treats us!"

Duchess Han was angry too and said, "Yes, indeed. We came specially to see her, but she goes to the other room. Next time you go to the Wangchun Pavilion make sure you don't behave like that." Duchess Guo blushed at this.

CHAPTER FOUR

Longing and Recall

AFTER RUMINATING FOR such a long time, Li Longji was despondent. He took a stroll and saw the green grass growing by the marble steps. But there was no silken skirt and the pearl-decked shoes of Lady Yang were absent. He felt sad again. Gao Lishi saw him and knew that he must not act rashly. He hid by the door and waited for a chance.

A few steps beyond the palace gate Li Longji lowered his head and murmured, "I long for her here. I wonder whether she is thinking of me. Gao Lishi told me this morning that she was weeping when she left the palace. It breaks my heart to hear of it. That was several hours ago and there has been no more news. That scoundrel Gao Lishi has been keeping out of my way."

Gao Lishi heard him and knew that his chance had come; he advanced to kneel before the emperor, saying, "Your slave is here."

"Gao Lishi, what have you there on your shoulder?"

"Her Ladyship's hair."

Thinking that Gao Lishi was making fun of him, Li Longji smiled and said, "What hair?"

Gao Lishi said, "Lady Yang said that she was sorry that she had offended Your Majesty and that she deserved ten thousand deaths. She will never be able to look upon your face again. She has cut off this lock of hair which she asked your slave to present to Your Majesty as a token of her love." He presented the hair with both hands.

Li Longji took the hair and wept bitterly, "Ah, my darling! I smelt the perfume of your hair on my pillow two nights ago, but today it is shorn for me. Your glossy hair is obviously a token of your sorrow. It breaks my heart. This lock of hair is like the love between us which has been cut as if by a pair of scissors."

"Your Majesty, do not grieve. Lady Yang is your favorite so why begrudge her a small space in the palace and make her stay outside? This flower-like imperial lady would return to the palace anytime you wish." Gao Lishi was tactful.

Li Longji thought for a while and said, "But I have already dismissed her. How could I recall her?"

"It is nothing. To dismiss her because of her mistakes and then recall her because she has repented that would show the divine mercy of the Son of Heaven." Li Longji nodded and thought that what he said made sense. Seeing that the emperor was about to agree, Gao Lishi continued, "Besides, it was barely dawn when she left in a single carriage so no one knew. Now it is dusk. If we open the gate in Anqing Quarter we can let her in from the Taihua Residence and no one will know. Your slave begs that she be pardoned and recalled. Your slave will bring Her Ladyship back at once. Her return will surely alleviate Your Majesty's grief."

Li Longji gave his consent for he found reason in what Gao said and the arrangement was right. He said, "Gao Lishi, I order you to bring Her Ladyship back."

"As Your Majesty commands!" excited, Gao kowtowed and withdrew.

Alone in the palace, Li Longji pondered. "How shall I meet her when she returns? She always tends to be angry. What shall I say to her? Well! Well! Well! I am to blame, let her have her own way."

Gao Lishi returned swiftly and entered the inner court, followed by a fragrant carriage with Her Ladyship in it. He reported, "Her Ladyship is here."

"Let her in at once."

"It shall be done. Lady Yang calls on His Majesty," announced Gao. Yang Yuhuan entered immediately and said, "Your slave Yang pays her respects to Your Majesty. She is under a sentence of death." She knelt and prostrated herself on the ground.

Li Longji felt pity for her and told her to rise. Gao Lishi sensibly withdrew leaving them alone. Yang Yuhuan said, "As your slave I acted wrongly and was sent away. Now that I behold Your Serene Countenance, I shall die content." While she spoke, tears coursed down her cheeks. Li Longji also sobbed and said, "Do not say that, my love."

"My guilt weighs down on me as heavily as a mountain, yet Your Majesty is as merciful as Heaven. Now I should repent. In future I shall keep my proper place and never ever show my jealousy."

Li Longji saw that she had repented and stepped forward to help her up. He said, "I was unreasonable for a moment. Let us not speak of it again."

"Long live Your Majesty!" was all that Lady Yang could say. Li Longji took her hand and wiped away her tears. He said lovingly, "A taste of parting has increased our love tenfold."

Realizing that the emperor and Her Ladyship were on good terms again, the maids waiting outside came in. "A feast is ready in the west palace, Your Majesty, Your Ladyship." Li Longji took Yang Yuhuan's hand and they walked slowly. Ever since that moment, they returned to being deeply in love.

Li Longji favored Yang Yuhuan even more after she returned to the palace; the pair cherished the lost love and became more intimate. The emperor stayed with her all day neglecting state affairs and leaving everything, big or small, to Yang Guozhong. The three duchesses received higher honors and many gifts from the emperor and the Yang family's authority became higher than the throne. This made men with lofty ideals discontent.

Guo Ziyi, a native of Zhengxian County, Huazhou, had been a successful candidate in the provincial examination of military officers. Since childhood, he had held lofty ideals. He was well versed in both polite letters and the martial arts and he dreamt of becoming a mighty hero who helped to bring peace and stability to the country. After passing the examination, he went to the capital to wait for an appointment.

There were hardships on the trip but Guo Ziyi arrived in the capital and stayed in a hotel where he waited for instructions. People like him meant nothing in the capital but he did not realize it. It was boring sitting all day in the hotel so he sometimes took a stroll in the street or went to teahouses and restaurants. In this way, he learned many things about affairs of state and became much more knowledgeable. What worried him was power had fallen into the hands of the Yang family, An Lushan had become a favorite and the government was going to ruin. By himself he could do nothing about this.

One day when he had nothing to do, he went to Chang'an Market for a drink. As he walked there, the jostling crowds reminded him of drunkards and he thought it would be hard to find a sober man like Qu Yuan, a great patriot of the State of Chu in ancient times. He wanted to find someone who shared his ambitions and aspirations so that they culd accomplish great tasks together. It was sad that people like Lü Shang, who helped the emperor to establish Western Zhou, Li Guang, a famous general in Western Han, and Fan Kuai, a renowned general in the Han Dynasty, were nowhere to be found.

As he was pondering over this, he reached a place between the east and the west markets, a prosperous area in Chang'an. He looked up and saw a signboard – Xinfeng Restaurant. He entered and called out, "Do you serve wine?"

"Please go upstairs, sir." His manner had impressed the waiter who led him to a room upstairs.

"Are you drinking alone, sir, or are you waiting for other guests?"

"I will have a few cups by myself. Bring the best you have."

"We have the best wine. And you'll like it." The waiter went to bring the wine.

Guo Ziyi got up to look outside where large crowds hustled and bustled. A procession of people suddenly came from somewhere nearby. A eunuch led a group of richly dressed officials; attendants, carrying gold, silk, sheep and wine followed. He thought it strange.

"Sir, your wine is heated." Guo Ziyi turned and said, "Waiter, tell me where are those officials outside going?"

"Sir, I'll tell you while you drink. The emperor has ordered new mansions in Xuanyang Quarter for his brother-in-law Yang

Guozhong and the three duchesses. The four mansions are next to each other and each is like an imperial palace. Nowadays every family wants to outshine every other one. When one family sees that their neighbor's houses are better than his, he pulls his houses down and rebuilds until they have one exactly the same. In this way a single hall may cost millions. The new buildings were finished today so all the government officials are going there to offer their congratulations and give presents of sheep and wine. They will all pass this way."

"Ah, is it possible?" Guo Ziyi sighed. If the favorite concubine's relatives were indulging in such a display, what would it lead to! They vied with each other in ostentation; their displays of luxury came from hard-won wealth of the people. And none of the courtiers, hangers-on, ministers or men of influence dared tell the emperor that these vermilion roofs and brilliant tiles were stained with the people's blood. The more he thought about it, the angrier he became. The wine had gone to his head and he had to rest for a while in the restaurant. He stood up and slowly paced the room. On the wall, a few lines of poetry were written and one poem caught his eye.

When the people desert Yan city,
And no horses return from the Han Pass.
He comes to the ghost beneath the hill,
And there hangs a silken dress on a ring.

It surprised him and he said, "What a strange poem!" He read it carefully again. He thought the poem seemed rather sinister and looked for the name of the author, "Written by Li Xiazhou." His brows were knit in thought. The name sounded familiar. "Ah, yes," he finally got it. Li Xiazhou was a renowned fortune-teller who could tell the future. The poem must have a hidden meaning, but who could explain the riddle?

A noise downstairs interrupted his thoughts and without thinking he said, "Where is the waiter?"

"Yes, sir?"

"What is the meaning of that hubbub downstairs?"

"Well, sir, just take a look out of the window." He looked in the direction indicated by the waiter and saw a lord riding past preceded by retainers. "Who is that?"

"Sir, just look at the big belly! That is the famous An Lushan, a great favorite with the emperor. His Majesty even allowed An Lushan to sit beside him. Today he was made Prince of Dongping and he is on his way back from the court to his new palace outside Donghua Gate."

"Ah, so that is An Lushan, and what has he done to be made a prince? He has the face of a rebel; he will certainly bring ruin to the empire!" He wondered how the court had come to admit such a jackal. What was the difference between this fellow and the Yangs? It was hard to tell what would happen, but the poem of Li Xiazhou contained a bad omen. He was angry. "Why do you look so gloomy, sir?" asked the waiter.

"I am so angry that my hair stands on end and I am beside myself with rage. My sword on my waist has also been disturbed!"

The waiter did not understand what he meant and said, "Don't look so depressed, sir. Let me get you another pot of wine."

"A thousand cups and a hundred pots of wine could never wash away my gloom. Here is your money." He walked down the stairs. The waiter was perplexed and murmured, "After three cups other men are at peace with the whole word, but this gentleman has a thousand sorrows. It is none of my business; I just take the money to the counter."

After leaving the restaurant Guo Ziyi returned to the hotel; he had nowhere else to go. When he arrived his attendant who had come with him to the capital reported, "Master, the bulletin has come." He passed it to him with both hands. The bulletin read, "The Ministry of War announces that by Imperial Decree Guo Ziyi is now appointed military commissioner for Tiande."

"So the decree has come. We should pack our things and go to my post at once." The attendant went to prepare.

Guo Ziyi's mood changed from excitement to sadness. He was excited because he was able to serve the state, but he worried about the throne that appeared to be tottering and in danger. He thought, then decided. "Since I have been appointed by the emperor, I must not fear wolves ahead or tigers behind, even dark forces. I must dispel jackals and wolves and restore the great Tang."

CHAPTER FIVE

Passing on and Writing the Music

LI LONGJI AND Yang Yuhuan feasted and played day and night and the discontent of people outside the court reached fever pitch; upright officials were worried. But the emperor and Lady Yang knew nothing about that nor did they wish to know. All that interested them was carnal pleasure and sensory enjoyment.

Since Yang Yuhuan had returned to the palace, Li Longji showed her greater favor than before. The situation was like the poem: "His love for all his three thousand palace ladies seems to center on one, and none of the others in the six palaces can compare with her." Naturally Yang Yuhuan did her best to please Li Longji to consolidate her position.

One morning, when Yang Yuhuan got up, she ordered Yongxin and Niannu to clean the Lotus Pavilion because she wanted to compose music there. Niannu helped her dress and Yongxin set up the brushes, ink slabs, paper and ink stones. When all was ready, Yongxin smelt musk and heard the tinkle of jade pendants and said to herself in a low voice, "Ah, Her Ladyship is early this morning."

Since Lady Yang had come back to the palace, the emperor stayed with her in the morning and absented himself from his audience. Why should she come to the Lotus Pavilion so early this morning? It turned out that Lady Plum Blossom was good at singing and dancing and the emperor often praised the Frightened Swan Dance that she had written. Could Yang Yuhuan concede defeat? She planned to compose a music that would be better than that of Lady Plum Blossom. This would win the exclusive love of the emperor.

It is said that Yang Yuhuan in her previous life was a fairy on Penglai Mountain; she had lived in the moon and was very clever. Now she thought day and night about the melody and this moved Chang'e, the goddess of the moon. There was a melody called the Dance of the Rainbow and Feathery Garments that had stayed on the moon and was unknown to men. She thought, "Now the Tang emperor on the earth below is fond of music and Yang Yuhuan is his concubine. I will summon her spirit to hear the tune again. When she awakes she can transcribe it and bring the music of heaven to mortals on earth. This will be a praiseworthy deed!" She called her fairy maid, "Hanhuang, come here."

"What do you want, my lady?"

"Go to the Tang palace on the earth and bring the spirit of Yang Yuhuan to hear our music. When the dance has been played, you may send her back."

Hanhuang left the moon palace, crossed the Milky Way, passed the starry sky, and arrived at the Tang palace. She flew over the palace wall, reached the inner palace and stopped right beneath the window of Yang Yuhuan's palace. But the gate was locked and the curtains drawn. Yang Yuhuan looked like a cherry blossom and was fast asleep, cuddling a pillow. Hanhuang called gently, "Get up, Lady Yang. Get up, Lady Yang."

Yang Yuhuan was sound asleep, her hair to one side and her face covered with powder and rouge. She opened her sleepy eyes a little and then closed them again at the repeated calling of Hanhuang.

Seeing this, Hanhuang raised her voice, "Please get up, lady."

"Who is that calling from the palace gate?"

"Come quickly, my lady! Come quick."

Yang Yuhuan got up unwillingly and yawned. She went to the window, looked out and said, "Oh, it is a palace maid."

"I am not a palace maid who sweeps and waits on others."

"Not a palace maid? Are you a beauty from one of the other courtyards?"

"I am not a concubine either."

"Who are you?"

Hanhuang said proudly, "I am a fairy maid of the moon, and my name is Hanhuang."

Yang Yuhuan was startled and said, "Oh, so you are a fairy from the moon! How did you get here?"

"Chang'e, the goddess of the moon, ordered me to invite you to come with me and enjoy our cassia blossoms."

"Can it be true?" Yang Yuhuan asked.

"Don't hesitate, my lady; let me lead the way. Come with me." So saying, Hanhuang waved her hand, and Yang Yuhuan flew towards the sky with her. Clouds floated beneath their feet and the wind whispered softly into their ears; they gazed at the stars so near they could reach out a hand to pluck them. Before their eyes was a glorious palace. Cool breezes dispelled the summer heat.

Yang Yuhuan said, "Ah, this is mid-summer. Why do I feel so cold?"

"This is known to men as the Palace of Boundless Cold. You may enter now."

When she went in, she thought that she may have seen the decorations, the yard, the flowers and other things there some time before. But she had no time to recall it in detail and she smelt the fragrance of cassia. A group of fairies in white tunics and red skirts played music under the cassia tree. The music was sweet and Hanhuang told her that this was the Dance of the Rainbow and Feathery Garments. They both listened to it beneath the cassia tree.

The melody was moving and lovely and the fairies played earnestly. The music, though, could not remind Yang Yuhuan of her previous life or wake her from the nightmare of riches and power on earth; nor could the music help her free herself from the infatuations and greed of the mortal world. She could only go her own way, rising and falling with the world.

Yang Yuhuan did not know the intentions of Goddess Chang'e

but she was carried away by the fairy music and exclaimed, "Marvelous, it is so clear and melodious; it moves me. It certainly is not a tune from earth!" She asked Hanhuang whether she could meet Goddess Chang'e but the time was not right for her to return to the moon and Hanhuang declined saying, "The time for that has not yet come. It is nearly dawn, and Your Ladyship should return to the Tang palace." Hanhuang waved her hand and Yang Yuhuan woke from her dream. The fairy music and rhythms still rang in her ears and she got up early to order Yongxin to clean the Lotus Pavilion. She wanted to compose music in serene surroundings.

When Yongxin saw Lady Yang approaching, she went to greet her. "I beg to report to Your Ladyship that the brushes, ink slabs, paper and ink stones are ready."

"You and Niannu may stay here." Yongxin waved a fan and Niannu burned incense to inspire her.

Water surrounded the Lotus Pavilion; the scent of lotus came through the gauze-screened window and mixed with the smell of musk. Sitting at the table Yang Yuhuan straightened the paper and took up a brush to transcribe the music of the moon. She was inspired and expressed her thoughts carefully, considered all the details, made every word fit and wrote the stanzas in their proper sequence. An oriole sang on a willow branch. Yang Yuhuan put down her brush and was moved. She said, "Wonderful, wonderful," and altered the score. She wrote the music at her first attempt and it was soon finished.

Li Longji sat for an audience and thought about the inner palace. He hastily appointed a group of officials for various posts, concluded the audience, sent the officials away and went to the Lotus Pavilion when he learned that Lady Yang was there.

Niannu spotted the emperor in the distance and went to meet him, "Long live Your Majesty!"

"Niannu, where has Her Ladyship gone? What are these? Brush and ink stone?"

"Her Ladyship has been composing music and has just gone to change her dress."

Li Longji nodded and said, "My darling! My darling! You have all the accomplishments that could grace a lovely woman. What music have you been composing? Let me have a look." He sat down and read the score on the table. The words were written meticulously; they were excellent and there was not the slightest dissonance in the score. He hummed the tune and wondered. The melody had an unearthly quality, as if it came from heaven. It was rare music indeed. He could not help saying, "My darling, my darling not only is your beauty unsurpassed, but this music shows the talent of a genius. In intelligence alone you outshine the three thousand beauties in the inner palace."

The silk evening dress that Lady Yang had changed into made her look more delicate. She walked with light steps to the Lotus Pavilion accompanied by Yongxin. When she saw Li Longji sitting there reading the score, she knelt down and said, "Long live the emperor!"

Li Longji helped her to rise and said, "Take a seat, darling." Yang Yuhuan was not as restrained as she was the first time she came to palace and sat down as ordered.

Li Longji had not seen her for half a day and ran his eyes over her from head to foot. He said, "My darling, the silk dress makes you look more charming than ever. You are like a lotus glimmering in the lake and with the orchid in your hair, your face is doubly enchanting..."

Lady Yang was delighted to hear what he said, but tried to be modest and said, "Why has Your Majesty returned from court so late today?"

"Because I had to appoint a new governor for Lingwu Prefecture, an important post. I discussed the matter with my ministers the whole morning but we could not find a suitable man. Finally Guo Ziyi was promoted to the post. That is what delayed me."

"I had nothing to do while I was waiting for Your Majesty in the Lotus Pavilion and tried to learn a new tune. It falls far short of the Frightened Swan Dance which won much acclaim after it was performed." Lady Yang was jealous.

"I have just seen and hummed it; it is quite unique. How can that Frightened Swan Dance compare with this?"

"I wrote it hastily, without much thought; I hope Your Majesty will correct its mistakes."

"I shall go through it carefully with you." As Lady Yang sat beside the emperor, Yongxin and Niannu crept out of the Lotus Pavilion.

Li Longji became passionate and sat close to Yang Yuhuan; each pointed to the score with one hand. Li Longji said, "You are a rare beauty and the music you wrote is flawless. Tell me, what do you call it?"

"Last night I dreamt that I was on the moon and saw a group of fairy musicians dressed in rainbow colored feathery garments. I want to call it the Dance of the Rainbow and Feathery Garments."

"Good. The Dance of the Rainbow and Feathery Garments is a good title. It is certainly a music of the moon." Li Longji looked at her again and said, "Your unearthly beauty makes me think that you must once have been a fairy on the moon. We must give this tune to the conservatory. But I am afraid ordinary musicians will not fully appreciate its excellence. I would like Yongxin and Niannu to copy the script and learn it from you. After that they can teach Li Guinian and he will pass it on to his musicians. We should do it that way."

"Yes, Your Majesty."

Li Longji stood up and looked around. He held Lady Yang's hand and said, "It's getting dark; let us return to the palace."

After Yang Yuhuan returned to the palace, Li Longji constantly indulged himself in pleasure. He paid little attention to state affairs; it was a peaceful time in the country. He did not know that in his absence, royal relatives and civil and military officials in the court contested for privileges and wealth; they formed cliques to further their own interests.

An Lushan had been favored by the emperor and received several promotions. He was a changed man; his wild ambitions became apparent; he was arrogant and overbearing. Other officials allowed him to have his way, but he and Yang Guozhong were antipathetic, like fire and water. Yang Guozhong looked on An as an ingrate who had forgotten that he had saved his life. Moreover, An often opposed him and this made him unsatisfied. Earlier Yang Guozhong had warned His Majesty that An was an ambitious fellow with treason written on his face. He would be trouble in the future, but the emperor had not listened. He was determined to warn the emperor again and was bent on having An Lushan dismissed by the emperor.

One day when he was approaching the palace gate, he told his attendants to withdraw and went in alone. There was a sudden uproar and he wondered who dared make such a noise inside the palace. When the procession came near, he sneered, "Oh, it's An Lushan!"

"Old Yang, did you call me?" An Lushan answered back sarcastically, because Yang Guozhong had called him by name.

Yang Guozhong made no reply to this but reproached him. "This is the palace. How can you make such a noise here?"

Rejecting the reproach An Lushan pointed to his clothes and said, "Old Yang, see here. The robes I wear were given to me by the emperor; the horse I ride is from the imperial stable. I have been summoned to confidential discussions on important matters and am leaving the palace after all the others have left. What can you do with me? Since I am a prince there can be no objections when my attendants call out to clear the way for me. Can you, a prime minister, compare with me? Can you tell your attendants to call out to clear the way for you?" He looked triumphant.

"What? An Lushan, when have you become so high and mighty?" Yang Guozhong laughed coldly.

"I have always been like this."

"An Lushan, think back a little."

"To what?"

"To the time when you first came to see me. Were you like this then?"

An Lushan did not mind Yang Guozhong laying bare the past. He was brazen and said, "Old Yang, that was different. There is no comparison. Why harp on the past?"

"Well, An Lushan, you lost an army and should have been beheaded for your crime. You knelt at my feet to plead and I covered up your offences in the memorial to the emperor and thus saved your life. How could you forget all that?" Yang Guozhong was uneasy.

An Lushan did not take this into account in his rebuttal. "His Majesty in his mercy pardoned me and restored me to my post. What did you have to do with it?"

"Well said, indeed! You sin against your conscience! You are ungrateful." Yang Guozhong had not convinced him so he scolded him.

This made An Lushan angry, so he touched a sore spot. "Yang Guozhong, things are changeable; fame and disgrace depend upon chance. Do not think that because you have power and influence you can bully colleagues in the court. You mentioned my failure but do you remember your attack on Nanzhao? Did you not hide the truth from the emperor and cover up for Xianyu Zhongtong, the defeated general?"

"Who would dare deceive our sovereign? This is slander." Yang Guozhong was touched to the raw and gave a weak defence.

"Have you never deceived him? How many posts and official ranks have you sold?"

Yang Guozhong could not withdraw and had to fight head on. "Hold your tongue. You talk about the sale of official posts. How did you get your wealth if not through such means?"

"That is not all by any means. How many tricks have you played while relying on your cousin's influence? You are guilty of thousands of crimes against the state." An Lushan's attack avoided the matter of selling positions.

Yang Guozhong shouted himself hoarse. "These are baseless slanders!" He seized An Lushan and said, "Come with me to see the emperor!"

"Who is afraid of you? Let us go! Let us go!" An Lushan also seized Yang Guozhong and gripping each other they went before the emperor.

Yang Guozhong spoke first. "Your Majesty, An Lushan is disloyal and hides a dagger in his heart. He poses as a simple man but is at heart more treacherous than Shi Le." To convince the emperor, he added, "Once An Lushan did not bow when he saw the crown prince; he is cocky and impolite. Such insolence is not to be endured and evil must be struck down. I beg Your Majesty to mete out justice immediately while there is time!"

Not bowing to the crown prince just showed that An Lushan was loyal only to the emperor and Li Longji knew this.

An Lushan refuted him. "The royal favor shown to me has made Yang Guozhong jealous. I am simple, unable to protect myself and sooner or later I shall be his victim." He seemed to be in a state of fear and his story and his tears contrasted with the haughtiness shown by Yang Guozhong in his capacity as brother-in-law of the emperor. This impressed Li Longji favorably.

An Lushan saw that the emperor did not intend punishing him and said, "Only the emperor knows my loyalty. I beg permission to leave the capital to serve Your Majesty at the frontier."

The pair had often accused each other and Li Longji was unable to reconcile them. A military general and prime minister who are at odds cannot work together in the court. As An Lushan wanted to work at the frontier, wouldn't this be a good way of solving the conflict? So he appointed An Lushan Military Governor of Fanyang, and ordered him to proceed at once to his post. After kneeling to receive the imperial edict, Yang Guozhong and An Lushan said together, "Long live the emperor!" but their minds were on other matters.

When they left the palace, An Lushan bowed merrily to Yang Guozhong and said sarcastically, "Veteran prime minister, I am going now. You will be troubled no more by my insolence. In future, you can bare fangs and brandish claws and run amuck in the court, while I build my principality in Fanyang and do as I please." Yang Guozhong did not know what to say and just gave a sarcastic laugh.

An Lushan started leave and turned back to mock Yang Guozhong, "One last word, prime minister. I suppose my new appointment comes through your help." He saluted by bringing both hands together and said, "Well, when I arrive at Fanyang, I will bide my time to see the end of you." He left without saying goodbye. Yang Guozhong was stupefied.

It was only after An Lushan had gone that Yang Guozhong realized what had happened. He reflected, "Ah, what a bad business! How can I rid myself of the hatred I feel in my chest? I wanted to overthrow him, but added to his accomplishments. Will

I become a laughing stock? I honestly hope that An Lushan will make trouble this time; then the emperor will see that I was right in warning him. Your Majesty, Your Majesty, when that happens you will regret the decision you made today."

CHAPTER SIX

Paying a Tribute of Lychee

AFTER LI LONGJI sent An Lushan away, no one in the court dared provoke Prime Minister Yang. He thought the country was at peace and stayed all the time with Yang Yuhuan in the inner palace trying to please her and satisfying her desire for good food.

Yang Yuhuan was fond of fresh lychee, a delicate fruit that grows in Hainan and Fuzhou thousand miles from the capital. How could he bring lychee to the capital to please his imperial concubine? Was this a problem for an emperor? Certainly not. He just ordered the two places to pay a tribute of lychee each year.

Some things are easier said than done. Fuzhou was in Sichuan Province, far away from the capital, while the distance to Hainan was further. Fresh lychee usually loses its flavor seven days after it is picked so it would have to be sent to the capital before the first day of the sixth moon, Lady Yang's birthday. Only a feudal emperor who did not care about the misery of his people would make such an order.

Each year in the second half of the fifth moon special envoys from Fuzhou and Hainan galloped towards the capital carrying a basket of lychees suspended from a pole. It was especially hard for envoys from Hainan, which is further from the capital; they had to offer the tribute the same day.

Usually, the envoys took shortcuts off the road, sometimes across wheat and rice fields. They had a hard time but the ordinary people along the road suffered more.

An old peasant of East Village, in Jincheng County, not far from the capital, and his family of eight lived on a few *mu* [one *mu* equals to 1/15 of an acre] of infertile land. He heard that envoys would pass that morning and was afraid that his crops would be trampled; he got up early and kept watch on the field. He waited and saw no envoy but a man with a bamboo stick and a woman with a stringed instrument walked slowly towards him. When they came near, he saw that they were a couple of blind fortune-tellers, and heard what they said.

"We have traveled a long way today, husband, and my feet are aching. I can't go any further. We do not tell other people's fortunes; we are struggling for our own lives."

"There is someone there, wife. Let me ask him where we are." He took a few steps and called out, "Pray, sir, what district is this?"

The peasant replied, "This is East Village, Jincheng County, next to the West Village, Weicheng County." The blind man bowed and thanked him.

While they were talking, horse bells rang. The peasant at once looked up and saw a group of people on galloping horses. Leaving the blind man and woman, he ran towards them shouting at the top of his voice. "Commander, keep to the highway, and don't trample on the grain!" But who listens to a peasant? The commander just took them through the green field, as that was the shortest way.

The blind couple continued walking along a path, talking. The man said, "It is not far to the capital, wife. Let me go ahead and I may be able to hire a donkey for you." There was a beat of hooves and a group of envoys from Fuzhou rushed past. The blind man at once stepped aside, but before he had stopped moving, another group of horses with envoys from Hainan rode up. Unable to avoid them, the blind man was trampled to death and lay on the ground.

No thought was given to the living, still less to the crops.

The peasant staggered after the horses crying out, "Heaven! My crops have been trampled and destroyed by these people. There is nothing left for us to eat. What can I use to pay tax? The peasant's lot is hard!" He sat down and beat the ground with his fists.

The blind woman's husband was silent and she crawled on the ground feeling with her hand. Finally she touched her husband's body but it did not stir and she exclaimed, "Alas, something is wrong. Someone has been trampled to death! It is my husband. Save his life please. Let the local authorities know."

Only then did the peasant stop howling. He looked round and said, "Oh, the fortune-teller has been killed." When the blind woman heard this, she cried, "Please sir, call the local authorities and asked those on horse back to pay for my man's death."

"You have no sense of propriety. You'd better not do that! Do you know who those people on horseback are? They are sending fresh lychee as tribute for Lady Yang. No one knows how many people they have trampled to death on the road, but who dares to ask for compensation? What chance would a blind woman have?" The peasant was resigned to his lot and advised the blind woman.

"What's to be done, then?" The woman cried and said, "Oh, my husband, how am I going to bury your corpse?" The peasant had a generous nature and said, "I will help you to bury him nearby."

Ordinary people were not the only sufferers. Low ranking officials in feudal bureaucratic offices could not escape the mayhem.

One example of this was the posting station in Weicheng near the capital, a place where officials changed horses and had a rest. The station had spent its budget on envoys sending tributes of lychee each year and only had a skinny horse left. It was time for the lychee tribute again and the station master cleared off leaving a groom in charge. He had difficulty managing the station and did not know what to do with the envoys.

One afternoon envoy from Fuzhou galloped up and called out, "Station master, give me a new horse quickly." The groom left the room to hold the reins while the envoy carefully lowered his fruit basket and dusted his clothes. Another envoy from Hainan arrived at a gallop and cried out, "Station master, a change of horse for me." He carefully put down his fruit basket and after greeting the envoy from

Fuzhou said, "Groom, where is our meal?"

"It is not ready."

The envoy from Fuzhou wanted to make up time and was not worried about the food. "Never mind, we won't eat now. Just bring out the horses quickly."

"I am sorry, gentlemen, but there is only one horse left at the station. You yourselves can decide who will have it."

The envoy from Hainan had come a long way and his horse was not fit. The groom's reply enraged him and he shouted loudly, "What! Such a big station and only one horse? Call your rogue of a station master out and I'll ask him what he's done with the horses."

The groom spread his hands out helplessly and said, "The station had many horses. In the last few years they have been ridden to death by envoys with the fruit tribute. The station master was at his wit's end. That's why he made off."

The envoy from Hainan pressured him, "If the station master is not here, we can demand horses from you."

Although the groom was angry, he dared not talk back. Pointing to the stable he said, "Is there a horse in the stable?"

The envoy from Fuzhou was clever and he knew that as long as they argued there would not be another horse. He wanted to have the one that was there and said, "I got here first; let me have it."

"I come from Hainan which is farther away; you should let me have it."

The Fuzhou envoy went to change his horse; he did not want to quarrel with the envoy from Hainan. Angered, the Hainan envoy pulled him back. Immediately the envoy from Fuzhou picked up his basket of lychee to defend himself and said, "Don't you dare touch my lychee basket!" The envoy from Hainan also picked up his fruit basket and moving towards the envoy from Fuzhou saying, "Don't you dare touch my basket!" They were locked in a stalemate.

"Please keep your temper, gentlemen," the groom said. "Why don't both of you ride the horse?"

The envoys reacted to his suggestion by venting their anger on him. The Hainan envoy roared, "Nonsense! I'm going to beat you, you rascal!"

"I'm going to beat you too, you trickster!" The Fuzhou envoy was not one to lag behind.

The groom protected his head with his hands and knelt down, begging for mercy. The envoys said in unison, "If you want us to let you off, bring the horse quickly."

"There is only one horse."

"We need another."

"I can't get you another."

The two beat him again. The groom could not escape and took off his clothes saying, "Please don't beat me, gentlemen. Even if you beat me there is still only one horse. Please take my jacket to buy wine." The envoy from Fuzhou wanted the horse and not the coat. The envoy from Hainan examined the jacket, put it on and said, "All right, I must hurry. I shall change my horse at the next station." The envoy from Fuzhou mounted the skinny horse and rode off.

The horse had gone and so had the groom's jacket. He was very sad and sighed, "Oh, Lady Yang, Lady Yang! This happens all for your lychees!"

The lychees arrived at Chang'an, the capital, on time, but Li Longji had taken Lady Yang to Mount Lishan to spend summer there.

The emperor ordered a feast to be held in the Palace of Eternal Youth on Lady Yang's birthday, the first day of the sixth lunar moon. He sent Gao Lishi to summon the musician, Li Guinian, and his orchestra to play the Dance of the Rainbow and Feathery Garments which had been composed by Lady Yang. They would enjoy themselves from morning to night.

Ever since she had returned to the palace, Yang Yuhuan had done her best to keep Li Longji's favor and strengthen his love. The Dance of the Rainbow and Feathery Garments had been composed for this purpose.

When the score was finished, Yang Yuhuan had followed the emperor's instructions and had taught it to Yongxin and Niannu, who learned it quickly.

The two palace maids passed what they had learned on to Li Guinian, the orchestra leader, each night at the Chaoyuan Pavilion. One night when they had taken the score to the pavilion and were waiting for Li Guinian, Yongxin pushed open the window and said to Niannu, "Look, the moonlight lights up the outside as if it were under water and there is a cool breeze. This is a perfect night to learn music."

Niannu said, "We have finished the prelude and will begin the main parts." Li Guinian soon arrived.

He was an outstanding figure and had been appointed head of the orchestra by the emperor. There were excellent musicians, such as Lei Haiqing a famous lute player, in his group. After Li arrived the three started.

The Dance of the Rainbow and Feathery Garments was music from heaven and not only officials, but ordinary people in the capital all knew about it and longed to be the first to hear it. A certain young man by the name of Li Mo from area south of the Yangtze River heard of it during his visit to the capital. He was young and talented. As a child he had studied music and was known for his fine flute playing. He did his utmost to find a way to hear the music.

His efforts paid off. Someone told him that Chaoyuan Pavilion had been built by the palace wall and that music played in the palace could be heard from the outside. Taking his flute, he went that particular moonlit night to Lishan where he walked around the red palace wall and leant against a spot near the pavilion. He looked up to see the dancing light from the red lanterns and moving shadows. Patiently he waited.

After a while the mixed sound of pipe, flute, gong, drum and other musical instruments floated through the air. It was very pleasant to the ears, like the sound of scattered pearls falling on jade plates. After listening for a while, Li Mo grasped the essence. He took out his flute and lightly played the tune accompanied by music from the pavilion that sounded like the clatter of autumn bamboo and the crackle of spring ice. He listened to the music, played his flute then left happily when the lights and people in the pavilion had gone and the moon had moved to the west.

No one knew that Li Mo had stolen the music while Yang Yuhuan was preparing to dedicate the piece to the emperor on her birthday.

Now that the emperor was sitting in the center of the Palace of Eternal Youth giving orders to others to request Lady Yang to come.

Helped by Yongxin and Niannu, Lady Yang was gorgeously attired and walked slowly to the Palace of Eternal Youth. She curtseyed to the emperor and said, "Your slave Lady Yang is here. Long live the emperor! May Your Majesty live ten thousand years."

"Long live to you, my love." Li Longji said happily and added, "This is your birthday. I have prepared a feast to celebrate it. Let us spend the day in pleasure."

"I am overwhelmed by your royal favor, and would like to drink to your eternal life." Eunuch Gao Lishi at once handed Lady Yang a cup of wine and she presented it to Li Longji with both hands. Li Longji drank it and ordered a cup of wine for her. Lady Yang drank kneeling to show her thanks and kowtowed, saying, "Long live the emperor."

After the ceremony, Gao Lishi took a red scroll from an attendant and presented it to the emperor. The prime minister and the three duchesses had come to congratulate them and had brought gifts; they were waiting outside the palace.

Li Longji said, "Give them our thanks. The prime minister need not stand on ceremony and should return to his office to attend to affairs of state. The three duchesses may wait and feast with us later in the palace."

After he sent Gao Lishi away, another eunuch entered and reported that the lychees from Fuzhou and Hainan had arrived. Li Longji gave an order that they be brought in at once. At this a eunuch presented a large plate of lychees covered with a piece of yellow silk. Li Longji passed a sprig to Yang Yuhuan and said, "I know your fondness for them. I ordered the local authorities to send them here posthaste and they have arrived on time for your feast. For this I have to drink to you." Yang Yuhuan could only say, "Long live the emperor."

After drinking the wine she took a red lychee that held a white and translucent fruit inside; it tasted cool and sweet to her mouth. It was heavenly fruit and the emperor had given it to her. Lady Yang was overjoyed.

Seeing that she was in a happy mood the emperor heightened their enjoyment by saying, "Gao Lishi, order Li Guinian and his musicians to play for us."

Li Guinian and his men had waited outside for a long time. Hearing this order, he led the other musicians in and they kowtowed to the emperor and Lady Yang. They then played the Dance of the Rainbow and Feathery Garments which they had rehearsed many times.

Yang Yuhuan did her best to explain the music saying, "Every word and every note should match the dance. This part I have called light singing and graceful dancing."

"You have explained the dance very well."

Yang Yuhuan was overwhelmed with the praise and said, "I have had an emerald disk made and I would like to dance on it for Your Majesty's amusement."

"I have never seen you dance. It must be an entrancing sight. Yongxin and Niannu, Zheng Guanyin and Xie Aman, accompany Her Ladyship as she dances on the emerald disk." Li Longji's spirits were doubly enhanced.

While Lady Yang was putting on a dancing costume, attendants prepared the emerald disk. Li Longji also changed into less formal clothes and said to Gao Lishi, "Let Li Guinian and his men play according to the score and I will beat the drum myself."

Lady Yang was helped on to the emerald disk by palace maids and, when she stood in the center, the others withdrew. She looked like a red cloud descending from the sky. Gao Lishi knelt down to hold the drum and the emperor beat it to start the music. The other musicians played their own instruments. Sometimes the beat was quick and sometimes it was slow. Yang Yuhuan followed it closely changing her movements so that sometimes she was like a lotus swinging amid green leaves, and at other times, like a whirl in the wind. The dance stopped immediately when the emperor stopped playing. Yang Yuhuan curtseyed and said again and again, "Long live the emperor!"

Li Longji rose and stepped forward to take Yang Yuhuan's hand. He said, "That was an exquisite dance and proves that there is no end to your charms. You were like a swallow in flight and a swimming dragon." He turned and called, "Maids, bring the wine! Let me offer you a cup." Li Longji took the wine from a maid, handed it to Yang Yuhuan and said, "I hope you will taste and bottom up this cup. This is my thanks for your dance."

"Long live the emperor!" Yang Yuhuan took the cup and was modest. "Your slave is not worthy of drinking the wine given by you."

A little drunk and affected by the allure of Yang Yuhuan's charms Li Longji said, "I shall give you ten rolls of silk and a golden headband from Jinshajiang for your dance." He took a scented pouch from his chest and gave it to Yang Yuhuan. Hand in hand, they went to the sleeping palace.

CHAPTER SEVEN

Shift of Affection Triggers
a Grudge

THE DEEPEST AFFECTION will diminish and the most profound love will brew a grudge. Although Yang Yuhuan had been in favor with Li Longji for a long time, there were three thousand beauties in the inner palace who coveted his affections and tried every means of winning his favor. Lady Plum Blossom, Jiang Caiping, had been Li Longji's favorite, but she accidentally offended him and was moved to the east wing. She would not give up and Yang Yuhuan did all that she could to guard against her. The emperor, however, still had feelings for her. Jiang was extremely clever and she would surely find a way to get back to the emperor. Yang Yuhuan knew very well that she and Jiang Caiping were incompatible, like fire and water. It was not that she could not tolerate Jiang; she was afraid that Jiang could not tolerate her. As a result, she was often on tenterhooks.

One day the emperor did not return to Lady Yang's palace after attending the morning court. At dusk, she was very worried and sent Yongxin and Niannu to find out what had happened. The two maids did not return for some time and Yang Yuhuan sat alone in the palace feeling wretched. Normally the emperor would have returned long before and the two would have sat together holding each other's hand chatting merrily. She had no idea why he had not returned that day. Just then, there was a cry, "The emperor is here!" She got up at once, but there was no one; the words had been spoken by a parrot that had learnt the phrase. She stood by the rails looking around, helpless; it was already dark. Worried, she paced up and down. Suddenly she heard footsteps approaching; it was Yongxin coming back to report. "Your Ladyship, His Majesty is sleeping in the Emerald Pavilion tonight."

"Ah, can it be true?" she exclaimed. Tears rolled down her cheeks. "How shallow is the emperor's love! I wait to chat with him and he suddenly neglects me!"

Yongxin consoled her, "It is by chance that His Majesty hasn't come, my lady. He can't be staying away deliberately. Don't be sad, Your Ladyship."

"If his affections have not shifted how could he sleep alone in another palace? The emperor never passes a night alone; can it be no one lies by his side tonight?" Lady Yang was not simple and did not believe what Yongxin said to console her. Just then, Niannu returned and said, "Your Ladyship, I have found out the truth."

"What is it?"

"Your Ladyship, I heard that His Majesty secretly ordered a eunuch to fetch someone."

"Fetch whom?"

"Lady Plum Blossom, Jiang Caiping."

"Ah, so it is Lady Plum Blossom, the devil!" Her worst fears had come true. But she was still in doubt and said, "Are you certain of what you are saying?"

"Quite certain."

"Ah, heaven. Is that devil Lady Plum Blossom in favor again?" She sat silently wiping her tears.

Yongxin and Niannu said, "Don't be distressed, Your Ladyship."

Lady Yang said with feeling, "How can I not be sad or tremble at the news?" She wiped her tears away but they came again. She gave a long sigh and said, "My love and favor have turned to tears today. On other days, he loved me so dearly, but his heart has suddenly changed. If I had done wrong, he should have told me and pointed out my faults! After all the time he has been here, his heart has gone to another. He has deceived me for I am simple and innocent."

Niannu told her what she knew. "My lady, a eunuch told me that yesterday the emperor sent a parcel of pearls to Lady Plum Blossom from the Blooming Flower Pavilion. She wouldn't accept them and sent them back with a poem saying that since her dismissal she had not dressed her hair and that pearls would not console her in her grief. That accounts for what has happened tonight."

"So that is it! How could I know?"

Yongxin advised her to accept the emperor's wish and pleaded the case for Lady Plum Blossom's return. This would please His Majesty and Lady Plum Blossom would be grateful. But how could Yang Yuhuan tolerate someone else? She said no and asked the pair to go to the Emerald Pavilion with her.

Niannu panicked and said, "Why do you want to go there, my lady?"

"I'll see what magic she uses, what spell she casts to charm my lord and how she so fascinates the emperor."

Niannu was even more worried and said, "The emperor doesn't want you to know what has happened tonight, my lady, and it is now nearly midnight; His Majesty will be asleep. If Your Ladyship suddenly arrive there, it may embarrass him. You had better rest and deal with the matter tomorrow."

Although Lady Yang wanted to go to the Emerald Pavilion to vent her anger, what Niannu said was reasonable. If she went there now, it would certainly enrage the emperor. She wept and sighed. "Very well. I won't go ... but what sleep will I get tonight?"

After a sleepless night, she went to the Emerald Pavilion alone the following morning.

Lady Plum Blossom was there with the emperor. Her real name was Jiang Caiping, but Li Longji had granted her the title Lady Plum Blossom because she liked plum blossom. She had been the emperor's favorite in the past. After Lady Yang's arrival, she fell from favor and His Majesty had her moved to the east pavilion of the Shangyang Palace. The night before, however, the emperor had pretended to be sick and slept in the Emerald Pavilion. Secretly he sent a eunuch to summon Lady Plum Blossom. The maids had been told not to let Lady Yang know about this and Gao Lishi was ordered to stand guard outside the pavilion; he was to allow no one in.

Lady Yang came looking for the emperor and when Gao Lishi saw her from a distance, he was taken aback. Lady Plum Blossom was still in the pavilion. What could he do?

Before he could react, Yang Yuhuan arrived and said, "Gao Lishi, where is His Majesty?"

"In the pavilion, my lady."

"And who is with him?"

"No one."

"Open the door and let me see for myself."

Even though he was experienced in handling such things, it was a difficult situation. All he could say was, "Please take a seat, Your Ladyship. His Majesty was busy with state affairs. He felt a little tired and took a rest here. I was ordered to guard the door so that no one went in."

"Very well! How long will you keep up this farce? I know you fix your hopes on someone who is on the way up and insult me now that I am out of luck. Very well! I shall have to knock at the door myself." Gao Lishi had no choice and called out, "Lady Yang is here! Quickly open the door!" This warned the couple inside and startled Li Longji, who immediately hid Lady Plum Blossom behind a curtain and lay on the bed pretending to be asleep.

Lady Yang entered the inner room directly through the opened door. When she saw the emperor she said, "I heard that you were unwell, Your Majesty, and have come to ask about your health."

"I was feeling slightly indisposed, so I did not go to the palace. But why should you take the trouble of coming here so early?" Li Longji acted as if nothing had happened.

"I think I can guess the reason for Your Majesty's sickness."

The emperor could only laugh and say, "What do you guess?"

Lady Yang said that it was because of Lady Plum Blossom; Li Longji denied it. Yang Yuhuan did not believe him and looked down to see a pair of women's slippers. Li Longji lowered his head, pretending to look for something and an emerald trinket fell from his chest. When Yang Yuhuan saw this, she pressed for an answer.

Gao Lishi saw what was going on and at once ordered a eunuch to take Lady Plum Blossom through a gap in the wall at the back and then to the east pavilion. Lady Yang thought that Lady Plum Blossom was still in the pavilion and said, "The sun is high in the sky. Why hasn't Your Majesty gone to court? Those who do not know what is happening will think that I, the ugly imperial concubine, have kept you back. I shall wait here till you return." Li Longji was worried about Lady Plum Blossom and used every means to delay having to go. "I am not feeling well today; I shall not go to court."

When he finally found the opportunity, Gao Lishi discretely whispered to the emperor that Lady Plum Blossom had gone. Lady Yang kept urging him to go and Li Longji nodded and said, "Since Lady Yang wishes me to go, I will make the effort." He had nothing to worry about and left. Lady Yang found nothing and vented her anger upon Gao Lishi, "Gao Lishi, a fine trick you played behind my back. Now tell me where did the slippers and trinket come from?"

Gao Lishi explained truthfully, "Your Ladyship, His Majesty's love for you is unparalleled; he tries at all times to please you. As for these slippers and trinket, you would do well to say nothing of Lady Plum Blossom, the emperor's former favorite or even of some new beauties. Don't blame me for speaking out of turn. Even high officials have concubines so why cannot the emperor have one night of pleasure?"

Lady Yang could not refute him and offered a weak excuse for her behavior. "I do not begrudge him sharing his bed with someone else, but I hate the others who play tricks on me."

Yongxin arrived and Gao Lishi asked her to persuade Her Ladyship to return and not be distressed. Before Lady Yang had taken a step, Li Longji came back from the court. He was embarrassed and tried to please Lady Yang by asking her to go to the Blooming Flower Pavilion to view flowers. Lady Yang was not in the mood and said, "Are the flowers there as lovely as those in the east pavilion? Since the plum tree is the first to flower in the spring, you don't need the clinging willow."

Li Longji knew what she implied and said, "I love you truly.

Don't you know where my true love lies?"

Lady Yang became coy and ventured to ask the emperor to send her back. She took out the hairpin and jewel box and gave them back to him. In the emperor's eyes, she was demure and lovely and he again explained, "My love, how can you speak like this? We will love each other for a hundred years and still that will not be enough. Why should you speak of parting? It is my fault and I beg you not to be angry." Then he smiled and said, "When you shed tears and frown you are doubly charming. My love, put away the hairpin and box. We will go to the west palace where I have something to tell you." He held her hand and walked slowly.

The emperor had admitted that he was wrong and Yang Yuhuan realized that she had gone far enough. "If Your Majesty really wants me to stay, what more can I say?" Side by side, they walked to the west palace.

CHAPTER EIGHT

Peeping a Bath and Secret Vow

IT WAS MID-SUMMER and extremely hot. Li Longji decided to take Lady Yang to bathe in the Huaqing Pool. Eunuchs and maids busied themselves to prepare after the order was given.

The Huaqing Pool was at the foot of Mount Lishan and the people who worked there had been at the imperial palace but had been moved there for various reasons. For instance, one of the two maids now on duty had a loud voice and was plain, stout, clumsy and unfit for singing and dancing. The other had waited on Lady Plum Blossom who had been angry after she returned from the Emerald Pavilion and fell ill. So they were sent here. Usually there was little to do there but today everyone as busy because the emperor and Lady Yang were coming to bathe in the spring. After cleaning the palace and the pool, the maids had changed the beds and as everything was ready, they were waiting outside.

Mount Lishan was on the outskirts of Chang'an. The scenery there was unique and from a distance, it could be seen that it was surrounded by green trees. A red wall had been built round the Huaqing Pool and the Hot-Spring Palace so ordinary people could not see inside.

Inside there were small gardens, and carved beams with beaded curtains that covered corridors and a spring. It was an ideal place for bathing in the summer.

Li Longji and Yang Yuhuan arrived surrounded by eunuchs and maids, then headed for the Hot-Spring Palace and the Huaqing Pool. In the palace, Li Longji dismissed the eunuchs and all the maids except Yongxin and Niannu.

The others left and Li Longji said to Yang Yuhuan, "My love, the clear spring water ripples in the pool. It is soothing to the skin, fragrant and soft. Let us bathe here."

Yongxin and Niannu heard this and helped them take off their outer garments. The pearl-bright, jade-fine beauty of Lady Yang was at once revealed and Li Longji could not help murmuring, "My love, I cannot help feasting my eyes on you or stop loving, caressing, and cherishing you."

He held her arm and they walked into the pool. A screen separated them from the maids. Yongxin said to Niannu, "Look, how fond the emperor and Lady Yang are of each other. Don't you envy them?"

"Yes, I do."

"They caress each other among the flowers by day and lie together under the moonlight at night; they taste all the joys of love."

Yongxin suddenly added, "We have waited on Lady Yang for several years and see her each day; yet we have never seen her naked. Shall we peep through the curtain?"

"Yes, let's."

Despite the possible anger of the emperor and Lady Yang, the two took a furtive look. Yang Yuhuan's slender body floated like a lotus on the waves. She was lovely, with a slim waist, alluring breasts, light arms and snow-white skin. Niannu spoke in a low voice. "Look, how the emperor ogles her with a smirk on his face as if he had taken leave of his senses."

Yongxin said, "Look, the emperor holds her tight and kisses her again and again."

While they were peeping, two other maids who were carrying

out their chores came in and said, "You are having fun. Let us have a look too."

Startled, Yongxin and Niannu retorted, "We are just waiting on Lady Yang while she takes her bath. What is there to see?"

The other two were not satisfied by this and said, "You are not just waiting on Lady Yang, you're taking a good look at the emperor too."

"Pah, Pah, nonsense!"

While they were bickering, Li Longji helped Yang Yuhuan out of the water and called out, "Yongxin, Niannu."

At once, the pair emerged from behind the screen. Lady Yang came from the spring looking fresh and radiant with her dark hair lying disheveled on her shoulder. The two maids at once supported her to a couch. They helped her to dry her body and put on her clothes. Yongxin went out to call eunuchs to come with a carriage and said, "May it please Your Majesty, the carriage to take you and Her Ladyship back to the palace is here."

Li Longji was in high spirits and said to the eunuchs, "Let the carriage follow us. We'll take it when we are tired." To Yang Yuhuan he said, "Let us saunter slowly together, hand in hand and shoulder to shoulder in the cool breeze."

Ever since the day they had bathed in the Huaqing Pool, Li Longji's love for Yang Yuhuan had grown stronger. Yang Yuhuan, however, was uneasy after what had happened to Lady Plum Blossom. As the saying goes, "Being close to a tiger is like being close to an emperor." No one knew how it would end. In the palace it was quite common for someone to be quite happy one day and discarded the next. Whenever she thought about it, she was deeply worried and tried her best to keep in favor with the emperor.

The seventh day of the seventh lunar month was approaching. Legend has it that the Cowherd and the Weaving Maid, two stars in the heavens, are only allowed to meet that night each year. The Weaving Maid walks across the Milky Way over a bridge formed by magpies. This beautiful legend has intrigued men of letters and inspired enthusiastic young people who have left behind many moving stories and poems. The most popular verses handed down from generation to generation are "The rendezvous of gold phoenix and dew fare better than mortal lovers for all their meetings", and "When love is true, it makes no difference how seldom lovers meet." The Double Seventh was near and Yang Yuhuan would do something to celebrate it.

When she did, her activities attracted the attention of the Cowherd and the Weaving Maid in the heavens. The Weaving Maid had just crossed the Milky Way and, when she saw a wisp of smoke from burning incense rising high in the sky, she asked a fairy maid, "Where does it come from?"

The fairy maid looked around and replied, "Your Ladyship, it is Lady Yang, concubine of the Tang emperor, who is in the palace praying for happiness on this Double Seventh night." Since the story of the Cowherd and the Weaving Maid had spread among people on earth, women had prayed in courtyards for skill and happiness on the night of the Double Seventh.

"She is so reverent," the Weaving Maid said with a smile, "Let us go and have a look." They drifted to the sky above the Tang court.

The conversation and laughter of mortals not only reached heavens, but it was also heard by Li Longji, who was resting in a side hall. He spoke to the eunuch standing by. "Who is laughing and talking there?"

The eunuch called to a eunuch outside. "His Majesty asks who is laughing and talking there?" The eunuch on duty replied, "Lady Yang is going to the Palace of Eternal Youth to pray for happiness."

Li Longji heard this and said to the eunuch, "You don't have to relay this to me, and don't light the lantern. I will go there quietly." He left the side hall followed by eunuchs.

Yongxin and Niannu had already made the arrangements in the hall. Displayed on the table were a golden basin, a silver vase with fresh flowers, fruit and burning incense; candles lit up the hall. Li Longji looked on quietly and listened attentively as Lady Yang held burning incense and prayed. "I, Yang Yuhuan, reverently burn this incense, the offering of a true heart, as I pray to the twin stars above. May our love pledged by a hairpin and jewel box last forever and I not be cast off like a fan when autumn comes."

While Her Ladyship was praying, Yongxin and Niannu looked around and suddenly saw the emperor. They cried in astonishment,

"Ah, His Majesty is here!" Lady Yang turned hastily to kneel to him.

"What are you doing here, my love?"

"It is the evening of the seventh day of the seventh moon, so I prepared some fruit and was praying to the Cowherd and the Weaving Maid for grace and skill."

The emperor made fun of her. "You are already cleverer than any heavenly weaving maid. What more do you have to ask for? My love, look at the Cowherd and the Weaving Maid. Separated by the Milky Way they can only meet one night each year. How they must long for each other!"

"When you speak of the twin stars' grief at separating, sire, it makes me sad. It is a pity we mortals do not know what happens in heaven. They must be lovesick too." She wiped away tears.

"Ah, darling, why are you weeping?"

"Though the Cowherd and the Weaving Maid meet only once a year, their love will endure for all eternity. But our love, I am afraid, will not last as long."

"Why should you say that, my love?" He moved close to her and whispered, "Can the stars enjoy the same pleasure as us?"

"Your Majesty has been very kind to me, but there is something I beg to be allowed to say tonight…"

"Don't hesitate. What is it?"

Sobbing, Yang Yuhuan said, "Now I am the most favored of all Your Majesty's servants. But I am afraid that as time passes you will stop loving me. I will be forsaken and we will not live together till our hair turns white. If only our love would endure, I would die content." Her tears streamed down.

Li Longji wiped them away with his sleeve and said, "Don't be so sad, my darling. Ours is no common love."

"If you love me so much, sire, I beg you to vow under the twin stars to make our love eternal."

Li Longji promised and said, "Let us go then to offer incense and make a vow together." He took her hand and they walked together. The emperor offered incense and bowed with Yang Yuhuan, "May the twin stars in the heavens be our witness! We, Li Longji and Yang Yuhuan, love each other so dearly that we wish to be husband and wife in every new life and never be parted." Li Longji raised his hands and bowed, saying, "In the sky we will be two love birds, flying together." Yang Yuhuan bowed and responded. "On earth we will be twin branches on one tree." Together they said, "Though heaven and earth may end, may this vow last for ever and for ever." Yang Yuhuan turned and thanked Li Longji, saying, "I thank the emperor from the bottom of my heart. I shall remain true to this vow in life and death." She asked Li Longji, "Who will be our witness tonight?"

Li Longji thought a while and pointed to the sky, "The Cowherd and the Weaving Maid that shine beside the Milky Way can be our witnesses."

Moved by this the Cowherd said to the Weaving Maid, "See, my lady, how devoted the Tang emperor and Lady Yang are to each other. We lovers in heaven should watch over lovers on earth as we are entrusted to do. As they have asked us to witness their secret vow of love, we should protect them."

"There is a sad fate ahead of them; they will soon be separated by death. If they remain true, we can bring them together again."

"You are right. But now the night is nearly done and we must go back to our palace." The Cowherd and the Weaving Maid left hand in hand.

CHAPTER NINE

Fanyang Rebellion

AN LUSHAN, PRINCE of Dongping Prefecture, was made military governor of Fanyang and left the capital after the emperor mediated in a dispute between him and the prime minister, Yang Guozhong.

Though appointed a prince, An Lushan had started his career as a military man and felt constrained in the capital where he was unable to realize his ambitions. Now at the frontier, far from the court, he could act independently and do as he wished - plot to seize the throne.

There were 32 districts under the jurisdiction of the Fanyang military governor. Half the district commanders had been Hans and the others were Tartars. As the two nationalities had different characteristics, An Lushan found it hard to work with them and he presented a memorial to the emperor asking if he could substitute Tartar chiefs for the Chinese generals. Li Longji approved his request. Now An Lushan had under him Tartar chiefs and generals and they had become his confidants.

Of the 32 generals, the fiercest were He Qiannian in the east, Cui Qianyou in the west, Gao Xiuyan in the south, and Shi Siming in the north; the four generals were also the closest to An Lushan. When autumn came and the men and the horses were ready, it was time to drill and train. An Lushan ordered the four generals to take their men hunting and they followed his command.

Did An Lushan actually send them hunting? No. It was a pretext for drilling and training his men. He inspected his troops so he could launch the rebellion when the time came. Naturally, the four generals knew what was on his mind and each trained his men to be like fierce tigers and brave dragons. An Lushan was happy to see this and knew that he was prepared and that he could accomplish what he wanted. He murmured to himself, "Tang emperor, Tang emperor, there is no way that you could stop my men and horses!"

As the saying goes, if you don't wish anyone to know what you've done, it is better not to have done it in the first place. Someone was aware of An Lushan's activity. It was Guo Ziyi, the newly appointed governor of Lingwu. When he had first met An Lushan in the capital, he realized that An was a rebel and harbored ill intent. The emperor, however, trusted An and made him military governor of Fanyang, which was like letting the tiger return to the mountain. Guo Ziyi was even more worried when he learned that Tartar generals had been appointed. After he took up his new post, Guo Ziyi became aware that Lingwu was a place of great strategic importance and should be well defended. In the meantime he sent scouts to Fanyang to find out what was happening so that he could take precautions.

Guo Ziyi was sitting in the hall thinking when an attendant reported the return of a scout. He summoned him in at once and said, "Scout, you've been back there?"

"Yes, governor. I gathered a great amount of important information and returned as quickly as possible to report to you."

Discreetly, Guo Ziyi asked his attendants to close the door and said, "Step forward. Tell me, what is An Lushan's military strength? How powerful is his army?"

"My lord, when I reached Fanyang, I found a host of army tents, numerous spears and swords, and military curfew is strictly observed."

Guo Ziyi interrupted him, "What is An Lushan doing now?"

"He has dismissed his Chinese generals and appointed Tartars in their places. Pretending to hunt each day, they in fact improve their horsemanship."

"What else?" Guo Ziyi knew about this and was anxious to find out what new moves An Lushan had made.

"You would scarcely suspect such treacherous behavior. By underhand and sinister means he has rallied the barbarians and secretly gathered outlaws and criminals; many are hiding in his lair."

This surprised Guo Ziyi, who said, "Ah! Indeed! But has no one informed the government of this?"

"I heard that a month ago someone in the capital accused him of plotting rebellion and the emperor secretly sent a eunuch to Fanyang to watch him. But when An Lushan met the envoy, he pretended to be stupid and behaved politely, bribing him to say nothing. The eunuch was happy. He returned to court and completely cleared An Lushan of every charge. Now the emperor trusts him implicitly and had the informer sent to An's camp as punishment. Who dares to breathe a word against him any more?"

Guo Ziyi sighed and said, "What will this lead to?"

"Recently the prime minister presented a memorial to the throne, which declared that An Lushan's treason was obvious and asked His Majesty to have him executed. An Lushan heard of it and was a bit worried. But the emperor declared that he was loyal and told the prime minister to stop suspecting him. When An Lushan heard of it, he laughed aloud and said he would destroy the powerful minister."

Guo Ziyi said, "So he wants to destroy the prime minister! That means he is ready to rebel. How is it that I have never seen the memorial from the prime minister in the bulletin?"

The scout said, "It was marked confidential and was not published in the bulletin; the prime minister had a copy sent to An Lushan to goad him into revolting."

This made Guo Ziyi angry and he said, "A rebellious general at the frontier and a treacherous prime minister at the court! I cannot contain my anger!"

The scout added, "An Lushan has another scheme of presenting horses which is even more dastardly."

Guo Ziyi said, "How? Explain it to me."

"An Lushan sent his general, He Qiannian, with a memorial to the throne asking to be allowed to present three thousand horses, each of which would be accompanied by two armed guards, two trainers and one groom; that amounts to fifteen thousand men taking the horses to the capital. It would cause a huge disturbance along the way and ordinary people will suffer. Who could check them? Once these troops and horses reach Chang'an, they will cause much trouble."

Startled, Guo Ziyi said, "Ah, if he succeeds in this plan, the capital will be in danger."

"The memorial has just been sent but the emperor has not yet agreed to his request. It is obvious that An Lushan is plotting against the throne." The scout told Guo Ziyi all that he knew.

Guo Ziyi rewarded him with a jar of wine, one sheep and fifty taels of silver, as well as a month's leave. He then ordered maneuvers the following day.

Guo Ziyi's careful defensive measures did not stop An Lushan's plot to overthrow the Tang Dynasty. To further his ambitions, An Lushan had entered into a league with the tribes of the north and rallied outlaws and vagabonds from all parts of the empire. He gave them military training and waited for the time. As Li Longji had always trusted him, he intended to revolt only after his death. However, Yang Guozhong kept warning the emperor of An Lushan's disloyalty and asked to have him executed. Although the emperor did not listen to Yang Guozhong, An was vulnerable because he was far away at the frontier while Yang was present at the court. For this reason An could not postpone the revolt too long, as sooner or later he would be stabbed in the back. Acting on this, An Lushan ordered his troops to march on the capital, regardless of the consequences.

At first An Lushan dared not show his hand and employed deception by forging a decree in the emperor's name. The decree ordered him to march secretly to the capital with his army and kill the prime minister. By this means, he would seize the capital and ordinary people would not realize that his ambition was to overthrow the Tang Dynasty.

The situation in the frontier was critical, and urgent missives about An Lushan's rebellion were detained by ministers in power. The country had been at peace for a long time and civil officials had become indolent and officers frivolous. When war suddenly broke out, no one knew how to deal with it properly. Geshu Han, a retired general, once working as a military general in Hexi and Longyou, was appointed deputy marshal in haste and was made responsible for the defense of Tongguan Pass, a place of strategic importance as it guarded the route to the capital.

Although a deputy marshal, Geshu Han could not make independent decisions; he had to listen to a eunuch appointed as an army inspector and sent by the court. When An Lushan's army arrived at the Pass, they were opposed by a weak Tang force. The rebel army was large and strong, and under the circumstances, Geshu Han thought it the best to defend the city by closing the city gates, which would make it impossible for it to be taken quickly or easily. But the army inspector insisted that they fight and Geshu Han had no choice but to go out and fight as best he could. They were no match and An's officers captured him after a few skirmishes. As a result of the surrender, Tongguan Pass was lost. Ecstatic, An Lushan led his irresistible force on towards Chang'an.

The love between Li Longji and Yang Yuhuan deepened after that day they bathed together in the Huaqing Pool and later made a secret vow in the Palace of Eternal Youth. The emperor completely continued to neglect state affairs and knew nothing of the seizure of the Tongguan Pass by An Lushan. He just spent the days and nights with Lady Yang.

Autumn comes when summer goes. Autumn painted the imperial garden in many colors; willow leaves turned yellow, the duckweed grew less green and the red lotus shed all of its petals. The cassia flowers were in bloom. Clouds drifted across the blue sky and high up wild geese were flying. It was a time to appreciate natural scenery and the emperor ordered Gao Lishi to prepare a small feast in the imperial garden. He and Lady Yang visited it.

They arrived holding each other's hand in a carriage pushed by eunuchs. Gao Lishi was waiting to greet them at the west gate and said, "May it please Your Majesty and Your Ladyship to alight here." He helped them down and withdrew, as there were no new orders from the emperor.

"My love, let's take a walk."

"As you wish."

Hand in hand they wandered among flowers and trees. There was a cool gust of wind and a row of trees cast long shadows by the railings. Swallows still lingered by their nests, and a duck and a drake slept on the pond. They walked slowly, the only people in the garden.

"Gao Lishi, bring wine! I shall drink a few cups with Her Ladyship."

Gao Lishi came at once and said, "The feast is already spread and ready in the pavilion. Please step over there."

They forwent the sumptuous food of the imperial garden, ordering instead a simple meal of vegetables and fruit. He dismissed the imperial musicians and asked Lady Yang to sing a song composed by Li Bai, while he accompanied her on the flute. It was a small feast; they did as they liked without ceremony.

In a while, words from the song, "Her dress is like a brilliant cloud," could be heard. The couple came to the part, "The famous flower and the beauty are delighted, and the emperor enjoys the scene with a smile," and they gazed at each other; Lady Yang was grateful for the thoughtful arrangement. She drank a few more cups and was intoxicated, intoxicated by wine and affection. She looked so lovely in that state that Li Longji could not take his eyes off her; he was drunk himself.

But extreme joy begets sorrow. The sound of drum could be heard and Gao Lishi and some eunuchs came running. The drum woke Li Longji and he said, "Where did the sound of drum come from?" No one answered. The prime minister, Yang Guozhong, rushed in, saw Gao Lishi and asked loudly, "Where is the emperor?"

"In the imperial garden."

Yang Guozhong continued walking and said, "The situation is serious. I must go straight in." Gao Lishi followed him and as soon as Yang Guozhong saw Li Longji he said, "Your Majesty, I have had bad news! An Lushan has revolted and his army has entered the Tongguan Pass. He is marching on the capital."

Li Longji was alarmed and said, "What of the troops defending the Pass?"

"General Geshu Han was defeated and has surrendered to the rebels."

Li Longji did not know what to do and stammered, "Ah, ah, ah, Geshu Han has been defeated. How could it be that An Lushan has rebelled? He must have left Fanyang, taken Luoyang rapidly and then marched on to Tongguan Pass. The news strikes dread into my heart and I quake with fear. What plans do you have to resist them?"

Yang Guozhong had calmed down and said, "In the past I repeatedly warned Your Majesty that An would rebel, but you would not listen to me. Now what I predicted has happened. At the moment we are powerless to resist him. For the time being Your Majesty should go to western Sichuan and wait there until the generals from the provinces rally to defend the throne."

Li Longji had nothing to contribute himself and said, "Very well, very well. I'll do as you say. Put out the order for all princes and ministers to prepare to accompany me." Yang Guozhong left and Li Longji spoke to Gao Lishi. "Quickly order Chen Yuanli, Commander of the Imperial Guards, to muster three thousand men to escort us." Gao Lishi left.

A eunuch spoke out, "May it please Your Majesty to return to the palace for a rest?" Li Longji paced forward and murmured, "While we were feasting merrily in the garden, I had no idea that this would happen. What shall I do? Maids, has Lady Yang slept?"

"Yes, she is fast asleep."

"Do not wake her. We shall wake her when we leave at dawn tomorrow. Ah, heaven, how unfortunate I am to be overtaken by such a disaster and how distressing it is to think of her taking to the road with her flower-like beauty!"

Early in the morning Li Longji, Yang Yuhuan and many eunuchs and palace maids left the palace. Ministers including Yang Guozhong went with the emperor and they traveled day and night heading for western Sichuan. As the capital became more and more distant, they saw mountains and rivers and deserted houses with broken tiles and withered crops. There was chaos everywhere, totally unlike the Kaiyuan period. Li Longji was sad to see it.

Gao Lishi suddenly arrived. "Your Majesty, we are at Mawei Station. Would you please take a rest here." He helped Li Longji and Lady Yang alight and went inside. Li Longji spoke to Lady Yang. "I was wrong in believing the scoundrel An who has forced us to make this move. There is no point in regretting it. The only thing I feel sorry about is that you, my love, have to take this hard journey with me. There is nothing else I can do."

Although tired and not properly dressed, Lady Yang kept up proprieties and said, "I, your servant, shall follow you and not shrink from any hardship. I only hope that the rebels will soon be defeated so that Your Majesty can return to the capital."

Let us leave the pair pitying and consoling each other. The three thousand imperial guards led by Commander Chen Yuanli had enjoyed a good position and had lived in comfort. Now that they experienced hardships, they complained and grumbled. At Mawei Station they ran about shouting and sighing and plotting in groups. Finally the general outcry was that An Lushan's rebellion and the flight of the emperor from the capital were all Yang Guozhong's fault. If the treacherous minister were not put to death, they would not escort His Majesty .

Chen Yuanli heard the commotion and came out of his quarters and said at the top of his voice, "Stop shouting and pitch camp quietly. I shall report to the emperor and ask for his orders." The commotion died down but soon started again.

Before Chen Yuanli had reported to the emperor, small groups of soldiers carrying swords were searching for Yang Guozhong. They shouted out that he had been the cause of the trouble and was now secretly scheming with western tribesmen. They vowed to kill him. The leader of the group cried out, "Whoever wants to kill Yang Guozhong join us!"

Yang Guozhong ran but the guards surrounded him and there was nowhere to hide. He was arrested quickly and without any further ado his head was chopped off.

In the inner room, the roaring startled the emperor. He called out, "Gao Lishi, who is shouting outside? Call Commander Chen here at once."

Gao Lishi met Chen Yuanli at the door. Chen knelt before the emperor and said, "Long live the emperor!"

"Why are the soldiers shouting?" The emperor was apprehensive.

Chen Yuanli spoke truthfully. "Your Majesty, by trying to take over the reins and usurp all power Yang Guozhong endangered the state. When the guards discovered that he had been secretly negotiating with western tribesmen, they were indignant and killed him."

"What!" Li Longji panicked and could not utter a word. When Lady Yang heard it, she turned her head to wipe the tears away. Li Longji thought for a moment. He had to accept what had happened and said to Chen Yuanli, "Very well. Give orders to resume our journey." He knew that it was most important that they reached western Sichuan in time.

Chen Yuanli came out and announced, "His Majesty pardons the guards for killing the prime minister and orders you to set out once again."

CHAPTER TEN

Death at Mawei Station

L I LONGJI HAD misread the situation. After killing Yang Guozhong he thought that the soldiers would be pacified; he had pardoned them. The soldiers, however, were restless and called out together, "Though Yang Guozhong is dead, his cousin Lady Yang is still with the emperor. Until she is killed, we will not go a step further!"

Chen Yuanli had to make a report to Li Longji. He knew that the soldiers were afraid that Lady Yang would later take revenge for Yang Guozhong's death. He advised the emperor, "I hope Your Majesty will put aside your love of Lady Yang and have her executed to satisfy the guards."

"Aya! How could they request this?" Li Longji was thoroughly alarmed. Yang Yuhuan grieved; she shivered and tugged the emperor's sleeve. Li Longji said indignantly, "If Yang Guozhong was guilty, he has already paid with his life. But his cousin only served in the inner palace. What can the army suspect her of?"

Chen Yuanli could only say, "Your Majesty is right. Yet the troops are in an ugly mood. What can we do?"

Yang Yuhuan listened attentively and was sad and frightened. She said, "Your Majesty, this has taken me by surprise and I feel distressed. As I grieve for my cousin's death, I find that I too am involved. I must have been fated to suffer. I beg you, sire, give me up at once." She was choking and could say nothing.

Helpless, Li Longji consoled her, "My love, don't be sad." From outside the cry came, "We shall not move a step unless Lady Yang is executed!"

Chen Yuanli knew that the situation was urgent and said, "Though Lady Yang is innocent, Your Majesty, she is the prime minister's cousin. As long as she is at your side, the troops will feel unsafe. Only when the troops feel safe will your own safety be assured. I hope Your Majesty will consider this carefully."

Li Longji's mind was in a muddle and for a moment he was unable to say anything. Yang Yuhuan clung to his robes crying sadly, "I can't bear to leave Your Majesty. I never expected them to be so cruel!" Li Longji sobbed and the shouts outside became louder. He took hold of her and said, "My love, I don't know what to do."

Seeing that nothing had happened the soldiers surrounded the station making an uproar. Gao Lishi had to urge the emperor. "Your Majesty, the troops have besieged the station. If we hesitate, they may become desperate. What is to be done?"

Li Longji knew that there was no other avenue for him to explore. He could only save the situation by giving up Lady Yang and he said, "Chen Yuanli, quickly pacify the troops while I find a way out."

After Chen Yuanli left Li Longji and Yang Yuhuan clung to each other and cried; both knew that it was time for them to part forever. Li Longji sighed and said, "It would have been better for you to have loved an ordinary person rather than an emperor. Then you could have lived till your hair turned white. How can we abandon the love between us so suddenly?"

Yang Yuhuan shared his feelings but the situation forced her to choose death. So she knelt down and said, "Your Majesty has shown me so much favor that even if I kill myself I cannot repay your kindness. The situation is desperate and I beg you to allow me to commit suicide to pacify the troops. Then you will arrive at western Sichuan safely and I shall die comforted." She fell to the ground weeping.

Sorely afflicted Li Longji held her to his bosom. He said, "How can you say that, my love? If you die, what are my throne and empire to me? I would rather lose my empire than abandon you."

"I will never forget Your Majesty's kindness. But things have come to such a pass that there is no other way out. If I hesitate any longer, we may both be destroyed and then my guilt will be greater. Please give me up and preserve your empire."

Hearing what they said Gao Lishi sobbed in sympathy, but under the circumstances he had to remind the emperor of his duties. Kneeling he said, "Since Lady Yang shows such spirit and wishes to sacrifice herself, I beg Your Majesty to think of the empire and force yourself to agree to her request."

The cries outside became louder and louder and Li Longji knew that this was the only thing that they could do. He sobbed, stamped heavily and said, "Well, well, so be it then! If she insists, I cannot forbid her. Let Her Ladyship do as she thinks right!" Weeping he went to another room and covered his face.

Although she had made up her mind to die, when Yang Yuhuan heard this she was sad and cried out bitterly, "Long live the emperor," before falling to the ground. Gao Lishi shouted to the soldiers outside, "Listen men! His Majesty has ordered Lady Yang to commit suicide."

"Long live the emperor! Long, long live the emperor!" The troops were relieved.

After calming the troops, Gao Lishi helped Yang Yuhuan to rise. She murmured sadly, "I thought that we would live till we were old. Who would have expected that soon we will be parted forever or that I was going to die for the emperor?" When they walked past a shrine, she wanted to go in and pray. Gao Lishi did not have the heart to refuse the request of a person about to die. Kneeling before the image of Buddha Lady Yang said, "Great Buddha! My sins are many; have mercy on my soul!" She wept openly.

Gao Lishi knelt down and said, "May Your Ladyship enter paradise! Have you any last commands for me?"

"Gao Lishi, the emperor is growing old. When I am dead, you

will be the only one who can understand him. You must look after him and tell him not to think of me any more."

Her sincerity moved Gao Lishi and he said, "I will, my lady."

"Gao Lishi, there is something else." She unfastened the hairpin from her hair and took out the jewelry box. She said, "The emperor gave me these to pledge his love. Bury them with my body and be sure not to forget!"

Gao Lishi took them and said, "Yes, my lady."

She knew that the time for death was near and wept again. Chen Yuanli and a few soldiers arrived. He ignored her distress and said, "Lady Yang has been ordered to commit suicide. Why is she still here delaying His Majesty's journey?" The soldiers pressed forward and Gao Lishi who stretched out his hand to stop them said, "Keep back! Lady Yang is about to die."

Yang Yuhuan was angry and said, "Ah, Chen Yuanli! Why don't you pitch yourself against the rebels instead of against me?" The soldiers pushed forward and Gao Lishi did his best to stop them.

Yang Yuhuan looked round. There was a pear tree. She removed her white silk belt and sighed, "I will end my life here with the pear tree." She bowed to heaven and said, "Yang Yuhuan thanks the emperor for his past kindness; we shall never meet again. Although my body will lie in the earth, my spirit will follow the imperial pennants!" She then hanged herself.

Chen Yuanli shouted to the soldiers, "Lady Yang has died, men, withdraw!"

Gao Lishi took down the silk belt that Lady Yang had used to hang herself with and took it to Li Longji. "Your Majesty, Lady Yang is dead."

Li Longji looked dazed and said nothing. Gao Lishi tried again. "Lady Yang is dead, sire. Here is the silk belt with which she hanged herself." Only then did Li Longji accept the fact and he cried bitterly, "Aya, my love! my love! How can I bear this?" He slumped onto a chair and said, "She was like a peach blossom, but now…"

Gao Lishi showed him the hairpin and the box and said, "Her Ladyship asked me to bury these two articles with her." Li Longji looked at them and recalled the pledge of love they made in the

Palace of Eternal Youth. He cried aloud.

"Your Majesty, where shall we find a coffin at such a time?"

"Never mind that. Wrap her in a silk quilt and bury her deeply for the time being. Mark the place well so that we can remove her body later. The hairpin and the box can be fastened to her clothes." He covered his face and cried out, "I shall never see her again in this life."

Gao Lishi made these arrangements. Chen Yuanli entered and knelt down. "May it please Your Majesty, your horse is ready."

Li Longji stamped and said bitterly, "What do I care if I never reach western Sichuan?"

Outside trumpets sounded, men cried out and horses neighed; the troops were ready to go west. Gao Lishi knew that although the emperor was disconsolate he had to move on to western Sichuan. He came in quietly, advised him and helped him mount his horse. Along the road they encountered thick mists, cold winds and yellow dust, which together with the long distances compounded Li Longji's sorrow and bitterness.

After Yang Yuhuan hanged herself, General Chen Yuanli led the guards to escort Li Longji to go to western Sichuan. They were worn out many days in the hard journey. Li Longji complained and yearned desperately for Lady Yang. At times he blamed himself bitterly because he was an emperor and had been unable to protect his beloved imperial concubine.

The guards marched slowly on and arrived at Fufeng, where Li Longji rested in the Fengyi Palace while the soldiers camped around it.

Incessant wars in the past had emptied almost all the houses; deserted fields produced no grain. The soldiers plundered and looted all the way so that there was practically nothing left when they passed. At Fufeng no one had anything to eat. That included Li Longji.

An old peasant arrived shivering and carrying a bowl of oatmeal. He said to Gao Lishi, who was guarding the gate, "Please, sir, would you let His Majesty know that the peasant Guo Congjin has come to present oatmeal."

Gao Lishi was overjoyed; he had sent eunuchs to seek out food some time ago and they had not returned. He had been worried that the emperor would be angry. He told Guo Congjin to wait there and reported it straight away to emperor. Li Longji said at once, "Let him come in."

Guo Congjin followed Gao Lishi into the hall and he kowtowed to the emperor, saying, "Your humble subject Guo Congjin salutes Your Majesty."

"Where are you from?" asked the emperor.

"I live here, Your Majesty."

"How do you make a living?"

"I tilled the land and was happy to live here when times were peaceful; harvests were good, I had enough to eat and was clothed. Now there has been a sudden rebellion at Fanyang and I am much afraid. I heard that Your Majesty was flying to the west and feared that there was nothing for you to eat in this desolate place. I still have some oats at home, so I present you a bowl of oatmeal and hope that you will not find our simple country fare too rough or coarse."

Li Longji was moved. He said, "Thank you. Bring it to me, Gao Lishi."

Gao Lishi took the bowl from Guo Congjin and presented it to the emperor.

Inside the bowl was a yellow and white gruel and though the emperor was hungry, he did not eat. His thoughts flew elsewhere and he murmured, "Ah, after living in luxury in the palace all these years I have never tasted anything like this. I had more than one hundred dishes of rare delicacies and fresh vegetables and fruit each day and yet I often thought them ill prepared. Who would have thought that I would have to satisfy my hunger with this? How can I swallow it?" He ate a little, sighed and put down the bowl.

Seeing that he could not eat the oatmeal, Guo Congjin said, "Your Majesty, who do you consider responsible for the trouble we are in today?"

"Who would you say?" Li Longji was surprised by the question.

"I hope you will forgive me if I speak frankly." Guo Congjin was persistent and seemed to have made up his mind.

"Don't hesitate. Go on."

"It was Yang Guozhong's fault. He relied on his relationship with Your Majesty to accept bribes and strengthen his evil power until he had corrupted the whole empire. For many years he waged a feud with An Lushan and eventually provoked An Lushan to revolt."

Li Longji defended himself saying, "How could I know of Yang Guozhong's challenge and An Lushan's rebellion?"

"An Lushan has been planning to revolt for a long time and everyone knew of his treason. Last year when someone informed on him, Your Majesty had the informer put to death. After that who would risk his life to warn you?"

Li Longji had to admit to his faults and said, "Yes, I bear much of the blame. I remember when Yao Chong and Song Jing were ministers of state they gave me such good advice that I felt that my subjects from all over the country were before me and that I could see them. After they died, the new ministers simply tried to seize power or curry favor with me. They were not like you, a loyal citizen."

"But if Your Majesty had not come here, what chance would I have of seeing you?"

Li Longji sighed and nodded. "I profusely regret it."

Guo Congjin saw that the emperor felt remorse and said no more. He gave a few words of consolation and took his leave.

Just then an envoy with one hundred thousand rolls of silk tribute, which had been sent by the military governor of western Sichuan and was on its way capital, arrived at Fufeng. When the envoy heard that the emperor was at Fufeng, he asked Gao Lishi to report his presence to the emperor.

Li Longji told Gao Lishi to accept the rolls of silk and sent the envoy back. He then said to Gao Lishi, "Order the guards to gather. I have something to say to them."

Chen Yuanli went inside the hall while the guards gathered outside the palace. Li Longji asked Chen Yuanli to pass a message onto the guards and he addressed them, "Soldiers, listen to me. The Fanyang rebellion was unexpected. We have traveled far to western Sichuan to avoid attacks and I thank you for your escort. Today, however, I have a proposition."

"What are Your Majesty's orders?"

Li Longji showed his human side and said, "I know that while you have been on the road to western Sichuan and you have been longing for your parents, wives and children. The journey is arduous and the road is as hard as the road to heaven. We are going to a remote destination; you are cold and hungry and have experienced every kind of hardship. I have thought about this for some time. I cannot settle with you as I am not in the capital and I have no money. Today an envoy from western Sichuan brought a hundred thousand rolls of silk tribute and I want to distribute it among you in lieu of a salary so that you can go home and be reunited with your families."

"Then what about Your Majesty?"

"I have decided to proceed slowly to western Sichuan with the eunuchs and young princes."

Li Longji was surprised at the reaction. After they had heard what he had said, the guards said in a chorus, "We are heartbroken at Your Majesty's words. Soldiers are trained for crises but after receiving our salary, we proved useless and could not destroy the foe. We want to follow you to western Sichuan. As for the silk, we would not dare accept it; please use it for rewards when the rebellion is suppressed. Your Majesty, if we do not mean it, heaven will punish us."

Li Longji was deeply moved and said, "You are so loyal that I will always remember you, but I cannot bear to keep you for too long. You must go home."

"Can it be that Your Majesty suspects us of being disloyal because of Lady Yang's death?"

"No, that is not the reason. But the citizens of Chang'an are concerned about us. Go back and tell them that I am safe and well."

The guards did not waver and said that they wanted to follow the emperor to western Sichuan. They would return to the capital together when the rebels were swept away. Only then did Li Longji give his consent and said, "It is getting late; we will spend the night here, and start early tomorrow."

CHAPTER ELEVEN

The Spirit Followed

AFTER YANG YUHUAN hanged herself at Mawei
Station, her spirit drifted from the station and followed Li
Longji to western Sichuan.

Moved by Li Longji's attempt at distributing the silk tribute
the guards pledged to accompany him to western Sichuan. They
walked slowly; they had traveled a long time, the road was desolate
and they had little food. Yang Yuhuan's spirit drifted with the wind
and soon caught up with them. It saw the banners fluttering from
the imperial canopy and when it approached, it wanted to cling to
the robe of Li Longji. A drum sounded, the spirit was startled and
stopped. A black wind covered the road and when it died, Li Longji
had gone. The spirit could only return amidst the dust.

A little later, Yang Yuhuan's spirit saw the ghost of the Duchess
of Guo coming her way. It was being beaten by two devils who were
taking her to the City of Avenging Spirits. There was another ghost,
a male dripping with blood and running. Yang Yuhuan's spirit looked
at it and saw that it was her cousin, Yang Guozhong, who was being
dragged by two devils to the Forest of the Hills of Swords and Knives
in Fengdu, a city of ghosts. The spirit of Yang Yuhuan thought of her

sister in the Pei Family who had enjoyed every luxury in her life and of her cousin Guozhong who had seized power and ruined the state; they had both come to this end. If this was the case with her sister and cousin, she must be guilty too. The future looked bleak; what would her end be? She had no option but to return to Mawei Station and repent.

At the time, the Tutelary God of Mawei Station had been summoned by the God of the Eastern Mountain and told to watch over the body and spirit of Lady Yang. In a former life she had been a fairy on the fairy mountain and had died in his territory; he had to wait for further orders from heaven. The Tutelary God went to inspect the place where Yang Yuhuan had been buried.

Yang Yuhuan's spirit drifted back to Mawei Station and hovered above the pear tree where she had hung herself. There was some writing on it -- Lady Yang lies here. Was it not the writing of Gao Lishi? So she was buried there! Ah, Yang Yuhuan, Yang Yuhuan, in the past you lived such a life of luxury and pleasure. Now you are lonely, covered by yellow earth instead of silks and brocades. It is very sad! Where are the hairpin and the jewelry box you asked Gao Lishi to bury with you? Did he do what you asked, or did he just throw them away. If he threw them away, how could you prove your love? But it is meaningless; even if he had buried them, how could your decayed body reunite with the emperor? The spirit wept sadly.

The Tutelary God who had just arrived heard her weeping, "Is that the ghost of Lady Yang crying there?"

"Yes. What god are you? Please pardon me for being here."

"I am the Tutelary God of Mawei."

"I beg you to help me."

The Tutelary God told her about his instructions from the God of the Eastern Mountain. "You were formerly a fairy on the fairy mountain; you were sent to earth to expiate some faults. And now, though you have ended your span of life on earth, you are not permitted to return to heaven yet." He unfastened the white belt she used to hang herself and said, "By the order of the God of the Eastern Mountain, I deliver you from your sins to save you from hell."

"I thank you. May I ask if I will ever meet the emperor again?"

"That I do not know. For the time being you may stay at the station and wait for an order from heaven. I shall be leaving you now." The god suddenly disappeared. After what he had told her the spirit of Yang Yuhuan had no choice but to stay.

The Tutelary God left but he frequently came back for his rounds. The local temple had been prosperous. After An Lushan rebelled, the local people ran away; now it was deserted and no more incense burned there. Many wandering spirits roamed around nowadays so he had to make more inspection tours and see to it that everything was all right. One night when he arrived at the station on an inspection tour, he saw the spirit of Yang Yuhuan sitting, weeping alone on the tomb and murmuring under the pale moon and cold stars. He hid and listened to what she said.

The spirit of Yang Yuhuan sighed and said, "In life I enjoyed great favor and honor and took pleasure with the emperor in the west palace. Now my corpse is buried in the ground and I am sad. Who would recognize this ghost as the former Yang Yuhuan!" The spirit took the hairpin and the jewelry box out from her sleeve and gazed at them murmuring, "These pledges of love taken from the grave were given to me by the emperor. I feel sad when I see them. I thought that our love would remain as solid, but it has been severed just as a thread is snapped. If I had known that our love would end like this, I would never have kept them. I remember the jewelry box giving off a fragrance at night and the hairpin glittering in the morning mirror. What joy and love we had. When I think of our former love, how can I bear to close my eyes in death?"

The spirit was lost in thought and repented murmuring, "Ah, Yang Yuhuan, although I died a sad death, all that I did in my life was bad; the crimes that my cousin and sisters committed in their greed for power will be laid at my door. How can I be forgiven? The Tutelary God said that I was once a fairy on the fairy mountain but since I have been so sinful, I have no hope of rejoining the fairies. All I ask for is to return to my former lover, then I will be content."

When the Tutelary God saw that she was sincerely repentant he showed himself and said, "Lady Yang, I am here."

Startled, the spirit said, "So the Tutelary God is here."

"I heard you repenting. Your penitence will move the gods on high to pardon you and restore your love."

"Thank you for your sympathy. But I fear my faults were too many and that I cannot be pardoned. It makes me sad."

"Do not be sad. I will give you a travel permit allowing you to wander around at will for a hundred miles. However, I must remind you that you were once an immortal and that you were sent to earth for minor faults. When you went to the palace, you were led astray by love that led to this catastrophe. Now that you have repented and awoken from your dream, I hope that you will forsake your old ways and return to heaven as soon as possible."

Yang Yuhuan's spirit was pleased to hear that she would receive a permit. But how could she, an unhappy ghost, go to heaven? With the travel permit, she could travel at night and vanish by day; guided by the moon and stars she could find her former love.

The Tutelary God did not know what was on her mind and gave her the permit before leaving.

The spirit of Yang Yuhuan rose from the grave and hovered around the pear tree. It thought about the day that she had been forced to hang herself and again wept sadly.

The Weaving Maid from heaven passed by on her way to present silk to the Heavenly Palace. When she saw a gloomy aura rising to the sky she said to the angels, "Do you see that sad and foggy atmosphere? What place is that down below?"

"That is Mawei Station, my lady."

"Tell the carriage to stop, and summon the Tutelary God of Mawei."

The Tutelary God arrived, kowtowed to the Weaving Maid and said, "The Tutelary God of Mawei greets you, my lady. May you be blessed forever."

"God of Mawei, as I passed by I noticed a sad atmosphere from your territory penetrating to the sky. What is the cause?"

"I will tell you, my lady. That was Yang Yuhuan, the concubine of the Tang emperor, who was lamenting her death on her grave."

"So it is Yang Yuhuan. I remember the evening in the tenth year of the Tianbao period; she and the Tang emperor swore to be husband and wife all their future lives at the Palace of Eternal Youth. But now, poor thing, she is an unhappy spirit. Tell me how she died."

The Tutelary God told her the whole story, including the mutiny of the guards and the suicide of Lady Yang. After hearing the story, the Weaving Maid felt sympathetic and said, "Though she was to blame for her own death, the Tang emperor, the son of heaven, was unable to protect a woman. What of his pledge at the Palace of Eternal Youth? How heartless he is!"

"My lady, Lady Yang does not blame the emperor. She was thinking about how she could renew her union with her lover."

"Even when she is in such a state she still remembers the pledge in the Palace of Eternal Youth. I find this very touching."

"She has repented her former sins too, my lady."

"Well, if she repents all her sins she could be forgiven. I shall speak for her in heaven and have her restored to her position among the fairies."

The Tutelary God said, "My lady, even if you restore her to her old position, she will not renounce her pledge to the Tang emperor."

This touched the Weaving Maid and she said, "Well, she is very steadfast in her love." She added, "You may go back to your post now. I shall see to this." She ordered the angels to drive her carriage to the heavenly palace.

CHAPTER TWELVE

Hearing Bells and
Mourning the Image

A FTER LI LONGJI left Mawei Station, there was no beautiful Lady Yang to accompany him. He rode on horseback closely followed by Gao Lishi. The guards marched westward in front of him day after day past mountains, gorges empty houses and deserted fields. Poplar leaves rustled in the autumn wind and sometimes one or two lonely geese lamented overhead. It all increased Li Longji's sorrow.

After Yang Yuhuan committed suicide, Li Longji lost interest in life. He and his government faced a hopeless exile and an arduous journey as a result of the rebellion of An Lushan. He thought the matter over and decided to cede the throne to Li Heng, the crown prince, leaving him to restore peace.

The procession had gone on and on for a whole month and was nearing western Sichuan. As the crown prince was now the ruler, Li Longji ordered Gao Lishi to go slowly. But it was autumn and the mountains, water and fallen leaves on either side of the road made him sad and he sighed often.

Gao Lishi worried about this and frequently offered advice. "Your Majesty, you are tired after the long journey and the weather is cold. You must not grieve, but keep up your spirits."

"Ah, Gao Lishi, you know that Her Ladyship and I always sat together and walked shoulder to shoulder; we were never apart. Now the westward exodus has killed her and I cannot but think of her." He sobbed as he spoke of her death and murmured, "It makes me sad to think of the past and I feel hatred when I look back towards Mawei Station."

The guards were just ahead and Gao Lishi thought it improper to mention the subject. He said, "Your Majesty, the path ahead is steep. Keep a firm grip on your reins, sire, and ride slowly."

Li Longji realized what he implied and knew that he had been careless. He said no more, held the reins tight and moved on slowly. Looking around he saw horses and men picking their way along a path beneath towering and precipitous mountains that almost touched the sky while monkeys and wild birds wailed in the background. Dark clouds gathered, engulfing the mountains; the wind was cold and the sky dark. It was a frightful scene.

"It is going to rain, sire. Will you go into the Jian Pavilion to take shelter?" Gao Lishi got down first and helped Li Longji to dismount and walk up to the pavilion. After Li Longji sat down, Gao Lishi told the soldiers to take shelter as well.

Li Longji sat for a while in the pavilion then stood up and looked at the scene around them. He improvised a poem and recited to himself:

> *I walk here alone in my grief,*
> *My sorrow as endless as the hills and streams.*
> *The wind has driven storm clouds over,*
> *Rain falling endlessly makes me sick at heart.*

He spoke to Gao Lishi, "Where does that irritating sound come from? Find out what is causing it."

Gao Lishi walked to the railings and looked around. "Your Majesty, it is the rain in the forest and the bells hanging from eaves; they make a noise in the wind."

97

"The dripping of the rain and the tinkling of the bells are dismal and frightening. And the glowworms in the wet grass disturbed by the wind are like spirit lights. Ah, I sit alone on the empty mountain unable to be with my love. The raindrops and the bells have rekindled my sadness."

Gao Lishi had to distract him. He saw that the rain had stopped and said, "Your Majesty, do not grieve. The rain has ended. Will you come down now?"

When Li Longji left the pavilion and mounted his horse, Gao Lishi called out, "Guards! To horse. The emperor is on the horseback." The procession continued along the narrow mountain track now green after the rain.

The day that Li Longji entered western Sichuan he learned that Guo Ziyi had been victorious and would soon suppress the rebellion. Since he was no longer in charge of state affairs, he just passed the day mourning over his love. It was just like the poem that reads:

> Green the hills and streams of Sichuan,
> Where day and night I mourn.
> I should never have given up my love,
> Not though she cost me my empire.

Li Longji ordered the authorities to build a temple in Chengdu and sought out skilled artisans to make a life-size image of Lady Yang sitting down. When it was finished, he told Gao Lishi to bring it to the palace; he would escort it to the temple himself.

While he waited, he thought of Lady Yang and blamed himself for breaking their pledge. He had promised to become her husband all their future lives, but he had deserted her on the road. He hated An Lushan who rebelled and forced him to go westward; he hated the imperial guards who had pressed him hard and had drawn their swords and spears at Mawei Station just after they had left the western gate of the palace; he also hated Chen Yuanli, the general of the imperial guards, who forced him, a powerless emperor, to give her up. All of them were hateful. He blamed himself for losing his head. Had he shielded her with his body, they might never have dared to attack the emperor. Suppose they had struck him down, what would it have mattered? They should be together at least in the nether world. Now he lived on alone and his life had no meaning. He had nothing to do all the day, but pine with endless tears and infinite sorrow. "Ah, my darling, whether I'm on earth or in heaven, this sorrow will never end!"

"May it please Your Majesty, Lady Yang's image has arrived." Gao Lishi's words awoke Li Longji from his reverie but he was still confused. When he saw the wooden image, he immediately stood up and cried, "My darling, we've been apart for some time. I am glad that you have come today. Let me tell you all about my sorrow." He approached the image and said, "My love, why don't you answer me..." He stretched his hand and when he realized it was only an image, he gave out a cry in disappointment.

"The carriage is ready, Your Majesty, for you to escort Her Ladyship to the temple." Gao Lishi reported.

"Very well," said Li Longji. "Give the order that my horse goes to the left of the carriage carrying the image so that we can proceed side by side." On the road, when he thought of their past pleasure trips and how they contrasted with the sorrowful procession today, he was sad.

"We have reached the temple. Will Your Majesty alight?" asked Gao Lishi. Eunuchs and maids escorted the image into the temple.

After a while Gao Lishi reported, "The auspicious hour has come. Your Majesty, we are waiting for your order to carry Her Ladyship to her throne." Maids placed the image to the throne and when everything was ready Li Longji stood up and stepped forward. He took incense from Gao Lishi but before he burned it in front of the image, his thoughts turned to the pledge made before the Cowherd and the Weaving Maid on the night of the seventh day of the seventh lunar month at the Palace of Eternal Youth. Who would think of the broken incense-stick today? Tears coursed down his cheeks; he trembled as he stood before the image.

"The first libation." Gao Lishi appeared to remind the emperor, who recovered and took the goblet from a eunuch saying, "May your spirit come to the libation. You were buried in haste and at a time of confusion at Mawei Station. No sacrifice was offered at your grave."

"The second libation."

"I offer you this cup. I hope to move your grave back to the imperial mausoleum one day and we'll be buried together."

"The third libation."

"Now the libation is over, but there is no end to my sorrow. Why do you not move or say something? My heart seems slashed with a knife and my entrails burn with fire."

Gao Lishi, the maids and the eunuchs all wept when they heard this. When Li Longji stopped crying, he looked at the image and gave a cry. "Look, Gao Lishi! Are those not tears on her face?"

The maids and Gao Lishi looked at the image and actually saw tears falling down the cheeks of the image. They all knelt and cried, "Her Ladyship!" After a long pause Gao Lishi said, "Will it please Your Majesty to burn the sacrificial paper money?"

Li Longji burned the paper money handed to him by Gao Lishi, took another cup of wine from him and poured the final libation.

"It is growing late, Your Majesty. Will you return to the palace?" Gao asked.

Li Longji knew it was time to leave. He looked again at the image and ordered the maids to lower the curtain. He then mounted his horse and left the temple, his sorrow undiminished.

CHAPTER THIRTEEN

The Reburial on the Way Back

AFTER AN LUSHAN took Tongguan Pass, he marched straight to Chang'an, the capital. Li Longji and Yang Yuhuan had left for western Sichuan, and the ordinary people of the capital were trampled by An Lushan's soldiers who burned and looted everything in their way. Palace maids and musicians from the Pear Garden Conservatory also fled.

Yongxin and Niannu, personal maids of Yang Yuhuan, fled the palace and followed a group of refugees. They arrived at Jinling [Nanjing today] after crossing the Yellow and Yangtze rivers. There they became nuns in a Taoist temple and settled down. Li Guinian, the orchestra leader, also went south with his lute and made a living singing in the streets and lanes of Jinling. Fairs were held in front of the famous Vulture Peak Monastery on the riverside where Li Guinian often sang songs about Li Longji and Yang Yuhuan to the ordinary people. His songs also expressed his yearning for the capital and his native place.

Lei Haiqing, the famous lute player from the Pear Garden Conservatory, stayed in the capital. He became angry when he saw the court officials who had received high positions and huge salaries.

Their sons and wives had also been given titles, but they now feared death and forgot their gratitude to the former emperor. They had all surrendered to the rebels and thought only of their present comfort. They did not care for history's verdict. To him this was shameful and disgusting. Though he was only a musician, he would not lose his self-respect as they had.

An Lushan appreciated imperial music and kept a large number of musicians to play for him. He decided to celebrate his victory and feast with the traitors at the Frozen Azure Pool. There was to be music and Lei Haiqing was naturally among the musicians summoned.

An Lushan gave an audience to the officials in the inner court. Those who waited outside the palace were his former colleagues; they were now his subjects. When they were told to go in, they vied with other to be first and knelt down, saying, "Long live the emperor, long, long live the emperor!"

An Lushan was happy and said, "You may rise. Today I have a little leisure and invite you to feast at the Frozen Azure Pool to celebrate the pacification of the empire." The officials thanked him and followed their new master to the feast.

Proudly An Lushan sat at the table, while the officials flattered him by kneeling and offering him wine. He was in an ecstatic mood and ordered music. The Dance of the Rainbow and Feathery Garments, Li Longji and Yang Yuhuan's music, was played. An Lushan was pleased to hear it and said, "Bravo! Well played!" The puppet officials said, "The Tang emperor went to great pains to have this dance rehearsed, but it is now played for the pleasure of Your Majesty. Your Majesty is indeed favored by heaven!" The flattery went to An Lushan's head and he said, "True. More wine!"

Suddenly the noise of weeping was heard at the convivial gathering. Both the emperor and the officials were surprised and listened. Someone was not only weeping but singing also. "While the rebellion began at Fanyang, the beacon fires are gleaming. Thousand of homesteads lie in waste and the people are in utter misery." Another verse of the song asked, "Emperor of Tianbao, where are the former officials now?" An Lushan became angry and said, "Who is that crying out there?"

"It is the musician Lei Haiqing."

"Bring him in."

When the guards brought Lei Haiqing in, An Lushan shouted, "Lei Haiqing, we are drinking here to celebrate peace. How dare you be so woeful out there?"

"Ah, An Lushan!" Lei Haiqing stood there fearlessly and berated him. "An Lushan, you were an officer who was defeated in battle and you should have been sentenced to death; yet the emperor was merciful and spared your life. He even made you a prince! Instead of trying to serve the government well, you rebelled with your army. You have befouled the capital and forced the emperor to flee. You are an arch criminal who will soon be put to the sword when the imperial army returns. Who are you to talk of feasts and pacification?"

"Aya!" An Lushan had not expected this and he was furious. "What insolence! Since I ascended the throne, no one has disobeyed me. How dare you, a common musician, defy me? Men, draw your swords." The guards took out their swords but they were no threat to Lei Haiqing for he had made up his mind to die. He went even further, cursing and pointing at An Lushan, "An Lushan, you are a heartless monster and a beast with a human face! Though I am only a common musician, I am not as shameless as these turncoat officials. An Lushan! You have defied the will of heaven, you will soon fall, a corpse bespattered with blood!" He threw his lute at An Lushan and it was immediately seized by the guards.

An Lushan roared, "Take him and kill him quickly!" The guards dragged Lei Haiqing off. An Lushan was still angry when the puppet officials came forward to say, "Do not be angry, Your Majesty. Why pay any attention to a foolish musician?"

"My pleasure is spoiled. You may leave."

"Your Majesty's orders shall be obeyed. Let us see the emperor back to the palace." They knelt.

An Lushan left in a towering rage. The officials at once rose, all talking. "That musician deserved to be killed. Fancy a musician posing as a patriot! What's wrong with us coming to the feast? He positively tried to put us in the wrong! All of us simply acting a part; how much, after all, is a loyal minister worth? Lei Haiqing, Lei

Haiqing, you were foolish because you have never been an official!"

Although An had seized the throne, people like Lei Haiqing had not accepted him and generals of the Tang empire still fought against him. He was in a difficult situation.

After the Crown Prince Li Heng ascended the throne in Lingwu, he struggled to restore the Tang empire. He made Guo Ziyi Military Governor of the Northern Circuit and ordered him to lead his troops in the fight against the rebels. Guo Ziyi had defeated Shi Siming and He Qiannian, An's generals, and was advancing on Chang'an. The great Yan empire of An Lushan had not only been defeated militarily, but there were also conflicts in the inner court. An Lushan's favorite concubine Lady Duan had wanted to make her son, An Qing'en, the crown prince, which enraged An Qingxu, An Lushan's elder son. He colluded with Pigsy Li, An Lushan's favorite general, and had An Lushan killed.

The puppet empire collapsed soon after An Lushan died and Guo Ziyi and his troops marched into Chang'an. Guo Ziyi made the office of the imperial guards his temporary headquarters. When Guo Ziyi had entered the capital, he saw the desolate scenes and remembered how it had been. It made him sad. He suddenly recalled the restaurant and the poem written on the wall. He said to his generals, "When I first came here there were lines written by Li Xiazhou, a fortune-teller, on the wall of restaurant. I did not understand them then but realize now that all his prophecies have come true."

The generals asked him to explain the meaning of Li Xiazhou's poem and Guo Ziyi said, "An Lushan led all the troops from the north against the capital. That explains the meaning of 'When the northern town is deserted'. Then General Geshu Han was defeated at the Tongguan Pass, which explains 'And no horse returned from the Pass'. The third line, 'He comes to the ghost beneath the hill' refers to Mawei Station, while the fourth line 'And there hangs a silken dress on the ring' predicted how Lady Yang would die."

"So that's it. But thanks to your might the capital has been recovered; that was a wonderful achievement," the generals said.

Although the victory made Guo Ziyi happy, the job was not finished. He said to the generals, "The capital has been recovered, but the reigning emperor is still at Lingwu and the old emperor is far away in western Sichuan; ministers have fled and citizens dare not return to their homes. We must clean up the palace and sweep the imperial tombs so that the reigning emperor and the old emperor can return." The generals bowed and said, "Yes." Guo Ziyi gave an order asking the refugees to return and take up their former tasks. He also called on the former officials to work together for reconstruction. A general was appointed to lead five thousand fully equipped imperial guards to Lingwu and escort His Majesty, Suzong, back to the capital. Obeying an order of the new emperor, Guo Ziyi himself went to western Sichuan to welcome Li Longji, the old emperor, back.

Li Longji had been in western Sichuan for more than a year before Li Heng, now Emperor Suzong, had suppressed the rebellion and sent someone to welcome his father back to Chang'an. He had arrived at western Sichuan in haste and distress but the procession that left was leisurely.

Very soon they arrived at Fufeng where they stayed in Fengyi, the pleasure palace. Li Longji recalled that this was where an old peasant had offered him a bowl of oatmeal. He stood quietly in the dusk; the palace looked desolate and he was gloomy.

It was getting dark and Gao Lishi advised him to enter and have a rest. Li Longji paid no attention to this and said, "How far is it to Mawei, Gao Lishi?"

"Only a few dozen miles."

"I have ordered the local authorities to make a proper grave for Lady Yang. Go there at once and see that the work is done quickly. When I arrive, the reburial can take place."

Gao Lishi had left and there was no one close talk to him; Li Longji was doubly sad. Although it was dark and quiet, he did not feel like sleeping. He stepped down to the courtyard and raised his head to see the moon. It was rising slowly and light from it fell on the green grass on a corner of the wall. He felt lonely; there was no one to share the view with. He was heart-broken.

He thought of Yang Yuhuan lying cold in her lonely grave. In the past, if he had left her even for a moment it was hard to bear;

now death separated them forever. How sad it was! When they pledged their love with the hairpin and the jewelry box, little had he thought that they would buried with her. Thinking about this, he cried aloud, "Ah, my darling. How shall I ever forget the way you looked and spoke?" He thought of how she was not only lovely when she was happy; she was also charming when she was angry with tears in her eyes. No other woman had understood or delighted him so much. They loved each other and there was no other beauty who could compare with her. She was dead. He too was more dead than alive. If he could meet her after death, he would rather die than continue living alone. He wanted to leave this world and enter the nether regions to rejoin her under the earth.

He looked up and saw the moon high in the sky. He remembered how they prayed to the Cowherd and the Weaving Maid on the seventh day of the seventh moon and made a secret vow. Now he was alone beneath the moonlight! Ah! Circumstances changed so quickly. "Ah, Moon! When we made our vow, you must have heard it too; you were there by the Milky Way. I hope you will not deny it and persuade the Cowherd and the Weaving Maid to help make our pledge of love come true."

It was cold and late. After experiencing wars and parting from Yang Yuhuan, Li Longji was old and frail. He was tired and went into the palace.

The master of Mawei Station, after receiving the imperial order, was busy with preparations. He went from door to door finding people to tidy the house and the yard and make a new grave for Lady Yang. While he was bustling round, Gao Lishi came to oversee his efforts, and that made him work harder. The imperial order stated that Lady Yang's body was not be seen by any men so the stationmaster had to get four hundred women to work as gravediggers. He and his men had spent a whole day conscripting four hundred women. But the women did not know how to use a hoe or pick so they had to be trained during the night.

Li Longji arrived in a carriage escorted by eunuchs and imperial guards the following day. Gao Lishi, the master of Mawei Station and other officials waited on the road to welcome him. He sat down in the hall and they withdrew to wait outside.

It was late in the afternoon and after resting Li Longji walked past the Buddhist shrine. It was silent, no one chanted scriptures there. The pear tree on which Lady Yang had hung herself was still there, covered with green leaves that made it look somber. Somber thoughts came into Li Longji's mind. "The surroundings are unchanged, but you are dead. All my sighs are useless. The nights are long but you have never appeared in my dreams. Your face was as fresh as spring but where will I see it again?"

"As Your Majesty directed, I have overseen the work on a new grave for Lady Yang. Now everything is ready for you to begin the ceremony whenever it pleases you." Gao Lishi woke Li Longji who had not slept properly the whole night. He answered, "Order my carriage."

After a while Gao Lishi said, "Your Majesty, it was under this poplar tree that Lady Yang was buried."

Li Longji looked around and said sadly, "Ah, the weeds have grown rank and the wind sighs. Take pity my darling, I am most wretched!"

The women workers who had been gathered by the master of the station appeared and Gao Lishi said at once, "The women workers have come." Li Longji ordered that the guards be withdrawn and asked Gao Lishi to inspect their work.

Gao Lishi passed on the order. The guards marched out and the women started to dig. With great care, they removed the grass and earth from the top, but when they reached the depths, there was no sign of Lady Yang's body. The women were surprised and spoke among themselves. Suddenly one of them found a pouch and cried, "Oh, look! It is a scented pouch."

"Bring it to me," Gao Lishi ordered and the woman handed it to him. When Gao Lishi saw it he cried out, "Alas, My Lady." But he stopped, for it was an inappropriate time for him to show emotion. He ordered the woman worker to withdraw and reported the find to Li Longji. "Your Majesty, the grave has been opened, but it is empty. Even the silk quilt wrapped round the body and the gold hairpin and the jewelry box that were buried with her have disappeared. There is nothing left but this scented pouch."

He presented it to Li Longji. They had no idea that the heavenly emperor had made Lady Yang a fairy and raised her to heaven.

"How could that be?" Li Longji took the pouch from Gao Lishi and cried out, "I gave her this pouch on her birthday, after she performed the Dance of the Rainbow and Feathery Garments at the Palace of Eternal Youth. Where are you now, my darling?"

His head was lowered in thought and suddenly he raised it. "Could you be mistaken, Gao Lishi?"

"That day I peeled off part of the bark on the poplar and wrote on the tree to mark the place. How could I mistake it?"

"Could her body have been exhumed?"

"If that were the case, why would the scented pouch have been left?" Li Longji thought this reasonable and reflected in silence.

"There have been many cases, sire, of immortals who were raised from the dead. Perhaps Her Ladyship has attained immortality. Since this pouch was worn by Her Ladyship when she died, if we bury it in the new grave it will serve the same purpose."

"You are right. Wrap this scented pouch in the pearl-decked garments, put them in the marble casket and let the burial take place with due ceremony."

Gao Lishi did as he was told. He placed the pouch in the casket, ordered the women to put the casket in the grave and sealed up the tomb. He then gave them a string of cash apiece as a reward and sent them away. Only Mistress Wang, a woman worker, was still there, and Gao Lishi asked why she did not go. The woman said that she had picked up one of Lady Yang's silk stockings the previous year and wanted to present it to the old emperor. Gao Lishi reported this at once to Li Longji and took her to see him. When Li Longji examined it, he realized that it actually was one of Lady Yang's stockings. He wept and ordered Gao Lishi to give the woman five thousand strings of cash as a reward and allowed her to stay watching over Lady Yang's grave.

Gao Lishi tried to console Li Longji who was still lamenting when envoys sent by the reigning emperor arrived. Commander Guo Ziyi and four soldiers kowtowed to Li Longji. "Your subject, Guo Ziyi, Military Governor of the Northern Circuit, has come on His Majesty's command. We have an escort for your welcome return, sire."

Li Longji at once wiped away his tears and replied, "Yours was a truly remarkable achievement, my lord. You succeeded in wiping out the rebels and recovering the capital so that the imperial sacrifice could be renewed and the empire rebuilt."

Guo Ziyi replied humbly, "I was late in crushing the rebels, therefore, I deserve punishment and can claim no credit."

"No one could say that, my lord. Gao Lishi, order the carriage to proceed."

In no time, Gao Lishi had everything arranged. Led by Guo Ziyi and other officials, and escorted by soldiers, Li Longji returned to the capital in a carriage.

CHAPTER FOURTEEN

Making Amends
and the Lover's Reunion

AFTER THE TRIALS of a long and arduous journey, Li Longji finally returned to Chang'an, the capital. He took no part in affairs of state and just stayed in the southern part of the western palace where he spent his time in leisure. However, he found it hard to cope with leisure and thought of Yang Yuhuan all the time. On some particular rainy nights, when leaves fell from the plane trees and the wind moaned, grief overcame him.

On one such night, when raindrops were beating against the windows, Li Longji sat alone by a lamp; Gao Lishi was in the other room. Li Longji was lost in thought. He had hoped to see his darling one more at Mawei, but the grave had been empty except for her scented pouch. He did not know if she had been carried to heaven or whether her body had decayed. Was there any way for him to see her again?

"Ah, where does the singing come from?" He was surprised to hear a melody that came from far away and went to the window. "It is a sad song. Can it be one of my musicians?" He listened again and said, "Ah, it is Zhang Yehu singing." He paced a few steps and stopped. "Let me listen to his singing."

"The steep path winds across a thousand hills, and the way is rugged; when a squall of rain sweeps over the treetops, the bells on the pack-horse start ringing," the song came over the air. Li Longji heard the words and murmured, "That is a tune I composed called 'Bells in the Rain'. When I was traveling through the mountains, I heard bells ringing in the rain and thought of her so I put the sounds into music. Hearing this reminds me of that sad journey and I feel more broken-hearted than ever." The rain outside fell fast then slow, heavier and then lighter by turns. Li Longji could not sleep.

Gao Lishi did not sleep either. He listened carefully to the sounds from the inner room. Li Longji was in a sad mood again, so he entered quietly. "It is late, Your Majesty. Won't you rest?" In the distance the third watch sounded. "So it is midnight already," Li Longji said. "Do you know what is on my mind? How can I sleep? Gao Lishi, arrange the couch. I will sleep on it. I only hope that I'll have a sweet dream and see Her Ladyship."

When Li Longji had fallen asleep, Gao Lishi left the room quietly. Li Longji slept soundly on the couch.

Suddenly two eunuchs entered the room; they knelt down and said, "Wake up, Your Majesty!"

"Who are you?"

"Lady Yang ordered us to invite Your Majesty to visit her."

"What? So she did not die after all!" Li Longji asked in surprise.

"The day that trouble broke out among the guards she changed her dress and slipped away through the crowd. She has been a wanderer ever since."

"So she is still alive! Where is she now?"

"She is staying in a post station for the time being. She heard that Your Majesty had been longing for her day and night, so she sent us to welcome you. She wishes to fulfill the pledge she made with Your Majesty in the seventh night of the seventh lunar month."

"So that is it! Lead me there quickly. We will bring her back to the palace this very night."

In spite of the lateness, the dew, the cold wind, and the black sky, Li Longji left his bedchamber and followed the two eunuchs to the gate. A military officer suddenly barred his way. "Your Majesty should be inside the palace. Why are you wandering out at night incognito?"

Li Longji fell into a rage and said, "Who is this rough officer who stops me so rudely?"

"I am Commander Chen Yuanli. Will it please Your Majesty to return to the palace?"

When he heard his name, Li Longji became more irate and said, "Curse you, Chen Yuanli! At Mawei Station you incited the guards and forced Lady Yang to commit suicide. Execution is too good for you. How dare you oppose me again. You ignore my authority and behave with such arrogance!"

"If Your Majesty does not go back, the troops may mutiny again."

"Curse you again! You think that I have no more authority because I have given up the throne. You rely on your troops to take such liberties. This cannot be forgiven. Attendants! Cut off this rebel's head!"

The two attendants immediately drew their swords and killed Chen Yuanli, and then led Li Longji out of the gate. After a while they said, "Your Majesty, we have reached the station. Will it please Your Majesty to enter?"

Li Longji looked around. In the wilderness stood two or three desolate houses. When he approached a gate, he saw tall wild grasses and moss growing on the steps. A wind sighed and insects emitted shrill notes. Where was Lady Yang? Suddenly he seemed to be in the station at the riverbank. What a great flood! A monster was coming out of the water! It had the head of a pig and the body of a dragon. It was rushing towards him. Startled, Li Longji gave out a cry and woke from his dream. He was in a cold sweat. He sat on the couch and realized that it was a dream. He called out, "What is that noise outside, Gao Lishi?"

"It is only rain on the plane trees. It is the fourth watch now. You are awake?"

"Just now I had a dream, Gao Lishi. Two attendants came to tell me Lady Yang was in Mawei Station and wanted me to go there to fulfill our pledge. Gao Lishi, in ancient times when Emperor Wu of the Han Dynasty mourned for Lady Li, a necromancer by the name of Li Shaojun summoned her spirit for him. There must still be such necromancers. As soon as dawn breaks, try to find one to summon Lady Yang's spirits."

Gao Lishi carried out the order and posted imperial edicts in streets to summon necromancers. On the second day, a necromancer who responded to the call was invited to the palace.

He was called Yang Tongyou and he came from Linqiong. He said he was able to summon the wind and rain, and spirits and ghosts. The task would be a test of his magic power for he had learned that the old emperor was longing to see Lady Yang.

His magic power, however, was limited; the genies he sent all returned empty-handed. Gao Lishi urged on by Li Longji frequently pressed him for results. There was no other way out he told his attendant; he would have to go into a trance and complete the search himself.

After his spirit left the altar, it went directly to Fengdu. At Senlo Hall it called out in a loud voice, "Where is the officer on duty?"

"Who is making such a noise?" asked the Judge. He saw the necromancer and said politely, "What do you want here, sir?"

"I have come to search for Lady Yang's spirit."

"Please take a seat. That is easy. We have a special book for the registration of queens and court ladies." He asked the ghostly attendants to bring the book. The necromancer went through the book from beginning to end twice, page after page, but did not find Yang Yuhuan's name. He had to leave and said to the Judge, "Since she is not in hell, I must search for her in heaven."

He went to a number of places in heaven and found nothing either. Just as he was about to leave he saw the Weaving Maid and bowed, "Madam, my respects."

The Weaving Maid said, "What brings you here?"

"I am searching for Lady Yang's spirit. The old Tang emperor asked me to. She is not in hell and I came to look for her in heaven, but she is not there either… I wonder if my lady can tell me where she is."

"Since you cannot find her, you had better go back and say that you have failed."

"Yes, my lady. Only I boasted at the court that my spirit will find the fair one in the void."

"Who told you to boast?"

"It is as if I was looking for trouble. The emperor was so constant in his love; he thought of her each day."

The Weaving Maid became a little angry when she heard this and said, "He let her die at Mawei; what love and affection can he have for her?"

"No, my lady, you wrong him. A mutiny broke out as they fled in confusion. Even though he was the Son of Heaven, the guards were insolent. No one would carry out his orders and this was the cause of the tragedy."

"Now that they have been separated so long I expect the emperor feels her loss less keenly."

"Oh, no, the emperor is broken-hearted and feels bad day and night. He longs for her and wants to meet her spirit."

When she heard this the Weaving Maid recalled that the Cowherd had pleaded for Li Longji the other day. If that were so, it was a pitiful situation. The necromancer wanted to continue searching somewhere else while the Weaving Maid thought about it.

Moved by the necromancer's determination she said, "Tongyou, wait. If you really want to find Yang Yuhuan, I may be able to help you."

The necromancer was astute enough to realize that the Weaving Maid could tell him where Yang Yuhuan was and he bowed at once saying, "My Lady, where is Yang Yuhuan?"

"Have you ever heard of other worlds outside this one?"

"I have. But which one do you mean? And how can I reach it?"

"Well. Beyond the Eastern Ocean there is a fairy mountain named Penglai. If you go there, you will hear news of her."

"Thank you for your help. I will go there at once and find Her Ladyship." He said goodbye and flew away with the clouds.

After he had left, the Weaving Maid went into her palace and sat down. The Cowherd had asked her to assist in the reunion of Li

Longji and Yang Yuhuan so that they would keep their trust in them. She had wanted to help but thought that Li Longji was hard-hearted. The Cowherd had defended him and now the necromancer was also saying that Li Longji was firm in his love and sought high and low for her spirit. It was touching, but she wanted to know what Yang Yuhuan thought before she would do anything.

She ordered her attendant to send for Lady Yang and Lady Yang arrived at Xuanji Palace in a minute.

"I am here, Your Ladyship," said Yang Yuhuan.

"Don't stand on ceremony. Please be seated."

"You sent for me, my lady. What are your instructions?"

"Yuhuan, I asked you to come just for a chat. I have never asked you to tell me your story. I would like to hear all about your love for the Tang emperor during your life on earth."

The request made Yang Yuhuan sad. She breathed in and said slowly, "Let me tell you the whole story." But before she came to the important part, she sobbed, stopped for a while and then continued, "We loved each other deeply and pledged to remain together throughout our various lives. But during the unforeseen Fanyang rebellion, I died at Mawei Station and we parted forever."

The Weaving Maid said, "I have been told that your love continues even after death. If that is so, how could he be so heartless as to give you up at the Mawei Station?"

Yang Yuhuan wept and defended Li Longji. "It was indeed sad but not because the emperor was heartless. During the mutiny, swords were unsheathed and the emperor was in peril. How could he protect me at such a time? I was willing to die and the situation forced me to. It was nothing to do with him." As she cried, she covered her face with her sleeve.

For a moment they looked at each other and said nothing. Yang Yuhuan then showed the Weaving Maid the hairpin and jewelry box saying, "He gave me these when we pledged our love and I had them with me when I died. I took them to the fairy mountain to keep with me forever. I long so much to resume our love, but how can it be possible?"

"That is indeed a sad story! But now that you rank as an immortal you should free yourself of earthly desires. If you allow them to entangle you, you may be banished to the world of men." the Weaving Maid wanted to know what she really thought.

"Your Ladyship, though I am ranked with the immortals, I dream all the time of the Tang palace. And come what may, my love will never die." She suddenly stood up and said, "I would gladly be banished from heaven of only we could love again."

Moved by her sincerity, the Weaving Maid left her seat and touched her shoulder. "Yuhuan, be calm and sit down. The Cowherd and I have wanted to help you for a long time, but after what happened at Mawei I felt that Li Longji must be quite heartless. I just met Yang Tongyou, the necromancer, who told me that Li Longji was longing for you; he had sent him to find you under the earth or in heaven. As the emperor is still true to you, I told the necromancer to go to your fairy mountain. I also thought that you might bear some grudge against the emperor and called you here to find out what you thought. Now that I know you are both true in your love, I think that you should stay together. I shall put your case to the Heavenly Emperor and ask him to make amends for your past unhappiness by living together forever."

Yang Yuhuan was overjoyed to hear this, but she still had doubts. "I am only afraid that our sins were too great and will become a barrier that will keep us from each other. I will be content if I can just see him once more."

"Very well. I have heard that at the Mid-Autumn Festival they will be playing a new version of the Dance of the Rainbow and Feathery Garments that you composed. You will certainly be invited. On that night, the emperor will leave the world of men. When you return, tell the necromancer to lead the emperor to the moon that night to meet you there. Does that suit you?"

Yang Yuhuan still found it unbelievable and said, "Are lovers' meetings allowed in the palace of the moon?"

"It can be arranged. I shall tell the mistress of the moon beforehand. By the time you meet, I shall have procured an imperial decree so that your wishes will be fulfilled."

Moved and grateful, Yang Yuhuan bowed deeply and said, "I thank Your Ladyship. I must go now."

The spirit of Yang Tongyou, the necromancer, followed the

directions of the Weaving Maid and arrived at Penglai, the fairy mountain, after flying across the eastern ocean and many mountains. He walked over hills, by springs and flowers and along paths and came to a building with an inscription, The House of Lady Yang, carved on a board hanging above the gate. He knew that this must be the residence of Lady Yang. He took a hairpin from his hair to knock lightly on the door. No one answered. He knocked again and a fairy attendant opened the gate and asked, "Who are you?"

"I am Yang Tongyou, the necromancer. I salute you." He bowed.

"What do you want here?"

"The Tang emperor asked me to send his regards to your mistress."

"Her Ladyship has gone to Xuanji Palace. Please wait for a moment."

As an immortal, Yang Yuhuan could go anywhere at will and much faster than the necromancer. She had returned to her residence at almost the same time that Yang Tongyou arrived. When she saw the necromancer standing in the yard, she knew at once who he was, but said to the attendant, "Where does this necromancer come from?"

"I was just going to report to you, madam. He brings a message from a Tang emperor in the human world."

Yang Yuhuan walked into the hall and said, "Since he comes from the emperor, let him approach." The pair entered, the fairy attendant leading the way.

"Please be seated. May I ask the purpose of your visit?"

"On the emperor's command, I have come to bring you his regards."

"How is the old emperor?" Yang Yuhuan was anxious to know about Li Longji.

"He has become ill from thinking of you day and night."

This broke the heart of Yang Yuhuan and tears coursed down her cheeks. His love moved her deeply but as they were separated, she could do nothing except ask the necromancer to send him her love.

"I will. But I beg you to give me some token."

This was reasonable and Yang Yuhuan said, "When we pledged our love, the emperor gave me a double hairpin and a jewelry box. I will give you half of the hairpin and half of the box. Please tell the emperor that if we remain true, we shall be able to fulfill our pledge." She could now say such a thing because she had the assurance of the Weaving Maid. She then took out the hairpin and the box and divided them into two asking the attendant to give one of each half to the necromancer.

"There is still something on my mind, My Lady."

"Say it."

"These tokens were made on earth. If I give them to the emperor, how can he be sure that I received them from you? Can you tell me something which none but yourselves know?"

"You are right." She lowered her head in thought then raised it and said, "Ah, I have it! At midnight on the seventh day of the seventh moon in the tenth year of the Tianbao period, when everyone else was sleeping, the emperor and I were at the Palace of Eternal Youth. As we stood shoulder to shoulder thinking of the Cowherd and the Weaving Maid in heaven, we vowed to love each other throughout all our future lives." She wept when she spoke of this.

"With this, I can report back to the emperor. Now I must leave you."

Yang Yuhuan suddenly remembered the words of the Weaving Maid. "Wait, there is something else! On the fifteenth night of this eighth moon, there will be a big celebration on the moon when the Dance of the Rainbow and Feathery Garments will be performed. That night the emperor will leave the earth. I shall wait for him on the moon. Will you please guide him there? If he misses the opportunity, he will never see me again. You must remember this."

"I shall certainly tell the emperor about this grand celebration on the fifteenth night of the eighth moon." He then took his leave.

Even though Yang Tongyou had not wasted a moment in his travels to heaven and hell, Li Longji had already become impatient. His longing made him ill and he was now afraid that the necromancer was either lying or not doing his utmost. It was late autumn. The limbs of semi bare trees bent from the wind and rain that had fallen all night. He had not slept a wink and was not sure about the future.

Just then Yang Tongyou returned and reported to him. When he said that he had not found Lady Yang in heaven or hell, Li Longji became stricken with grief and wept. "That means I will never see her again. It is sad!"

"Your Majesty, don't grieve. Listen to me. I met the Weaving Maid in front of her palace, and she told me that Lady Yang was on Penglai Mountain…"

"Did you see her?" Li Longji interrupted.

"Yes. Lady Yang cried when she heard that you were ill. She asked me again and again to convey her love to you."

"Is this true?"

"Yes. I brought half a hairpin and box as a proof." He took them out of his sleeve and gave them to Gao Lishi, who handed them to the emperor.

Li Longji carefully examined the tokens that he had given her. They made him think about Lady Yang and he wept again and said, "The separation of the hairpin and box signifies our parting. Now we are alone and apart, unable to meet again." He held the tokens in his hands, then spoke to Gao Lishi, "These are earthly things. How could they have been taken to heaven? When we rebuilt the grave, they were not in it. How can we be sure they came from Lady Yang? How did the necromancer come by them?"

Gao Lishi had already spoken with Yang Tongyou and told him what had been said. "Lady Yang told the necromancer about a secret vow Your Majesty and Her Ladyship had made on the seventh night of the seventh moon in the Palace of Eternal Youth."

"Yes, that happened." Li Longji now believed him.

Yang Tongyou said, "Take comfort, sire. Lady Yang has another message for you."

"What is it?"

"She said that during the Mid-Autumn Festival the Dance of the Rainbow and Feathery Garments will be performed on the moon and she will be present. She asked me to lead Your Majesty to the moon to meet her."

"Why didn't you tell me that earlier?" Now he was completely convinced and said to Gao Lishi, "What is the date today?"

"It is the end of the seventh moon; there is only half a month till the Mid-Autumn Festival. Please rest now, sire."

"As she has consented to see me again, I no longer feel ill." Happy, he waved the necromancer away.

Time flew. Half a month passed in the wink of eye. There was a clear sky on the fifteenth night of the eighth lunar month and the Milky Way could be seen clearly. Necromancer, Yang Tongyou, waited a long time outside the palace gate to fly to the moon with the old emperor.

After a while the moonlight was joined by lights shining from the palace. When the old emperor left the palace, Yang Tongyou advanced a few steps. "Your Majesty, the necromancer greets you."

"Master, don't stand on ceremony. Please take me to the moon palace tonight. I have waited from noon to dusk to see the moon. Now I am depending on you to lead me up to the sky." Li Longji was full of hope.

"Your Majesty, the moon is high; let us go up into the sky."

"It is a long way to heaven, master. Are we going to fly there?"

"Set your heart at ease, sire, I'll manage." As he said this, he threw out the magic duster in his hand and it changed into a bridge. Li Longji saw the necromancer walking on the bridge, which went on and on and almost disappeared. He followed him closely. On either side, there was nothing but mist. After a while, he heard fairy music and was happy.

Lady Chang'e, the mistress of the moon, had already made arrangements for Lady Yang to meet Li Longji.

When Yang Yuhuan arrived, she asked to see Lady Chang'e and the fairy attendant replied, "Her Ladyship left word for you to wait here, madam. After you have met the emperor, she will join you both."

Presently the emperor arrived. He hesitated and the fairy attendant asked, "Are you the emperor from the earth?"

"I am."

"Lady Yang is waiting for you. Please come in and meet her."

"Where are you, my darling?" His legs carried him in giant strides.

"Where is the emperor?" Lady Yang went out to greet him.

They met, fell into each other's arms and wept. They talked and wept and wept and then talked without end. All those standing nearby were deeply moved.

"The mistress of the moon is here!" announced a fairy attendant. Li Longji ceased crying to meet Lady Chang'e and thank her.

Lady Chang'e asked them to sit down and said, "I congratulate you both on attaining godhood which means that you can love for ever. Say no more of the past. The Weaving Maid has asked the Heavenly Emperor to make you lovers in heaven. As the night is excellent and the moon is round, I shall give you a congratulatory feast." The fairy attendants then brought in wine.

They heard the music of the Dance of the Rainbow and Feathery Garments and Lady Chang'e said, "This is the music of heaven and Lady Yang improved it. Now I have borrowed it to accompany the two of you to the heavenly palace."

And thus, the lovers met each other again in the palace of the moon and reigned there forever, as a reward for their devotion to each other. And this is how this story of the lover's vow in the Palace of Eternal Youth has since been passed down from one generation to the next.

The Peony Pavilion

About
the Original Work

PEONY PAVILION WAS written by Tang Xianzu (1550-1616), a native of Linchuan, Jiangxi Province. Tang Xianzu was a famous writer and dramatist of the Ming Dynasty (1368-1644) who styled himself Yireng, Hairuo and Ruoshi. He also called himself Qingyuan Taoist, after a Qingyuan Tower that stood in his house. In his later years, he styled himself Jianweng.

Tang Xianzu was a famous man of letters in his youth. In the fourth year of the Longqing reign (1570), he passed the imperial examination at the provincial level at the age of 21. In the fifth year of the Wanli reign (1577), he prepared to sit the highest imperial examination. Senior Grand Secretary Zhang Juzheng, who tried to help his son Zhang Sixiu become a successful candidate in the imperial examination, recruited outstanding scholars from all over the country to keep his son company. Zhang Sixiu followed his father's instructions and tried every way to make friends with Tang Xianzu and Shen Maoxue, two young scholars enjoying a high reputation all over the country. However Tang Xianzu, an upright young man, was not willing to curry favors with the powerful, and subsequently failed the examination. Shen Maoxue, who was happy to be a friend of both Zhang Juzheng and Zhang Sixiu, came first in the examination and Zhang Sixiu came third. Tang Xianzu became a metropolitan graduate in the 11th year of Wanli reign (1583). Later he was appointed adviser of the Court of Imperial Sacrifice in Nanjing and five years later he served as administrative aide of the Ministry of Rites. In the 19th year of Wanli reign (1591), he submitted a petition to the emperor to impeach Shen Shixing, grand secretary of the Grand Secretariat, and exposed the court's failure in administration. As a result he was demoted to a clerk of Xuwen County in Guangdong Province. Two years later, he was transferred to Zhejiang to be the magistrate of Suichang County. As an upright local official, Tang Xianzu did not attach himself to those in authority and was more concerned about ordinary people's lives. Other officials attacked him and he was so unhappy as a magistrate that he left his post for home in the 26th year of Wanli reign (1598). Three years later, he was formally removed from office. Then Tang Xianzu moved home from the suburbs to the city proper and built Jade Tea Studio where he devoted himself to writing.

His teacher in his youth was Luo Rufang, a disciple of the Taizhou School. He was also friendly with Li Zhi and Da Guan. Both Li Zhi and Da Guan were ideologists opposed to traditional ethics and exerted great influence on Tang Xianzu who thought highly of them and regarded them as "two heroes". In addition, Tang established good relationships with Yuan Hongdao, Yuan Zhongdao and Yuan Zongdao. The three men were outstanding representatives of the Gong'an School, and advocated new ideas and opposed simple imitations. Influenced by them, Tang Xianzu founded the Linchuan School with his theatrical circle.

The dramas written by Tang Xianzu include *The Purple Hairpin, The Peony Pavilion, The Story of Nanke,* and *The Story of Handan*, which are known as *The Four Dreams of the Jade Tea Studio*. Tang Xianzu also wrote many poems, some of which are included in *Collected Works Written at Jade Tea Studio*, which was published before his death. Five years after his death, *Book of Jade Tea Studio* edited by Han Jing came out. Later, *Collected Works by Tang Xianzu* edited by Qian Nanyang and Xu Shuofang was published.

Of all the traditional dramas written by Tang Xianzu, *The Peony Pavilion* is the best and the most famous. Tang Xianzu once said, "I have had four dreams in my life, and the dream of *The Peony Pavilion* is my favorite." As a matter of fact, the drama was warmly received as soon as it was performed and became "known to every household, almost making *The Romance of the Western Bowers* appear inferior". At that time, many famous writers, such as Lü Yusheng, Shen Jing, Zang Maoxun and Feng Menglong, adapted *The Peony Pavilion* for such work as *Two Dreams the Same* (by Shen Jing) and *A Love Dream* (by Feng Menglong). The former has been lost, the latter still exists. And there still remain other various versions of *The Peony Pavilion*. *The Peony Pavilion* is almost always performed as a *kunju* [a local operas style from Jiangsu Province] opera. Some opera repertory, such as "Chunxiang Makes Trouble in Class," "Startling Dream of Wandering Through the Garden," and "Picking up the Portrait and Speaking to It," are all derived from *The Peony Pavilion*.

During the Song (960-1279) and Ming (1368-1644) dynasties, a Confucian school of learning, devoted to the study of classics, was in vogue. It stressed "preserving heavenly principles and getting rid of people's desires". The people in the Ming Dynasty attached great importance to a women's virginity, and spared no effort in praising virgin girls and women who did not marry in widowhood. The number of eminent women included in *Biographies of Eminent Women of the History of the Ming Dynasty* is much more than those in *History of Eastern Han* and the history books of the following dynasties. The scholars of the Taizhou School opposed the traditional Confucian school of learning and Tang Xianzu created dramas to criticize traditional ethics. In the preface to *The Peony Pavilion*, Tang Xianzu proposed that, "a person could die for love and a dead person could revive after death. If a person does not die for love, or does not revive after death, it means he or she has not devoted themselves to love". In reality, it was impossible for Du Liniang to revive after death, but Tang Xianzu believed that "it is impossible only according to your beliefs and it could happen if one was deeply in love". Tang Xianzu highly praised sincere love between men and women and through the description of Du Liniang's experience of romantic love, he criticized the inhuman society in which she lived. After Du Liniang returns to life and marries Liu Mengmei, her father, Du Bao, who strictly adheres to traditional ethics, refuses to approve his daughter's marriage. This shows how stubborn the traditional forces were and how hard it was for young men and women to struggle for their own love and happiness.

The publication of *The Peony Pavilion* had a great influence on society and caused huge upheavals for women. In one extreme case, Yu Erniang, a lady of Loujiang, cried so bitterly after she had read it that she died. Shang Xiaoling, an actress of Hangzhou, was so sad when performing the drama that she died on stage.

It should also be noted that some characters in the story are fictional and should not be compared to figures in history.

CHAPTER ONE

Du Bao Employs a Tutor

PREFECT DU BAO (styled Ziyun) of Nan'an Prefecture of Jiangxi Province in the Song Dynasty (960-1279) was a descendant of Du Fu, a famous poet of the Tang Dynasty (618-907). He started studying when young and became a successful candidate in the highest imperial examination at the age of 20. As an honest and upright official, who never encroached on the interests of others, Du Bao was held in high regard by the local people. Now that he was over 50 with grey hair, he thought many times of resigning his post and returning to his hometown to live a quiet and peaceful life. However, he had not yet submitted his resignation. His wife Lady Zhen, a descendant of Empress Zhen of the Wei Dynasty (386-550), was a kind and virtuous woman. They had a daughter by the name of Du Liniang and the old couple adoved her. Du Liniang was beautiful, dignified and unmarried. Whenever Du Bao thought of his daughter's marriage, he became anxious. One day, when he was not busy with official affairs, he asked his wife to come in and discuss it. The subject had also worried Madam Du. As a woman, she relied on her husband to decide on all family affairs. She had only taught her daughter how to do housework.

After his wife was seated, Du Bao said, "I agree that a girl must learn how to do housework. However our daughter is very intelligent and housework is easy to learn. She should be well educated and well brought up. When she is married to a scholar, she and her husband will need a common language. What do you think about it, Madam?"

"Master, I think you're right," Madam Du said.

Just then, their daughter Du Liniang arrived followed by her maid, Chunxiang, carrying dishes and wine. She greeted them saying, "Hello, Mother and Father!"

"Daughter, why have you prepared these dishes and wine?" Du Bao asked.

"It is a fine spring day today. It is also unusual for you not to be busy. I wanted to see you happy and healthy and treat you to dishes and wine."

Du Bao and his wife were very pleased and both said, "It's very kind of you."

Du Liniang presented the first cup of wine to her parents, saying, "To your health!" She held the second cup of wine high and said, "Wishing Father smooth sailing in his official career." She then made a third toast to her mother, "I hope Mother will give birth to a younger brother for me!"

Du Liniang's words moved her parents. Du Bao allowed Chunxiang to pour a cup of wine for Du Liniang then he turned to his wife and said, "Madam, compared to my ancestor, Du Fu, I am unlucky. He had a son, but I have only a daughter." There were tears in his eyes.

Afraid that Du Liniang would be upset by this, Madam Du comforted her husband, "Don't worry, Master. If we get a good son-in-law, he will be like a son."

Du Bao laughed, "Like our son?"

Madam Du retorted, "A daughter can also bring glory to family. There is an old saying, 'Don't be happy to have a son, and don't be sad to have a daughter.' Sometimes a daughter is better than a son. Why are you talking about this?"

Du Bao had realized that he should not discuss these things in front of his daughter. He asked her daughter to clean the table and leave and after she had gone, he stopped Chunxiang to ask what Du Liniang did each day in the embroidery room.

Chunxiang also thought that her master had said too much and answered, "What else can she do in the embroidery room? She does needle work."

"Does she do it all day long?" Du Bao asked curiously.

"She sometimes falls asleep," Chunxiang said.

Du Bao became very angry when he heard this and turned to his wife saying, "Madam, you are in charge of teaching our daughter to do a woman's tasks. How can you allow her to be idle and fall asleep during the daytime? Go and summon Liniang."

When Du Liniang arrived at the Rear Hall, she asked her father what the matter was.

Du Bao pulled a long face and said, "Chunxiang told me you fall asleep during daytime. After your finish your needlework, you may use the time reading books on the bookshelves. We would be proud of you if you were well educated and made a good match for a scholar. However you're idle and it's because your mother does not discipline you strictly enough."

Madam Du agreed but was afraid that such stern words would upset her delicate daughter. She said gently, "Master, look at your daughter. She is a real pearl and she is beautiful. I am her mother and will see to it that she is well educated." She said to Du Liniang, "My daughter, you must consider your father's words carefully. Though you're a girl, you should also learn to read and write."

Du Liniang felt wronged and said, "Father and Mother, you should not blame me. I have just finished drawing the embroidery manual. From now on, I'll find time to read the books on the shelves."

Madam Du was very pleased and encouraged her daughter saying, "You won't be able to read all the books on the shelves, but you must read The Ritual of Zhou [book of ceremonies and proper conduct]. You're from an official family. You must be skilled in needlework and understand etiquette like Ban Zhao [a historian during the Eastern Han Dynasty (25-220)] and Xie Daoyun [a poet during the Eastern Jin Dynasty (317-420)] of ancient times." Then she turned to say to her husband, "Master, do you think we should find a tutor for our daughter?"

Du Bao replied, "Female teachers are not available. We may get an old male teacher but we must not neglect him. First, we should show our daughter how to pay him proper respect and second, we should take good care of his board and lodging. I have learnt all of my skills from books too."

The news that Prefect Du would employ a teacher for his daughter quickly spread far and wide. All scholars were excited at the prospect and tried their best to win the position, except for one old scholar who did not take much notice.

He was Chen Zuiliang who started learning books by Confucius in his childhood and went to school at the age of 12. He later passed the imperial examination at the county level and the local government regularly supplied him with grain. In the following 45 years, he took part in the imperial examination at the provincial level 15 times. The exam was held once every three years and he failed on every occasion. After the low scores in his last examination, the official in charge of the provincial examination decided that the local government should stop providing him with grain. From then on, no one employed him as a teacher and he had no source of income. Fortunately his grandfather was a doctor and ran a drug store. He had some medical knowledge and began practicing medicine to make a living. Some of his income came from the drug store left by his grandfather.

To everyone's surprise, old and ugly Chen Zuiliang was the lucky one. More than ten outstanding scholars had been recommended to Prefect Du by the professor of the local academy, but the prefect was not satisfied. He insisted that he would employ only an experienced and prudent scholar. The professor, who did not know what to do, discussed the matter with the academy's messenger who recommended Chen Zuiliang. When Chen Zuiliang's name was mentioned, the professor burst out laughing but he thought for a while and agreed. Chen Zuiliang was the oldest scholar in the county and, although talkative, he was good enough to be a girl's teacher. The professor recommended him to Prefect Du and the prefect agreed to employ him. The professor then asked the academy's messenger to send an invitation to Chen Zuiliang.

The messenger was overjoyed; his suggestion had been accepted. He felt light-hearted as he headed for Chen Zuiliang's home to tell him the good news. As soon as he entered the drug store, he shouted out in a loud voice, "Congratulations to Mr. Chen."

"What's the good news?" Chen Zuiliang asked. He was most surprised when the messenger told him everything.

When Chen Zuiliang realized that the appointment was a fact not a joke he frowned and said, "The evil of men is that they like to be other's teachers."

The messenger could not understand what he meant and said, "From now on, you'll have enough to eat."

Chen Zuiliang, who did not want to offend the messenger, said, "All right, I'll go with you."

"Mr. Chen, I found the job for you. You must show your gratitude to me," the messenger said, asking for some form of reward.

"You want me to thank you? I am not sure if the prefect will accept me or not!" Chen Zuiliang was not a generous man.

However the messenger urged him, "If you are accepted by the prefect, you should give me some gifts."

They talked as they walked and soon came to the prefect's residence.

Prefect Du Bao had been told that Chen Zuiliang would come that day. He decided not to handle any official affairs, asked the cooks to prepare a banquet, and told the janitor to give him good warning of the teacher's arrival.

For the meeting Chen Zuiliang put on a special blue robe that had not been used for a long time. The robe did not fit him, nor did it match with his hat, but he looked like an old scholar. He thought to himself: "This is not the same as a meeting between a scholar and an official. As a tutor, I shall meet the host." With these thoughts in mind he raised his head, which gave him an impressive bearing when he entered the prefect's residence.

A shout of "Scholar Chen Zuiliang is coming!" accompanied him as he made his way into the entrance hall. There he knelt down on the ground and said, "Humble scholar Chen Zuiliang pays his respects to Your Highness."

Prefect Du saluted him in return, and said to his runner, "I'll talk with Mr. Chen. Have servants from the Rear Hall attend to us."

Acting as the host Prefect Du said, "I have heard that Mr. Chen is a learned scholar. May I ask how old you are and whether your ancestors are also scholars?"

"I am 60 years old."

"How do you make your living?"

"I come from a long line of doctors. I am practicing medicine now."

"Oh, you come from a doctor's family. What else are you good at?"

"I also know something about divination and geography."

"You're really an erudite scholar. Although this is the first time we have met, I have long known about you. A large country is full of talented people."

"Thank you."

"I have a daughter who is fond of reading books and I invite you to be her tutor."

"It would be my duty to teach her, but I am afraid that I have too little learning and talent for the position."

Prefect Du ignored this and knew perfectly well that Chen Zuiliang feigned modesty. He said, "You are qualified. Today is a lucky day. Let my daughter meet her teacher."

When the servant heard this, he began to beat a clapper to inform Miss Du Liniang. Meanwhile the band started preparing.

Du Liniang had dressed herself for the occasion and was ready to come out. Her servant Chunxiang was uneasy and said, "Now that the tutor has arrived, what shall we do?"

Du Liniang, who knew that she would be meeting her teacher that day, looked relaxed. She comforted Chunxiang, "I have to go out to meet my teacher. Even the virtuous young ladies of ancient times knew how to read and write. A maid should also learn to read books." They came to the entrance hall while she was speaking.

"Miss is coming!" a family servant reported.

Du Liniang came to the hall where she bowed to her father who said, "Come here, my dear. There is an old saying, 'Jade must be cut and chiseled to make it a useful vessel and a person must be disciplined and educated to become a useful citizen.' I have found a teacher for you. It is an auspicious day. Come and meet him."

The band began playing and Miss Du Liniang bowed to Chen Zuiliang. She said, "I am an ignorant student. I hope that my teacher will often instruct me." Chen Zuiliang replied in a modest way and Prefect Du ordered Chunxiang to kowtow to the teacher and said that she could keep her company.

Chen Zuiliang turned to Prefect Du and asked which books Du Liniang had read.

"She has read *The Four Books* for both men and women. I think *The Book of Changes* and *The Spring and Autumn Annals* are very difficult and are of no use to women. I hope she will start with *The Book of Odes*. The first chapter of the book is about the virtue of the consorts and it suits her well. What do you think of it?"

"It's a very good idea. I'll start with it." Chen Zuiliang nodded his head.

Prefect Du said, "Tomorrow will be an auspicious day. You'll start teaching and if my daughter and Chunxiang misbehave, you must not allow them to have their own way. Discipline them strictly." Chen Zuiliang agreed without hesitation.

Prefect Du gave permission for Du Liniang and Chunxiang go back to their room then banqueted and drank wine with Chen Zuiliang.

CHAPTER TWO

Chen Teaches *The Book of Songs*

WHEN CHEN ZUILIANG became Du Liniang's tutor, he explained *The Book of Songs* to her in the study everyday. Du Liniang was intelligent and worked hard at her studies. She also conducted herself with decorum and Chen Zuiliang liked her very much. Chen also taught Chunxiang, but she was too fond of play and often made him angry.

Early one morning, Chen Zuiliang went to the study and found no one there. He murmured angrily to himself, "What a spoilt girl! She has not shown up." He was determined to discipline her and banged the table with a ruler shouting, "Chunxiang, let Miss Du Liniang come to the study."

Du Liniang had in fact already got up. She was putting on a simple and elegant dress in exchange for a colorful one. Hearing the teacher, she and Chunxiang hurried to the study. Chunxiang seemed unhappy and grumbled, "Why does he make us go to school so early?"

Du Liniang ignored her. She quickened her steps and entered the study. "Good morning, Mr. Chen!" She saluted her teacher.

"Please don't blame us, teacher," Chunxiang said.

Chen Zuiliang ignored her and turned to Du Liniang and said, "As a girl, you should get up when the cock crows. After dressing you pay your respects to your parents. You should start study as a student at sunrise."

"From today I won't be late," Du Liniang said.

Chunxiang was not happy and retorted, "All right, we will stay up all night. We'll sit until midnight listening to your instructions."

Chen Zuiliang knew that Chunxiang had a very sharp tongue and ignored her. He turned to Du Liniang and asked her if she had reviewed the poem that they had studied the day before.

"Yes, and now I am waiting for you to explain it to me," Du Liniang replied.

"Could you please recite it?" Chen Zuiliang asked.

Du Liniang said calmly:

> *The sound of turtledoves cooing*
> *Rises over the islets in a river.*
> *The modest, retiring, virtuous, young lady*
> *Makes for our prince an ideal mate.*

"Good," the teacher nodded his head. "Now let me explain the poem to you. The first sentence describes the cooing of turtledoves."

"Could you show me how a bird coos?" Chunxiang interrupted. She was trying to cause trouble and, although irritated, Chen Zuiliang showed them how a bird cooed. Chunxiang followed his example and cooed, which made Du Liniang laugh. Embarrassed, Chen Zuiliang stopped her and went on to explain the second sentence. "Turtledoves like a quiet environment and live on the islets in a river."

"I remember it was yesterday, or the day before, this year or the last year. There was a turtledove in the prefect's residence. Then Miss Du Liniang set it free, and it flew to the home of Magistrate He (*he* in Chinese means river)," Chunxiang cut in.

"Stop that nonsense! We are in the middle of a lesson," the teacher said. Then he explained that the last two sentences meant that a gentleman would seek a quiet and virtuous lady.

"Why does a gentleman need to seek a girl?" Chunxiang asked.

Chen Zuiliang had no answer to the question and was embarrassed and angry. He said, "Keep your mouth shut!"

Du Liniang came from a literary family. Though she had spent much time learning needlework, she knew some poems, and was very unsatisfied with her teacher's explanation. She said, "Teacher, it is not difficult to explain the poem according to the notes. I can do that by myself. Could you please tell me the meaning and purpose of *The Book of Songs*?"

Chen Zuiliang did not know this himself and attempted to divert her with a vague answer. "Of the six most important ancient books, namely *The Book of Changes, The Book of Songs, The Book of History, The Book of Rites, The Book of Music,* and *The Spring and Autumn Annals, The Book of Songs* is the best." He had to think of something. "The Cooing of Turtledoves" in *The Book of Songs* is a song of love, but Chen Zuiliang said it sang the praises of elegant girls and virtuous consorts. Du Liniang could not agree. When Chen Zuiliang realized that his student would not accept his explanation, he tried to end the discussion. He said, "Confucius once said, to sum up, his 300 poems contain no sinister thoughts. In short, the connotations of the 305 poems in the book are innocent. You must learn this by heart."

Then Chen Zuiliang asked Chunxiang to fetch paper, brush and an inkstone so that Du Liniang could practice calligraphy. Chunxiang went and came back a moment later saying that she had collected all the materials. She deliberately put them down in front of Mr. Chen.

Chen Zuiliang had never seen the elegant things placed before him. He was surprised and asked, "What ink is this?"

Du Liniang smiled and said that Chunxiang had made a mistake. "It is a black pigment used by women to paint their eyebrows."

Chen Zuiliang pointed a pen and asked, "What pen is this?"

"It is a pen used for painting eyebrows."

Chen Zuiliang frowned and said, "I have never seen them. Take them away! What is this paper? What inkstone is this? Why is there a double inkstone?"

"This is Xue Tao Paper and that is Mandarin-Duck Inkstone." Du Liniang replied.

Chen Zuiliang was interested and moved closer, "Why are there so many holes on the inkstone?"

"They are called tear holes," Du Liniang said.

"Why does it weep? Hurry up, take it away." Chen Zuiliang waved his hand.

"These things are not for Miss. I brought them for you to enjoy." Chunxiang smiled and took them all away. Mr. Chen cursed and said that she was a naughty girl. Chunxiang brought back the brush, ink, paper and inkstone for writing a moment later. Du Liniang began to write.

Chen Zuiliang was surprised that Du Liniang's handwriting was so beautiful, but he did not know what style of calligraphy it was. He asked her.

"It is Beauty's Hairpin Style handed down by Madam Wei," Du Liniang replied earnestly.

Chen Zuiliang nodded and Du Liniang noticed that Chunxiang wasn't in the room. When she called her, Chunxiang came in and said excitedly, "I've been to the Back Garden. It is so big with colorful flowers and green willow trees."

Chen Zuiliang flew into a rage. "How dare you go to play in the garden rather than stay here to attend to Miss. I'll get a twig and give you a lesson."

Chunxiang was not frightened and replied, "What do you want to do with the twig? Beat me? We are women. We won't take the imperial examination. We only want to learn some of the characters. There is no need to be so serious."

Chen Zuiliang began telling them stories about some ancient scholars who took their learning seriously. However Chunxiang was not listening and heard a flower girl crying her wares. Du Liniang began listening too. Chen Zuiliang was so angry that he raised the twig to beat Chunxiang but she was very nimble and the old teacher missed her. She seized the twig and threw it to the ground.

As they were arguing fiercely, Du Liniang stood up to intervene. "Chunxiang, you've offended the teacher. Kneel on the ground!" Chunxiang dared not disobey Miss Liniang and fell on her knees. Du Liniang pleaded for her, "Master, please forgive her. I'll punish her for you." Chen Zuiliang was pleased and nodded.

"From now on, you are not allowed to go to the Back Garden," Du Liniang said sternly.

Chunxiang got on well with Miss Liniang. To show respect, she knelt on the ground, but when she realized that Miss Liniang was scolding her in earnest, she would not stand for it and began arguing.

The old teacher, who had never handled a dispute between women, tried to stop them as quickly as possible. He waved his hand and said, "Stand up, Chunxiang. I forgive you this time. It is true women do not take part in the imperial examination. However women should study as hard as men." He turned to Du Liniang and said, "You may return to your chamber after you finish your homework. I'll have a chat with your father." Then he walked out of the study.

Seeing Chen Zuiliang walking away, Chunxiang pointed at his back and cursed him saying, "You are an old idiot, an old bookworm. You're stupid!"

Du Liniang scolded her, "Stop this nonsense! An old saying goes, 'One who serves as my teacher one day will be like my father all of my life.' He has the right to beat you, but you should not curse him!" Chunxiang didn't dare argue with her. She was sulky and stood there silently. Suddenly Du Liniang asked Chunxiang excitedly, "Where is the garden?"

Chunxiang deliberately ignored her. Du Liniang had to ask her again and smile. Angrily, Chunxiang pushed open the back window and pointed with her hand. "It is over there!"

"Is the scenery in the garden beautiful?"

"Scenery?" Chunxiang wanted to tease Miss Liniang and hesitated. Du Liniang asked her several times and she said, "There are six to seven pavilions, a swing, a winding stream, a rockery, and many rare flowers and grasses. I don't know their names, but they are very beautiful. The whole garden is very beautiful!"

Du Liniang was taken by Chunxiang's description and said to herself, "There is such a beautiful garden over there!"

CHAPTER THREE

Miss Liniang Begins
to Think of Love

WHEN SHE RETURNED to her room, Du Liniang did not want to do needlework. She held a copy of *The Book of Songs* and kept reading: "The modest, retiring, virtuous, young lady / Makes for our prince an ideal mate." Soon she threw the book away, stood by the window, sighed deeply and said, "These two sentences display fully the sage's love in ancient times. It is also true of people today."

Chunxiang did not understand what the sage's love was, but she knew Miss Liniang well. She said, "You've studied for quite a long time. Why don't you take a break and enjoy yourself?"

Du Liniang thought for a while then went up to her and said, "Chunxiang, how can we enjoy ourselves?"

Chunxiang knew what was on her mind, and replied without hesitation, "Shall we go to the Back Garden and enjoy the scenery?"

Chunxiang's suggestion struck the right note, but Du Liniang was worried, "My father will be angry if he hears of it."

"Your father has gone to the countryside for a few days. You don't need to worry," Chunxiang said.

Du Liniang walked up and down the room slowly thinking. Suddenly she came to a bookshelf, took out an almanac and said to Chunxiang, "This will be the first time that I will be going to the Back Garden. I must pick an auspicious day. Tomorrow and the day after tomorrow are not suitable. Three days from now will be auspicious. Please go to tell the gardener that I'll make a visit in three days."

The next morning Du Liniang told Chunxiang to ask Mr. Chen if they could be excused from classes for several days. Chunxiang was pleased with the idea and left straight away. As soon as she entered the winding corridor, she saw Chen Zuiliang in the distance. Chen was near-sighted. He did not see Chunxiang until the maid was very close. "Hello, Chunxiang. Do you know where the master has gone? Where is Madam Du? Why hasn't Miss Liniang come to class?"

"Hi, Mr. Chen. Miss Liniang doesn't have time to study."

"Why?" Chen Zuiliang did not understand.

Chunxiang tried to tease him, "Mr. Chen, you're too clever to understand. You've stirred up trouble and the master blames you."

"What for?"

"You gave such an earnest explanation of *The Book of Songs* that Miss Liniang begins to think of love!"

Chen Zuiliang was surprised. "I only explained to her about the cooing of the turtledoves."

"After the class, she felt quite emotional. She sighed deeply and said that even turtledoves loves to stay on islet, and then asked why she was not as free as a bird. Now she has asked me to tell the gardener that she will visit the garden in three days."

"She wants to visit the garden?" Mr. Chen could not understand.

"It all comes from your explanations of *The Book of Songs*. Spring comes and leaves in such haste that it makes Miss Liniang sad. She decided that a visit to the garden would make her feel less melancholy." Chunxiang's explanation made Mr. Chen appear responsible for Miss Liniang's condition.

"She should not do that. A girl should cover her face when she goes out. How can Miss Liniang go anywhere she wishes? I'm 60 years old and have never gone sightseeing in spring." Chen used hackneyed and predictable excuses and Chunxiang ignored him. When he realized that Miss Liniang would not attend classes for a few days, he said to Chunxiang that he would ask for a few days' leave. He told her to clean the classroom and books everyday. He then left.

Chunxiang was so pleased that she sent the old teacher on his way with a few words of her own. Afterwards she headed for the garden and on entering it shouted, "Gardener!"

The gardener was drunk and answered, "Sister Chunxiang, I'm here!"

As he was tipsy, Chunxiang made fun of him. "You sneaked out of the house to drink wine and neglected your own work. Have you sent the vegetables to the kitchen?"

"The vegetable grower did."

"Have you watered the fields?"

"The water keeper did."

"Have you sent flowers?"

"I send flowers to Madam and Miss every morning."

"Why don't you send some flowers to me?"

"Oh, that's my fault. I'd forgotten." The younger gardener loved to make fun of young girls. However Chunxiang, who was very sharp, stopped him from going too far. Then she told him that Miss Liniang would come to the garden in three days.

On the day Chunxiang got up early to attend to Du Liniang who said, "Chunxiang, have the servants cleaned the path to the garden?"

"Yes," Chunxiang replied.

Then Du Liniang asked Chunxiang to fetch the rhombus mirror before she sat in front of the dressing table. Chunxiang helped her comb her hair and opened the jewel case, picked out the most beautiful ornaments and helped Miss Liniang put them on. After she had dressed herself up, Du Liniang looked in the mirror and gazed at her beautiful face. She could not help sympathize with herself.

Finding her still in front of the mirror Chunxiang said, "Miss, it's time for early tea already. Let's go!"

Du Liniang stood up slowly and looked at the mirror once more before walking out to head for the Back Garden with Chunxiang.

After they had passed the courtyard, the winding corridor, and the moon-shaped gate, they arrived at the garden where colorful flowers were in full bloom, birds chirped and the trees grew thickly. Goldfish swam in the pool and Du Liniang sighed and said, "What beautiful spring scenery! Without coming to the garden, I would never have seen it. Why has my father never mentioned it to me?"

She went into the Peony Pavilion, sat down, looked at the flowers and thought, "If there were no green leaves to contrast with the red flowers, the colors would be dreary." She turned to look at the goldfish in the pool. They all swam in pairs happily but after seeing them she was sad and said to Chunxiang, "Chunxiang, let's go back to our room!"

"Why? It is such a large garden. You haven't seen it all. Why do you want to return?" Chunxiang could not understand why she wanted to go back half way.

"Don't mention the garden any more! It will be useless even if we visited all of the pavilions, terraces, towers and buildings here. We'd better go back!" Du Liniang turned and walked towards her room followed by Chunxiang.

After Chunxiang had attended to Du Liniang she told her to take a rest while she went to see Madam.

Alone, Du Liniang sat lost in thought. She remembered the love poems that she had read and thought that although she was a girl of 16, she had not found a lover. What a waste of youth! It made her very sad. Soon she felt drowsy; she leant on the table, closed her eyes and fell asleep.

She dreamt that she had returned to the garden. Suddenly she saw a handsome young scholar enter with a willow twig in his hand. He stood there looking around then caught sight of her. Overjoyed, he shouted, "Hello, Miss!" and stepped forward to bow to her. "Miss, I have followed you all the way here. I was very disappointed when I lost sight of you. I'm so happy to find you."

Du Liniang thought the scholar looked appealing but she was so shy that she did not know what to say. The scholar raised the willow twig high and said, "You know much about poetry. I have just broken off a willow twig. Could you please compose a poem about it?"

The request pleased Du Liniang. She raised her head and looked at him closely. He was young and handsome. She thought, "I have never seen him before, why has he come to the garden?" She said nothing and as she did not seem to be offended, the young man said boldly, "Miss, I love you with all of my heart."

Du Liniang did not respond, but the expression on her face showed that she was pleased. The young man became bolder. "Miss, you're so young and pretty. I have looked for you everywhere and finally I find you here. However you hide and feel sad. It is a waste of youth." He took a step forward and suggested that they go somewhere else to talk.

Du Liniang stood there and blushed. The scholar reached out to hold her sleeve. "Where shall we go?" Du Liniang asked.

The young scholar pointed and said, "Behind the Chinese herbaceous peony garden and on the other side of the Taihu rockery there is a very quiet place." Du Liniang found the invitation irresistible. She stood up and began to walk.

The scholar whispered to her: "Miss, we are a natural pair. Let's be engaged right now. The opportunity is too good to miss."

Du Liniang blushed red and was too shy to say anything. The scholar lifted her up and carried her to the luxuriant flowers and trees.

All of a sudden, the flowers and trees shook and the leaves and petals fell. Du Liniang and the young man could not be seen. It happened that the Goddess of Flowers had come down to protect them. The god knew that Miss Du was fated to marry the young man, but they had no chance of meeting each other for some time. The god arranged a meeting by allowing the scholar to enter Miss Liniang's dream so that they could enjoy themselves.

The Goddess of Flowers knew well that the young man was not just an ordinary person. The young man's ancestor was a famous poet of the Tang, Liu Zongyuan.

Liu Zongyuan, styled Zihou, was a native of Yuncheng in Shanxi Province. He once served as governor of Liuzhou Prefecture. The

Liu family's fortunes declined later and his descendants lived south of the Nanling Mountains. One of them was the young man, now in his 20s, a brilliant scholar and a man of learning. However, after he had passed the imperial examination at county level, he found no opening for an official career. Without an income he lived a hard life. Fortunately, his ancestor Liu Zongyuan had a faithful servant, Hunchback Guo, who was good at planting trees and growing flowers. Guo handed on his horticultural skills to his grandson who supported the young man by growing trees and flowers. Though they had adequate simple food all the year round, it was no life for a learned scholar. Low in spirits, the young man often past time by sleeping in the daytime.

In his dream, he entered a beautiful garden where he found a slim beauty beneath a plum tree. The young man fell in love with her at first sight. He went over and held her in his arms. The beauty said, "Master, you will have a happy marriage and a bright future only if we meet." After he woke up, he changed his name to Liu Mengmei (Mengmei means: Dreaming Plum-Like Beauty).

Let's return to the dream of Du Liniang and Liu Mengmei. In the flowering shrubs the two young people stuck to each other like glue and finally fell asleep. The Goddess of Flowers, who had guarded for them for quite a while, decided to wake them by dropping a shower of flower petals.

Liu Mengmei woke first. He shook Du Liniang lightly and said, "The weather's been fine and we took a nap on the lawn." Du Liniang, both timid and shy, lowered her head without uttering a word. Liu Mengmei bent down to help her tidy herself, asked her never to forget the day, then disappeared.

Du Liniang opened her eyes. Liu Mengmei had gone and half asleep, she said in a low voice, "Young scholar, are you really gone?" Then she turned over and went to sleep again.

Just then Madam Du accompanied by Chunxiang came to see her daughter. She was angry to find her asleep during the day. She walked over to pat her on shoulder. "Liniang, how can you sleep at this time?"

Still half asleep, Du Liniang thought Liu Mengmei was calling her and murmured, "Young scholar." Fortunately Madam Du did not hear her clearly and Chunxiang hurried to wake her up.

"How are you feeling, my girl?" Madam Du asked.

Du Liniang, who had woken up completely, was frightened and cried out, "Oh, mother, you are here!"

"Liniang, why aren't you doing needlework or reading history? How can you sleep in broad daylight?" Madam Du scolded her daughter.

"I went to the garden early in the morning. The beautiful scenery upset me and I returned to my room not wanting to do anything. I fell asleep suddenly without realizing it. It was remiss of me not to come out to greet you. I hope you will forgive me, mother."

When Madam Du learned that her daughter had gone to the garden, she said seriously, "My daughter, the Back Garden is spacious and quiet. You shouldn't go there anymore."

"Yes, mother."

"Why didn't you go to class?"

"Mr. Chen asked for time off, so I am taking a break."

Madam Du sighed and said, "My daughter has grown and her mind is full of ideas but she won't tell me what they are. I'll just have to let things run their course." She left for her own room.

After her mother left, Du Liniang began to recall her dream: "Mother always urges me to study, but knows nothing about my need for love. I am glad to have met Liu Mengmei in my dream. How nice it is to be with the young scholar. Mother, you only let me read books. But no book can drive away the emptiness in my heart."

Night fell and Chunxiang saw that Du Liniang was still lost in thought. She went to help her take off her ornaments and make up her bed.

Madam Du felt very uneasy after learning that her daughter had visited the garden and from then on often went to see her. One day, she walked towards her daughter's room after supper and found Chunxiang sitting outside the house. She asked where Miss Liniang was.

Chunxiang was surprised to see her and said, "Madam, you're up very late. Is there something you wish me to do?" Madam Du insisted on knowing where Du Liniang was and Chunxiang pointed to the inner room. She said, "She talked to herself for quite a long while, then fell asleep. I think she is dreaming now."

Madam Du became very angry. "It is you who lured Miss Liniang to the Back Garden. What will we do if something happens to her?"

"It's all my fault. I'll never do it again," Chunxiang said obediently after seeing how angry Madam Du was. Madam Du still warned, "Chunxiang, don't you know that the Back Garden has been left untended for many years. Most of the pavilions and towers are dilapidated and people do not go there very often. Old people like me think twice before venturing in, so how can a young girl wander in alone? What would I do if something happened to my dear daughter? I hope you will take good care of her rather than lead her astray." Madam Du stood up and Chunxiang hastily followed to see her off.

CHAPTER FOUR

Du Liniang Draws a Self-Portrait

THE NEXT DAY Chunxiang rose very early and, after washing and dressing, went to ask Miss Liniang to get up. Then she went to the kitchen to make breakfast.

Du Liniang got up reluctantly. She sat in front of the dressing table and began to comb her hair. Soon the hand stopped in mid-air and she sat there staring blankly. She said to herself, "Who is the young man I met yesterday in my dream? He is tender and soft like water. It seems that we knew each other very well. Now he is gone, leaving me alone and I feel so bored staying here all by myself."

"It's time for breakfast!" Chunxiang came in holding a tray on her palm. Her voice distracted Du Liniang from her thoughts.

"I'm in no mood to have breakfast. How could I swallow such food?"

"Madam Du said you missed your supper yesterday. Today you must have your breakfast."

Suddenly Du Liniang felt that she had a grudge against Chunxiang and said, "Oh, I don't have the energy to touch these bowls and plates. I ate yesterday, and I am not hungry now. You may eat it yourself." She waved her hand. Chunxiang had no choice but to leave taking the tray with her.

After she had driven Chunxiang away, Du Liniang wished that her dream would continue but it would not and she became more unhappy. Suddenly she had an idea. There was nothing for her to do that day, why not go to the Back Garden again and search for her dream without telling Chunxiang? She walked out of her room, turned several corners and came to the garden. Finding that the door was open and no gardener in sight, she entered without any difficulty.

The scenery in the garden was as beautiful as before; the paths were covered with flower petals, the Chinese herbaceous peonies leaned on the rockery, and the winding stream ran silently. Everything in the garden reminded her of the happy time with the young man in her dream. A flower by the path caught her skirt made her think that just like human beings, flowers also liked to hold onto beautiful things. "What a great waste of my young life to stay in the embroidery room all day long." She was lost in thought.

Let's turn to Chunxiang. After having had breakfast, she returned to the room to find that Du Liniang had disappeared. It frightened her, but she guessed that young Miss must have gone to the garden and she hurried there. When she saw Du Liniang standing by the plum tree, she cried out, "Alas! Miss, you are here. How could you come here by yourself?"

Du Liniang tried to divert her with a vague answer. "I found a swallow on the painted corridor busy building a nest. Following it, I found myself in the garden."

"Let's go back, Miss. Madam will scold me if she knows you are here. I'll be blamed again," Chunxiang said, trying to convince her.

"Stop that nonsense. What's wrong with me visiting the garden occasionally?" Du Liniang said angrily.

"It's not me who talks nonsense. It's Madam Du's instruction. She said a girl should stay inside to do needlework, read books or practice calligraphy."

"Anything else?"

"She said the garden is desolate. There are flower and tree spirits here. If you want to get rid of boredom you'd better go to the front yard."

"I'll do as you say. You can tell my mother that I'll return soon," said Du Liniang impatiently. Chunxiang left.

After she walked away, Du Liniang began looking for her dreamland. She thought to herself, "Alas! There is the rockery; the Peony Pavilion is over there; close to the pavilion is the Chinese herbaceous peony garden. In front of it is a willow tree. To its left stands a plum tree. The young handsome scholar led me to the rockery and then carried me in his arms to the flowering shrubs beside the pavilion. How happy we were when we were together! However, now the pavilions and towers are dilapidated; the garden is desolate; the grass and flowers have withered and there is no sign of human habitation. It is quite different from the scene I saw in my dream!" Looking around her, Du Liniang suddenly caught sight of a big plum tree. She moved towards it without thinking. It looked like a big umbrella, tall and straight and covered with green leaves and plums. In the breeze Du Liniang could smell a pleasant fragrance. But, when she thought that lovely plums had bitter kernels, a symbol of her own fate, she felt sad. She said to herself, "I would be happy if I was buried by the tree when I die."

She thought that there would be fewer unhappy people if everyone could control their own fate and love whoever they pleased. No one in the world would blame God or man. Feeling tired she leaned on the plum tree and rested. Her hand fondled the tree's root and she made up her mind that she would see the young scholar again no matter what happened.

Chunxiang came back to the garden looking for Du Liniang and finding her asleep tried to wake her up.

Half asleep, Du Liniang murmured to herself, "Looking at the boundless sky I feel sad. I am so sorry that I did not compose a poem for him!"

Chunxiang, who did not understand her, said, "Don't make me guess! Miss'let's go back to your room."

Du Liniang was slowly lead towards her room by Chunxiang. She heard a bird singing and said sadly, "Listen, the cuckoo is saying 'let's go back'. Where can I return? I'm afraid I will not meet him in the garden again, unless in a dream or after my death." Ignoring what she said, Chunxiang took her back.

After her return to the garden to look for her dreamland, Du Liniang was disheartened and often went without food and sleep. As time went by, she became thinner and thinner. Chunxiang, who was very worried, said to her, "Since you've been to the Back Garden, you have no appetite and your nights are without sleep. You lose weight every day. How do you feel? Are you sick? No wonder Madam Du said you should not go there Miss, from now on you should never enter it again."

"You don't know why I want to go to the garden. I put on bright clothes and make up with great care every day, but I only sit in the room all day long by myself. To whom can I express my feelings? How can I get rid of my worries?"

"Miss, after visiting the garden, you always shed tears. You're so sad all the time and you look wan and sallow. Madam Du will be very worried if she sees you."

Du Liniang walked to the dressing table and looked herself in the mirror. She was surprised to see that she had lost so much weight. "Alas! I used to be very beautiful. Now I am so thin and pallid." Her eyes were full of tears. Chunxiang comforted her, but failed to cheer her up. Both of them sat there, silent.

Suddenly Du Liniang said, "Chunxiang, fetch a piece of silk and a brush. I'll paint a picture."

"It's a good idea, Miss. What will you paint?"

"I'll do a self-portrait. I want to paint a portrait of myself while I'm young. Otherwise I'll regret it when I'm old. Who would know Du Liniang was such a beauty if I died young?"

Chunxiang did not know what to say to the depressed girl and went to the inner room to get a piece of silk and a brush. Chunxiang thought to herself, "It's easy for Miss to paint her own portrait but it will be difficult for her to portray her sadness in the painting."

Before she began to paint, Du Liniang cried continuously, sighed, "I, Du Liniang, am only 16 years old. My life has only just begun. But I must paint a self-portrait."

She thought for a while, began to clean the mirror carefully and looked at herself in it. Then she took a piece of silk, and started drawing with great concentration. Chunxiang stood by and could not help exclaiming, "Wonderful!"

Soon she had finished and Du Liniang allowed Chunxiang to hang it up. It was truly an excellent painting; there were elegant Taihu rockeries, weeping willows, and green palm leaves. A slim, pretty girl leant on a willow tree with a plum branch in her hand.

"Does it look like me?" Du Liniang asked Chunxiang.

"It looks just like you. You're really a gifted painter. No one can compare with you." Du Liniang was also very satisfied with her work. Chunxiang sighed, "It's a great pity that there is not a young man beside you. After you get married, you may do a painting of a happy couple."

When she heard this, Du Liniang could not help telling Chunxiang everything. "I don't want to hide the truth from you. I did meet a handsome young man in the garden. However, he was only a dream."

Chunxiang was surprised and asked if it was the truth.

Du Liniang said, "I met a young scholar in my dream. He broke off a willow twig and gave it to me. Does that mean I will marry a man whose surname is Liu [willow]? I have finished my self-portrait and told you everything about my dream. Shall I inscribe a poem on the painting?"

"That sounds good."

Du Liniang picked up her brush and wrote a poem on the painting. It read:

Seen closely, she is an extraordinary beauty,
And seen at a distance, she is like a goddess.
One year she met a handsome young
man from the moon,
By a weeping willow rather than a plum tree.

As soon as she had finished, Du Liniang threw down the brush and sighed, "In ancient times some beautiful women were married when they were young and their husbands would draw portraits of them. Some beautiful women drew self-portraits and sent them to their lovers. No one was like me. I drew my self-portrait and have no one to send it to. Chunxiang, could you please ask the gardener to have this painting mounted?"

Chunxiang picked up the painting and left to look for the gardener.

CHAPTER FIVE

Du Liniang Dies for Love

DU LINIANG BECAME anxious and sick after going to the Back Garden. After almost six months she had not recovered. Sometimes she seemed better, sometimes worse, but there was no sign of complete recovery.

At 50 years of age Madam Du only had one daughter. Seeing her daughter become thinner and thinner made her very anxious. Du Liniang showed no signs of a chill or a temperature and Madam Du had no idea of what disease her daughter was suffering from. One day she decided to ask Chunxiang about the illness.

Chunxiang was a smart girl and knew what Madam Du would ask her. On her way to the hall she decided what to say to her. She knelt in front of Madam Du and said, "Humble maid Chunxiang pays her respects to Madam."

"Chunxiang, you wait on Miss Liniang every day. You must know what has made her ill. Tell me the truth!"

"I don't know anything at all, except that since Miss paid a visit to the Back Garden, she has not been well."

"How about Liniang's appetite?" Madam Du asked.

"All I can say Madam is that whenever I give Miss drink of tea or take in a meal, she always refuses it. She seems to be always in a trance, laughing and crying without reason. I'm afraid she is seriously sick."

"We have invited an imperial doctor to treat her, haven't we?"

Chunxiang said in a quiet voice, "She suffers from lovesickness. No doctor can cure her."

"What disease?" Madam had not heard what she said.

"I don't know. Maybe she has a chill," Chunxiang said cautiously.

Sensing that Chunxiang was hiding the truth, Madam raised her voice and said sternly, "Stop this nonsense. You know full well that she has not got a cold. Kneel down and tell me the truth!"

When she saw how angry Madam Du was, Chunxiang fell to the ground and told her everything. She said, "One day six months ago Miss went to the Back Garden. It was the very day that you happened to come to see her. She told me that she met a young man in the garden with a willow twig in his hand. The young man asked Miss to write a poem for him. It was the first time that Miss had met the young man, so she declined."

"What happened later?"

"Later ... later ... the young scholar took Miss to the Peony Pavilion."

"What did they do there?" Madam Du was alarmed.

"How do I know?" Chunxiang said. "Miss said it was only a dream."

"A dream?" Madam was surprised.

"Yes, it was a dream."

"It seems that she ran into a ghost. Let me discuss it with the Master."

Chunxiang went to fetch Prefect Du and Madam Du told him everything about Liniang's sickness. She asked him to invite a wizard to drive the ghost away from Liniang.

Prefect Du blamed his wife. "I employed Mr. Chen Zuiliang to teach her and make her concentrate on books. But you, her mother, let her have her own way. Now she is sick as a result of a visit to the garden. In my opinion, she has just caught a cold. Let Mr. Chen take her pulse and write out a prescription. She will recover after taking medicine. We may also invite Nun Shi from the Ziyang Palace to chant scriptures to drive evil ghosts away."

One day after Du Liniang woke up Chunxiang helped her move and sit by the window. Chunxiang rolled up the curtain for her and a sweet smell greeted them. A pair of swallows flew freely in the sky.

"Chunxiang, I'm very sick and have become very thin and pallid. I am afraid I won't live very long. Now I'm very concerned about the young scholar I met in my dream. How is he?"

"Miss, he only appeared in your dream. Please stop thinking about him."

Du Liniang did not listen to her and was longing to see her young lover. She wished he would appear in her dream again and thought, "Maybe the young man really lives somewhere. But how can I find him?"

As Du Liniang was not listening, Chunxiang said, "Miss, a dream is not real. It's useless to think about him. You should think about your own health. Your illness is very troubling. It makes you muddle-headed all day long. Oh, when will you have a clear head?" Chunxiang was most anxious.

"Is Chunxiang in?" Their chat was interrupted by Chen Zuiliang who entered the room without waiting for Chunxiang to greet him. He had come to diagnose Du Liniang's disease as requested by Prefect Du.

When she saw him, Du Liniang tried to get up. "Master, I'm sick and I cannot come to greet you. Please forgive me," Du Liniang said.

Chen replied, "Miss, according to an old saying, a rich knowledge and great ability come from learning. You were sick after your visit to the Back Garden and since then you have neglected your studies. When I learned that you were sick, I was very worried. Fortunately today the Master allowed me to diagnose your disease and I have a chance to see you. I didn't expect to find you so thin. When will you get better and return to school? Miss, tell me what's wrong with you?"

Chunxiang tried to make him appear responsible for the illness and said, "Mr. Chen, it is all your fault. You explained the love poem from *The Book of Songs* in detail, asked Miss to recite it and learn it by heart. That's why Miss is sick."

"How come?" Chen Zuiliang could not believe what he heard.

"You said, 'The modest, retiring, virtuous, young lady makes for our prince an ideal mate.' She pines for the prince."

"Who is the prince?" Chen Zuiliang did not understand.

"No one knows who he is," Chunxiang replied defiantly.

As Chunxiang was being rude to Teacher Chen, Du Liniang cut in, "Mr. Chen, you may feel my pulse now."

Chen Zuiliang reached out and placed three fingers on the back of Du Liniang's hand and Chunxiang said bluntly, "How can you take Miss Liniang's pulse by feeling the back of her hand?"

Chen Zuiliang realized that was wrong and said, "Miss, you may turn your hand over." He felt Du Liniang's pulse with great diligence and cried out, "Alas! Your pulse is very weak. I had not expected you to be so seriously ill." He sighed and said to Chunxiang, "Chunxiang, you take good care of Miss. I'm going to prepare some medicine."

When she heard this, Du Liniang sighed and said sadly, "Master, I know myself well. Neither acupuncture nor medicine can cure me. Thank you very much for coming to see me." Tears ran down her face.

Chen Zuiliang and Chunxiang were also very sad but could say nothing. They comforted Du Liniang and told her not to think too much. "You will get better and please don't worry. You'll recover after the Mid-Autumn Festival."

After Chen Zuiliang left, Nun Shi from the Ziyang Palace arrived to drive the ghosts from Du Liniang. She asked Chunxiang what disease Miss suffered from.

Chunxiang did not like Nun Shi and said defiantly, "An embarrassing one."

"Where did she get the disease?"

"In the Back Garden."

Nun Shi struck a pose by raising three fingers then five. Chunxiang ignored her and when she saw Miss lying there showing no response, she went close to her and heard her murmur, "My dear! My lover!"

"Listen," Nun Shi said to Chunxiang, "she talks incoherently. A ghost must have caught her." She took out a piece of yellow cloth and mumbled, "Go away wild ghosts and idle souls."

Nun Shi's voice woke Du Liniang who saw the yellow magic figure and said, "It does not work. My lover is not a young ghost attached to a flower or a tree."

"All right, if the magic figure does not work, let me call the palm thunder to hit him."

Though seriously ill, Du Liniang had a clear mind and tried to send the nun away politely. "Nun, I think you must be very tired from chanting scriptures. Could you please leave me alone and allow me to have a good rest?"

Nun Shi had to take her leave.

The Mid-Autumn Festival came. Thick black clouds hid the bright moon and the wind blew. There is an old saying that if it rains during the Mid-Autumn Festival, someone will die. With Du Liniang suffering from an illness at such a time, Chunxiang was very worried about how long she will live. The maid was determined to help Miss get up so that she could attend a family reunion for the festival. With her help, Du Liniang sat down on a chair by the window.

Still sick, Du Liniang did not know which day it was and felt chilly as raindrops fell down the window. "Chunxiang, how long have I been sick? What's the date today?"

"It is Mid-Autumn Festival."

"Oh, it's a family reunion festival. I expect that my parents are worrying about me. Have they celebrated it?"

"Yes," Chunxiang replied.

"I remember when Mr. Chen came to see me last, he said I would have recovered by the Mid-Autumn Festival. Now that the festival is here my health has gone from bad to worse. What can I do? My illness must have spoiled your appreciation of the moon. Chunxiang, open the window. Let me see the bright moon."

"There is no moon tonight." Chunxiang gently pushed the window open.

Raising her head, Du Liniang saw dark clouds and no bright

moon. She felt sad, sighed deeply and said, "Today is the Mid-Autumn Festival. Where do you hide yourself, bright moon? I feel so sad!"

Chunxiang who was standing by heard everything Miss said. She thought to herself, "Miss was cheated by a young scholar in a dream. I first thought that she would forget him. However as time goes by, she has sunk deeper and deeper into an abyss. She is such a beauty, but she will die for an unworthy man. I must go to comfort her." She helped Miss Liniang lie down and soon after feigned delight crying out, "Miss, the moon has come out. The bright moon will help you fall into a sound sleep. You'll have a good sleep tonight."

Chunxiang failed to cheer her up and she sighed deeply and said sorrowfully, "For a long time I have looked forward to the Mid-Autumn Festival. However, when the festival comes, I cannot appreciate the moon. Probably I am fated to be afraid of it. Maybe my life will end in this autumn rain that goes on and on. Oh, even with this bright moon on the Mid-Autumn Festival, I can only hear a plaintive whine in the distance, autumn insects chirping at night and the wind blowing through the Chinese parasol trees. All of these make my heart even heavier..." Before she had finished she became cold, shivered and her hands and legs became stiff.

It frightened Chunxiang. "Miss, Miss!" She cried at the top of her voice. And then she walked out of the door shouting, "Madam, could you please come right now? Miss is not well."

Astonished, Madam Du rushed to her daughter's bedroom. "My dear daughter, how are you now?"

"I have to tell you Madam, Miss is not well."

Finding that her daughter was unconscious, Madam Du could not help but weep. She held Du Liniang's cold hands gently and said, "Oh, my child, no one would believe that since the day you went to the Back Garden and dreamt, you have been in a state of delirium. If I had known earlier that you longed for a lover, I would have found a young man for you. Then you would not feel lonely, nor sleep by yourself every night. My sweet child, if you leave us, an old couple, I don't want to live either."

The bells hanging on the eaves rang in the wind, and Madam Du wept sadly by the bed. Du Liniang woke up. Seeing her mother she tried to get up but was so weak that she could not. When she spoke, she rambled. "Mother, I'm very grateful to you for bringing me up. You have given me boundless love since I was born. I'm not a dutiful daughter. I will not wait on you in your remaining years. Please don't be too sad over me. You must take good care of yourself." Her eyes brimmed with tears and Madam Du and Chunxiang both wept. They resented Heaven; it had destroyed good things on earth and ruined Du Liniang's life.

After a while Madam Du wiped away her tears, lifted her head and said, "I have no sons, only you, my daughter. I have placed all my hope in you and thought that you would support your father and I when we are old. But now you're seriously sick. I'm so unlucky..." Madam Du stopped abruptly and comforted her daughter. "My daughter, don't be so upset, take a good rest."

Knowing that she would never recover, Du Liniang spoke of something that worried her. "Mother, I'm afraid I won't get better. Where do you plan to bury me?"

Though filled with deep sorrow, Madam Du immediately said that she would be sent to their hometown.

Du Liniang tactfully told her mother of her wish. "Though I miss my hometown very much, it is far away; I would like you to bury me here."

Her mother did not understand what she meant and said, "I'll try every way to ship your body back."

Du Liniang had to tell her frankly, "I have a wish. You must listen to me whether it is right or wrong."

"Go ahead and tell me. I'm listening to you."

"There is a plum tree in the Back Garden. I like it very much. You must bury me under it," Du Liniang said.

"Why do you want to be buried under the plum tree?" Madam Du did not understand.

Du Liniang answered her vaguely. "I'm not as lucky as Chang'e who lives among sweet-scented osmanthus. I love plum blossoms very much. I do hope you will bury me under the tree. It's my last wish."

Madam Du was too sad to know what to say. She hated to hear the words spoken by her dear daughter, but she had to face reality. She thought she should tell her husband immediately. After instructing Chunxiang to take good care of her daughter, she went to see her husband.

After Madam Du left, Chunxiang was alone with Du Liniang who beckoned her to the bedside and said, "Chunxiang, we have been congenial companions for many years. After I die, you must take good care of my parents for me."

"That's the least I can do," replied Chunxiang.

"Chunxiang, may I entrust you with another thing?"

"I'll do everything you want."

"I wrote a poem on my self-portrait. I don't want any one else to see it. Could you please place the portrait in my purple sandalwood box and hide it under the Taihu Rock."

"Why do you want me to put it under the rock?" Chunxiang did not understand.

"I drew a self-portrait with great care just for a man who will be my lifelong companion."

Chunxiang thought that she should not discuss arrangements that would be made after Miss Liniang's death. She tried to comfort her. "Miss, you take it easy and rest. I'll speak to the Master. We'll find a young man for you; whether he is Mr. Mei [plum] or Mr. Liu (Willow), he will be your lifelong partner. Does that sound good?"

"I'm afraid I will not see the day. Oh, oh!" Probably tired after talking so long, Du Liniang felt pain in her heart. "Chunxiang, will you miss me after my death?"

This made Chunxiang very sad and before she could reply, Du Liniang lost consciousness again. Shocked, Chunxiang shouted, "Master and Madam, come quickly! Miss has passed out!"

Prefect Du and his wife had had a premonition that their daughter was dying and, when they heard Chunxiang, they lost no time in rushing to her bedside. They wept as they walked and cried out, "My dear daughter, how can you abandon your old parents!" Standing by the bed, Prefect Du shouted, "Please come to, my dear. Your father is here."

After a while Du Liniang regained consciousness and said in a low voice, "Father, I'm dying. I hope you will set up a tablet in front of my tomb." Then she died and her parents were choked up with sobs.

Prefect Du, his wife and Chunxiang grieved deeply. Chunxiang cried and said, "Miss, how sad I am. No longer can I burn joss sticks, light candles, pick up flowers, feed birds or move the mirror for you. You often did needlework until midnight and got up early to paint." She remembered Miss Liniang's instructions before her death and put the portrait in a purple box.

Nun Shi and Chen Zuiliang arrived soon after and cried bitterly.

Just then the housekeeper came in to say that an edict had arrived. Prefect Du received it and ascertained that it was an imperial edict passed on by the Ministry of Personnel. It read: "The Kin troops are invading our border. Prefect Du Bao of Nan'an is promoted to Pacification Commissioner of Huaiyang. Du Bao will set out for his new post immediately. This is an order from the emperor himself." Though Prefect Du had been promoted, he was not at all happy. His dear daughter had just passed away, and he had not yet made arrangements for her funeral. However he dared not disobey the emperor's order and after uttering a deep sigh, sent for Chen Zuiliang.

Chen Zuiliang was waiting at the outer room and, when he heard his name mentioned, hurried in. Prefect Du said, "Mr. Chen, my daughter has gone." Chen Zuiliang said sorrowfully, "Now that Miss Liniang has gone, I have lost a student. Master Du has been promoted so I have no one to rely on."

Prefect Du had no time to listen to him and said, "Mr. Chen, I have something to discuss. At the emperor's command I will soon leave for the post. My daughter had a wish. She wanted to be buried under the plum tree in the Back Garden, but I'm afraid this does not suit the new prefect of Nan'an, so I told my housekeeper to build a nunnery in the Back Garden. It will be called Plum Blossom Nunnery and will house my daughter's tablet." He turned and said to Nun Shi, "Could you please stay in the nunnery to take care of it?"

Nun Shi was pleased. She knelt on the ground and said, "I'll take good care of the nunnery."

Prefect Du also allocated one hectare of land to Mr. Chen and told him that he could share the harvest with Nun Shi after they had paid the costs of the Plum Blossom Nunnery. Chen Zuiliang and Nun Shi were delighted. Finally, Prefect Du urged them again and again to take good care of his daughter's tomb and offer her a bowl of rice on the Pure Brightness Festival every year. Too sad to continue, Prefect Du left, consoling his wife.

CHAPTER SIX

Liu Mengmei Visits His Friend

A FTER LIU CHUNQING dreamt of meeting a beauty under a plum tree, he changed his name to Liu Mengmei. Although he had been disappointed to find himself alone after waking up, he remembered clearly that the beauty in the dream had said that he would gain fame and fortune. He had studied hard for many years and had thought that it would not be difficult to get an official post. He thought that once he became an official, it would be easy for him to find a beautiful wife.

However reality was quite different. He was poor. The grandson of Hunchback Guo supported him by growing trees. Life dragged on and Liu Mengmei was very lonely. He did not have any close friends with whom he could converse in the city except for Han Zicai. Both Liu and Han were descendants of famous writers in the Tang Dynasty. Liu's ancestor was Liu Zongyuan while Han was descendant of Han Yu. According to Han Zicai, his ancestor, Han Yu, had been demoted to Chaozhou in southern China because he offended the emperor by submitting a petition. On the way to Chaozhou, he had been delayed by heavy snow in Languan, Shaanxi Province, and his horse could not go on. Han Yu thought that it was not a good omen. Suddenly one of the Eight Immortals in the form of his nephew, Han Xiangzi, came to see him. Han Yu, more depressed and in low spirits, picked up his frozen brush, softened it by blowing on it and wrote a poem at the thatched post of Languan:

> A petition was submitted to the emperor,
> And I was demoted to Chaozhou 8,000 li away.
> To help the emperor correct his errors,
> I would devote my remaining years.
> Where is my home? Mount Qinling is covered
> by clouds
> And my horse is held by heavy snow in Languan.
> I know why you came here from afar.
> You came to gather my bones by the river.

The last two sentences referred to Han Xiangzi and, when he saw the poem, the Immortal Han Xiangzi burst out laughing, tucked the poem into his sleeve and left on a cloud. Later Han Yu died of miasma in Chaozhou. As he had no relations in Chaozhou, Han Xiangzi, who already knew of his uncle's death, came on a cloud and buried his body. Then the Immortal Han Xiangzi went to the county government office and found no one there except a woman who became his lover. He was completely taken by her and spent a night with her. Later the woman became pregnant and gave birth to a son. Han Zicai was a descendant of both Han Xiangzi and the woman. Later when war broke out, Han's descendants wandered destitute from Chaozhou to Guangzhou. As Han Zicai was a descendant of Han Yu, the local official of Guangzhou submitted a memorial to the court suggesting that he be given a post. Later Han Zicai was appointed a petty official in charge of sacrificial rites at the Changli Shrine and lived on the Prince Yue Terrace built by Zhao Tuo.

Both Liu Mengmei and Han Zicai had passed the imperial examination at the county level and lived in the same city. Though Liu Mengmei looked down on Han Zicai, they had a few things in common and often visited each other. One day, when Liu Mengmei was still quite upset over the dream he had had a few days earlier, he had nothing in particular to do. As he could not concentrate on books, he walked slowly towards Prince Yue Terrace. Han Zicai was doing nothing except looking into the distance from the terrace. Seeing Liu Mengmei coming up, he greeted him, "Hello, I haven't seen you for quite a long time. What wind has blown you here today?"

"I had nothing to do at home, so I came to see you." Liu Mengmei made an obeisance by placing his hands together before his chest.

"You'll get a good view from the terrace," Han Zicai said proudly.

Liu Mengmei knew that the terrace gave a panoramic view but he was low in spirits and said, "It does not make me very happy to climb up."

Han Zicai, who did not know what he was implying, said in great delight, "I'm living in ease and comfort here."

"I believe those who are not intellectuals live a happier life than we do," Liu Mengmei said expressing dissatisfaction.

"Who in particular are you talking about?"

"Zhao Tuo who had the Prince Yue Terrace built is a good example."

"What makes you think that?" Han Zicai still could not understand.

"Originally Zhao Tuo was only a commandant of Nanhai. After Emperor Qin Shihuang died, the country fell into great disorder and many heroes rose up. Zhao Tuo, relying on the natural defense, set up a separatist regime by force of arms and called himself emperor. After that he had a grand palace built and lived there happily in his remaining years. Look at us. Though we have read thousands of books, we cannot gain a foothold." Liu Mengmei became more indignant and said, "Our ancestors said, 'One who has read the first half of *The Analects* by Confucius can occupy the country, while one who has read the second half of the book can administer it.' However I have read the book time and time again, but I haven't found a way out for myself." He paced back and forth on the terrace, now looking ahead, and now standing still. He turned to Han Zicai and said, "It is no use for us worrying about the present and cherishing a memory of the past. Brother Han, look! Only a few ancient trees can stand the wind and rain around the terrace."

As a long-standing friend of Liu Mengmei, Han Zicai knew that Liu was rather conceited and fancied himself as a gifted scholar. When he heard him grumbling, Han Zicai tried to talk him out of it. "Lord Changli once said, 'Be concerned that your article is good enough rather than worrying that officials do not understand you. Be concerned that you are not an outstanding scholar rather than worrying that officials do not know you.' Brother Liu, I think the reason why you have not started on your official career is that you have not worked hard enough."

Liu Mengmei was not convinced and continued, "Brother Han, what you say is not right. For instance, both my ancestor Liu Zongyuan and your ancestor Han Yu were learned scholars. Your ancestor Han Yu offended the emperor by submitting a memorial and was then demoted to Chaozhou; my ancestor Liu Zongyuan frightened the emperor when he was playing chess with Prime Minister, Wang Shuwen. He was sent to be commander of Liuzhou. Both Chaozhou and Liuzhou are in the border areas far away from the capital. Han Yu and Liu Zongyuan traveled together at that time and whether they were on a boat, or on horseback, they always kept their books. Every night they sat up late to read books and discuss articles." Liu Mengmei described their ancestors in great detail as if he had seen them himself. As he spoke he became more excited and said in a high voice, "As for the articles they wrote, they were well-matched. Han Yu said to my ancestor, 'Liu Zongyuan, I wrote the *Biography of Wang Nishui*, and you followed suit and created the *Biography of Ziren*. Later I wrote *Life of Palace Secretary Mao*, and you *Hunchback Guo*. I wrote *A Funeral Oration for Crocodiles,* and you *Snake Catcher's Words*. I once wrote an article praising the emperor. So did you. You always compete with me. Now I am sent into exile and you keep me company. Are we fated always to be together?' "

After a while Liu Mengmei calmed down and said gently, "Brother Han, let's forget the past. But why are we treated coldly by the court? My ancestor once wrote an article called 'Begging for Skills.' So far I haven't gained any skills for my career. Your ancestor once wrote an article 'Sending Away Poverty' and you haven't rid yourself of poverty yet. Both of us have had bad luck."

Moved, Han Zicai said, "What you say is true. You studied very hard all of those years and spent your family property on books but your knowledge is not worth a penny. However Lu Jia was also a Confucian scholar. When Emperor Gaozu of the Han Dynasty (206 BC-220 AD) sent him here to make Zhao Tuo Prince Nanyue, Zhao Tuo held him in great esteem and gave him lots of gold. After he returned to the court, he was promoted to Grand Master."

Both young men envied Lu Jia very much. Han Zicai said, "Lu Jia was a scholar who had good luck. Emperor Gaozu of the Han Dynasty had a strong dislike of scholars. Whenever a Confucian scholar came to see him, he would take the scholar's scarf and urinate on it. One day when Lu Jia went to see the emperor in a robe and scholar's scarf, Emperor Gaozu could not help saying, 'Another scholar is sending his scarf for me to pee on.' Lu Jia pretended not to hear him and continued walking towards the emperor. The emperor looked at him and shouted, 'I won the country by military force. I don't need any scholars like you.' Instead of becoming angry, Lu Jia, a very capable and brave man, said, 'Your Majesty, you can win the country with your skills on horseback. However can you administer the country with the same skills?' Emperor Gaozu, who had not expected Lu Jia to reply, was rendered speechless. After a pause, he smiled and said, 'All right, that sounds reasonable. If you have any good articles, please read them out to me.' Lu Jia was happy to oblige and calmly took a roll of 13 articles from his sleeve. He had written them with painstaking effort and opened and read them in a loud voice. The emperor was very pleased as the articles had many new ideas and he thought them extraordinary. The emperor praised him at the end of the first article, and, after Lu Jia had finished reading all of them, Emperor Gaozu appointed him a marquis. Scholar Lu did well that day. All the officials and officers at the court were most delighted that the emperor had found a gifted scholar."

Liu Mengmei knew the story and was very depressed by Han Zicai's description of how Lu Jia read his articles to the emperor.

He said, "Oh, I'm so unlucky. I've also written many articles, but I have no one to read to."

"Brother Liu, how do you make a living?" Han Zicai asked.

"I have no choice other than to depend on my gardener, the grandson of Hunchback Guo."

Liu Mengmei was at the end of his tether. Han Zicai suggested that he ought to visit some well-known people who might give him a chance.

"Brother Han, don't you know that it's very hard to find someone who is willing to help me."

"Brother Liu, Mr. Miao is an imperial envoy in charge of treasures. He is experienced and prudent, and always ready to help others. I have been told that his term of office will end this coming autumn, and he will hold the Treasure Exhibition Assembly at the Duobao [numerous treasure] Temple in Xiangshanao. Why don't you go there in autumn to meet him?" Han Zicai suggested this with great sincerity.

Liu Mengmei was persuaded and said, "Thank you very much for your advice. I'll do as you say and do my best to meet him." He took his leave.

After Liu Mengmei had returned home, he thought to himself, "As a result of my hard study in the past 10 or so years I'm now the most outstanding scholar in Guangzhou, but my knowledge has not earned me any rewards and I still live in a vegetable garden relying on my gardener. I am ashamed of myself." The more he thought about it, the more sensible Han Zicai's suggestion seemed. He was determined to walk out of his house and hew out his own path. He hoped that he would be fortunate.

He began preparing and one day called in his gardener, the grandson of Hunchback Guo, saying that he wished to speak to him.

"What is it?"

"I'm over 20 years old without any hope of gaining fame or fortune. You work very hard to support me all the year round, and both of us live a poor life eating simple food every day. Though young, I already know how inconstant human relationships are, and after careful consideration I have decided that I should not waste my youth carrying firewood and water every day. I have much to do…"

The gardener interrupted him saying, "Young Master, although I am not a man of great ability, I've done my best."

"I am not blaming you. I am going to give you all of the fruit garden."

The grandson of Hunchback Guo was very upset and said, "Then where will you make your living?"

"There's an old saying, 'Eating three meals a day without toiling at home is not as good as making a living outside it'," Liu Mengmei said.

"But, Young Master, it's not a good idea for you to make a living somewhere else. I think you'd better concentrate on your studies and try to pass the imperial examination at the provincial level. Then you'll bring honor to your ancestors." The gardener tried to advise him, but Liu Mengmei had made up his mind, and said bluntly, "Please don't stop me!"

Left with no choice, the gardener began to pack for him and before Liu Mengmei went he asked him many times to return after he had gained fame and fortune. The gardener said that he would be there waiting for him.

Liu Mengmei started his journey with a bundle wrapped in cloth on his back.

Imperial Envoy Miao Shunbin's term of office had expired. Before leaving for the capital to make a report to the emperor he intended to hold the Treasure Exhibition Assembly at the Duobao Temple.

Located in Xiangshanao, Guangzhou, the Duobao Temple had been built from funds raised by foreign business people to welcome the treasure-collecting official who was sent by the court. The temple had a bishop and joss sticks and candles burned every day. Before the Treasure Exhibition Assembly, the bishop, who had received notice from the imperial envoy, made various preparations. Early on the morning of the opening ceremony, he made another tour of the temple to see if everything was ready. Then he walked out of the temple to greet the imperial envoy.

Mr. Miao Shunbin soon appeared, climbing the flight of stone steps to the temple followed by an interpreter, a retinue and many foreigners. The bishop went to him and fell on his knees.

Then he got up and led Mr. Miao to the main hall. Everything was ready and Mr. Miao smiled with satisfaction. After he had taken a seat, he allowed the foreign merchants to show their treasures. The foreigners vied with one another to guide the imperial envoy to their sandalwood shelves on which rare treasures were placed.

Mr. Miao walked slowly by the shelves examining them with great interest. There were so many rare treasures that Mr. Miao, an expert judge, was full of praise and said, "All the rare treasures of the world are gathered here. The Duobao Temple deserves the reputation that it enjoys." Soon Mr. Miao came to the statue of Avalokitesvara. He asked the bishop to burn some joss sticks for him and standing in front of the statue he bowed deeply several times, praying that Avalokitesvara would bless and protect the coastal areas and territorial seas and that foreign merchants would keep coming to China to present their treasures.

When Mr. Miao looked back, he saw that many merchants from the West and Arabia were watching him intently and he was touched. He asked the bishop to pray for the foreign merchants in front of the Buddha and the bishop, who was good at singing praises and blessings, spontaneously recited:

> *The sea holds numerous treasures,*
> *But boats will meet storms at sea.*
> *Merchants who bring precious treasures with them*
> *Are afraid of traveling on the sea.*

Then the bishop turned to the foreign merchants and said, "Gentlemen, if you encounter a storm at sea, you will be safe from danger only by repeating over and over again, 'My infinitely merciful Avalokitesvara.' Be sure to remember this!"

When the Treasure Exhibition Assembly was almost over, Liu Mengmei arrived at the gate of the temple. He was determined to meet the imperial envoy and hoped to persuade him to help him in his official career. Though the guards in front of the temple stopped him, he insisted that they report his coming to the imperial envoy.

He said to one of Mr. Miao's attendants, "Brother, could you please inform the imperial envoy that Liu Mengmei, a student of the Academy of Guangzhou, asks to see the treasures."

The attendant knew that Mr. Miao was very fond of scholars and when he heard that Liu Mengmei was a student of the Academy of Guangzhou, he was more favorably disposed and went inside to report. Mr. Miao heard that the scholar wanted to come in to appreciate the treasures and retorted, "These treasures belong to the court. All and sundry are not allowed to see them." However, after a while he changed his mind and said that he would make an exception for a scholar.

Liu Mengmei walked in and bowed to Mr. Miao and before he had had time to say anything, Mr. Miao asked him why he had come to the assembly that day.

"My name is Liu Mengmei. I am a poor scholar. I am bored to death at home. When I learned that Your Highness was holding the Treasure Exhibition Assembly here, I made a special trip here to see the treasures and enrich my knowledge," Liu Mengmei replied.

"If that is so, you may start appreciating the treasures." Mr. Miao stood up and led Liu Mengmei to the shelves. Liu Mengmei was most surprised.

"I know something about pearls and jade but compared with you, I'm only a pupil. What are the names of the treasures on the shelves? You're experienced and knowledgeable, could you please tell me about them?" Liu Mengmei was courteous and very modest.

Mr. Miao, who was immensely proud, said, "This is a magic grit. That is the Sea-Boiling ruby. Over there is the cat's eye, and the emerald…" Liu Mengmei praised his knowledge and after a tour of the exhibition hall, Mr. Miao allowed him to sit down and his attendant served tea.

Liu Mengmei sat with ease and confidence and after sipping tea, he thanked Mr. Miao. "If I had not come today how else could I feast my eyes on so many treasures? I'm very grateful to Your Highness for giving me such an opportunity."

Mr. Miao replied courteously. Realizing that the imperial envoy was not arrogant and rude Liu Mengmei said, "May I ask Your Highness from how far away these treasures came?"

"It all depends. The farthest is 15,000 kilometers and the nearest is over 5,000 kilometers."

"Did they fly or walk here?"

Mr. Miao could not help laughing at such a ridiculous question, but replied earnestly, "How could they fly or walk here? The court bought some at a high price, and others were contributed to the court by foreign merchants."

Liu Mengmei sighed and said, "Your Highness, these lifeless treasures can come from afar without feet. I am a student of the Academy of Guangzhou and have much knowledge. It is only 1,500 kilometers from Guangzhou to the capital, but no one is willing to buy me, which means that though I have feet, I can't walk. I cannot help wondering whether the official at the Maritime Trade Commissioner in charge of foreign trade can really find treasures for the court."

Mr. Miao, who didn't understand the meaning of Liu Mengmei's words, said, "You don't suspect that these treasures are false?"

"No, they are real, but they cannot be eaten when we are hungry, and they cannot be used as clothes when we are cold. What's their use?"

"Then, what, in your eyes, are real treasures?" Liu Mengmei expected this question and replied loftily, "I would not dare cheat Your Highness. If you want to see a real treasure, I am one of the world's rarely seen treasures."

Mr. Miao thought that Liu Mengmei was boastful and sneered at him. "I'm afraid that the court has too many rare treasures like you."

"Please don't tease me, Mr. Miao. A rare treasure like me can even win the championship at the Lintong Treasure Competition held by Lord Mu of the Qin State.

Realizing that Liu Mengmei was serious, unlike some poor scholars who cheated others for their food and drink, Mr. Miao assumed a benevolent look and said, "According to what you say, treasures like you can only be presented to the emperor. Is that right?"

Liu Mengmei knew that he must grasp this critical moment to enlist Mr. Miao's help. He said, "I can say to Your Highness, if it's hard for poor scholars like me to meet local officials, how dare I dream of meeting the emperor?"

Mr. Miao told him the truth. "There's an old saying, 'The lackeys are even more difficult to deal with.' It will not be very difficult to see the emperor."

Liu Mengmei then gave an account of his situation. "The capital is 1,500 kilometers from here. I have no way of finding money for the journey."

"It's easy. In ancient times the gentry often gave gold to heroes. I can give the regular silver I draw from the government to pay your expenses on the way to the capital." Mr. Miao was very generous.

Overjoyed, Liu Mengmei bowed low to Mr. Miao and told him that as he had no parents or wife to care for, he could leave for the capital immediately. He stood up and took his leave. Mr. Miao asked his servant to take out some silver to give to him and offered him a cup of wine, wishing him a good trip and hoping that he would achieve his desires.

Before Liu Mengmei accepted the wine cup, he said, "Mr. Miao, I'm still worried. Although the emperor is wise, high-ranking officials around him will not appreciate my talents."

Mr. Miao comforted him. "Don't worry, there are people around the emperor who can tell good from bad and know what's what. Please drink this cup of wine and I hope that your talents will be useful to the imperial court."

Liu Mengmei went home, picked up some clothes, packed them up and left Guangzhou holding an umbrella. He first took a boat and then crossed Mount Meiling on foot.

CHAPTER SEVEN

Liu Mengmei Falls Ill

LIU MENGMEI HAD lived south of Mount Meiling for many years and had never traveled far. He did not know that the weather north of Mount Meiling was quite different from that in the south. In the south, it was like spring all the year round and there was no snow in the winter; the north had distinct seasonal changes with rain and snow in winter. When Liu Mengmei took his leave from Imperial Envoy Miao at Xiangshanao, it was autumn. After he arrived north of Mount Meiling he encountered cold winter weather and a strong wind from the north.

Liu Mengmei was eager to start his official career and traveled from dawn to dusk, often braving wind and rain. Before soon, he caught a cold and shivered all over. He had not realized how difficult the long journey would be and wished that he was at home south of Mount Meiling. But when he thought of his hard-earned funds, he was determined to go ahead. Fortunately the city of Nan'an was not far away.

The strong wind broke his umbrella, his old scarf was almost blown away and snow fell in large flakes. Shivering all over, Liu Mengmei struggled along the rough and bumpy snow-covered paths between the fields. Looking around, he saw that there were no houses nearby for him to stay the night. He had to walk towards the city, braving heavy snow.

The snow blotted out the sky and covered up the earth. Liu Mengmei took each step with great care. Soon he came to a river, over which there was a broken bridge. How could he cross it? He was at the end of his tether and walked back and forth carefully surveying the broken bridge. Finally he decided that he could cross the river with the help of a willow tree by the bridge. The challenge of crossing the river preoccupied him and he had not expected the surface of the bridge to be so slippery. He fell from the bridge into the river crying "Help! Help!" at the top of his voice.

Usually there would have been no one around in such an open area and on such a bad day. Yet, he was not destined to die, for his shout was heard by a man. It was none other than Chen Zuiliang, who used to be the tutor of Du Liniang, daughter of Prefect Du.

As it turned out, after Du Liniang died and Prefect Du Bao had been transferred to north China, Chen Zuiliang received no regular income and, although he was in charge of one hectare of land, he often ran short of money. When he learned that a village school was looking for a teacher, he rode a donkey and braved heavy snow to apply for the job. Suddenly he heard a voice from the river and said to himself, "Where is the voice coming from in such a bad weather?" He got off the donkey and near the broken bridge found a man struggling in the river.

"Help! Help!" Liu Mengmei caught sight of him and shouted at the top of his voice.

"Who are you? How did you fall into the river?" Chen Zuiliang asked.

"I'm a scholar."

On hearing that it was a scholar, Chen Zuiliang was determined to save him and said, "As you're a scholar, let me help you." He walked with great care towards the end of the bridge, but he was over 60 and he had great difficulty helping Liu Mengmei out of the water. He stretched out his hand and was just about to grasp Liu's hand when he fell down on the ground himself. Fortunately Liu Mengmei was near the shore and finally escaped from the river with

Chen Zuiliang's help.

When Liu Mengmei was out of danger, Chen Zuiliang asked him where he was from.

"I'm from Guangzhou."

"Where are you going?"

"To the capital, Lin'an."

"What for?"

"To present a treasure."

"What treasure?"

"I am a rare treasure. I'm braving wind and snow to take a trip to the capital, seeking an opportunity." Despite the fact that Liu Mengmei had been rescued from a desperate situation, he immediately started to boast.

Chen Zuiliang had his doubts and said, "You must be very sure that you'll pass the imperial examination or you would not hurry on such a journey in the freezing cold winter."

When Liu Mengmei realized that Chen Zuiliang doubted him, he boasted, "To tell you the truth, I'm an extraordinarily learned man, like a white jade pillar supporting heaven or a purple-golden beam of the sea."

Chen Zuiliang burst out laughing and said, "Alas, heaven has no eyes. It has almost broken the pillar that supports it and the purple-golden beam!" Then he turned to Liu Mengmei and said with great concern, "I'm just kidding you. I know something about art of medicine and your hands are freezing, which means that you are suffering from cold. The Plum Blossom Nunnery is not far from here and, if you go there with me, you could live there for the time being. You could continue your journey north in the spring, what do you think?"

Liu Mengmei knew that he was too weak to continue his journey and happily accepted Chen Zuiliang's invitation. He thanked Chen Zuiliang. The pair stumbled on through the snow supporting each other.

After saving Liu Mengmei from the river, Chen Zuiliang took the young man to the Plum Blossom Nunnery and allowed him to live there. As time went by, he gradually recovered under the careful medical treatment of Chen Zuiliang and soon had no difficulty getting about.

Before very long winter passed and spring arrived. One day when Liu Mengmei woke up, he was pleased to find the room full of sunshine. He had lain on bed for quite a long time and now found it better to get up and move around. He jumped up and took up the bundle that he had thrown in the corner of the room many days ago. His winter clothes still had stains of rain and snow and he hung them up by the window to dry.

He was not in the mood to read books and pulled a chair over by the window and sat on it. The warm spring sunshine made him drowsy and he yawned again and again. He was bored but had no idea how pass the time. Just then Nun Shi, the head of the nunnery, visited him. "Young Master, how are you getting on these days?"

"Thank you very much for coming to see me. I'm much better now but I do feel very bored. Look, without having anything to do, I have to sit in the sun." Liu Mengmei usually had no one to talk to and was very happy to see Nun Shi. He said, "Aunt, the nunnery is not small. Does it have a garden or a pavilion? I would like to spend some time in a pavilion or tower."

There was a pause, then Nun Shi replied, "There is a garden at the rear. However, as the pavilions and towers have not been renovated for years, most of them have collapsed. The flowers, trees and grass grow thickly but you could go there to relieve boredom. But please don't feel sad."

"How could I feel sad walking in a garden?" Liu Mengmei did not understand.

After sighing deeply, Nun Shi said, "I only made a casual remark. Please don't take it seriously. Go there and enjoy yourself. Walk along the painted corridor in the west and you'll see a bamboo gate about 100 paces in front of you. It is the gate to the garden, which is quite large. You can spend a whole day there. I'm sorry that I'm too busy to go with you today."

Liu Mengmei dismissed from his mind what Nun Shi's had first said and was eager to find a diversion. He said happily, "As there is a garden, I will go there right away." He said good-bye to Nun Shi and headed for the garden along the painted corridor.

Soon he came to a bamboo door surrounded by bushy trees; one part of the door lay on the ground. He pushed the door open and entered. "Oh! What a huge garden!" He was delighted. Preoccupied by the scenery, he did not notice green moss beneath his feet and slipped and fell. The garden, he thought, must have been neglected for quite a long time.

Walking along a narrow path, he came to another bamboo door that was bolted. He reached out, took off the bolt and walked in. When he saw the groves of bamboo, small lake, wild flowers in full bloom and thick grass, he became suspicious. There was only one nun at the Plum Blossom Nunnery how could such a small place have such a large back garden? The more he thought about it, the more he wondered.

However he wanted to see all of the garden and stopped thinking about it. Following a path, he went deep into the garden and found pavilions by the water, all of them collapsed, a pleasure boat by a leaning pavilion and a swing hanging in the air. What a scene of decay, he thought. There has been no war recently, why was it so desolate? Was there a sad story connected to it?

As he could find no answer to his questions, he simply gave up and started to enjoy the scenery. Soon after turning several corners he came to a rockery made of Taihu rocks. It was oddly shaped but elegant, and he liked it so much that he walked round it again and again, examining it with great care. Finally he found a cave and entered without hesitation. One of his feet kicked something hard and he looked down to see a sandalwood box on the ground. He bent down, one hand holding a stone, and picked it up. When he opened it, he was surprised to find a portrait of Avalokitesvara and could not help shouting, "Wonderful! Wonderful! The portrait is so magnificent. I'll take it to my room, hang it up and worship it every day." He left the garden in high spirits and headed for his room. He immediately put the sandalwood box on the table, and started to burn joss sticks to pay genuine homage to it.

Nun Shi knew that Liu Mengmei had come back from the garden when she heard a sound in his room. She had nothing to do and had returned to Liu Mengmei's room; she liked talking to the young scholar and said, "Young Master Liu, are you back?"

"Yes, I am back. Aunt, you said I would feel sad if I visited the garden. Could you please tell me which place would make me happy?" After exchanging casual remarks, Nun Shi took her leave and Liu Mengmei went to bed.

It drizzled for more than 10 days after Liu Mengmei visited the Back Garden. As soon as it cleared up, he opened the sandalwood box, carefully unfolded the portrait and looked at it again and again. He thought that he was very lucky. It was said that Avalokitesvara used to be on Mount Putuo in Zhejiang Province. People in Guangzhou seldom had a chance to see her, but he, a man living to the south of Mount Meiling, had obtained a portrait of her. It was a good omen. Also, the portrait had been painted with great care and was extraordinarily beautiful.

He could not keep his eyes off it and examined it carefully. Finally he spotted something that was not right; Avalokitesvara should have had natural feet while the beauty had three-inch feet deformed by foot-binding. He started to doubt that it was a portrait of Avalokitesvara and then concluded that it was not.

He continued looking at it and found the woman's elegant shape was just like that of Chang'e, a goddess in the moon. "Since she is a goddess who has come down to the world, I should prostrate myself before her," he said to himself. He wished he could be one of goddess' lovers in the moon. He took a step back to view it at a distance and saw that it was not Chang'e. There were no auspicious clouds around her and the beauty leant on a willow tree rather than a sweet-scented osmanthus tree. (Legend has it that there were only sweet-scented osmanthus trees on the moon.)

She was neither Avalokitesvara nor Chang'e. Who was she then? Liu Mengmei was attracted by the girl and thought that there was nothing on earth to equal her beauty. Looking up he stared at the girl's face. Oh, she looked familiar. "I must have met her before. But where have I seen her?" Liu Mengmei asked himself. "Was the portrait done by a master painter or by the beautiful girl herself?"

After some thought, Liu Mengmei went closer to the portrait, examining it carefully. He was surprised to find a four-line poem was written on it. It read:

Seen closely, she is an extraordinary beauty;
And seen at a distance, she is like a goddess.
One year she met a handsome young man from
the moon,
By a weeping willow rather than a plum tree.

After reading the poem, Liu Mengmei was more surprised and thought, "How strange it is! The poem mentions willow and plum trees. The beauty leans on a willow tree holding a plum twig, and both are related to my own name. In addition, it seems that I have met her before. Is she really the girl who once appeared in my dream?"

The beauty in the portrait reminded him of his dream and he remembered the beauty saying, "Only if you meet me, will you have a happy marriage and gain fame and fortune." He said joyfully, "Are you the beauty? If it is true, good luck is not far away."

The more he looked at the portrait, the more he was attracted by the elegant beauty. Holding a plum twig, the girl looked at him with tenderness and love. Liu Mengmei longed to hold the beauty's hands but it was only a daydream. He had no choice but to pick up a brush and write a poem on the portrait expressing his feelings.

The surpassing quality of this painting is natural;
The beauty in the picture must be a goddess.
If you would like to accompany a man from the
moon,
You may find him by a willow or plum tree in
spring.

After writing the poem on the painting, Liu Mengmei threw his brush aside and sat down.

He thought to himself that the woman in the portrait was not only beautiful; she could paint pictures and compose poems. The more he thought about it, the keener he was to hold the beauty in his arms. He could not help saying to himself, "Beauty, beauty! Sister, sister! In your company from now on I shall lead a happy life and worship you day and night."

CHAPTER EIGHT

Du Liniang Meets Liu Mengmei

IT WAS CLOSE to the third anniversary of Du Liniang's death. Entrusted by Du Bao and his wife, Nun Shi of the Plum Blossom Nunnery was busy preparing for a rite to save her soul. An auspicious day had been chosen. On the day Nun Shi got up very early; a flag was hung outside the nunnery to call back her spirit and a yellow notice pasted to the wall. A sacrificial altar had been set up as well. When everything was ready, Nun Shi began the ritual. At the time two nuns were walking towards the nunnery, an older mistress and her younger disciple. The disciple said, "Mistress, night is falling. Shall we stay the night at the Plum Blossom Nunnery ahead of us?" The mistress, the head of the Biyun Nunnery in Shaoyang Prefecture, had been traveling round the country with her disciple. Seeing the flag and the yellow notice and smelling the fragrance of joss sticks, she happily accepted her disciple's suggestion.

When they came to the gate of the nunnery Nun Shi asked them, "Where are you from, nuns?"

The mistress smiled sweetly and said, "We are from Shaoyang Prefecture. Could we please spend the night at the nunnery?"

Nun Shi was pleased to take in the two nuns but the guest room was occupied by Liu Mengmei and she hesitated. "You are welcome to stay in our nunnery. However a young scholar lives in the eastern wing room. He is sick and has not recovered completely. You will have to live in the western wing room."

The mistress thanked her and pointing to the flag and the yellow notice asked, "Are you holding a rite for a dead person tonight? Who is it?"

Nun Shi sighed deeply then replied, "The dead person is Du Liniang, daughter of former Prefect Du. She was an extraordinary beauty."

The mistress, who was keen to repay Nun Shi's hospitality, said, "Oh, what a pity. If we can do anything to help with the rite, we shall be very pleased."

"Thank you." Nun Shi was pleased with the offer.

While they were talking, bells were rung and drums beaten urging Nun Shi to go up the altar and offer a sacrifice. Nun Shi, who knew of Miss Liniang's fondness for plum blossoms, plucked a branch from Du Liniang's tomb, put it into a vase and placed it on the sacrificial table. Then she led the two traveling nuns in bowing to Du Liniang's tablet again and again. The rite continued all day and at dusk a whirlwind blew from behind the sacrificial altar. Nun Shi, frightened, said nothing about it and, allowing the others have their supper first, cleaned up the altar.

After the whirlwind, the soul of Du Liniang appeared. How could her soul travel so freely? It was not usual. As it happened, after she died, she went to the hell where Judge Hu who acted under the King of Hell received her. When he saw that she was such a beauty, not like the other ghosts in the hell, he showed concern for her. He asked her if she had been a dancer or a prostitute, whether she had died of sickness and who were her parents. Du Liniang's soul replied politely, "I never married and have not been a dancer or a prostitute. One day I paid a visit to the Back Garden of residence and had a dream under a plum tree. In my dream, a young man came, broke off a twig of a willow tree, and asked me to compose a poem. We fell in love with each other. After I woke, I missed him very much. From that day on, I became weaker and weaker and finally I died."

"You're telling a lie. No one in the world would die because of a dream." Judge Hu did not believe her. He sent for the Goddess of Flowers from the Back Garden of Du Liniang's residence who then told him it was true. Judge Hu wanted to turn Du Liniang into a swallow because she died only for love. The Goddess of Flowers begged him to show her mercy. "I wish say to Your Highness that the girl made a mistake in her dream. What she dreamt did not really happen, so you should not punish her. Also her father is an honest and upright official. He has only one daughter. Please set her free."

"Who is her father?" Judge Hu asked.

"My father is Prefect Du Bao. Now he is the Pacification Commissioner of Huaiyang," Du Liniang's soul replied.

"Oh, you are a young lady from a wealthy family. As your father is an upright official and has done much good work, I'll report the case to the Heavenly Court and let it to make a decision."

"I beg Your Highness to investigate my case. It's such a sad story," Du Liniang's soul appealed.

"Your case must be in the Broken Hearts Records," Judge Hu replied.

Du Liniang's soul insisted on appealing to the judge. "Could you please check if my husband's surname is Liu or Mei?"

Judge Hu, who could hardly decline her request, opened Marriage Records and began to go through them. "Oh, it is here. Your husband is Liu Mengmei, the latest Number One Scholar. Soon you will meet him at the Plum Blossom Nunnery. You two are fated to marry. If this is so, let me set you free. You may go out of the city of the ghosts of wronged people. You may go anywhere with the wind to look for your lover." Then Judge Hu ordered the Goddess of Flowers to take good care of Du Liniang's dead body in preparation for the day when she would return to the world. After Judge Hu had finished, Du Liniang's soul expressed heartfelt thanks to him and flew away with the wind.

Du Liniang's soul arrived at Nan'an City at the time when Nun Shi and the other nuns were performing the rite for her. Dusk was deepening and the Back Garden was quiet. She went through the bamboo door, passed Peony Pavilion and the railing, then stood in the center of the garden. Looking around she saw a scene of desolation. It had been three years since her parents had left and no one had taken care of the pavilions or towers in the garden. No one remembered her, Du Liniang. She was so sad that her tears ran down her face.

Suddenly she heard a sound, smelt burning joss sticks and saw candles in the hall. She was so curious that she went over to look. She found a tablet on the table inscribed with her own name. All of this told her that Nun Shi, who came to her room three years ago to drive away ghosts, was holding a rite for her. A vase with a plum blossoms branch stood on the table. "Oh, plum blossoms. They're my favorite!" she said to herself. "Since I have come here, I should make them aware of my presence." She waved her sleeve and made all the plum blossom petals fall to the table.

When she was about to leave, she heard a voice saying, "Oh, my lover, my beauty!" It surprised her and she listened attentively. She heard a young man's voice, saying, "I love you so much and call you day and night but you never answer. Why didn't you write your name on the portrait? I don't even know who you are."

The passionate voice stopped Du Liniang, and after a pause the young man went on to say, "My lover, my beauty, I love you with all of my heart." Du Liniang thought that the young man was probably talking in his sleep but an idea formed in her mind. Was he Master Liu or Master Mei who appeared in her dream?

Dawn was almost breaking and Du Liniang's soul had to return to her tomb right away before the sunrise. As she hurried away her garment knocked down the embroidered silk flag making a loud noise and startling the nuns. The young nun ran out shouting at the top of her voice, "Come quickly, mistresses!"

Nun Shi and the mistress of the Biyun Nunnery hurried in and asked together, "What's the matter? What has happened?"

"I saw a goddess leaving, waving her sleeves elegantly. She disappeared in a twinkle. I am so frightened," the young nun said.

"What does she look like?" Nun Shi asked.

After the young nun had described what she had seen, she asked Nun Shi, "What goddess could she be to come down to earth?"

"Well, it seems she looks just like Du Liniang, the dead daughter of Prefect Du. She must have come to the rite to make her presence known," Nun Shi sighed.

Just then the mistress of the Biyun Nunnery found the scripture table covered with flower petals. Surprised, all the nuns began to pray again, wishing Du Liniang's soul would soon go to heaven.

After Liu Mengmei found the portrait in the Back Garden, he fell in love with the beauty in the picture. From then on he hung it up every day and often looked at it with great interest, wondering who she was.

Late one night Liu Mengmei took out the portrait again, read the poems and gazed appreciatively at the beautiful girl. She looked back at him with soft eyes and he could not help asking himself who she was. Why did she always look at him with love but say nothing? How he wished he could meet her in his dream!

Suddenly there was a blast of cold wind that lifted up the portrait. Liu Mengmei hurried over to hold it with both hands, fearing that the wind would damage it. He thought to himself that he should take great care of this hard-won portrait; it would be a great pity if the wind spoiled it. He had considered looking for a master painter to have it copied but thought again and gave the idea up; there was no such beauty on earth and it would be pointless. He went to lie down in his bed. It was possible that he might meet her in his dreams.

There was a gust of cold wind but Liu Mengmei had already fallen into a sound sleep and did not feel it. Du Liniang's soul came with the wind. A few days earlier, when her soul had gone to the Plum Blossom Nunnery, she heard a young man's voice calling, "My sister! My beauty!" The pitiful sound had attracted her and this time she made a special trip to the eastern wing room. Peeping through a window into the room, she was astonished. Her own portrait hung on the wall and on it, was the poem that she had written. Beside her own poem was another with the signature of Liu Mengmei.

While Du Liniang was lost in thought, the young man muttered in his dream, "One year she met a handsome young man from the moon. By a weeping willow rather than a plum tree. My love, the man you mentioned in your poem was me, Liu Mengmei. But you're only a beauty on paper and how can I be close to you and touch you?" Amazed, Du Liniang thought, "I wrote that poem. The scholar calls himself Liu Mengmei. Is he the man I met in my dream?" She was overjoyed and knocked at the door.

Liu Mengmei woke up and said, "The bamboo is being blown about by the wind. Is there anyone knocking at the door or is it the sound of the wind?"

"It's me," Du Liniang replied.

Liu Mengmei thought to himself that it was very late and no one would be visiting him at this hour. It must be Nun Shi coming with some tea. He called out, "I don't need tea, Nun Shi. Thank you very much."

"No, I'm not Nun Shi."

"Are you the young nun from the Biyun Nunnery?"

"No, I'm not her either."

"That's very strange. Who is it then? Let me open the door and take a look," Liu Mengmei murmured to himself.

He rose from his bed, draped a robe over his shoulder, unlatched the bolt, opened the door and found an extraordinary beauty standing there. Before he knew who she was, the young lady had passed him by and entered the room, smiling sweetly. Liu Mengmei closed the door in a hurry.

The lady tidied herself up, bowed to Liu Mengmei and said, "Young master, all blessings."

"May I ask where are you from? Why do you come here so late at night?" Liu Mengmei was suspicious.

"Can you guess, young master?" Du Liniang said with a smile.

Liu Mengmei was very curious and guessed that she was a goddess from heaven, a concubine who had escaped from her husband's residence, or someone who had eloped but lost her way in the night.

As Liu Mengmei could not answer her question, Du Liniang had to introduce herself. "I'm not a goddess from heaven, nor a concubine, nor an eloper. Young master, have you ever met a young lady under a plum tree in your dream?"

"Yes, I once had such a dream."

"During your dream, you came to my home on the eastern side of the nunnery."

Liu Mengmei suddenly realized and said excitedly, "You're the beautiful girl who once appeared in my dream. I thought a dream was not real. It really surprises me that we can meet with each other today."

Du Liniang was also pleasantly surprised and said, "How happy I am to meet you here. I was born into a good family. Since childhood, my parents have subjected me to strict discipline and I have never met a young man before. As for our meeting in front of the rockery by the Peony Pavilion in our dream, you know what happened later." Du Liniang lowered her head and was too shy to continue.

"Oh, you're really the beauty in the picture? My lover, my darling, I have missed you very much." Delighted, Liu Mengmei grasped Du Liniang's hand, went to the portrait and said, "God blesses me, and brings you to life." Like two familiar friends they sat down and spoke to each other earnestly expressing their love for one another. Afraid that it would frighten him, Du Liniang did not tell him that she was dead. Du Liniang left at about four o'clock in the morning and before she went she said, "I have a few words to say to you. I hope you will understand me."

"Say anything you want," Liu Mengmei said, smiling broadly.

"I'm a young lady from a wealthy family. Once I give myself to you, I hope you will never betray me. My only hope is that we shall be an affectionate couple forever." These matters worried Du Liniang.

Liu Mengmei promised seriously. "How dare I forget you since you sincerely love me?"

"In addition, please let me leave every morning before the cock crows. You don't need to see me off. It is chilly in the morning and you would be cold."

"Please don't worry, I'll do what you say. May I ask you, what is your name?"

Du Liniang could not avoid a deep sigh. As a dead person she dared not tell him her name. She had to equivocate. "I'm from a good family, Master Liu, don't worry about it. For the time being, I can't tell you my name as it might cause trouble. I'll tell you later."

"That's all right," Liu Mengmei said. "I hope you will come to see me every night."

CHAPTER NINE

Du Liniang Tells the Truth

HEAD OVER HEELS in love, Du Liniang and Liu Mengmei were inseparable every night. They did not expect others to spread exaggerated stories and malicious gossip. Nun Shi, the head of the nunnery, was suspicious and kept an eye on Liu Mengmei's room.

For several nights in succession she heard Liu Mengmei talking to somebody with a woman's voice. She could not help suspecting that there was a woman living in his room. She thought to herself that Prefect Du had built the Plum Blossom Nunnery for his dead daughter. In the past three years nothing had happened and the nunnery had been peaceful. However, since Chen Zuiliang had introduced Liu Mengmei, a young man who called himself a scholar from Guangzhou, to the nunnery, it had not been peaceful. When Master Liu came, he had been sick and weak. But after he recovered, he took a walk in the Back Garden rather and has been absent-minded, restless and in low spirits since. The day before yesterday, two nuns from Shaoyang had come to the nunnery. According to Taoist rules, nuns should not marry, nor give birth to children; they should devote their lives to Taoism and worship the

191

three Taoist founders. However the young nun was only 16 years old, a pretty girl with a flirtatious manner. Her Taoist dress did not hide her beautiful face and features. With this in mind, Nun Shi could not help suspecting that the young nun was having an affair with Liu Mengmei.

"Aunt Shi," someone was calling her. Nun Shi looked up and saw that it was none other than the young nun. She said without thinking, "Young nun, you go out every night. Did you visit Master Liu last night?"

"Alas! Why do you ask me this? Who saw me entering his room?" the young nun replied angrily, blushing and knitting her brows.

"I saw for myself. Why do you dress up beautifully every day? Don't you go with a young man?"

"Aunt Shi, that is even more objectionable to my ears. Please point out whom I'm going out with? Though I'm young and like to dress myself simply and elegantly, I have always preserved my purity. How could you suggest that I would do such a thing? Though you're over 50, you're still charming. Maybe it's you who wants to find a boyfriend."

"You, you... How can you falsely accuse me?" Nun Shi was so angry that she did not know what to say.

"You may think what you want. Why do you allow a young scholar to live in a nunnery? That is simple evidence." The young nun did not let Nun Shi off easily.

"Alas! Don't you accuse me of having an affair with the young scholar? You're traveling nuns and he is a traveling scholar. The two of you can stay here, why can't he? Before you came the young scholar's room was quiet after he went to bed. But in the past two days, the young man has opened the door late at the night and talked to a woman all night. Who does he talk to if it is not you? I'll take you to the official government and let the local official decide on it." Nun Shi reached out trying to seize the young nun.

The young nun, who was not at all frightened, grasped Nun Shi's robe and said, "All right! Let's go right now. As the head of a nunnery, you let a local ruffian live here. I don't believe the local official will let you off so easily."

While the nuns were quarreling, Chen Zuiliang walked in, saw them and made fun of them. "What are you doing? Fighting for the right to win over believers?"

Nun Shi said, "Mr. Chen, let me tell you, I heard Master Liu open his door and talk with a woman at midnight. Then I asked the young nun if she visited Master Liu at night. Instead of giving me a proper answer, she falsely accused me by asking why I let a young man live in my nunnery. Please tell her who brought the young man here and I'll take her to the local government and let the prefect decide who is right and who is wrong."

The two nuns were really angry and Chen Zuiliang tried his best to calm them. He told them to stop quarreling and consider Master Liu who should not be put in a position where he would lose face.

"All right, I'll listen to you." Nun Shi let go of the young nun.

"Let's work together to find who talks with the young scholar at midnight," the young nun suggested and the two nuns finally reached agreement. The lovers had no idea that the two nuns were watching them and, as usual, they met that night.

Liu Mengmei prepared everything after dark and sat by the table waiting for his lover to come. Soon he dozed off, one hand supporting his head.

Du Liniang arrived and saw him sleeping soundly on a chilly spring night without any cover over his body. She felt tender affection towards him and went up and called him gently, "Master Liu! Master Liu!"

Liu Mengmei woke up and seeing his lover he stood up and bowed to her. "I should have come out to greet you but I fell asleep while waiting for you. Your footsteps were so light that I didn't hear you coming. Darling, you are late tonight."

"I wanted to come earlier, but I had to wait for my parents to go to bed. I put the needles and threads for my needlework into order and dressed myself up before coming. That's why I'm late," Du Liniang explained.

"I appreciate your deep feelings and love for me," Liu Mengmei said. He paused then continued, "It's a wonderful night, but it's a pity we don't have wine or cakes."

"Oh, I forgot to tell you that I brought a pot of wine and two boxes of cakes and snacks with me. I left them outside. I'll bring them in. We shall have a good time tonight." Du Liniang had prepared for everything.

They sat down to drink wine and chat but soon they both blushed, revealing their thoughts of love. Liu Mengmei urged Du Liniang to make love but Du Liniang, who was shy, tried to say no. Happily engaged in their conversation the two young people were unaware of the eavesdroppers. Nun Shi and the young nun from the Biyun Nunnery had been standing by the window of Liu Mengmei's room for quite a while. The young nun said to Nun Shi, "Listen, the young man is talking to somebody now. But I'm standing by you so there is no reason to suspect me."

Nun Shi put her ear close to the window and said, "It's a woman's voice. Knock on the door." The young nun did as was told.

"Who is it?" Liu Mengmei asked.

"It's Nun Shi. I'm bringing you some tea," Nun Shi replied.

"It's very late at night. I don't want tea, thank you, Nun Shi." Liu Mengmei answered, slightly unnerved.

"Do you have a guest in your room?" Nun Shi asked.

"No, no, there is no one here." Liu Mengmei was flustered.

"I heard a woman's voice," Nun Shi said.

When they heard this, Liu Mengmei and Du Liniang knew that they had been found out. They were so frightened that they did not know what to do. Liu Mengmei's face turned white and in a low voice he asked Du Liniang what to do.

Nun Shi urged him again to open the door and warned that if their voices were heard by the local people, they would all come.

Panic-stricken, Liu Mengmei rubbed his hands and said once more, "What shall we do?"

Du Liniang appeared calm, smiled and said to her lover, "Don't worry. I'm only a girl from a neighboring family. If Nun Shi will not forgive me, I'll accuse her by saying it is her who seduces me. Master Liu, don't be frightened. Open the door. I'll hide myself behind the portrait."

When Liu Mengmei opened the door, Nun Shi and the young nun competed with each other to enter the room while congratulating him.

"Why do you congratulate me?" Liu Mengmei asked holding his arms wide and trying to stop them from entering.

The nuns shouted, "In the dead of night when the nunnery is locked you are sporting with a girl."

Du Liniang was invisible and Liu Mengmei said firmly, "What are you talking about? Where is the girl? How can a girl hide herself in my room?"

The nuns pushed Liu Mengmei aside and came to the center of the room. Suddenly the candle became dim. Nun Shi was very surprised and said, "We saw a shadow of a woman with our own eyes. In a twinkle, she disappeared and there is only a portrait of beauty. Has this ancient portrait turned into a spirit, Master Liu? What is this portrait?"

"Every night I burn joss sticks and candles in front of it. Late at night I pray for her. But you think I have a woman in my room. How rude you are!"

"So, that's how it is! I heard you talking with someone the night before last. I suspected it was the young nun. Now all is clear, Master Liu, you're lonely by yourself. Let the young nun stay behind and keep you company." Nun Shi was embarrassed, and was trying to get into Liu Mengmei's good graces.

"It's unnecessary. Please don't bother me from now on. I am an honest scholar. Nun Shi, you woke me up from my dream." The two nuns went away, depressed. Liu Mengmei felt angry and out of sorts. He said to himself, "Those nuns spoilt my enjoyment. How disappointing!" Leaning on the door of his room, Liu Mengmei looked out and saw the shadows of dusk lengthening. Flags fluttered in the wind and the sound of bells and drums subsided. The young man became excited when the sun set. When he recalled how the two nuns spoilt his happy reunion with Du Liniang the night before, he was quite upset. He had looked forward to the arrival of his lover the whole of the previous day, but the irritating nuns had frightened her away. He thought to himself, "It's nighttime. My darling will come at any moment. I hope the clouds will make it darker when she is comes, otherwise the nuns will find her and cause a disturbance again. Why don't I go to the main hall and have a chat with Nun Shi so that she won't be suspicious before my lover comes?" He went into his room to light an oil lamp leaving the door open for Du Liniang. Then he walked towards the main hall.

Du Liniang's soul soon appeared. Fearful, she flew slowly towards Liu Mengmei's room. On the way she was startled by a sound and the shadow of a tree that looked like a man. She kept looking around fearing that there was someone hidden in the dark. Finally she came to the eastern wing room.

"Oh, Master Liu is not in the room. Where has he gone?" She took a risk and entered to find that the oil lamp that he had brightly lit with two parallel strands of wick--a good omen for a marriage. Du Liniang sighed and said, "How I wish that Master Liu and I will become a happy couple! All ghosts know that I come here to meet my lover, but none of the people on earth know what is going on. Though I belong to the hell, my body is well preserved. I died for Master Liu three years ago and now I will return to the world for him. I should tell my lover the truth and end all the secrecy." Though she was worried that Liu Mengmei would be frightened when she told him that she was actually a ghost, she had made up her mind to tell him the truth.

After exchanging a few casual remarks with Nun Shi, Liu Mengmei took his leave and headed for his room. He passed the winding corridor shaded by bamboo and his footsteps woke up several sleeping birds, which flew into the dark sky causing flower petals to drop to the ground. The door opened automatically before he stepped into his room and Du Liniang's soul walked out to greet him. "You're back," she said.

Liu Mengmei bowed low at the sight of his beautiful goddess and said happily, "How are you, Miss?"

Du Liniang said that she had been making the oil lamp brighter while waiting for him.

"Thank you for your kindness." Liu Mengmei held her hand and entered the room.

"Master Liu, I thought of a Tang poem while I was waiting for you." Du Liniang was determined to tell him the truth through a poem.

"That's fine. I'll listen to it with my full attention," Liu Mengmei said.

Du Liniang walked to the young scholar slowly and recited a Tang poem in a low voice:

I feel sad when planning to find a go-between;
Cold is the moon and grey is the mountain.
I wonder who is singing a love song now,
Trying to seduce my lover on earth.

"It's a wonderful poem," Liu Mengmei said. The last sentence hinted at Du Liniang herself, but unfortunately, Liu Mengmei did not understand. He was intent on enjoying time with his beauty and Du Liniang had to try again. "Master Liu, where have you been at such a late hour?"

"Last night I was most annoyed by the two nuns who disturbed us and I went to Nun Shi's room to see if there was anything suspicious before you came. I didn't expect that you would arrive so much earlier than last night," Liu Mengmei answered.

"I was longing to see you so much that I came earlier than usual."

When he heard this, Liu Mengmei felt most grateful to Du Liniang and said, "As a poor scholar, I am very lucky to have you. You're as beautiful as a goddess and love me with all of your heart. I'm the happiest person in the world. Oh, I felt so outraged when the nuns disturbed us last night and I am so sorry for it. You must have been very frightened. Let's enjoy every minute tonight and make up for last night. What do you think, my dear?" Liu Mengmei looked eagerly at her.

"Yes, I was very frightened last night. I didn't expect them to be so rude. Fortunately, I hid behind the portrait and when they entered the room, I sneaked out under the cover of the black clouds so that they didn't see me. However, I slipped and fell on the stairs and have never suffered so much in my life. I'm very worried that my parents will hear about our relationship. If my mother finds out, she will punish me severely." After what had happened the previous night she had became really scared.

Liu Mengmei said nothing, but stood up and bowed to his lover saying that he was very sorry for what had happened that night. Then he said, "May I ask why you love me so much? I am a poor scholar but you seem to be concerned about me all the time."

"That is obvious. I love your outstanding character and morals."

Then Liu Mengmei asked frankly, "Have you been promised to any man?"

"No, I haven't," Du Liniang replied.

"What kind of man do you want to marry?"

"I want to marry a young scholar who genuinely loves me."

"I love you from the bottom of my heart and will love you forever."

"I believe you. That's why I risked my life to come to see you every night."

Then Liu Mengmei came straight to the point and said, "Would you please be my wife?"

"Your home is far away from here and I fear that you already have a wife and want me to be your concubine."

"I've never married. Why would I make you my concubine? You'll be my wife."

This made Du Liniang happy and she asked with a smile, "Are there anyone in your family?"

"My father and mother. My father used to be a court official."

"Oh, you're from an official family. If you are from a good family why haven't you married much earlier?"

The question made Liu Mengmei sad and he said, "My parents died when I was a child and as an orphan I lived a poor life roaming about. That's why I haven't married before. You're such a beautiful and intelligent lady and from a good family. I'm really no match for you. If you are willing to be my wife, I'll love you all my life and will never abandon you."

Liu Mengmei's frankness set Du Liniang's mind at rest. She said to him, "Why don't you ask a go-between to make an offer of marriage since you're so determined to marry me? After we marry, we could be together all the time."

Liu Mengmei thought that this was a good idea and said that he would visit her parents the following day to ask for her hand.

This went further than Du Liniang expected and she was

startled. She said, "Tomorrow you will see me, not my parents."

"Does that mean you're really a goddess from heaven?" the young man asked. Du Liniang smiled and gave no answer. "It's no wonder you're extraordinarily beautiful, totally different from the girls on earth," Liu Mengmei added.

"I'm not a goddess."

"If you're from a good family why doesn't a maid accompany you when you walk at midnight? And what is your name? You have never given it to me." Liu Mengmei raised question after question and Du Liniang who had difficulty answering lowered her head and sighed. The longer it took her to answer, the more Liu Mengmei suspected that she was a fairy maiden. He urged her to tell the truth and said, "If you're from heaven, I would not dare have you as my wife. Even if you love me wholeheartedly, you'll never escape heavenly punishment. Let's put an end to our personal relationship."

Du Liniang denied that she was a fairy maiden and Liu Mengmei said that if she was not from heaven or earth, she must be a flower or moon spirit.

"All right, let me tell you everything."

"That's good! I'll listen to every word," Liu Mengmei encouraged her. Du Liniang thought about it but still did not know how to start. "My darling, who can you tell your story to if not me?" Liu Mengmei persuaded gently.

Du Liniang was moved by his sincerity and love. She sighed and said, "Where shall I start? Master Liu, I'm so worried that if I tell you the truth, you won't marry me and will take me as your concubine instead. You must swear on this before I tell you everything about myself."

"Oh, that's easy," Liu Mengmei said without hesitation. "Since you want me to promise to marry you, I'll do it." Then he lit some joss sticks, held them high, knelt on the ground and said, "I shall live with you in the same room while I'm alive and I shall be buried with you in the same grave after I'm dead. If I can't keep this promise, I'll die right away."

This oath so moved Du Liniang that her eyes filled with tears. She was determined to tell the truth. She warned him first not to be frightened to her story. Then she described in detail how she died after a dream in the Back Garden and how Judge Hu in the hell allowed her to be free and look for her lover. "Tonight is the time for me to be brought back from death. I hope you will help dig up my grave tomorrow, then I can come back to life," she said excitedly.

Liu Mengmei was not at all frightened, but he did not know how to help her. "You're my wife and I'm not afraid. I just have no idea how to help you out of the tomb. I fear that my efforts may be in vain."

"My body has been well preserved as if I were asleep."

"Oh, that's wonderful. But where is your grave?"

"Please learn it by heart. Beside the big Taihu rock in the Back Garden there is a plum tree. My tomb is under the tree."

Just then there was a gust of cold wind, and Liu Mengmei trembled all over with cold. "What can I do if I frighten your soul while digging the grave?"

"Don't worry about it. Though my grave is surrounded by twisted roots and gnarled branches, there is an air hole leading to the world. Also, my cold body has already been warmed up by your body so my soul won't be frightened."

The subject had been broached after they had chatted for several hours and they both realized that they could talk the whole night through. Liu Mengmei suggested that they should discuss the most important things right away. He said, "I believe every word that you have said. However I'm only a scholar, not a laborer. I am afraid that I'm not strong enough to dig your grave by myself."

"You could let Nun Shi to help you."

Liu Mengmei thought that this was a good idea and asked how deep the grave was. He feared that it might be too deep to be dug out.

"My coffin is buried only one meter under the ground. You will certainly need to dig it out with all of your might. My darling, I rely on you to save me." At this moment a cock crowed in the distance, startling Du Liniang's soul. It was the time for her to go back to the grave. Before leaving, she entreated him over and again, "My darling, I died for you. I love you with all of my heart.

Now I place all of my hope in you. Whether or not I come back to life all depends on you. You must try everything to save me. Please remember your promise. Otherwise I'll hate you forever." Du Liniang disappeared with a gust of cold wind.

Standing in the middle of the room, Liu Mengmei pinched his arm to make sure that he was not dreaming. Then he said to himself, "It's strange. I, Liu Mengmei, became the son-in-law of Prefect Du overnight. Am I just indulging in wishful thinking? She told me she was 16 years old. After she died she was buried under a plum tree in the Back Garden and looks just like a living person but insists she is a ghost. It's strange. Since she told me everything in detail, I have no reason to suspect her and should do as she asks. I'll have to discuss the matter with Nun Shi." Dawn had broken and Liu Mengmei walked out of the room to see Nun Shi.

CHAPTER TEN

Du Liniang Is Saved

WHEN PREFECT DU built the Plum Blossom Nunnery for his dead daughter, he also bought sacrificial fields. Chen Zuiliang was instructed to collect rent and Nun Shi took care of the nunnery. Chen Zuiliang was able to earn some income from the rents, but Nun Shi, who was in charge of cleaning up the nunnery every day, had no chance of earning anything extra. Not long before, Chen Zuiliang had proposed that the local people build a temple to Prefect Du. His proposal had been accepted and he benefited from its construction. The more Nun Shi thought about it, the angrier she became. Early one morning, when she was sitting and cursing Chen Zuiliang, she heard someone calling her. "Good morning, Aunt Shi." She looked up and saw that it was Liu Mengmei.

"Young Master Liu, what can I do for you?"

As it happened Liu Mengmei had been pacing up and down outside the hall for a while. After he decided how to explain things to Nun Shi, he entered the hall and said, "Aunt Shi, since I came to the nunnery, I have never been to the hall. Today I want to take a look at it."

Nun Shi went over to greet him, delighted to find him so reverent and respectful; she volunteered to show him around and introduced him to every statue of Buddha. However Liu Mengmei's mind was elsewhere and, while pretending to listen attentively, he searched for something he needed. Suddenly he saw Du Liniang's tablet and said, "Aunt Shi, the inscription on the tablet reads, 'The sacred tablet of Miss Du.' Who is Miss Du? Is she a queen?" Liu Mengmei pretended to know nothing about her.

"No, she is not a queen. Don't you know why the nunnery was built? Former Prefect Du constructed it for his beloved daughter Du Liniang. Miss Liniang died when she was 18 years old. Just after she had died Prefect Du was promoted and, before leaving for his new post, decided to build this nunnery for his daughter."

When Liu Mengmei heard this, he covered his face with his sleeve and cried, "Actually Miss Du Liniang is my charming wife."

"Master Liu, is it true?" Nun Shi was surprised.

"Absolutely true," Liu Mengmei said firmly.

Thinking it very odd, Nun Shi began asking Liu Mengmei all about Du Liniang, when she was born, when she died, how Liu Mengmei met her, and how they were married. Liu Mengmei did not know how to reply but suddenly had an idea. He said, "Let me show you. If I add a character to her tablet, the table will move and prove that my words are true."

Nun Shi did not believe him but she was curious. She brought a brush from the inner room and gave it to Liu Mengmei who began to add the character to the tablet. As it turned out, Liu Mengmei had not been sure himself, but as he had made the claim, he had to do it. How strange it was when the table actually began to move! Dumbfounded, Nun Shi bowed to Du Liniang's tablet and said, "Oh, Master Liu is really your husband. I did not know. Please forgive me." Then she turned to Liu Mengmei and said, "Since Miss Liniang is your beloved wife, you should guard her tomb."

After seeing the tablet move by itself, Liu Mengmei asserted that he would help her revive and return to the world. Then he told Nun Shi of his plan to dig up Du Liniang's tomb.

"Do you have magic power? Are you the king of the Hell?" Nun Shi still did not believe him.

"Don't argue with me. You just find a laborer and you could give me a hand too," Liu Mengmei said.

"According to the law, anyone involved in opening a dead person's coffin is liable to be executed. It does not matter whether they are the culprit or an accomplice. I dare not help you."

"Don't worry about it. It was suggested by Miss Liniang herself. She also told me that your help is indispensable."

"If Miss Liniang wants me to, I'll take the risk. Let me find an auspicious day for her."

"I have looked for it in the almanac and tomorrow will be an auspicious day. We shall dig the tomb tomorrow." Liu Mengmei did not want any further delay and Nun Shi agreed. Then Liu Mengmei sent Nun Shi to Chen Zuiliang's drug store to buy soul-saving medicines. On the way there she called on her nephew to ask him to come to the Back Garden of Plum Blossom Nunnery to help dig up the coffin.

Early in morning of the following day, Nun Shi's nephew came to the Back Garden by himself carrying a string of paper money. He hung it up by the Taihu rock, burnt some joss sticks and prayed to all the heavenly gods. "We shall be digging up Du Liniang's tomb today and I am doing what I have been told to do. If it is not right, please don't blame me."

When he had finished praying and burning the paper money, he saw Nun Shi and Liu Mengmei arrive. On the way there the nun talked incessantly, but Liu Mengmei, who was smoldering with impatience, was not in the mood to chat. He walked straight to the Taihu rock to look for the tomb, but found only a pavilion full of broken tiles and bricks and garden covered with thick grass. He said anxiously to Nun Shi, "Aunt Shi, I remember picking up the portrait by the Taihu rock. However, now I cannot find the place. What can we do?"

"Master Liu, don't worry. Look, the mound under the plum tree is Miss Du Liniang's tomb." Nun Shi pointed to the mound ahead of them.

Liu Mengmei sped to the tomb and threw himself onto it crying bitterly, "Alas, my darling, I'm so sad to find you lying here by yourself in a desolate garden. You must be very lonely." Nun Shi followed closely behind and her nephew limped along. Nun Shi said, "It's not the time for crying. Let's make the best use of our time and dig up the tomb."

Nun Shi's nephew began burning another string of paper money while Liu Mengmei knelt on the ground to pay homage to the local god of the land. Nun Shi's nephew was very experienced. He walked around the tomb and said to the other two, "Let's start digging here. It's the end of the tomb." Nun Shi and her nephew dug with all of their might and soon their spades touched the coffin. "You two must be very careful. Please don't frighten Miss Liniang." Liu Mengmei was worried.

"Alas!" A sound from the coffin startled them. "Oh, it's the voice of Miss Liniang!" Nun Shi said after she had calmed down. Her nephew was very brave. He jumped into the pit, pulled the snails off the coffin, brushed the dust off the lid and pried it open. Du Liniang lay there peacefully. She looked as if she were sleeping and a pleasant smell rose from the coffin. At the sight of the sleeping beauty, Liu Mengmei lost his fear. He jumped into the pit, gently raised Du Liniang in his arms and lifted her out of the coffin. Just then Du Liniang's eye-lids moved. Nun Shi, who had sharp eyes, shouted in surprise, "Miss Liniang is opening her eyes."

"Oh, my darling, open your eyes and look at me," Liu Mengmei said with emotion.

Gradually Du Liniang came to. She opened her eyes and asked, "Is it real or false?" There was a gust of wind and Du Liniang closed her eyes hurriedly. Liu Mengmei hastened to carry her to the Peony Pavilion to shelter from the wind. He asked Nun Shi to put the soul-saving medicine that she bought the previous day from Chen Zuiliang's drug store into warm wine and gently poured the medicine into Miss Liniang's mouth. Soon Du Liniang's cheeks turned red and the three around her exclaimed, "She's come back to life. It's wonderful!"

With the help of the medicine and wine, Du Liniang gradually recovered consciousness. When she opened her eyes and saw the people around her, she was startled and said, "Who are you? Have you robbed my tomb?"

"Miss Liniang," Liu Mengmei called out happily and astonished,

"I'm Liu Mengmei."

Excited Nun Shi said, "It's a miracle that has not taken place since ancient times. Today you came back to life after you had been dead for three years." Then she went to Du Liniang and asked, "Do you remember me, Miss Liniang? I'm Nun Shi." Du Liniang stared at her for a while, but could not remember who she was.

Liu Mengmei was anxious and said, "Do you remember the Back Garden?" Du Liniang was silent and but after a pause asked, "Who is Liu Mengmei?"

"It's me," Liu Mengmei answered. Du Liniang looked at him with tenderness and love. "You've kept your promise. Your great love has moved heaven and earth. That's why you could save me from death. Your love for me is utterly honest. I'm so grateful to you."

Liu Mengmei put his palms together and said: "Amitabha!"

After Du Liniang awoke from death, she felt very weak and lacked the strength to do anything. Her body felt like jelly, but with a few days rest and the care of Nun Shi and Liu Mengmei, who prepared various kinds of nutritious food and fresh fruit for her, her energy gradually improved and her health recovered. One day when she was with Nun Shi, she thanked her. "Aunt Shi, I died three years ago for love. Now that I am back from Hell and restored to life, I'm very grateful to you and Master Liu. Without your help, I would still be in the tomb. I owe my life to you and I'll remember your help and kindness forever."

"Don't mention it. It's the least I could do," Nun Shi said. "I have something to tell you. Master Liu has urged me many times recently to speak to you of marriage."

"I think it's too early to discuss. First of all I have to ask for my parents' approval. They are in Huaiyang. Then they must find a go-between for us," Du Liniang said.

Nun Shi was not pleased with her answer and said, "How can you say that? Isn't it something for you to decide? Do you remember what happened before your death?"

"Yes, it is still fresh in my mind. I fell ill because I missed Liu Mengmei whom I met in a dream. Then I drew a self-portrait and asked it to be buried under the Taihu rock. Master Liu found the portrait and from that day on, he burnt joss sticks before it, bowed to it and called for me day and night. Although I was buried, I'll never forget his sincerity."

Nun Shi saw Liu Mengmei coming and said, "Look, Master Liu returns."

Liu Mengmei visited Du Liniang several times a day. He saw Du Liniang's face glowing with health and was overjoyed. After a deep breath, he exclaimed, "My dear wife Liniang, how are you today?" Du Liniang blushed a deep red.

Liu Mengmei was pleased with himself and said, "I retrieved a goddess from a tomb."

"Thank you very much, Master Liu. It is you who gave me another life. I can never thank you enough for what you've done," Du Liniang said.

"Let's get married tonight," Liu Mengmei said eagerly.

"According to Chinese tradition, a marriage between a man and a woman should be approved by their parents and arranged by a go-between," Du Liniang replied.

"Oh, Miss, now you want to act according to tradition. Do you remember when you visited me every night? We had many happy times together."

"Master Liu, things have changed. Before I was a ghost. A ghost needn't follow human rules. Now that I have returned to life, and as a lady from a good family, I must follow traditions." Then she bowed low to Liu Mengmei and said, "I'm very grateful to you for granting me a second life. But as far as marriage is concerned, we must have my parents' consent and it must be arranged by a go-between."

"That's not a problem. After we marry, we can visit your parents. They will be very glad to see their dead daughter has returned to life. As for a go-between, Nun Shi is qualified," Liu Mengmei said firmly.

Du Liniang was about to say something when someone knocked on the door. "Is anyone home?"

All the people in the room were alarmed. "Who is it?" Liu Mengmei asked.

"It's me, Chen Zuiliang. I come to pay you a visit, Master Liu."

The three people were panic stricken. "What shall we do now, Nun Shi? Mr. Chen is knocking at the door." Liu Mengmei did not know what to do.

Du Liniang was startled, but calmed down and said to Nun Shi, "Aunt Shi, I'll hide myself first."

Chen Zuiliang was surprised at hearing a woman's voice in the room. He kept on knocking.

"It's very nice to see you," Liu Mengmei said after opening the door. "I was not properly dressed so I didn't come to the door straight away. I hope you will forgive me."

"It's very strange," Chen Zuiliang said.

"What's strange?"

"I heard a woman's voice."

When she heard this, Nun Shi walked out from the inner room to greet Chen Zuiliang. "Oh, Mr. Chen is here. How are you?"

"Aunt Shi was in my room. That's why you heard a woman's voice," Liu Mengmei explained.

Chen Zuiliang did not know what was happening and said to Liu Mengmei, "Tomorrow will be the Mid-Autumn Festival. It is also the anniversary of the death of Miss Du Liniang. I have prepared some sacrificial offerings for her and came to invite you to go with me to pay our respects to Prefect Du's daughter tomorrow."

"Yes, I'll wait for you tomorrow," Liu Mengmei said.

"Well, I'll take my leave now." Chen Zuiliang left.

After he had gone, Liu Mengmei closed the door and Du Liniang came out of the inner room. Nun Shi said to the two young people, "What shall we do then? Tomorrow Chen Zuiliang will go to the Back Garden to sweep the tomb. If he finds that the tomb is empty, he will report it to the local officials. They will think that Miss Liniang is a spirit and criticize Mr. and Mrs. Du for not educating their daughter. Master Liu will be suspected of luring Miss Liniang. I will be punished for digging up the tomb. We have to find a way out."

As it happened, Nun Shi had already thought of something but she used the opportunity to urge Du Liniang to marry Liu Mengmei. Du Liniang was so worried that she begged Nun Shi for a solution. "Aunt

Shi, what shall we do then? You must find a way for us to cover our tracks."

Du Liniang was very anxious and Nun Shi said calmly, "Miss, don't be alarmed. I have an idea, but I'm not sure if you agree with it."

"I'll agree with you. Please tell me, Aunt Shi," Du Liniang said keenly.

"Master Liu is going to Lin'an [now Hangzhou,Zhejiang Province] to take the highest imperial examination. I suggest that you marry him right away, then the two of you leave for Lin'an by boat tomorrow morning. You'll be gone without a trace. What do you think of it?"

"Yes, that's a good idea!" Liu Mengmei exclaimed, looking anxiously at Du Liniang.

After some time, Du Liniang nodded her head; she had no choice. Nun Shi took out a wine jar and two cups then presided over the wedding ceremony. The bride and bridegroom kowtowed to Heaven and Earth, to each other and then drank wine from nuptial cups. They were thus married.

Early next morning Nun Shi's nephew, who had already hired a boat, waited for Nun Shi, Liu Mengmei and Du Liniang at the wharf. He saw them coming and the boatman urged them to hurry. After Liu Mengmei had helped his wife board the boat, Nun Shi took her leave saying, "Master Liu, and Miss Liniang, you must take great care during the trip."

Liu Mengmei invited Nun Shi to go with them. "There is no one to attend to my wife on the way. Could you please do me a favor and go with us? If I pass the imperial examination and become an official, I'll repay you for everything you've done."

After while Nun Shi agreed. She thought that it would be better for her to leave as there could be trouble if she stayed. She said, "All right, I'll go with you but, Master Liu, could you please give something to my nephew and let him go home?"

Liu Mengmei, who had not much money, took off an article of clothing and gave it to Nun Shi's nephew. After thanking him Nun Shi's nephew asked, "What shall I do if they ask me about it?"

"You just tell them that you know nothing about it." Liu

Mengmei boarded the boat, the boatman untied the rope and it floated down the river.

Du Liniang looked at the scenery on both sides of the river and shed tears. Liu Mengmei said, "Why are you weeping, my darling?"

Du Liniang said nothing for a while then in low spirits replied, "I'm thinking that I once lived in this city for many years, then was buried here. But after I returned from death, I have to leave. I don't know when I shall come back again."

Liu Mengmei and Nun Shi tried their best to comfort her and Du Liniang overcame her sadness. Liu Mengmei went to her and whispered, "How nice it is to enjoy a honeymoon in a small boat!"

Du Liniang blushed and said in a low voice, "Master, I did not realize until today that life on earth is so full of happiness. After so much trouble, the love between us is as deep as the sea!"

Now let's turn to Chen Zuiliang in Nan'an Prefecture. Mr. Chen got up early the following morning, put some joss sticks, candles, wine, cakes and fruit in a basket and carried them to the Plum Blossom Nunnery. When he arrived, he found the door of the nunnery open and no sign of Liu Mengmei and Nun Shi. Miss Du's tablet had disappeared too. He was astonished and thought that they must have paired up and run away. He had never come across such a callous nun and immoral scholar.

He had to go to the Back Garden by himself and, when he approached Du Liniang's grave, he was stunned to find the coffin open and Miss Liniang's body gone. The scene made him call to mind that the people to the south of Mount Meiling were good at robbing tombs. Liu Mengmei came from there. He was sure that he had robbed the tomb and escaped with Nun Shi. Chen Zuiliang lost no time in reporting the case to the local government of Nan'an Prefecture and asked the prefect to have Liu Mengmei arrested. Then he packed up his things, and started his journey to Huaiyang to report it to Mr. Du Bao.

CHAPTER ELEVEN

Liu Mengmei Takes
the Imperial Examination

O N THE DAY that his beloved daughter died Du Bao, the prefect of Nan'an, had been designated by the court as the Pacification Commissioner of Huaiyang. Since then three years had elapsed.

When Du Bao assumed his post, the Kin minority in the north were a serious menace to the Song Dynasty. After Wanyan Aguda annihilated the State of Liao and established the Kin Dynasty, the Kin people controlled all the northern area and challenged the Song Dynasty. Emperor Zhao Gou of the Song Dynasty crossed the Yangtze River in panic, and fled to Lin'an [now Hangzhou, Zhejiang Province]. This period was known in history as the Southern Song Dynasty. Time flew swiftly and 30 years later Wanyan Liang distinguished himself as Emperor of the Kin Dynasty, while Zhao Gou, the lotus-eating emperor, never thought about reclaiming the central plain but concentrated on building up the Lin'an city. In this man-made paradise the emperor and ministers enjoyed themselves to their hearts' content, celebrating peace with song and dance.

At that time many poets composed works depicting the green

hills and water of West Lake and the splendor of Lin'an. One of the best known poems was called "Viewing Sea Waves". It described the beautiful scenery of Hangzhou city and boasted of "three seasons of laurel and 10 miles of lotus flowers". The image so tempted Emperor Wanyan Liang of the Kin Dynasty that he could not restrain his desire to invade it.

After he came to the throne, Wanyan Liang secretly sent a painter with the envoy to the Song kingdom to paint a panoramic picture of the West Lake. The painting was made into a screen for his room. Painted on the screen was a portrait of him standing beside a horse on the top of the Mount Wu by West Lake. There was also a poem inscribed on the screen:

> *I want to rule the whole country,*
> *What difference is there between the Kin's land*
> *and the south?*
> *Millions of troops will head to the West Lake,*
> *I'll ride a horse and stand on the Mount Wu.*

The screen allowed him to enjoy the scenery of West Lake and at same time reminded him of his plan of annexing the Southern Song Dynasty.

Wanyan Liang never ceased his attempt to conquer the Southern Song Dynasty. He thought that in war, it was a good strategy to mix falsehood with the truth, and nothing could be too deceitful. Hence, he decided that a Han would lay the ground for his invasion by sowing dissent. After careful selection, Wanyan Liang finally picked a robber named Li Quan from Huaiyang area. Li Quan was brave enough to defeat 10,000 men and the local Song official could do nothing to stop his attacks. So Wanyan Liang decided to use him to pave the way to Lin'an. Li Quan always fawned on Wanyan Liang who called him "sweet mouth king".

Li Quan had been a hooligan in Huai'an, Jiangsu Province and had gathered round him a group of local ruffians called the Five Hundred Gangsters. They incessantly harassed local people. The Southern Song court could not appease them or wipe them out; it could not prevent the gang from wreaking havoc on local people at their whim and pleasure. Nevertheless, Li Quan was not content with being a robber; he had ambitions of taking up a post in the court. The Southern Song court would not accept him and the Kin beckoned him, so he fell into their arms and called himself "a Han who knows the Kin language and teaches the Kin to curse the Han".

Although Li Quan was brave enough to defeat 10,000 men, he was in fact bold but not crafty. Fortunately, his wife, Lady Yang was resourceful and good at strategy. All of Li Quan's soldiers were in awe of her. This husband-and-wife duo colluded in evil acts, causing anger and discontent in the Huaiyang area.

After Du Bao had been made Pacification Commissioner of Huaiyang, he first of all reassured the people, and then tried to eliminate the gangsters. However, the gangsters outnumbered imperial soldiers and it was not an easy task to manage in the short term. Du Bao instead focused on keeping the enemy at bay. After careful investigation Du Bao decided to build new fortification for Yangzhou. Under Du Bao's instructions, the soldiers and the people of Yangzhou built a new wall around the old city wall. This provided strong protection to the inside wall. The new wall was high and solid with watchtowers on top. Built into the wall were several short walls with arrow holes from which the soldiers could shoot the enemy outside. On the day they finished building the wall, Du Bao held a riverside ceremony to celebrate with the civil and military officials and the soldiers and the civilians of Yangzhou. Followed by a couple of high-ranking officials Du Bao inspected the wall's quality and defense capability. He also invited local wealthy merchants to walk along the new wall with him. With a big enough army, sufficient provisions and fodder, Pacification Commissioner Du would not be afraid if Li Quan attacked.

However, Du Bao had not taken everything into account. Although, for the time being, Li Quan could not take Yangzhou City, he never gave up the idea. Emperor Wanyan Liang of the Kin Dynasty kept on pushing him to clear the way for an invasion of Hangzhou. It was three years since Li Quan established himself and his men in Huaiyang. And since then, Li Quan continued harassing the local people and provoking riots. Yet, he achieved nothing by taking over the city or occupying the land. As time went on, Li Quan found it harder to justify himself to his Kin masters, which placed him in a dilemma.

One day Li Quan received urgent instructions from the Kin court that left him with no choice. He went to consult his wife, Lady Yang, who had not slept well the night before. Her face was gloomy and Li Quan came straight to the point. "My lady, our Kin master is about to head south. I was supposed to pave the way by attacking Huaiyang, but the new Pacification Commissioner Du Bao of Huaiyang has accumulated funds and provisions in the city of Yangzhou of Huaiyang areas and has improved the city defenses making it difficult to take. I am desperate. Do you have any good ideas?"

Lady Yang was really capable. For her this was no problem and she said straight away, "In my opinion, we should first of all besiege another city of Huai'an of Huaiyang areas; Du Bao will definitely send for troops. Then we can deploy our elite men to cut off his reinforcements. In that way we will be assured of victory."

"You are really smart! My love, you have persuaded me! Let's attack Huai'an city right now!"

In the meanwhile, Liu Mengmei and Du Liniang finally arrived in Zhejiang, after a long journey. They rented an empty house in the capital city, Lin'an, and settled down. Liu Mengmei returned to his books and started preparing for the imperial examination.

As Liu Mengmei's wife, Du Liniang decided to help her husband achieve honor as a scholar and official rank. However, recently she had noticed that her husband was downcast and lost in thought. So one morning Du Liniang asked Nun Shi to go to the market to buy wine, which she hoped would help drive his gloom away.

The house in which they lived was beyond the urban area because Liu Mengmei was short of money and they had to find a place with low rent. Thus, although Nun Shi left early in the morning, Du Liniang knew that she would not be back for several hours. The young couple stayed in their room chatting about how they met in the dream and their reunion in the garden. As they talked, both of them felt love swelling up in their breasts.

Nun Shi bought the wine at the market and was about to return when she saw scholars from all over the country rush to the examination hall. It surprised her and she hurried back. As soon as she entered the room she shouted, "Master, Mistress, do you know what is happening?"

Liu Mengmei and Du Liniang had no idea asked her what the matter was. Catching her breath Nun Shi said, "When I bought wine at the market, I heard that the examination begins today. I saw all the scholars going to the examination hall. Master, you will have to be quick or you will miss this golden opportunity. Let's drink a cup of wine to the Number One Scholar. Drink your success!"

When they heard the news, the young couple did not dare waste a moment. Liu Mengmei prepared to go immediately and Du Liniang said to him, "My love, you have to concentrate in the examination. We will look for your parents-in-law the day you win."

Liu Mengmei arrived at the examination hall only to find that it had finished. The only person there was the chief examiner, Miao Shunbin, who was going over the papers recommended by the sub-examiners. The question asked in this examination was, "Which of the following deserves the most attention: suing for peace, fighting, or defending?" Obviously the question referred to the serious situation in the north, the threaten by the Kin, and asked the scholars for their opinions. His Excellency Miao read some of the papers. Some of them wished to sue for peace, some were for fighting and others were for defending, but none got to the point, which bewildered him; how could these scholars be so pedantic? However, the imperial examination was held once every three years and he had to enroll somebody. Reluctantly, he picked out three papers and went through the motions of ranking them.

He was pondering over his last choice when he heard a commotion outside the examination hall. The noise was getting louder and louder. He was very surprised and wondered who would be so barbaric as to make a disturbance here, and he ordered the doorkeeper to bring the offender inside for investigation.

The offender was non other than Liu Mengmei. When he found that the examination had ended, he took it for granted that the same rules applied as for local examinations in which those who missed the test would be allowed to sit it. Liu Mengmei had pleaded to be allowed to, but the doorkeeper just would not let him in and they had quarreled.

As soon as the doorkeeper hauled him in, Liu Mengmei said to the chief examiner, "Your Excellency, I must sit the examination. Please allow me to."

"Good Heavens! How can you be so stupid! This is the imperial examination! It is against regulations to take in one more paper after the Imperial Academy has sealed them."

"I came 10,000 miles from the south of Mount Meiling with my family to take part in the imperial examination. If there is no hope, I'd rather kill myself right here and now!" Liu Mengmei was desperate and would have bumped his head on the stone steps.

Fortunately the doorkeeper pulled him back in time. The phrase, "south of Mount Meiling," rang a bell in Miao Shunbin's mind. He took a good look at the young man; wasn't he the Liu Mengmei whom he had helped financially? He had given him the money to come to the capital to take the imperial examination and he had to make an exception. He said, "Come here, young man. Do you have the examination paper?"

"Yes, I do."

"In that case, you can take the examination and will be ranked according to your performance, just like other scholars."

Liu Mengmei was ecstatic. He kowtowed in gratitude and asked the chief examiner for the question. Miao Shunbin read it out. "It is known that the Kin in the north are about to invade our country. Now here are three strategies: suing for peace, fighting, and defending. Which one in your opinion is the best?" After thanking him, Liu Mengmei went to compose his answer in a nearby examination hall.

His Excellency Miao then brought out another three papers to mark. He had hardly decided on them when Liu Mengmei handed in his paper. Miao Shunbin gasped in admiration at his speed and said, "Oh, good for you! You finished your work in such a short time! I'll read it later. Now, just tell me, what do you think of the three proposals?"

Liu Mengmei expressed his views calmly and frankly. "I have no particular preference for any one of the three choices. However, it is advisable to act according to the situation and any changes in it. Our first step should be to fight and defend, and then peace will come. It is like the doctor curing disease with medicine. Fighting cures the outside, guarding cures the inside and making peace is something in between." Liu Mengmei stepped back and stood to one side.

Miao Shunbin found Liu's analysis fresh and penetrating, entirely different from the perfunctory and pedantic arguments put forward by other scholars. He could not help praising him. "Excellent! Brilliant! Now, what shall we do about the current situation?"

Gaining confidence from the chief examiner's praise, Liu Mengmei approached and declared, "As to the current situation, His Majesty should not sequester south of the Yangtze River and officials should not indulge themselves at the waters and mountains of the West Lake. If they do so, when will the northern land be reclaimed? If they kneel down and sue for peace, how could we overcome the disgrace? If they intend waging war against the enemy, His Majesty should head north and direct the frontline battles."

Miao Shunbin slapped the table saying, "Superb! How reasonable and convincing your speech is! Of the 1,000 scholars who took the examination, none showed a real understanding of the current situation. They don't deserve the title of a scholar. You have a rare talent and arrive at the crucial point with only a few remarks. Now please wait for the news outside."

Although the chief examiner Miao had recognized Liu Mengmei as the scholar he met before, it was not appropriate to acknowledge each other or talk about the old days on such an occasion. Nevertheless, Miao Shunbin had made up his mind to grant Liu first place in the examination. Collecting the papers, Miao ordered his attendants to go to the palace with him to have an audience with His Majesty.

While he was walking slowly to the palace he heard noises and neighing from the Bureau of Military Affairs. A drum was being beaten. His heart sank; the situation must be very serious in the frontier area and someone had raised the alarm. He looked back and saw the Minister of the Bureau of Military Affairs hurrying over. Miao Shunbin knew that the bureau was in charge of the military affairs for the whole country and had priority in reporting so he stepped back to allow the minister meet the emperor first.

The palace messenger heard the drum and came out. When he saw the minister in a panicky state, he said, "What do you have to report so urgently?"

"The Kin have invaded…"

"Who leads the vanguard?"

" 'Sweet Mouth King' Li Quan, Li Quan…"

"Where are the enemy now?"

"In the Huaiyang area."

So that he could give a clear message to the emperor, the palace messenger asked, "Which official is there now?"

"Du Bao, the ex-prefect of Nan'an, is the Pacification Commissioner of Huaiyang. He has strengthened the defense work and accumulated funds and fodder. But I am afraid the real battle will start sooner or later. We'd better arrange for reinforcements."

Noticing the presence of the chief examiner Miao Shunbin, the palace messenger asked about his report. Miao said that he had the result of the imperial examination and he would like to ask for the emperor's instructions on the right day to release it and when to hold the banquet for the successful candidate.

The palace messenger asked them to wait and went into the palace. A moment later he came out and announced the emperor's instructions: "In administering the country I have to take into account the urgency of a case, while paying equal attention to civil and military affairs. Now that the Huaiyang area is in imminent danger, I order the Pacification Commissioner Du Bao to fight the enemy without delay. As to publishing the imperial examination result and holding the banquet, this must be postponed until the war ends. Make my order known to all the candidates." The two officials kowtowed and went to do their own business.

CHAPTER TWELVE

Huai'an Rescued

THE PACIFICATION COMMISSIONER Du
Bao had guarded Yangzhou for three years. Although Li
Quan's gangsters had not been exterminated, their power and
bullying had been curbed. Generally it was peaceful. But the Kin
in the north were always ready to act and recently, they seemed
prepared to invade. This deeply concerned Du Bao.

However, Madam Du was not very concerned about the
emergent military situation. She only had one daughter and she had
died at a young age in Nan'an where she was buried. In her spare
time, Madam Du missed her dead daughter and felt most miserable
and resentful. One morning, she saw her husband alone in a tent
meditating. She approached slowly and said, "Hello, my dear."

"Hello, my lady."

"Master, we have been away from Nan'an for three years. You
see, time flies…"

Du Bao knew that his wife missed their dead daughter and
understood what she implied. He intentionally tried to divert her.
"Yangzhou is prosperous and almost as good as Nan'an."

"Master, whenever I mention our late daughter you have nothing

219

to say. You don't know how depressed I am!" Madam Du's words revealed her unhappiness.

"Well, it is not true that I don't miss our daughter. But the country is in such danger that I cannot always think about our personal misfortune!"

"Master, we are now both old and feeble. If we have no children, who will take care of us and attend to us on our death bed? I am thinking of finding a girl in Yangzhou to bear children and carry the family name for you. What do you think of the idea?"

"That is just not possible. I am an official in Yangzhou; I am the parent of the people. How can I behave like that!"

"Then how about finding a girl on the other side of the Yangtze River?"

"The enemy in the north poses a huge threat and could invade at any time; the situation at the frontier is so critical that I have no time to consider other things." Du Bao would not agree and Madam Du, who did not know what to do, shed tears.

"Master!" A messenger rushed into the tent distracting the old couple from their discussion.

"What's the matter?"

The messenger approached and handed over a memoir. Du Bao took it and read out: "The Bureau of Military Affairs has reported an invasion in Huai'an. His Majesty orders Du Bao, the Pacification Commissioner of Huaiyang, to go to Huai'an immediately." Du Bao said to his wife, "My lady, there is a crisis in the military situation. Imperial orders must be obeyed without delay. We must go to Huai'an right now. Go to pack quickly." Madam Du hurried to prepare and Du Bao ordered his subordinates to get ready.

After a while, an attendant came into the tent and reported that the ships had been assembled at the dock and were waiting for deployment.

"Start off!" Du Bao ordered.

When they heard the news, all the officials in Yangzhou came to bid farewell to Du Bao. He thanked them and boarded the flagship with Madam Du. Subordinates and attendants embarked on the other large ships and they left for Huai'an.

Not long after they sailed, they noticed a man on a horse

galloping alone along the embankment. He waved and shouted. A moment later he was close to the flagship. It was the messenger and Du Bao shouted, "What's happened?"

"Li Quan is assaulting Huai'an city and the situation is most critical! The city could be lost at any time!"

"Aren't there soldiers defending it?"

"The small armed force cannot hold on too long. The Bureau of Military Affairs is worried that traveling by boat may take too long and, if precious time is lost, Huai'an will be in real danger. So it orders you to leave the ship and make haste to rescue Hui'an on horse as fast as you can!"

Madam Du was unaccustomed to such things and was so scared that her whole body trembled. Du Bao was quick to reassure her. "My lady, don't be afraid. I will go on land to Huai'an. You can go back to Yangzhou by ship."

In the distance Madam Du saw a horse galloping towards them at full speed. She sighed and said, "Oh, here comes another messenger." The messenger shouted from the bank "Master, Kin soldiers are pushing into our country and will cut off our retreat. The soldiers defending Huai'an cannot hold on for too long. Master, the Bureau of Military Affairs orders you to move without delay!" The messenger wheeled his horse and galloped back along the way he came.

Madam Du could not help weeping. She said to her husband, "What shall we do? You are old and weak, where will you find the strength to resist the Kin invaders? Alas! Battle flames rage everywhere and we have to part!"

"My lady, the situation has changed suddenly and unexpectedly. I was afraid that the way to Yangzhou would be cut off. Now it has happened. Oh, where can we meet again?" He thought and then said, "My dear, I cannot stay long. I have military affairs to take care of and must leave for Huai'an now. It seems that Yangzhou is in danger too. Don't return to Yangzhou. Go directly to Lin'an and wait there for me to return."

"Oh, my God! What kind of life is this! In such dangerous circumstances we cannot stay together but have to spend the days separately!"

Du Bao felt sad too and said with regret, "It is because I am a military officer." Then he left without looking back. Left behind, Madam Du called out to her husband to take care of himself but did not know whether he could hear her or not. When Du Bao was out of sight, Madam Du sighed deeply. She said to Chunxiang, "Yangzhou must be full of battles and fires. We have no choice but to go directly to Lin'an." Thus they left for Lin'an together.

After Du Bao had transferred from Nan'an to the Huaiyang area, he had been stationed in Yangzhou city most of the time. He was not familiar with Huai'an city and after riding his horse non-stop he asked a soldier where they were.

"We are not far from the Huai'an City."

Seeing the weeds spread over the land and hearing the distant sound of the Kin music, Du Bao could not help shedding tears that fell like raindrops wetting his robes. He announced loudly, "Look everybody! Huai'an can be seen in the distance and it is in great danger. Let's not spare ourselves and charge into it! I'll ask the court for more reinforcements. All soldiers and officials, listen to my order! March on!"

Enemies blocked the way. Nevertheless, encouraged by their chief commander, the soldiers dashed on without stopping. Li Quan had so many soldiers that they surrounded the city in seven circles and were so tightly guarded that not a drop of water should have been able to trickle through. But, to the enemy's great surprise, Du Bao's troops rushed into the city at the first attempt. Li Quan's soldiers called in astonishment, "Du's army has broken into the city!" But Li Quan did not seem very concerned and said to his attendants, "Let them be. When they run out of provisions and fodder, they will surrender."

Du Bao galloped into the city at the head of his force. As the relieving force arrived in the city, all the civil and military officials rushed to express their thanks. But Du Bao had no time for such trivial formalities. He first asked about the deployment of the armed forces and their provisions. There were still 13,000 soldiers in the city and the provisions could last for another six months. Feeling assured he said to his attendants, "From today, civil officials will guard the city, and military officials will go out to fight the enemy. Working together and acting according to circumstances we can hold on till reinforcements arrive."

A subordinate said with concern, "One thing that I fear is that the Kin troops will make a massive invasion of the south."

Du Bao said, "We will not fear the Kin troops. Their attack will depend on the general situation and that is not settled yet. Don't give comfort to the enemy and dampen our own morale. At worst, even if they did come, we will risk our lives fighting them."

"Master!" A messenger entered interrupting Du Bao.

"What's happened?"

"M-m-master, Li Quan is attacking again."

"What an unreasonable hooligan! I know that he must have thought that it was a dirty trick letting me into the city. Let him be. Guarding the city is more important."

After entering Huai'an city, Du Bao strengthened the defenses, improved military discipline, and encouraged the morale of soldiers and civilians. Therefore, although they could not end Li Quan's siege, they could hold the city of Huai'an and the inhabitants could wait for the relief troops and for further developments.

Although Li Quan commanded a large army and surrounded the city, he was frustrated because he could not take it without waiting. A great amount of provisions were consumed everyday and he became really worried. On one hand, he was afraid that he could not hold out for long if the Song reinforcements arrived; on the other, he was worried that his Kin masters would accuse him of being incapable if he achieved nothing. The dilemma caused him to make one unwise decision after another, which disheartened the troops. Moreover, recently it was said that the Kin court had sent an envoy to negotiate with the Song imperial court. Li Quan wondered what they were conspiring and thought that if the Kin betrayed him he would be doomed.

One day Li Quan asked his wife for advice. "You see, my love, a rather long time has passed since we laid siege to Huai'an, but we just can't take the city. What can we do? I want someone to take a message to Huai'an and find out Pacification Commissioner Du's intentions so that we can decide what next to do."

"You are right. It's time to consider our options."

"But at the moment we don't have a suitable person to send."

His wife agreed, "Yes, those under our command are not suitable. We must find someone who enjoys Du Bao's confidence."

Just then they received a godsend in the form of Chen Zuiliang, the teacher who worked for Du Bao when Du was the prefect in Nan'an. Chen Zuiliang had arrived in Huai'an. He had made a special trip just to report to Du Bao that someone had dug up Du Liniang's grave. Chen heard first of all that Du Bao was in Yangzhou and he went all the way there only to be told that Du Bao had moved to Huai'an so he hurried there.

He had not anticipated the difficulties of leaving home particularly during the tumult of a raging war. Robbers and invading soldiers frequented the road from Nan'an to Huaiyang areas making walking almost impossible. What's more, Chen Zuiliang was not familiar with the road. He was fearful and rushed into bushes and down paths whenever he saw someone. One day he rashly plunged into the tent of some of Li Quan's men and was caught. He was brought immediately to Li Quan's tent.

Li Quan learned from the interrogation that the man named Chen Zuiliang used to work for Du Bao. He also extracted from him the fact that Du Bao had a wife and a maid. With his wife's help, Li Quan arrived at a plan. Two soldiers brought in a pair of women's heads and claimed falsely that they had killed Madam Du and her maid, Chunxiang. Chen did not look closely and assumed that what they said was true. He could not stop himself from wailing and Li Quan who was bluffing said, "Hey, stop crying, you pedantic old scholar! Very soon I will break into the city and kill old Du Bao!"

Chen Zuiliang did not know the truth and pleaded with him again and again not to kill Du Bao.

"I can spare his life, but he must give up the city of Huai'an." This was Li Quan's real intent but Chen did know it. And he said, "That is easy. Let me see him and tell him about your overwhelming power and he will do what you say."

Li Quan's wife then pretended to do Chen Zuiliang a favor. She said, "Since that is the case, the king will not kill you today. Tell Du Bao about this quickly." Chen Zuiliang ran off as fast as he could.

The Pacification Commissioner Du Bao stayed on the city tower day and night, observing every movement of the enemy. He guessed that Li Quan had 10,000 soldiers but was hesitant. He had not acted and there must be a reason for it. After an ill-considered movement by the enemy, Du Bao worked out a plan to frustrate them but there was no suitable person to carry it out. While he was thinking about it, an attendant reported to him, "Your Excellency, an old friend of yours has arrived. He calls himself Chen Zuiliang from Nan'an."

Du Bao was really surprised. "How did the old scholar get into the city? Ask him in immediately."

Chen Zuiliang rushed into the tent, crying out, "Where is Master Du?"

Du Bao stepped forward and said, "How unusual it is that an old friend arrives from afar."

Chen Zuiliang immediately saw Du Bao and his white hair and could not stop himself saying, "It is only three years since we parted, and your hair is all white." They saluted each other formally and a servant brought in two cups of tea. When they were seated Chen Zuiliang said, "Master, poor Madam Du was killed on her way to Lin'an."

Du Bao stood up astonished and said, "How did you know that?"

"On my way to Huaiyang I was captured by the enemy and I saw it with my own eyes! And Chunxiang was killed too!"

"Oh, my god! My lady…" Du Bao cried and was about to faint when a servant rushed over to support him. Those who were present and heard it were all extremely grieved. But Du Bao calmed down, wiped away his tears and said to them, "Alas, how can I behave like this? My wife was killed because she denounced the enemy. It was a worthy death. I cannot lose control and lower morale because of this. Please stop crying. We have more important military affairs to discuss!"

The others stopped one after another and Du Bao said, "Mr. Chen, as the enemy released you, did 'Sweet Mouth King' ask you to bring a message?" Du Bao was a truly capable officer and he knew Li Quan must have required Chen Zuiliang to bring information, otherwise, how could this feeble old scholar, who was not strong enough to tie a chicken, escape from the fiend?

"Yes, there is a message, but a bad one: he said that he will kill you!"

Du Bao was not angry. He sighed and said, "Why does he want to kill me? I'd kill him for the sake of the country."

Chen Zuiliang stepped forward and said, "What the 'Sweet Mouth King' asks for is just Huai'an city."

"Shut up!" Du Bao shouted angrily. After he had calmed down a little he said, "Mr. Chen, how many tiger-skin armchairs did you see in Li Quan's tent? One or two?"

Chen Zuiliang did not understand why Du Bao asked such a question and he answered honestly, " 'Sweet Mouth King' sat beside his wife."

Du Bao laughed and smacked the table. "If that is so, I can free Huai'an from the siege." The others did not understand what he meant and when they were about to ask he said, "Mr. Chen, why did you hurry to this chaotic battlefield from faraway Nan'an?"

Chen Zuiliang slapped his forehead and said, "What a dotard I am! I might have forgotten if you had not asked. I came to tell you that Miss Du Liniang's grave has been robbed!"

Du Bao was taken aback again and said in a pained voice, "Oh, my God! Why had my daughter's grave been robbed? It must be the funeral objects that tempted the robbers. Who robbed the grave?"

Chen Zuiliang had resented Nun Shi for a long time and he gave a detailed account implicating her. "It is Nun Shi's fault! After you left, she brought back a companion named Liu Mengmei, an idler from the south of Mount Meiling. When they saw the valuables, they were covetous, robbed the grave and fled the same night. What's more, they abandoned Miss Du's remains in the pond." He did not mention that it was he who first brought Liu Mengmei to the nunnery.

Du Bao sighed. He had no choice but to be philosophical. "My daughter's grave was robbed, my wife was killed. It fits the proverb, 'A death without a burial is not a perfect death, even after you are buried, the grave cannot be perfect.' Well, under the circumstances

I cannot do anything at the moment. However, I humbly thank you for your kindness."

Hearing the phrase, "humbly thank," Chen Zuiliang promptly complained that he had become much poorer after Du Bao left.

Du Bao nodded and said, "I understand. But as I am on the battlefield I cannot repay you right now. But I have a great opportunity at hand that will guarantee a meritorious service. It's yours if you want it."

"I am at your beck and call, Sir," Chen Zuiliang said without hesitating.

Since Chen had volunteered, Du Bao explained the task. "I have written a letter to Li Quan and hope to persuade him to dismiss his troops. However, there is no suitable messenger in my tent. Since you are here, I am asking you to carry the letter. If you succeed in talking Li Quan into surrendering, I will ask the court to record your meritorious deed. I promise that you will have your day." Du Bao then ordered the attendant to bring Chen some traveling expenses.

Chen Zuiliang humbly accepted the money. Nevertheless, he was very frightened at the prospect of returning to the enemy's tent. Du Bao assured him saying, "Don't be afraid. Although Li Quan is a ruthless man, he must act according to circumstances. Since he let you walk safely through the siege, he must regard you as a messenger. Please accept my reassurances and go. If you succeed, the court will surely reward you!"

Chen Zuiliang had to take the risk if he was to win glory and rank. Holding Du Bao's letter above his head and trembling with fear he approached the enemy's tents and asked to see the "Sweet Mouth King". The guard recognized him as the scholar that they had released two days earlier and went inside to report. "Respected king, the scholar has come back on his own from Huai'an and asks to see you about something urgent."

Li Quan had hardly begun to speak when his wife said, "Great! Bring him in!" Chen Zuiliang trembled as he walked through two rows of soldiers holding weapons. He entered the tent, saw "Sweet Mouth King" and his wife sitting on raised chairs and said hastily, "Chen Zuiliang comes humbly to see the respected king and his lady."

Paying no attention to his flattery Li Quan asked directly, "Did Du Bao agree to surrender?"

Chen Zuiliang did not answer the question and said, "Who cares about a city? A city is nothing! I came to present a throne to you!"

Li Quan laughed and said, "I have a throne already."

However, Chen Zuiliang continued, "This is a higher official rank--a promotion! Respected king, the Pacification Commissioner Du Bao has a letter for you. Please read it."

Li Quan opened the letter but found that it only tried to persuade him not to serve the Kin Dynasty and pledge loyalty to the Song Dynasty. In doing so, he could win glory and be loyal at same time, etc. At the end of the letter there was a line that read, "There is another secret letter for your lady." Li Quan chuckled. "This Du Bao is really funny, he knows how to revere my wife too." He passed the letter to her although he knew that she could not read.

"Read it to me. Read carefully," his wife said.

So Li Quan read the letter and explained the contents to her. The letter said it was quite unreasonable for the Kin court to offer an official post only to Li Quan and neglect his lady. In addition, Du Bao said that he had requested the Song court to guarantee her the title of the Lady of Fighting Kin.

Li Quan's wife thought for a while and said to him, "I have made up my mind. Let's do as the letter asks. We'll write a letter of surrender tonight and ask the scholar to take it back."

"But I am afraid that if we pledge loyalty to the Song, the Kin won't let us off lightly," Li Quan said much concerned.

Ignoring Li Quan, the woman turned to Chen Zuiliang and said, "Scholar, you must guarantee that all your promises will be realized."

Right away Chen Zuiliang answered, "Of course."

Li Quan knew that his wife would talk to him alone later, so he stopped questioning the scholar and spoke politely to him. "Would you like to come to our house, have a meal and take a rest. We will write the letter tonight so that you can leave tomorrow morning."

After Chen Zuiliang left, Li Quan's wife said to him that they had been attacking Huai'an city for a long time but had achieved nothing. The Kin would resent this. However, if they sought refuge with the Song court, the consequences would be unimaginable. Without the backing of the Kin, the Song court could punish them any time they wished. His wife's insights weakened Li Quan, and he immediately asked her what they should do.

"Let's be the Fan Li and Xi Shi." *

Li Quan thought for a while then clapped his hands and said, "Yes! Fan Li and Xi Shi wandered far and wide by rivers and lakes! But today all the rivers and lakes are under the control of the Song troops. It seems that the only choice left to us is to go to sea and be pirates!"

"That's right!" Once they had made up their mind, the couple ordered the soldiers to lift the siege of Huai'an. That very night they boarded boats and sailed off to sea.

---

* Fan Li was a politician from the Spring and Autumn Period, and Xi Shi was the favorite concubine of King Fu Chai of the State of Wu in the Spring and Autumn Period. They loved each other. Wandering by rivers and lakes is a famous love story about them in China.

CHAPTER THIRTEEN

Reunion of Mother and Daughter

AFTER LIU MENGMEI hurried off to sit his examination, Du Liniang waited patiently at home for the good news. She thought to herself that with all his talent her husband would surely become a first-rate scholar and obtain official rank.

When she saw Liu Mengmei stumbling into the yard, she immediately stood up and greeted him. "How are you, my darling? I expected to see you come back in official robes and in a splendid chariot. How is it that you have returned by yourself on foot?"

After drinking some tea, Liu Mengmei related the whole story in detail; he was late for the examination but was allowed to take it; he won the favor of the chief examiner, but publication of the result had been postponed because the court had to discuss the military situation in the Huaiyang area that was said to be serious. Liu Mengmei sighed and said, "My darling, I'm so sorry that I delayed the confirmation of your honorable title."

Du Liniang did not seem very concerned about her status, but the words "Huaiyang" and "serious" attracted her interest. Straight away she asked, "My darling, is Huaiyang the area that my father administers?"

"Yes, that's it."

When she heard this she burst into tears. "Oh, my God! I wonder what has happened to my parents?" Liu Mengmei hurried to comfort his wife and after she had calmed down, she thought a while and said, "Darling, I have something to say, but I find it difficult to speak out."

"Please speak, don't hesitate." Liu Mengmei always listened to his wife.

"As the examination result will not be published for a long time, could you go to Huaiyang and ask about my parents for me?" Du Liniang asked.

"Your wish is my bounden duty." Liu Mengmei said straight away and added with concern, "I am just worried about leaving you alone at home."

"You don't need to worry about me. I'll be fine and have the companionship of Nun Shi. But you must take care of yourself in the turmoil and chaos of war."

"I will."

Then Du Liniang and Nun Shi prepared Liu Mengmei for the journey by making up a bundle and fetching an umbrella. Suddenly, Liu Mengmei remembered something. "My love, when I meet my parents-in-law face to face, they will wonder where this new son-in-law came from. How can I explain your coming back to life?"

Du Liniang knew her father was very difficult to convince and might not believe what Liu Mengmei said. She thought for a while and said, "I know what to do. You take my picture with you. When my father sees it, he will ask what happened to us."

"Then what should I say?"

Du Liniang could not think of anything more convincing and exclaimed, "Just say that our marriage was predestined by God and, when you walked on my grave, the tomb suddenly opened!"

Liu Mengmei could not think of a better idea and had to agree with his wife. He picked up the bundle, said farewell and asked her to take care of herself. Du Liniang hated to see him go and walked part of the way with him. The pair were in tears when they said good-bye.

After Liu Mengmei left for the north, Du Liniang spent her days with Nun Shi waiting for him to come back. One day at dusk they sat in the room chatting about the time that they opened the grave and helped Du Liniang return life. They could not help sighing with emotion. Gradually it got dark, but Du Liniang still did not want to go to bed and she asked Nun Shi to light the oil lamp. Seeing the oil had run out, Nun Shi told Du Liniang to wait in the yard while she went to the owner of the house to borrow some.

After bidding her farewells to Du Bao, Madam Du and her maid Chunxiang traveled towards Lin'an. In the chaos and turmoil of war they had to stop from time to time; sometimes they took a boat and sometimes they walked. Finally they crossed the Yangtze River and sailed smoothly along the Grand Canal to Lin'an.

After the boat arrived at the dock outside the city proper, the boatman told everyone to get off and Madam Du and Chunxiang had to go ashore. It was dusk and smoke from kitchen chimneys rose all around. The two stood on the dock bewildered, not knowing what to do or where to go. They had no relatives or friends in the city to give help and they could not spend the night at the dock. Their only choice was to find an inn where they could stay for the time being. However, they were not familiar with the roads and just walked where their steps took them. Fortunately, Chunxiang had a good eye and noticed a house not far away. The door was unlocked and the pair made hurried steps to the house. Pushing open the half-closed door, Madam Du said in a faltering voice, "Anybody at home?"

"Who is it?" A voice answered.

Chunxiang was very surprised to hear a female voice and cried out, "Hello! Anybody there?" Madam Du called out that they were two woman passengers who were passing by and would like to stop in the house overnight.

Du Liniang listened carefully and decided they were indeed female voices. Nun Shi had not come back, so she cautiously opened the door. As soon as Madam Du, supported by Chunxiang, walked into the yard she thanked her and said, "Sorry to disturb you. We are on our way to Lin'an. Because it is late and we are not familiar with the roads, we came to your place to see if we could stay overnight. Could you provide us with accommodation?" As Madam Du said this, she lifted her head and caught a glimpse of the hostess in the moonlight. The girl's countenance stunned her and she said, "Young lady, do you live alone in this shabby house without any light?"

"This is an empty house and I am admiring the moon here."

When Madam Du heard this she felt doubtful and whispered to Chunxiang, "Look, who does this girl resemble?"

After taking a good look at her, Chunxiang was astonished too. She murmured, "Oh, Madam Du, this girl looks like Miss Liniang!"

"You check whether there is anyone else in the house. If not, I am afraid this girl is a ghost." Chunxiang moved stealthily and peeped into the room.

Du Liniang also examined the two women. She whispered to herself, "The old lady looks like my mother and the young girl looks like the maid Chunxiang." Tentatively she said, "Excuse me, Madam, could you tell me where you come from?"

Madam Du heaved a deep sigh. "Well, I came from Huai'an to seek refuge here. My husband is Pacification Commissioner Du Bao." Madam Du was testing Du Liniang too.

Du Liniang recognized the voice and said to herself, "Isn't this my mother? Should I recognize her or not?" While she hesitated, Chunxiang ran panicking to Madam Du. "It is a totally empty house! Not a trace of anyone! She must be a ghost! A ghost!"

At this Madam Du became speechless with fright. Involuntarily she backed away. Du Liniang saw her and approached with the intention of identifying herself and explaining the entire matter. But Madam Du thought Du Liniang's ghost was about to spring on her. She lost no time in trying to escape and cried over and over, "Aren't you the ghost of my dead daughter? I neglected you when you were alive. Now I know that I was wrong. Chunxiang, Hurry up! Throw her some of the ghost money we carry. Be quick!" Muddled, Chunxiang produced a wad of ghost money and threw it to Du Liniang.

"I am not a ghost!" Du Liniang asserted bluntly. She had no time to offer a better explanation.

"If you are not a ghost, then who are you?" Madam Du then asked Du Liniang to answer her call three times. If she were not a ghost, the voice would get louder each time. However, Du Liniang had not fully recovered her life energy and her three answers became fainter. During the jostle and hustle Madam Du touched Du Liniang's hands; they were really cold! Now Madam Du was even more convinced that the girl was a ghost. Chunxiang was so scared that she knelt on the ground and kowtowed again and again pleading, "Miss, please don't punish me!"

"Dear child, we didn't hold the ceremony to release your soul from purgatory. It is your stubborn father's fault," the old lady said desperately as she tried to get away.

Du Liniang heard her and held her mother's sleeve more tightly. "Mother, why are you so frightened? I can't let you go!"

Just then Nun Shi came back with the oil. She had been surprised to hear noisy human voices before going into the yard. She held the oil lamp high and found the ghost money scattered on the ground, which also surprised her. Chunxiang saw Nun Shi and beckoned her. "Look, Madam, isn't the woman coming in the door Nun Shi?"

"Yes, it is her!" The old lady looked at the door and was sure.

Nun Shi saw Madam Du and Chunxiang. She was surprised and said, "Oh! Aren't you Madam Du and Chunxiang? Where do you come from? Why are you so frightened?"

Du Liniang shouted, "Aunt Shi, come! Be quick! My mother is scared!"

Hearing them speak fluently, Chunxiang cried out, "Oh, my God! This aunt might be a ghost too!"

As the situation seemed to be getting more and more confusing, Nun Shi walked straight into the house and put the lamp on the table. Then she dragged Madam Du close to the lamp and asked her to look carefully. Gradually Madam Du calmed down, but she still remained suspicious. Then Nun Shi and Du Liniang explained in great detail what had happened during the past three years: how Du Liniang had been brought back to life and met Liu Mengmei; how they came to Lin'an; and how Liu Mengmei's left for Huaiyang to look for Du Liniang's parents after he had taken the imperial examination. Madam Du finally exclaimed that it was all most unusual and the four brought face to face sobbed with emotion. As it was really late,

Nun Shi made arrangements for the other three to rest.

It was well into autumn. With a bundle on his back, a scroll in his hand and an umbrella under his arm, Liu Mengmei headed for Huaiyang to carry out Du Liniang's request. In the confusion and chaos of war he had to make use of every available means of transport whether it was boat or cart. When there was nothing available, he walked. Having traveled day and night, he finally reached Yangzhou, only to find that his father-in-law had gone to Hai'an. Thus he had to begin another journey and on the way suffered many hardships. He had been cheated out of almost all the money that he had, and at the end of the journey, all that was left was the bundle and the umbrella. Although often hungry, he endured.

Finally he arrived at Huai'an city. It was dusk, the city gate was closed and he had to stay at an inn outside the city. However, when he sat down at the table, he found that he had no money for food and he asked the inn owner if he could trade his brush or umbrella for a meal but was refused. In the circumstances his only option appeared to be to reveal his identity.

"Sir, have you heard of Pacification Commissioner Du Bao of Huaiyang?"

"Everybody here has heard of Pacification Commissioner Du! He suppressed the rebellion and repulsed Li Quan's gangsters by strategy. Tomorrow a banquet will be held in a tent to celebrate his victory."

"That is great. You know, I am His Excellency's son-in-law. I came here especially to visit him."

This really surprised the inn owner who looked at the young man again. He examined him from head to foot and from back to front and, although he observed very carefully, he just could not make himself believe that this poor and dull looking young man was the son-in-law of Pacification Commissioner Du. After thinking, he decided what to do and grinned at Liu Mengmei. "Oh, why did not you tell me about this earlier? His Excellency has an invitation for you!"

"Where is it?" In such desperate circumstances, Liu Mengmei

clutched at any straw and was overwhelmed with joy, not realizing what the inn owner intended.

"Come with me and I'll show you."

They left the inn, walked along several streets, turned a few corners and arrived at an open ground. Nearby was a compound, slightly higher than ordinary civilian house, surrounded by a long wall from which the paint had peeled. On the wall hung a piece of white paper and pointing to it, the inn owner said to Liu Mengmei, "That is the invitation. Read it carefully."

Liu Mengmei took a few steps forward and saw that it was not an invitation at all, but a notice. The inn owner pointed to it and said, "Look, it reads, 'Stop Being an Idler and Defrauder.' This is a notice issued by Pacification Commissioner Du Bao. It says, 'I have neither nephews in the imperial court nor a son-in-law. Anyone who claims that they are related to me in this way will be arrested.' It not only refers to you, young man, it talks about me. 'Anybody offering help to the defrauder will be punished too.' How dare you intend such a thing! Leave quickly, I will not report you and don't you incriminate me." The inn owner walked off by himself.

Abandoned by the inn owner and without a penny, Liu Mengmei faced a dilemma. Du Bao's notice had stated clearly that he had no son-in-law. He did not know what to do; desperation and misery gripped his heart and he burst into tears.

After he had shed tears, he looked around and caught sight of a big house with a notice on which several characters were inscribed. He stepped forward and saw that they were the four golden characters that said: Mother Piao's Memorial Temple. Mother Piao was the woman who gave Han Xin {a general of the Han Dynasty} financial help. Liu Mengmei walked into the temple. It was empty and on the altar stood an everlasting oil lamp. Inscribed on the wall were a few lines by Han Xin expressing his gratitude for Mother Piao's meal. When Liu Mengmei saw this, he felt bitter. He bowed to the statue of Mother Piao and said, "When Han Xin was down and out, he met generous Mother Piao and had a meal. Now I am suffering from hunger and cold, but cannot beg even for a cup of cold water!" Full of emotion he stayed the night on the temple porch.

On the morning of the following day Liu Mengmei went into the city and walked straight to Pacification Commissioner Du's office. To muster up his courage, Liu Mengmei paced up and down in front of the door. Then he made up his mind. He said to the doorkeeper, "I am the son-in-law of Pacification Commissioner Du Bao. I have come especially to pay a formal visit."

The doorkeeper had been watching the young man in ragged clothes for a while. He carried a worn-out bundle, a broken umbrella and a torn picture; he could not believe what he claimed and said disdainfully, "What a day-dreamer you are! Look at you, shabby dress, wan countenance, how can you be the son-in-law of Pacification Commissioner Du? Hunger must have driven you out of your mind!"

Liu Mengmei saw that the doorkeeper was a snob and rebutted him indignantly, "Old and useless man, listen! I am a dignified scholar who has graduated from a regular school. I came from Lin'an to visit my father-in-law, but have spent all my traveling expenses on the way. That's why I am in such an awkward situation. You should not judge a person on appearances alone. Go and report that I am here immediately!" Liu Mengmei spoke so vehemently that the doorkeeper felt uneasy. He thought that if by any chance this man was indeed the son-in-law of Pacification Commissioner Du, and if he did not report him, he would be in trouble himself. He decided to report him, impostor or not.

At the time Du Bao was alone in a room deeply grieved by Madam Du's death. When the doorkeeper reported to him, he thought, "My daughter has been dead for three years. How could there be a son-in-law? He must be an impostor." Nonetheless, he said to the doorkeeper, "What does the man look like?"

"Nothing special. Oh yes, he has a scroll under his arm."

Du Bao concluded that the man must be a poverty-stricken painter seeking financial help. However, today was such a happy occasion that he did not feel inclined to punish such an idler. He said to the doorkeeper, "Tell him that His Excellency is busy with military affairs and has no time to meet him. Ask him to go on his way."

Although Liu Mengmei had been denied admission, he was

eager to try again. He knew that on that very day there would be a celebratory banquet, an occasion attended by all the civil and military officials. He sat on doorstep waiting for a chance to rush in.

After a while civil and military officials arrived one after another. The adjutant ordered the banquet to begin and drums rolled. Sitting at the head of the banquet, Du Bao addressed everyone there. "Although Li Quan's gangsters have been repulsed, the Kin still look at us like a covetous tiger. It is too early to sing songs of triumph. However, today, let's celebrate our small victory with a cup of wine." All the civil and military officials began praising Pacification Commissioner Du's great skill in outwitting the enemy. A messenger arrived and announced that the court had replied to His Excellency's memorandum. His Majesty instructed Pacification Commissioner Du Bao not to retire. He was to return to the court and be designated Joint Manager of Important National Affairs. Madam Du had been conferred a posthumous honor, Grade One Courageous and Virtuous Lady.

At once all the officials congratulated him. The position of Joint Manager of Important National Affairs was in fact that of Prime Minister and those present competed with each other in trying to flatter Du Bao and win his favor. After thanking everyone, Du Bao said modestly, "You are in the prime of your lives and have a bright prospects as officials. I return to the court in my old age and am not worthy of praise."

While Du Bao and his subordinates were exchanging toasts and eulogies, Liu Mengmei waited outside, famished and exhausted. He decided to disregard formalities and rushed towards the hall. Of course the doorkeeper tried to stop him and the two began quarreling. The noise carried through to the hall and Du Bao said to the adjutant, "Who is causing that commotion?"

"It is a man calling himself your son-in-law, Your Excellency. He said he was very hungry and wanted food. Our man tried to stop him but he beat him."

Du Bao was enraged at hearing this. "Damn! I announced a prohibition. How dare this poor idler behave as he likes here!" Without listening to his subordinates' conciliatory words, Du Bao ordered the adjutant to arrest Liu Mengmei immediately, place him in jail for the meanwhile and escort him to Lin'an for interrogation when he returned to the court. In this way, Liu Mengmei was maligned by his father-in-law when he tried to carry out a mission for his wife.

CHAPTER FOURTEEN

Family Reunion

WHILE THE BANQUET to celebrate peace was taking place in Huai'an, the capital city, Lin'an, was also in a jubilant mood. The emperor was overwhelmed with joy and the nobles of the court were extremely busy preparing the celebratory ceremony.

One morning, Chen Zuiliang, a subordinate of Pacification Commissioner Du Bao of Huaiyang and a former teacher in Nan'an, followed the minister of the Bureau of Military Affairs to the court to offer the letter of surrender from Li Quan. It happened that on the same day Miao Shunbin, the chief examiner of the imperial examination, went to the court as well. Miao wanted to ask the emperor to name the Number One Scholar so that the examination result could be released. The two ministers greeted each other, the palace drum was heard and a palace eunuch called, "Ministers who have a report, approach please."

Miao Shunbin knew that the suppression of Li Quan was a priority, so he asked the minister of the Bureau of Military Affairs to report first. The old minister accepted it as a gesture of goodwill and approached to kneel before the emperor, asking Chen Zuiliang to prostrate himself behind him. He reported loudly, "The minister in charge of national military affairs humbly reports. Congratulations, Your Majesty! Due to your imposing power, the bandits led by Li Quan in the Huaiyang area have surrendered and the Kin in the north dare not act rashly. Now, this is Chen Zuiliang from Nan'an. He was sent by Pacification Commissioner Du Bao to submit Li Quan's letter of surrender."

The palace eunuch announced the emperor's order. "Ask Chen Zuiliang to report in detail how Du Bao called on Li Quan to surrender."

Obeying the instruction Chen Zuiliang hastened to take a few steps towards the emperor. He gave a full account of how Du Bao had devised a trap to induce Li Quan to capitulate and told how when the Kin knew that Li Quan had surrendered they dared not to raise an army to invade the south. After listening to report, the emperor ordered Chen Zuiliang outside to wait for further instructions.

Then Miao Shunbin approached to report that the imperial examination had ended long ago and so had the marking of the examination papers. Because of the rebellion in Huaiyang, the publication of results had been delayed. Now that Li Quan had surrendered, and the country was peaceful again and the people happy, it was the best time to release the results and not let the candidates wait any longer. The emperor ordered them to wait outside too.

After the minister of the Bureau of Military Affairs and Miao Shunbin walked out of the palace, they began talking to each other. Miao Shunbin said, "The examination result ought to be released now. Those poor scholars have been waiting for too long." The old minister thought that the selection of talent was a matter of importance too. However, he looked down on Chen Zuiliang who had submitted the letter of surrender and said, "It seems far too easy for that scholar to obtain a position just for bringing a letter of surrender."

Before long the palace eunuch came out to announce the

imperial orders. "I am very happy to hear that Li Quan's gangsters were suppressed and the Kin enemy is now afraid to advance south. This is all to Du Bao's credit. I have already issued a decree ordering him to take up an official position in the capital. As Chen Zuiliang brought me the good news, I designate him the Memorial Processor at the Palace Gate and grant him official robes and hats." As to the imperial examination, the Emperor named Liu Mengmei as the Number One Scholar and ordered him to attend the banquet held for successful new candidates.

Ecstatic with such a change in fortune, Chen Zuiliang flew to the eunuch, took the robe and hat and in no time at all had changed out of his scholar's apparel. The old minister and Miao Shunbin had to congratulate him albeit in a perfunctory way. "Congratulations! Tomorrow we will count on you to publish the examination result!"

Chen Zuiliang had no time to reply and asked again and again, "Your Excellency, where does the Number One Scholar Liu Mengmei come from?"

"He is from the south of the Mount Meiling. As a matter of fact, the young man had a most unusual experience."

As their audience at the court had finished, the old minister felt like a chat and asked Miao Shunbin to tell him about it.

"That scholar is really lucky. On the examination day, just as I had finished going over the papers and was about to report to the emperor, there was a man wailing outside the hall pleading to take the examination. It was him. He explained why he missed the examination; he had traveled from the south of Mount Meiling to the capital with his wife. I pitied him and submitted his paper as a supplement. Who would have expected that His Majesty would name him as the Number One Scholar? Isn't that something unusual?"

The old minister nodded and agreed.

Chen Zuiliang thought to himself, "The Number One Scholar must be Liu Mengmei the grave-digger. How did he come to have a wife? Yes, perhaps he married Nun Shi." However, Chen Zuiliang said nothing about this and thought that now Liu Mengmei had become the Number One Scholar, the young man would surely enjoy bright prospects in the official hierarchy. Why not use the opportunity and claim a tie with him? He turned to the two ministers and said, "To tell you the truth, the new Number One Scholar, Liu Mengmei, is my friend."

"Oh, that also earns congratulations!" The two ministers made a few casual remarks and left separately.

The court picked out 200 to 300 outstanding scholars as the metropolitan graduates from each imperial examination. The candidates selected would be given a banquet by the emperor and were expected to compose a poem in the Apricot Garden. The best candidate was called the "Number One Scholar" and was paraded through the streets on horseback. It was a spectacular event and the scholars looked forward to it day and night. But this year was most unusual. All the metropolitan graduates attended the banquet except for the Number One Scholar, Liu Mengmei. None of the ministers in the court knew where he was. How could the banquet begin without the presentation of the Number One Scholar? The official in charge of the ceremony sent out two lieutenants to look for Liu Mengmei.

The lieutenants carried a board that read, "Liu Mengmei, named the Number One Scholar by the emperor, comes from the south of Mount Meiling. Age 27, medium height with fair complexion." They looked for him everywhere--boulevards, alleys, entertainment houses, even brothels--but just could not find him. After talking it over, they thought that if they failed to find him, they could replace him with someone else. But this was not possible because the Number One Scholar was expected to compose a poem and his place could not be filled by someone without talent. They had no choice but to return to the street and call his name. Nobody answered.

Just then a hunchback came hobbling along the street and heard a voice calling "Liu Mengmei". He thought that master Liu was nearby and dashed to where the sound came from. He went so fast that he bumped into the lieutenants and fell down still calling "Liu Mengmei".

The lieutenants, annoyed by their failure to find Liu Mengmei, were furious at being bumped into by a hunchback and angrily rebuked him. "Oh, this is wonderful! We call Liu Mengmei and you call Liu Mengmei too. There must be a connection. Come with us, we'd like to talk to you."

The hunchback was none other than the grandson of Hunchback Guo who used to take care of trees for the Lius. He had traveled from the south of Mount Meiling to Nan'an where he was told that Master Liu had fled to Lin'an after robbing a tomb. That is why he was in Lin'an. When he heard from the lieutenants that Liu Mengmei had won the title of Number One Scholar and that they were looking for him so that he could attend the banquet, the grandson of Hunchback Guo was overjoyed. He said, "Officer, as he has won first place, you will surely find him somewhere. Don't worry!"

The lieutenants thought that this was quite reasonable and said, "All right! We won't do anything this time. Come with us to look for your master!"

How could the lieutenants, who were looking for Liu Mengmei everywhere in the streets, ever know that the man they sought was in jail?

After Du Bao returned to the capital, he assumed the post of joint manager of Important National Affairs, which was equal to the prime minister. When he first took up office, there were dinners that he could not avoid and procedures for the transition. It was not until he had settled into office that he remembered the impostor who claimed to be his son-in-law. As he was free that day, Du Bao decided to cross-examine him and sent an usher to bring the prisoner from jail.

When the usher arrived, the jailor was extorting money from Liu Mengmei. He was disappointed to find that Liu Mengmei was as poor as a church mouse and found no money or valuables in his bundle. The jailor, though took a fancy to the scroll. He thought that it was a portrait of the Avalokitesvara and intended taking it home to place in a shrine. However, no matter how hard he tried, Liu Mengmei just would not let it go. He thought that when he was interrogated, he would produce the picture so that Du Bao would recognize it.

The usher arrived to fetch the prisoner just as the jailor was trying to wrest the scroll from him as he held it tightly in his arms. Seeing the usher, the jailor dared not misbehave and when Liu Mengmei told the jailor had tried to rob him, the usher commanded the jailor to return the item to Liu Mengmei. The jailor immediately obeyed.

Liu Mengmei held Du Liniang's portrait in his hand as he followed the usher to Du Bao's mansion. Du Bao was already sitting high up in the hall with two rows of court officials standing at either side. As Liu Mengmei was escorted into the hall, the officials all cried out but Liu Mengmei ignored them and strode into the hall with a dignity that surprised Du Bao. He asked, "Who on earth are you? You broke the law, how dare you not to kneel down before me?"

Liu Mengmei was not intimidated by the question and answered indignantly, "I am Liu Mengmei from the south of the Mount Meiling and the son-in-law of Your Excellency."

Liu Mengmei's insistence on maintaining this relationship enraged Du Bao. "My daughter died three years ago. When she was alive she was not betrothed to anyone. How can you be a son-in-law? It is not only ridiculous, it is abhorrent! Throw him into jail!"

"Don't anyone dare touch me!" Liu Mengmei shouted indignantly.

"I don't have a son-in-law like you. You are just an idler and a deceiver out for money!"

"I, your son-in-law, am both knowledgeable and talented. I can make a fortune by myself. Why should I seek financial help from you?"

Du Bao was almost speechless with rage. He shouted angrily, "How dare you answer back! There must be bogus stamps and letters. Search his bundle so that we may catch the thief with his takings!" The usher opened the bundle and found only a girl's portrait. Nevertheless, when Du Bao recognized that the girl in the portrait was none other than his own daughter, he became angrier and believed that Liu Mengmei was the grave digger. He ordered the court officials to torture Liu Mengmei to extract a confession.

Under the circumstances, Liu Mengmei had to relate the whole story: how he picked up the scroll; how Du Liniang's ghost asked him to open the coffin and how he helped her return to life. Du Bao had never heard such an odd story and was convinced that Liu

Mengmei was a ghost. He ordered him to be hung up and beaten with a peach tree's twig specially used to beat ghosts.

While Liu Mengmei was being beaten and crying out at the injustice, the lieutenants and the grandson of Hunchback Guo came by searching for Number One Scholar and were still shouting, "Where is the Number One Scholar Liu Mengmei?"

Liu Mengmei heard his name called and answered loudly. The grandson of Hunchback Guo said, "Alas, that sounds like my master's voice inside!" They forced their way into the hall. Hunchback Guo recognized Liu Mengmei straight away and cried, "Alas, the man hanging there is none other than my young master!"

Liu Mengmei saw the intruders and cried for help. Without a thought for his limp legs the grandson of Hunchback Guo rushed forward and lifted his crutch to hit Du Bao. There was pandemonium with the two parties bickering at each other. The lieutenants claimed that Liu Mengmei was Number One Scholar of the imperial examination while Du Bao insisted he was either a thief or a ghost. Each party stuck to its own view and neither would give way.

The chief examiner Miao Shunbin, who had been told where Liu Mengmei was, arrived holding the robes and footwear that the emperor granted to Number One Scholar. Although he explained what had happened, Du Bao just would not believe him but Miao Shunbin carried an imperial order and just took Liu Mengmei away. Du Bao had no say in the matter. He did not know what to do and asked Chen Zuiliang to explain the whole thing again. Afterwards he still insisted stubbornly that he should report to the emperor that Liu Mengmei was a grave digger and could not be called Number One Scholar.

Liu Mengmei paraded through the streets and later heard that his father-in-law had appealed to the emperor. So he submitted a memorandum to vindicate himself. The emperor knew from what Liu Mengmei said that Du Liniang was still alive and at once sent an official to summon her. Du Liniang, Madam Du, Chunxiang and Nun Shi learnt that Liu Mengmei had become the Number One Scholar. Of course, everyone was extremely happy and, when they learned that they had been summoned by the emperor, they took great care of their appearances, dressed in a hurry and followed the official to court.

Outside the palace Du Bao and Liu Mengmei waited to be summoned. Liu Mengmei smiled at Du Bao and called him "respected father-in-law". However, Du Bao did not consider himself a father to Liu Mengmei and sternly denounced him as a "criminal". Liu Mengmei replied in a relaxed way, "Why am I the criminal when, on the contrary, you are the criminal."

"I gave meritorious service by repulsing Li Quan. What charges can you accuse me of?" Du Bao had been goaded into fury.

"Well, isn't it funny? You can conceal it from the emperor but not from the whole nation. You have not suppressed Li Quan, you have suppressed only half of Li Quan." Liu Mengmei teased him intentionally.

Du Bao was puzzled. "What do you mean by half of Li Quan?"

"Well, you only induced Li Quan's wife to retreat. How can she be the complete Li Quan?" Du Bao's face turned purple and he became incoherent with rage.

Just then the emperor convened the court and Chen Zuiliang arrived with Madam Du and Du Liniang. Du Bao saw the two women and could not help crying out, "Ghost!" During the audience with the emperor, Du Bao still refused to accept that they were people and the emperor sent someone to bring a mirror to test them. Du Liniang's image appeared in the mirror and, when she was asked to stand under a tree, her shadow could be clearly seen. As a result they decided that Du Liniang was indeed human. However, Du Bao stuck to his own ideas and refused to admit it. After he had heard each side's account, the emperor agreed that it was a most unusual event and said that they deserved congratulations. He ordered every family member to recognize one another and they all obeyed except for the son-in-law and the father-in-law. The imperial order came just when they were laughing, crying, bickering, and arguing, so they stopped quarreling and knelt down to receive it. The order read: "I have heard the unusual story of the Du family. Now I grant the family a reunion; promote the Joint Manager of Important National Affairs, Du Bao, one grade higher; confer on Du Bao's wife the title, Lady of Huaiyin City; appoint Number One Scholar, Liu Mengmei, to Chancellor of the Imperial Academy, and confer to Liu Mengmei's wife the title, Lady of Yanghe County. I order the Chief Ceremonial Minister Han Zicai to send them to their mansion."

Listening to the imperial order, Liu Mengmei lifted his head and saw that the official messenger was his old friend Han Zicai. The two greeted each other and spoke of their experiences since they had parted. Han Zicai had benefited from his association with his ancestor, Han Yu, and had been sponsored by his local government to take the imperial examination. Now he held the post of Chief Ceremonial Minister. Liu Mengmei could not help marveling at the way that the old friends from the south of Mount Meiling had all met in the capital one after another.

Of course, the happiest person was Du Liniang. She thought that she was so lucky to have been brought back to life by Liu Mengmei. And all of this was due to her love for Liu Mengmei. Among all the ghosts, who had been more devoted than she? No one could have had an ending as perfect as hers.

The Peach Blossom Fan

About
the Original Work

KONG SHANGREN *(STYLE* name of Pinzhi), the author of *The Peach Blossom Fan*, was born in Qufu, Shandong Province, in 1648 and died in 1718. A descendant of Confucius (64 times removed), Kong Shangren came from a landowning and intellectual family. In 1667 he passed the county examination to earn the title of *xiucai* [one who passed the imperial examination at county level in the Ming and Qing dynasties] and enrolled in the Imperial Academy in 1681. During an inspection tour of south China, Emperor Xuan Ye of the Qing Dynasty traveled to Qufu to make sacrifices to Confucius. Kong Shangren came to notice when he gave a lecture on Confucianism that was much praised by the emperor. The following year he went to the capital and became a master of the Imperial Academy.

In 1686 Kong Shangren took part in a conservancy project at the mouth of the Yangtze River and spent three years in Yangzhou where he met many adherents of the former Ming Dynasty, survivors of the great upheaval during dynastic change. Through activities such as climbing the Meihua Mountain and visiting the grave containing the dress of Shi Kefa, Kong Shangren gathered raw material for his drama *The Peach Blossom Fan*. He also went to Nanjing where he visited the Ming imperial palace, the Xiaoling Mausoleum of the Ming Dynasty, the Qinhuai River, Sanshan Street, and other famous sights of that region. He made a special trip to the Baiyun Temple on Qixia Mountain, where he met Zhang Yi, a Taoist priest, who had been formerly a commanding officer during the Ming Dynasty.

Kong Shangren started to write *The Peach Blossom Fan* before he became an official. He continued writing when he was living in Yangzhou and Zhaoyang (now Xinghua, Jiangsu Province). It took him over ten years to complete the famous romance. After revising it three times, he finally finished it in June 1699. After its publication, Kong Shangren assumed office as a vice-director of the Ministry of Revenue in March 1700, but was dismissed from office soon after. No reason was recorded for the dismissal. In the winter of 1702 he returned home from Beijing. He toured Shanxi, Hubei and Huaiyang, and then returned to Qufu, where he died at his home.

Kong Shangren also wrote many poems and prose works. But only *The Peach Blossom Fan* won him great renown and many consider it his greatest work. The play, ostensibly a love story, outlines the history of the downfall of Emperor Zhu Yousong of the Ming Dynasty in south China. The principal characters are Hou Chaozong and Li Xiangjun. Hou was a man of letters and Li an educated courtesan. The separation and reunion of the lovers allowed the author to ruminate on the rise and fall of a dynasty. The drama is set in the period 1643 to 1645.

In 1643 Li Zicheng, a leader of a peasant uprisings, invaded and took Beijing, resulting in the suicide of Emperor Chongzhen of the Ming Dynasty on the Coal Hill, now Jingshan Park. In 1645 Emperor Shunzhi of the Qing Dynasty issued an invitation soliciting opinions from hermits and adherents of former regime. The play realistically reflects the complex contradictions of this historic period, giving the reasons for the empire's downfall. It also serves as a lesson in history. This is what the author means when he says: "It not only affects the audience with deep emotions. It also makes them profit from the salvation of the state."

The play specifically describes Emperor Zhu Yousong indulging in wine and women and ignoring the business of state. Corrupt officials seize power, forcing honest officials and loyal state servants out of office. The corrupt officials flatter the emperor and throw many innocent people into prison. They repress the critics and the dissenters, which leads to the collapse of the empire. The author's grasp of the circumstances gave him the ability to reveal as much as possible of the true situation.

Kong Shangren lived in the Qing Dynasty, which replaced the Ming. He was born into a landlord family and would not have had an objective view of history, nor would he have been able to give a full account of the reasons for the collapse of the Ming. Kong Shangren claimed that the fall of Ming was due to vagrants and bandits. This view owes much to the attitudes at the time and his class background. The author had formed an opinion of the Qing Dynasty that he could not give openly, and could only imply his true meaning.

Yet the social outcasts in the drama, such as Liu Jingting, Su Kunsheng and Li Xiangjun were portrayed positively, as people with integrity and a concern for the safety of the state: they showed courage in the struggle against corrupt officials and gave support to a just cause; they knew the difference between right and wrong. All this demonstrates the author's progressive thinking.

When *The Peach Blossom Fan* appeared in print in Beijing, it had a great impact on society. It was read by princes and wealthy merchants alike. Many copied the drama resulting in a huge increase in the price of paper. It was reported that when Emperor Kangxi of the Qing Dynasty read the excerpt on the court session to choose the beauties, he stamped his feet, frowned and declared that although Emperor Zhu Yousong did not want to perish, he could not escape his fate.

As an artistic achievement, *The Peach Blossom Fan* is universally acclaimed for its orderly composition. The verses are fluent and the dialogue polished, which gives life to the characters. The play's plot is also unusual in that it does not have a traditionally happy ending. The romance is a unique piece of writing that has taken its place in the history of Chinese drama. Kong Shangren's reputation is often compared to that of Hong Sheng, the author of *The Palace of Eternal Youth*. Many consider Hong Sheng the best playwright in southern China and Kong Shangren the best playwright in the north.

CHAPTER ONE

Hou Chaozong Stays in Nanjing

NANJING IN SOUTHEAST China is a land of beauty, and the capital of many dynasties. Because of its strategic importance, Nanjing served as the capital for eight dynasties in Chinese history. They included the State of Wu during the Three Kingdoms Period (220-280), the Eastern Jin (317-420), Song (420-479), Qi (479-502), Liang· (502-557), Chen (557-589), later Tang (923-936) and Ming (1368-1644) dynasties. Of them only the Ming Dynasty re-unified the country and turned Nanjing into a national political center under the leadership of Zhu Yuanzhang, the first emperor of the Ming. Nanjing became a magnificent city after two decades of renewal. Later Emperor Zhu Di of the Ming made Beijing the capital, but Nanjing still preserved the central organizations — the Six Boards [the Boards of Personnel, Revenue, Rites, War, Justice and Works]. It was an important southeastern Chinese city, prosperous, commercially active, and with arts and handicrafts as good as those in Beijing. Nanjing was also first in the country in terms of learning and civilized living. It attracted many Chinese and foreign scholars and was the place where the provincial examination was held once every three years. Scholars from east China gathered there during the examination period.

The imperial examination of the 14th year of the Chongzhen reign (1641) generated some lucky scholars who passed and many others who failed. Among those who failed was a young man called Hou Fangyu (styled Chaozong), a native of Shangqiu in Henan Province. He was a descendant of Hou Ying, a distinguished person of the Warring States Period (475-221 BC). His grandfather Hou Zhipu once served as chief minister of the Court of Imperial Sacrifices; his father Hou Xun had been the imperial secretary at the Board of Revenue and later joined the Donglin Party.

In the later Ming Dynasty, a group of eminent scholars in southeastern China renovated the Donglin Academy in Wuxi, Jiangsu Province, which was originally founded by Yang Shi, a philosopher of the Song Dynasty (960-1179). They gave lectures in the academy and not only spoke candidly about current affairs, but criticized contemporary leaders as well. They denounced the exploitation and brutal rule of the eunuchs, headed by Wei Zhongxian, and advocated protection of the interests of landlords, industrialists and merchants in southeast China. They were called Men of the Donglin Party.

Later many societies carried on the party's traditions and showed the same spirit. The most famous of them was the Restoration Society. Hou Chaozong was a member of the Restoration Society. In his early years he was well known for his literary gatherings and he considered his prose poems as good as those of Ban Gu (32-92 AD), a famous historian and writer of the Eastern Han dynasty, and Song Yu, a famous prose poet of the Warring States Period. His articles were as good as those of Han Yu (768-824) and Su Shi (1037-1101), two great writers in Chinese history. However, to his great surprise, he failed in the provincial examination and was most disappointed.

Instead of returning home, Hou Chaozong rented a house near the Mochou [not-to worry] Lake in the west of Nanjing and stayed in the city. Mochou Lake is a famous scenic spot in Nanjing and a place where the literati often gathered. Legend has it that during the Southern Song Dynasty (1127-1279) a girl, Mochou, from

Luoyang in Henan Province, was married to a rich and powerful man in Nanjing whose surname was Lu and had a home by the lake. Soon after the wedding, her husband went to fight in a war. Though lonely and distressed, she was kind and warm and always ready to help those in difficulty. To show their love and respect for this woman, people later named the lake after her. Hou Chaozong often invited friends to drink wine and compose poems in his house where they could enjoy the beautiful scenery through the window.

In February 1643, the 16th year of Chongzhen reign, Hou Chaozong stayed at his house. He had been going to bed early and getting up late; he was bored. There was a war in north China that stopped him receiving letters from home. Worry contended with boredom and he had not realized that the rainy season had arrived. Standing by the window looking at the lake in the rain, he sighed deeply and said, "I must not worry, I must not worry. But I can't help worrying!"

Fortunately he had close friends living nearby. Chen Zhenhui (styled Dingsheng), a native of Yixing, Jiangsu Province, and Wu Yingji (styled Ciwei), a native of Guichi in Anhui Province who lived in the famous Cai Yisuo Study in the Sanshan Street, not far from Mochou Lake. They were all members of the Restoration Society and frequently visited one another. One day the three men decided to go to the Mount Yeshan Taoist Temple near Mochou Lake to view the plum blossoms. Hou Chaozong rose early in the morning, got things ready and waited for his friends.

On the way to Hou Chaozong's house Chen Dingsheng asked, "Brother Ciwei, what do you know about the activities of the 'rebellious troops' these days?"

Wu Ciwei sighed heavily and said, "I read some articles in a newspaper yesterday. They have gradually moved on Beijing. The troops under Marquis Zuo Liangyu, who fought against Li Zicheng and Zhang Xianzhong (the leaders of the peasant uprisings of the Ming Dynasty), have retreated to Xiangyang. No troops in central China can defeat them."

When they came to Hou Chaozong's house, Wu Ciwei said that they should forget about the war and enjoy the beautiful spring scenery. Hou Chaozong came out to greet them. "Please come in.

My brothers have arrived really early today."

"We dare not be late when you invite us!" Wu Ciwei replied.

Chen Dingsheng said that he had sent a servant boy to prepare the temple and the wine.

CHAPTER TWO

A Visit to Liu Jingting, Storyteller

AFTER THEY SET out they ran into the servant who said, "Master, you're too late. You may as well return home."

"Are we late?" Chen Dingsheng didn't understand.

"Master Xu, the duke of the State of Wei, chartered the temple for his guests to view the plum blossoms."

Chen Dingsheng flew into rage and Hou Chaozong suggested that they go to the brothels by the Qinhuai River instead. "It will be fun to chat with beautiful girls of Nanjing."

Wu Ciwei, who didn't want to go to the brothels, said, "It's a long way to the bank of the Qinhuai River, Brother Hou. Have you heard about Liu Jingting from Taizhou? He is a wonderful storyteller. Even the former high-ranking officials, such as Fan Jingwen and He Ruchong, think highly of him. He lives near here. His stories would be a great diversion."

"That sounds good," said Chen Dingsheng.

Hou Chaozong became very angry. "Liu Jingting is a hanger-on of Ruan Dacheng, an adopted son of an eunuch. We should not listen to such a person."

Hou Chaozong did not actually know Liu Jingting so Wu Ciwei

said, "Brother Hou, you are not familiar with Ruan Dacheng, an evil man who refuses to step down from public view. He has recruited female entertainers in Nanjing to ingratiate himself with gentry and officials and I have written an article that exposes his crimes. Before I wrote it, Ruan's hangers-on did not know that he belonged to the eunuch clique headed by Wei Zhongxian and Cui Chengxiu. Soon after they read my account, they all left, one after another. One of them was Liu Jingting. I think we should take that into account when we judge his character and morals."

Hou Chaozong was very surprised and said ruefully, "I didn't know there was such a hero among the hangers-on. We should pay him a visit."

The three young men walked towards Liu's home, and stood before it as their servant boy stepped forward to knock on the door, "Is Liu Jingting home?"

"He is a famous person. You should call him Master Liu," Chen Dingsheng corrected the boy.

The boy repeated, "Please open the door, Master Liu."

Liu Jingting, a white-bearded man wearing a hat and a dark blue robe with wide sleeves, came to the door. "Hello, Master Chen and Master Wu. It was remiss of me not to come out to greet you." He turned towards Hou Chaozong and asked, "Who is this young man?"

"This is my friend Mr. Hou Chaozong, a distinguished scholar from Henan," Chen Dingsheng said. "He knows of your illustrious name and we have come to listen to your story telling."

Liu invited them in to sit down and drink tea. "You are very familiar with *Historical Records* and *Historical Events Retold as a Mirror for Government*. Why do you come here to listen to my folk stories?"

Hou Chaozong, who had never heard his stories, urged him not to be modest and to allow them to hear them.

Liu Jingting knew that it would be hard to turn them down and said, "Thank you for coming. I dare not decline. I expect that you are not interested in historical stories and folk tales. Let me tell you a section from *The Analects*, something that you would be familiar with."

This surprised Hou Chaozong who said, "That is strange. How

can you tell a story about *The Analects*?"

"If you can read it, why can't I tell it?" Liu Jingting replied with a smile. "Today I will act the cultured person and tell a story." He went to his special seat, stroked his wooden clapper on the table and began. "Today I would like to relate to you how the three Sun brothers cheated the king of Lu State..." The three young scholars found the story interesting, vivid and easy to understand.

"Bang!" At the sound of his wooden clapper, Liu Jingting stood up and made a bow by cupping his hands on his chest. He said, "I have made a fool of myself!"

"Wonderful! Wonderful!" Chen Dingsheng cried. "You explained ancient Chinese history so well. It's a unique skill indeed."

Wu Ciwei interrupted to say, "Brother Liu did not try to find refuge with another after he left Ruan Dacheng. Now he tries to advise others by using his own experience as an example."

After hearing Liu Jingting's story, Hou Chaozong felt that he knew him better. He could not resist saying that he was a moral person who shared their views. Storytelling was just one of his skills.

The three young scholars voiced their approval and Liu Jingting said modestly, "You are welcome to come again."

Hou Chaozong asked Liu about the others who left Ruan Dacheng.

"They have all left Nanjing," Liu replied. " Only Su Kunsheng lives nearby. He is good at singing *kunqu*[melodies that originated in Kunshan, Jiangsu Province, in the Ming Dynasty]. I heard he is teaching the adopted daughter of Li Zhenli, a famous courtesan, to sing *kunqu*."

Hou Chaozong said, "We'll see him too. I hope he and Brother Liu will come to visit us."

"I'll pay you a visit," Liu Jingting promised. Then he bowed and saw them off.

CHAPTER THREE

Li Zhenli's Adopted Daughter

ON THE BANK of Qinhuai River, close to the Temple of Confucius, there was a brothel run by the famous courtesan Li Zhenli. Its front gate faced the Wuding Bridge and its back door Chaoku Street. The Examination Office was across the Qinhuai River so that men of letters often came to the brothel. Li Zhenli, a natural beauty, was good at entertaining her clients. Handsome scholars attracted by her beauty had often visited her. However, though still good looking, she was getting older. She was now a middle-aged woman. She had adopted a graceful and charming girl who attracted many men who had not yet begun to accept clients. Of her admirers, Yang Longyou adored her most.

Yang Longyou, a native of Guiyang in Guizhou Province, was once a successful candidate in the imperial examinations at provincial level; he later became a county magistrate. He was a brother-in-law of Governor Ma Shiying of Fengyang and was on friendly terms with Ruan Dacheng. After he resigned his post, he frequently visited brothels in Nanjing and had an affair with Li Zhenli. Having once caught sight of Li's adopted daughter, he was determined to introduce her to a good man. On a spring day when plum blossoms withered and willow tree leaves turned green, he headed for Li Zhenli's home.

As it was warm and fine, Li Zhenli had allowed the maids to roll up the curtains and clean the receiving room. She was expecting Yang Longyou and soon he pushed the door open to walk in. Li Zhenli greeted him warmly. They exchanged words and she invited him upstairs. There, she burned joss sticks, served tea and invited him to view the inscriptions that celebrities had made on the four walls. However Yang Longyou, who was more interested in her daughter, asked where she was.

"She is making up in her room." Li Zhenli called out, "Daughter, Lord Yang is here."

The daughter hurriedly applied lipstick and rouge. Her hair done in a fashionable coil, she changed into new clothes and walked out of her room taking quick short steps.

With a cup of tea in his hand, Yang Longyou viewed the poems and paintings on the walls. Seeing the inscriptions by Zhang Pu and Xia Yunyi, two famous scholars, Yang Longyou was inspired to write a poem himself. He started composing one and heard a sweet voice saying, "Lord Yang, all blessings." He turned round and found a beautiful girl standing by him. He stared at her and said, "I only saw you a few days ago and now you are even more pretty. All these poems describe your beauty. Let me write one myself."

Li Zhenli offered a brush, an ink stone and a piece of paper for Yang's poems. With a brush in hand, Yang Longyou was lost in thought. Finally he put the brush down and said, "My poem cannot compare with theirs. Let me paint some orchids to decorate the white wall."

"That would be better!" said Li Zhenli.

Yang Longyou looked at the poems and paintings once again. "Oh, there are jagged rocks painted by Lan Tianshu," he said. "Let me paint orchids beside them."

He raised his brush and drew the orchids with great care. When he had finished he put the brush down and stepped back to examine his work. "Though it cannot compare with the works of the famous painters of the Yuan Dynasty (1279-1368), a famous beauty needs orchids as a comparison," Yang said proudly.

"It is excellent. It adds splendor to the room," Li Zhenli said enthusiastically.

"Please don't flatter me." However, Yang was very pleased with himself. He turned to the girl and asked, "What's your formal name? I would like to write an inscription for you."

"I'm too young to have a formal name," the girl answered.

"Would you please name her, Mr. Yang?" Li Zhenli cut in.

Yang Longyou wanted to show off in front of the two women; he had a fertile imagination. "There's a saying from *Zuo Zhuan*, or *The Spring and Autumn Annals*, 'The orchid has national fragrance and people admire its enchanting beauty.' Let's name her Xiangjun [Fragrant Lady]."

"Wonderful!" Li Zhenli said. "Xiangjun, come here and thank Lord Yang."

"I also have a name for your building—The House of Enchanting Fragrance." So saying, Yang Longyou picked up his brush and wrote an inscription on the painting that read: "In the mid-spring of the year of *Guiwei*, I painted these orchids in the House of Enchanting Fragrance, which won a smile from Xiangjun. Yang Wencong from Guiyang."

"Both the painting and inscription are excellent," Li Zhenli said. When Yang Longyou sat down she served him a cup of tea.

Yang Longyou wished to know more about Xiangjun and said, "I believe that Xiangjun is the most beautiful girl in the country. How well developed are her skills?"

"My daughter is elegant, but has not learnt any skills yet. A few days ago she started to learn *kunqu* from Su Kunsheng."

Yang Longyou said that he knew Su Kunsheng, the famous actor, and asked what she was learning from him.

Li Zhenli said that Xiangjun was learning *The Four Dreams of the Jade Tea Studio* [four operas written by Tang Xianzu, a famous dramatist in the Ming Dynasty], and that she had just learnt to sing half of *The Peony Pavilion*. She let Xiangjun take out the script to see it. At that very moment Su Kunsheng came in, saw Yang Longyou and said, "Lord Yang. I haven't seen you for a long time."

"Congratulations on having such a good student."

Yang Longyou stood up and saluted him and after the exchange of greetings, Su Kunsheng began to teach Xiangjun. "Today Lord Yang is here. We may follow his instructions."

Xiangjun began to sing an aria from *The Peony Pavilion* that she had learned. Sun Kunsheng often corrected her and taught her the song sentence by sentence. She also learned to sing a new scene from the opera.

"Your daughter is very bright. She will surely be a famous entertainer soon," Yang said after hearing her sing. Then he turned to Su Kunsheng and said that he had met Hou Xun's son, Hou Chaozong, the day before. "He is rich and well known for his literary talents. This young man is looking for a beauty. Do you know him, Mr. Su?"

"He comes from the same town as me and he's from an old and famous family."

Yang Longyou said, "We should introduce Xiangjun to him." Li Zhenli happily agreed and asked Yang Longyou for his help. Yang Longyou agreed to help. After drinking more tea they all left.

CHAPTER FOUR

Scholars Denounce Ruan Dacheng

T HE SWORN BROTHER of Yang Longyou, Ruan Dacheng, was hated and denounced by everyone. Ruan Dacheng (styled Yuanhai) was a native of Huaining in Anhui Province. He was good at writing *ci* [poetry written to certain tunes with strict tonal patterns and rhyme and rhyme schemes, in fixed numbers of lines and words] and *qu* [a type of sung verse]. However he was overly ambitious. To advance his career, he had thrown in his lot with Wei Zhongxian, the head of the eunuch clique. When the clique was crushed, he was cursed and hated by others. Instead of repenting, he then tried to seek another backer.

Every year, during the middle of spring, a memorial ceremony would be held at the Temple of Confucius. On the day, those who administered the temple rose early, cleaned the paths, set out sacrificial containers with meat, vegetables, fruit, wine and cakes, and lit candles and joss sticks. When all was ready, they waited for the officials in charge of the ceremony and other men of letters.

Amid the sounds of drums and music, officials of the Imperial Academy led many scholars to pay tribute to Confucius. During the Ming and Qing dynasties, the Imperial Academy was the highest educational body and, as Emperor Zhu Yuanzhang of the Ming had chosen Nanjing as the capital, the Six Boards and Imperial Academy were all located there. Later Emperor Zhu Di made Beijing the capital and founded another Imperial Academy there, but the one in Nanjing remained unchanged in its importance.

Ruan Dacheng attended the ceremony, skulking among the men of letters and looking for a way to execute his schemes. However the famous five scholars of the Restoration Society—Wu Ciwei, Yang Weidou, Liu Bozong, Shen Kuntong and Shen Meisheng— were there. After they had kowtowed to the statue of Confucius, the scholars stood up and exchanged greetings. Ruan Dacheng went over to salute Wu Ciwei hoping that he would salute him in return; he would then be accepted by other scholars. However Wu Ciwei, an upright man, could not tolerate such a despicable person. Instead of returning the salute, he denounced him: "You are Ruan Dacheng? How dare you come here to attend the sacrificial ceremony! You will offend Confucius and bring disgrace to our scholars! Get out of here!"

At this Ruan Dacheng became most irate and retorted, "I'm a successful candidate in the highest imperial examination, and a famous writer. What crimes have I committed? Why shouldn't I attend the memorial ceremony?"

"Your crimes are known to everyone. You're a person without heart. How dare you enter the temple and attend the ceremony?" Wu Ciwei scolded in a loud voice. "The notice to prevent insurrection, posted the day before yesterday, is directed at people like you."

Though discouraged, Ruan tried to defend himself. "I came to the memorial ceremony to lay bare my true feelings."

"Let me express your true feelings for you. You are Wei Zhongxian's adopted son, and a diehard follower of Cui Chengxiu and Tian Ergeng of the eunuch clique. You colluded with the Xichang secret service to arrest, torture and persecute upright men of the Donglin Party. All of your crimes are abundantly clear. Once the sun rises, the ice on the mountain melts. You have no way to go."

Wu Ciwei had exposed all of Ruan's crimes and Ruan Dacheng

could not deny the facts. He looked for an excuse. "Brothers, you only curse me, you don't understand my predicament. You did not know that I was a student of Mr. Zhao Nanxing [a politician and literati in the Ming Dynasty and an important member of the Donglin Party] who was persecuted to death by Wei Zhongxian. When the Wei clique ran wild, I stayed at home to mourn my parent's death. Have I hurt anyone?" He raised his voice. "You make groundless accusations. It's true that I was acquainted with Wei Zhongxian, but that was to prevent attacks on scholars of the Donglin Party. Why do you scold me?" He composed himself and pointed to Wu Ciwei and his friends. "How dare these frivolous young men start rumors here!"

On hearing this the young scholars at the ceremony became indignant. They shouted, "How dare this shameless man curse us at the Temple of Confucius. Let's teach him a lesson."

"Beat the traitor!"

"Slap his face!"

"Grab his beard!"

The scholars surrounded Ruan Dacheng, grabbed his beard and beat him badly. Ruan Dacheng ran away, holding his head with his hands.

As he ran off Wu Ciwei raised his voice and said, "We did well today. We avenged the men of the Donglin Party and brought credit to the Imperial Academy. From now on we should work together with one heart to prevent such shameless people coming back."

All the scholars supported him.

CHAPTER FIVE

Ruan Dacheng Tries
to Climb Up Again

RUAN DACHENG WAS not an ordinary man. Although the scholars had beaten him at the Temple of Confucius he had no intention of changing his ways; instead he planned revenge. He knew that to carry out his vendetta, he had to take up an official post and regain power. Night and day he thought of possible ways. Finally an idea came. He rented a large mansion in Kusifang where he established an elegant garden with several pavilions. There he kept a number of well trained, young and pretty actresses.

The opera troupe was expensive to maintain, but Ruan Dacheng decided to use it as a stepping-stone for his career. He curried favor with powerful officials by offering bribes to the greedy and providing actresses to those fond of beautiful girls. When the opportunity came he would use these favors to regain power.

One day when he was lost in thought, a servant handed him a letter from someone wishing to hire his theatrical troupe. Ruan Dacheng looked at it and was surprised to find that the hirer was

Chen Dingsheng, a famous young scholar in Nanjing. His servant said that Chen's messenger had told him that Chen Dingsheng, Fang Mizhi and Mao Pijiang were drinking wine at the Jiming Temple. The three young men wished to see Ruan's new opera *The Swallow's Love Note*. Ruan Dacheng realized that it was a good opportunity to show his talents. He said to the servant, "Go upstairs right away, pick out the best stage properties and tell the actors and actresses to make up immediately. Go with them to the temple to take care of everything."

Soon everything was ready. As the theatrical troupe was about to set off, Ruan Dacheng whispered to the servant, "You must listen to what the three scholars say and report it to me in detail." The servant, his reliable agent, nodded his head.

After they had left, Ruan Dacheng went to his study and sat at his desk. He then poured wine into a cup, and began to drink. He was in a good mood because the famous scholars still remembered him.

After a while, Yang Longyou paid a visit. Ruan Dacheng was famous for his poetry and sung verse while Yang Longyou was good at painting and calligraphy; the two men of letters had a good relationship. Yang Longyou knew that Ruan Dacheng had written a new opera *The Swallow's Love Note* and was eager to read it. During the past few days he had been so busy that he had not had time to visit him. Now that he was free he had taken a leisurely walk to Ruan's residence. He passed the Yonghuai Hall before the janitor had time to tell Ruan that he had arrived. At the study he saw Ruan reading an article. "Brother Ruan, don't work too hard," Yang boomed, "You must take good care of yourself!"

"Oh, it's you, Brother Yang." Ruan Dacheng came out of the study to greet him. "Please take a seat."

"Why do you stay at home by yourself on such a beautiful spring day?"

"My new opera *The Swallow's Love Note* will be sent to the press soon. I'm revising it."

"Oh, I came here to see the same masterpiece."

"I'm sorry to say that my theatrical troupe is away right now."

"Where has it gone?" Yang Longyou was surprised.

"A few young scholars have hired it." Ruan Dacheng wanted to keep Yang guessing and Yang Longyou had no choice but to say, "Then let me read your script while we drink wine."

The suggestion made Ruan Dacheng very happy because he already had wine and food prepared. Yang Longyou drank the wine and read the script. He lauded Ruan's work, and this made Ruan very happy, although he pretended to be modest: "Please don't laugh at it. It's not good enough."

The servant from the Jiming Temple walked in and said, "The three scholars have watched three scenes and the wine has gone ten rounds. All of them are full of praise."

On hearing this Ruan Dacheng could not help shouting, "Wonderful! They really know how to appreciate good work! What else did they say?"

"They said Your Lord is a gifted scholar. Your work is extraordinary."

"Oh, they really said that? What else did they say?"

The servant added exaggerated details to please his master. "They said that, as for literary talent, Your Lord should rank first in the world of letters."

It made Ruan Dacheng happy, but he pretended to be unsatisfied. "They flattered me. You go back to the temple and continue listening to what they say." The servant left. Smiling from ear to ear, Ruan Dacheng gave a toast to Yang Longyou and said proudly, "It is surprising that these young scholars know me so well."

"Who are these scholars?" Yang Longyou asked.

"They are Chen Dingsheng, Fang Mizhi and Mao Pijiang, all outstanding scholars, and they seem to admire my work," Ruan Dacheng said delightedly.

"They never give praise without reason. *The Swallow's Love Note* is a good work indeed..."

Before Yang Longyou had finished speaking, the servant returned. Ruan Dacheng was expecting more praise, but the servant said that though the young scholars praised his literary talents, they denounced him bitterly as an adopted son of the eunuch clique who used his powerful connections to bully people.

Hearing this, Ruan Dacheng flew into rage and said, "Damn, how dare these young villains curse me?"

"Why do they pick on you?" Yang Longyou asked.

Ruan Dacheng did not know what to say. He chattered for a long time then said, "I must find a way out or I will never be able to face people." While speaking he stood up, rubbed his hands and walked up and down sighing, but could not find an answer. He turned towards Yang and said, "What shall I do then?"

CHAPTER SIX

Ruan Presents Dowries
to Hou Chaozong

THE FORMER COUNTY magistrate, Yang Longyou, knew that Ruan Dacheng longed for power but was down on his luck. Nonetheless, he was still wealthy. Some of the scholars belonging to the Restoration Society were keen on courtesans. Why not get him to use his money to curry favor with them? He saw an opportunity with Ruan.

"Brother Ruan, I have an idea that may solve your problem but I'm not sure that you will agree."

"If Brother Yang is willing to help, I'll agree," Ruan Dacheng replied.

"Brother Yang, Wu Ciwei is the head of young scholars and Chen Dingsheng is the leader of the young masters. If both Wu and Chen let the matter drop, all the others will end their nonsense," Yang said.

Ruan Dacheng rubbed the table and stood up saying, "That's a good idea! But who's going to convince the pair?"

"Only Hou Chaozong from Henan can do it. He is an intimate

friend of Wu Ciwei and Chen Dingsheng. They always follow his advice."

"Who will convince Hou Chaozong then?" Ruan Dacheng asked anxiously.

Yang Longyou told Ruan Dacheng of his plan. "I discovered that Hou Chaozong was bored to tears in Nanjing. He wants a beautiful girl to keep him company. I have found the right one for him. Her name is Xiangjun. She is both pretty and skillful. It's a certainty that Hou Chaozong will fall in love with her at first sight. If Brother Ruan is willing to spend money to establish a good relationship with him, he will argue your case to Wu Ciwei and Chen Dingsheng."

Ruan Dacheng clapped his hands and shouted, "Wonderful! A really good idea." After thinking for a while he said, "As a matter of fact, our friendship spans two generations. His father and I passed the imperial examination at the same time. I should do something for him. But how much money will be needed?"

"Two hundred taels of silver will be enough for a dowry and a banquet," Yang Longyou replied.

Ruan Dacheng agreed readily. "No problem. I'll have 300 taels of silver sent to your residence and leave you to take care of it."

Yang Longyou thought that he had settled the matter and raised his wine cup. Ruan Dacheng, who finally saw a way out of his predicament, raised his as well. Both of them were very happy. After drinking his fill, Yang Longyou took his leave.

CHAPTER SEVEN

Hou Meets Xiangjun
for the First Time

THE WAR IN north China made it impossible for Hou Chaozong to return home. Lonely and bored, he wanted to visit the brothels in Nanjing but had no money. Although Yang Longyou had mentioned Xiangjun several times, Hou Chaozong had not dared visit the brothel to see the charming girl.

It was the time of the Pure Brightness Festival, which coincided with the warmth of spring. The city was transformed by the season and captivating scenery. Hou Chaozong, fed up with loneliness, threw down his book and walked out planning to visit Xiangjun in a brothel.

On the street he heard someone calling from behind. "Master Hou, where are you going?" He turned and saw Liu Jingting walking towards him, and invited him to come along with him. Soon they came to the bank of the Qinhuai River.

"That is the Waterside Pavilion and the Long Bridge. Let's slow down." Liu Jingting led the way. "The old brothel is quite close. A lot of famous courtesans live in that lane over there."

Following Liu Jingting's directions Hou Chaozong entered the lane. Red apricot branches spread over the pink walls and he heard the cries of flower sellers. He could not help saying, "It is quite different. Each household has a black door and tender willow branches."

Liu Jingting pointed and said, "That taller house is Li Zhenli's home."

"Where does Xiangjun live?" Hou Chaozong asked.

"She is Li Zhenli's daughter. She lives there with her."

"Wonderful, I just want to see her now that we chance to be here." Hou Chaozong's spirits rose and he thought that it was a good omen.

Liu Jingting came to the door and knocked. Someone inside answered saying that Li Zhenli and her daughter had gone to a box party at Bian Yujing's home.

Hou Chaozong knew nothing about box parties and asked Liu. Liu Jingting was tired after the long walk and sat down on a stone block in front of the house. He said to Hou Chaozong, "Famous courtesans from various brothels are sworn sisters, just like some men are sworn brothers. On festive occasions the sworn sisters get together, each bringing a box of fresh food. They taste each other's food, exchange cooking tips, and play musical instruments."

Hou Chaozong was pleased, "Oh, it must be interesting. Do they invite guests?"

"No, no!" Liu Jingting waved his hand. "They are afraid of the guests disturbing them. They lock the door and allow guests to watch performances from downstairs only."

"What would a guest do if he was fond of one of the courtesans?" Hou Chaozong asked.

"He may throw something upstairs. The courtesan he picks will throw fruit back to him. Then she will walk down to make an appointment," Liu Jingting explained.

"That's the way it is. We'd better go there and have a look."

Liu Jingting stood up and led the way. Hou Chaozong noticed that each household grew poplar and willow trees as well as colorful flowers. Limpid water ran under the bridges and the melodious sound of the xiao [a vertical bamboo flute] came from the deep lanes. The pair soon arrived at the Warm and Green Building, Bian Yujing's residence. In the doorway they ran into Yang Longyou and Su Kunsheng.

"How could Brother Hou condescend to come here? It's most unusual, most unusual!" Yang Longyou pretended to be surprised.

"I heard that Brother Yang went to see Ruan Dacheng. It's a surprise to meet you here!" Hou Chaozong teased back.

"Brother Yang comes here for you, Brother Hou." Su Kunsheng answered for Yang Longyou. Liu Jingting, who knew nothing of the affair, interrupted them and the three men sat down.

Soon Hou Chaozong stood up to look at the house, "How wonderful the Warm and Green Building is, but why can't we see Xiangjun today?"

Yang Longyou knew what Hou Chaozong was thinking. "Xiangjun is upstairs," he said.

"Listen," Su Kunsheng said. "They are playing musical instruments."

They also heard the elegant songs that the instruments accompanied. Hou Chaozong was so excited that he took a pendant from his fan and threw it upstairs. Soon cherries wrapped in a white silk scarf were thrown down.

"Who threw that?" Hou Chaozong asked anxiously. "How nice it would be if it were Xiangjun."

Yang knew quite well who it was. "I guess this white silk scarf belongs to Xiangjun."

No sooner had Yang Longyou said that than Li Zhenli appeared leading Xiangjun. Both gentlemen were surprised and overjoyed. Yang Longyou introduced them to Hou Chaozong.

Hou Chaozong said, "I'm Hou Chaozong from Henan and have long admired you. Today I'm truly fortunate to meet you." Hou Chaozong saw that Xiangjun was beautiful, and said over and over again, "Brother Yang, you have been a good judge."

Li Zhenli allowed the guests to sit down. They were served tea and other dishes. Soon, they began playing wine-drinking games. Su Kunsheng let Li Zhenli take over while Xiangjun held the wine cup. Li Zhenli did not decline; it was a rule in the brothel that the procuress gave orders. Then she said, "We shall take turns to drink wine. Each person drinks all the wine in the cup and then shows their talents. Here are the topics: the first is cherry; the second, tea; the third, willow; the fourth, apricot blossoms; the fifth, the pendant of a fragrant fan; the sixth, a snowy silk scarf." Then she turned to allow Xiangjun to cater to Hou Chaozong. "Xiangjun, drink a toast to Master Hou." Xiangjun poured a cup of wine for Hou Chaozong and another for herself; both emptied their cup.

Li Zhenli threw the dice on the table and called, "It is the pendant of a fragrant fan." She stared at Hou Chaozong and said, "Master Hou, drink this cup of wine and then say something."

Hou Chaozong drank the wine and said, "Let me compose a poem." He stood up while the others clapped. In a low voice he recited:

> The breeze of beauty in south China,
> Does not hide in the sleeve.
> Following the young man's fan,
> It will sway and give out a fragrance.

"A good poem! A good poem!" Yang Longyou exclaimed.

Liu Jingting knew that Xiangjun's nickname was Lesser Fan Pendant and he teased her. "A fragrant fan's pendant! Don't spoil it while swaying!"

Li Zhenli hurriedly changed the subject. "Xiangjun, prepare a cup of wine for Lord Yang!"

Yang Longyou took the cup and drank the wine. Then they drank in turn and enjoyed themselves.

But after a while Hou Chaozong stood up and said, "I've drunk enough wine. I must leave now."

Liu Jingting knew what Hou was thinking and stood up. "It's a rare chance for a gifted scholar to meet a beauty." Holding Xiangjun with one hand, and Chaozong with the other he said, "You're a born couple. Why don't you drink a cup of heart-to-heart wine?"

Su Kunsheng who also wanted to see the pair engaged stood up and said bluntly, "Xiangjun is very shy. I have to ask you, Master Hou, would you accept an engagement with Xiangjun? We spoke of it the other day."

"How can I refuse? Can a scholar refuse to be the best in the country?" Hou Chaozong answered excitedly.

When she heard that Hou Chaozong was to be promised to Xiangjun, Li Zhenli said, "If my daughter is to be united with the socially elevated, could you please pick an auspicious day?"

Yang Longyou, who had already chosen a day for them, said that the 15th day of the third lunar month would be best. But Hou Chaozong said that it was very hard for him to arrange for a dowry in such a short time. "Don't worry," said Yang Longyou, "I've arranged for a dowry and an engagement banquet."

Everything was settled and they left.

CHAPTER EIGHT

Hou United with Xiangjun

DAYS FLEW AND Li Zhenli waited anxiously. She was not young and would have to rely on her adopted daughter, Xiangjun, for the rest of her life. It had been hard to find the right man for Xiangjun, who was beautiful but haughty. Li Zhenli had arranged everything with great care. But still a lot of work had to be done; she had to prepare a big banquet and invite the guests. She hurried to finish her make up and went into the sitting room shouting to her male servant, "Bao'er, where are you? Come here!"

Bao'er walked in slowly, waving a palm fan. His languor angered Li Zhenli.

"Today is a day of great importance for our young lady. Distinguished guests will arrive soon, but you're still dreaming. Roll up the curtains and clean the house right now." Then she walked around the house, instructing her servants on this or that. The House of Enchanting Fragrance was bustling with activity.

While she was occupied, Yang Longyou walked in. He wore brand new clothes and was followed by several porters carrying gifts from Ruan Dacheng. He had made up his mind not to mention Ruan Dacheng's name on this occasion. He was familiar with the building, pushed open the door, walked straight to the sitting room and asked in a loud voice, "Where is Zhenli?"

Li Zhenli was so busy that she had not seen him enter. Hearing his voice, she turned and said, "Lord Yang, I'm very grateful for your services as a go-between." She saw Yang Longyou had arrived alone and asked, "Why has Master Hou not come?"

"He will come soon," Yang Longyou comforted her with a smile. He beckoned the porters in, and they carried cases of ornaments and clothes to the sitting room. "I have prepared several cases of clothes for Xiangjun as gifts. Please take them." The cases were sent to the bridal chamber.

"You are extravagant. Thank you very much."

Yang Longyou took a red package from his sleeve and gave it to Zhenli. "Here are 30 taels of silver for the banquet. Please ask the kitchen to prepare their best dishes and supply wine." Li Zhenli was overjoyed and thanked Yang Longyou again and again. "We really don't deserve this. Xiangjun, come here immediately!"

Xiangjun had risen early and taken extra care over her make up. She looked exquisite. Hearing her mother's call, she entered the room.

"Lord Yang gave you many presents. You must thank him."

Xiangjun bowed to Yang Longyou gracefully. Waving his hand Yang Longyou said, "They are mere trifles, hardly worth mentioning. You should not bother."

Just then Hou Chaozong arrived. He wore brightly colored clothes and Bao'er who saw him shouted in a loud voice, "The New Master has come!"

Yang Longyou walked to the gate to greet him. "Congratulations, Brother Hou. Xiangjun is an extraordinary beauty. I have prepared the dowry and the banquet. I hope you will enjoy yourself."

Hou Chaozong was very grateful. "You're most considerate, Brother Yang. However can I thank you?"

Yang Longyou bowed and Bao'er came to serve them tea. Yang Longyou asked, "How is the banquet coming along? Is everything ready?"

"Everything is ready," said Li Zhenli.

Yang Longyou was relieved. He stood up to take his leave. "Today is your day of happiness, Brother Hou. I must not stay long. I take my leave now and tomorrow I'll congratulate you on the happy occasion."

"Why don't you stay?" Hou Chaozong asked.

"It's not convenient, just not convenient." Yang Longyou stood up and walked towards to the door.

With the help of Bao'er, Hou Chaozong began to change his clothes.

Li Zhenli excused herself saying that she had to prepare for the banquet and help Xiangjun dress. After she had left, Ding Jizhi, Shen Gongxian and Zhang Yanzhu, some of the brothel's clients and their literary friends, entered the house and came to the room. They saluted and congratulated Hou Chaozong. He returned the salute and said in a friendly way, "Please excuse me today."

Just then some of Nanjing's famous courtesans headed by Bian Yujing arrived. Bian Yujing was very fond of Xiangjun. When she saw the bustle in the hall she thought that the ceremony was being held up and shouted, "Master Hou is here. Let's ask Xiangjun to come out!"

Li Zhenli heard her in the backroom and hurried upstairs to help Xiangjun, who was already dressed, to come down. Shen Gongxian, Ding Jizhi and Zhang Yanzhu played music to welcome her. Suddenly the room was filled with the sounds of *sheng* [a reed pipe wind instrument], a *xiao*, and *gongs* and drums. Surrounded by happy music, Hou Chaozong and Li Xiangjun saluted each other.

It was a rule of the brothel not to have a formal ceremony. After the courtesan viewed her man, it would soon be followed by a feast. Hou Chaozong and Li Xiangjun took the place of honor at the feast with men sitting to the left and women to the right. They sang, played musical instruments, recited poems and blew flutes while Bao'er served wine to everyone.

Smiling happily and holding wine cups, Hou Chaozong and Li Xiangjun looked at each other. To the laughter of clients and friends and courtesans, Hou Chaozong and Xiangjun drank the first cups of wine. Hou Chaozong felt pleased and fell into a reverie because the scene reminded him of Du Mu, a famous poet of the Tang Dynasty (618-907), who frequented the brothels in Yangzhou, and was known for his literary talents as well as his beautiful women.

In the meanwhile, Li Xiangjun thought to herself, "I'm only a girl driven to prostitution. Today I'm fortunate to receive a scholar as handsome as Hou Chaozong. He may not treat me as a concubine and may make me his wife eventually." She was happy, yet concerned.

Li Zenli's clients and literary friends, who often visited the brothel, were fond of making fun of the courtesans. Today with plenty of wine and food they were too excited to pay attention to Chaozong and Xiangjun. Ding Jizhi reminded them, "Look out of the window, the sun is setting. It's late. Let's send the lovers to the bridal chamber."

Shen Gongxian disagreed, "There is no hurry. Master Hou is a gifted scholar. Today he gets an unrivaled beauty. He has drunk wine. Now he should compose a love poem."

Zhang Yanzhu said that it was a reasonable idea. He spread a piece of paper on the table and began to rub an ink stick against an inkstone.

Hou Chaozong knew very well that he must comply and said, "I don't need the paper. I have a palace fan with me. I will write a poem for Xiangjun on it as a token of my love."

"That's a good idea!" the others said. Hou Chaozong walked to the table, bent down and wrote a poem on the fan. It read:

A red building is located in a sloping lane,
Where the nobility and scholars often go by cart.
The Qingxi River is lined with lily magnolia trees,
Which are not as attractive as peach and plum
flowers.

"A good poem! A good poem!" The guests were profuse in their praise and a bridal poem written by Yang Longyou was delivered to Hou Chaozong. Master Hou unfolded it and read:

Li Xiangjun was an unsurpassed beauty
And an elegant girl hidden by dress and sleeve.
Just like the goddesses of Mount Wushan

Who waited to meet Prince Chu in their dreams.

"Lord Yang is most affectionate," said Hou Chaozong, smiling.

Soon all the people at the banquet realized that it was late. Special music played by trumpeters sent the new lovers to the bridal chamber. Each of the other customers found his lover to enjoy.

CHAPTER NINE

Xiangjun Denounces Ruan

THE FOLLOWING MORNING Yang Longyou went to The House of Enchanting Fragrance. The gate was closed, and the courtyard silent. A male servant cleaned a stool outside. As a frequent guest of the brothel, Yang Longyou knew everyone. He shouted to the male servant, "Bao'er, go to the new couple's window and tell them I have come to congratulate them."

"They're not up yet. They went to bed late last night. Why don't you go home and come back tomorrow?" Bao'er teased Yang Longyou.

Yang Longyou didn't mind Bao'er's joke and said with a smile, "Stop the nonsense! Go quickly."

Li Zhenli, who was already up, called out, "Who's there Bao'er?"

"Lord Yang is here to offer his congratulations," Bao'er answered.

Li Zhenli quickly opened the door and went out to welcome Yang Longyou. "I'm most grateful to Master Yang for finding such a good man for my daughter."

Yang Longyou asked if the lovers were up. Li Zhenli answered, "No. They went to bed very late. Please take a seat, Master Yang, I'll wake them."

"Don't worry, it's unnecessary!" Yang Longyou said, but Li Zhenli woke them. While waiting in the sitting room Yang Longyou thought: They stick to each other like glue and want to stay in bed. I gave them such pleasure.

"That's interesting!" Li Zhenli said as she walked in. "Lord Yang, don't you think it interesting? They helped each other to dress, then looked at each other in the mirror. They have washed and dressed but remain in each other's arms. Lord Yang, you're not a stranger. You go in and bring them out."

Without hesitation Yang Longyou followed Li Zhenli to the bridal chamber where he bowed to Hou Chaozong, congratulated him and asked, "What did you think of the bridal poem I wrote last night?"

"Wonderful!" Hou Chaozong said with a smile.

"You must have composed an excellent one yourself?" Yang Longyou queried.

"I wrote a hurried poem. I wouldn't dare to show it to you," Hou Chaozong said modestly.

"Where is it?" Yang Longyou had to praise the poem before broaching the subject that was utmost on his mind.

Xiangjun took the fan out of her sleeve and handed it to Yang Longyou.

"Oh, written on a fan." Yang Longyou sniffed the fan and remarked on its fragrance. Then he unfolded it and read the poem. "It is wonderful. Only Xiangjun is worthy of it." He returned it to Xiangjun and told her to put it in a safe place.

Yang Longyou looked at Xiangjun and said, "Look, Brother Hou, Xiangjun is truly beautiful. You are blessed with good fortune, how else could you have such a beautiful lady?"

At first the young lovers flirted and ignored Yang Longyou, then Li Xiangjun said seriously, "Master Yang, though you're a relative of General-Governor Ma Shiying, you're not very well-off. How could you spend so much money to help someone in a brothel? I need to know so that I can repay you. I feel most uneasy accepting such expensive gifts"

Xiangjun's words struck a chord with Hou Chaozong. "What she says is reasonable. We met by chance, like patches of drifting duckweed. I feel uncomfortable about accepting such generosity."

Yang Longyou was not surprised to hear this. He said, "Let me tell you the truth. The dowries and banquet cost over 200 taels of silver. They were all paid for by a man from Huaining."

"Ruan Dacheng from Huaining of Anhui Province?"

"That's right." Yang Longyou felt embarrassed.

"Why did he spend money on me?"

"He only wants to be your friend."

Hou Chaozong recalled what he knew of Ruan Dacheng. "He passed the imperial examination at the same time as my father and knew him. But I despise him and have broken off relations for a long time. I don't understand why he did me a favor."

Yang Longyou hoped that his explanation would persuade Chaozong to forgive Ruan Dacheng and said, "Ruan Dacheng used to be a student of Zhao Nanxing and was one of us. Later after protecting the Donglin Party he sought refuge with Wei Zhongxian. To his surprise, when the Wei clique was crushed, members of the Donglin Party regarded him as an enemy. Recently the scholars from the Restoration Society have fiercely attacked him. A few days back they even insulted and beat him. Ruan Dacheng had many friends but no one has defended him; his background makes everyone suspicious. Everyday he has looked at the sky, cried bitterly and said, 'Brothers attacking brothers, how sad it is!' He says that you are only one who can save him and earnestly wishes to make friends with you."

Yang Longyou was a good speaker and Hou Chaozong was moved. "So that is what it's all about! Ruan Dacheng appears to be sincere. I feel some sympathy for him even if he did belong to the Wei clique. If he repents and mends his ways, we should welcome him; his crimes can be forgiven. Dingsheng and Ciwei are intimate friends of mine. I'll discuss it with them when we meet tomorrow."

Yang Longyou was pleased. "If you do, it will be good for us all."

Xiangjun had listened to Yang Longyou carefully and realized his true character. He was no better than a hired agent speaking for Ruan Dacheng. She refused put up with it; she stood up and said to Hou Chaozong, "What did you say, my dear. Ruan Dacheng is a shameless cur of treacherous court officials. All the people, women and children included, spit on him and curse him. Others attack him and you want to protect and save him? I would like know where you stand, Master."

The more she spoke, the more excited she became. Undeterred by the men's responses, she continued, "He paid for the dowries and for personal gain you wish to act wrongly? These ornaments and costumes mean nothing to me." She removed her hairpins and silk garments and said indignantly, "We are not afraid of being poor, but our reputation will never be soiled."

Yang Longyou was taken aback by the elegant young woman's stand. He was embarrassed and said, "Alas! Xiangjun is too tough and vehement."

After listening to the round of speeches, Li Zhenli picked up the things from the ground and merely said, "What a pity to throw out such fine goods."

Hou Chaozong felt ashamed. "All right! You have your own view and I have fallen below your standards, but we are friends and lovers." He turned to Yang Longyou. "I hope you understand me, Brother Yang. I do not like being looked down upon by women. If a courtesan of a brothel holds dear her reputation, how can I, a scholar, mix with treacherous court officials. I am loyal and enjoy great esteem from my friends in the Restoration Society. If I associated with an evil man, my friends would all turn their backs on me. I could not save myself, let alone others."

Left with no choice Yang Longyou said, "If that is so, I take my leave."

Hou Chaozong did not urge him to stay and said, "These presents belong to Ruan Dacheng. As Xiangjun will not use them there's no point in leaving them here. Please return them to him."

Hou Chaozong turned to Xiangjun who was still angry and said, "Xiangjun is a natural beauty. She'll look more lovely without pearl and jade ornaments or brocade garments." Xiangjun ignored him.

Li Zhenli was not happy. "Even so it is a great pity to give away precious things."

Hou Chaozong knew that the procuress loved money and comforted her. "Don't worry about those things. I will compensate you."

Li Zhenli was relieved and said, "Thank you."

CHAPTER TEN

A Boat Tour at
the Dragon Boat Festival

HOW TIME FLEW! The Dragon Boat Festival which fell on the fifth day of the fifth lunar month was taking place. During the festival it was the custom of each household to place cat-tail leaves on their doors to keep away evil. Everybody, men and women, old and young, would come out to view the lanterns along the Qinhuai River.

Chen Dingsheng and Wu Ciwei, two distinguished scholars of the Restoration Society, arrived at the Examination Office by the Qinhuai River. It was a scene rich in variety but they saw no members of the Restoration Society. Disappointed, Chen Dingsheng turned to Wu Ciwei. "Brother Ciwei, we were bored at the inn. We came here to enjoy the festival with other scholars. Where are they?"

"Brother Dingsheng," Wu Ciwei replied, "I guess all of them are now on the lantern boats." Pointing to a pavilion by the river, Wu Ciwei said, "That is Ding Jizhi's waterside pavilion. Let's watch the lanterns from there."

At the pavilion they lifted the curtain and climbed the steps. "Is Mr. Ding Jizhi home?" Chen Dingsheng called.

A boy attendant came out and said, "Master Chen and Master Wu, my master has gone to the lantern fair. But we have prepared wine and dishes. My master said before leaving that his guests should drink wine and feel at home."

"That is gracious of him," the scholars said happily.

"Your master is in an esthetic mood." So saying the two young scholars sat down and the attendant placed wine and food on the table. Chen Dingsheng was about to drink then put down his cup.

"This is a fine place to enjoy the lanterns but we are a select band and should keep unwanted people away." He turned and called, "Boy, bring me a lantern." He picked up a brush, dipped it into the ready-made ink and wrote eight Chinese characters on the lantern, "Only members of the Restoration Society are admitted." The attendant hung it on a high spot outside the pavilion.

"If members of the Restoration Society arrive, we invite them in," said Wu Ciwei.

"That's right. The lantern keeps out unwanted people and invites friends in," Chen Dingsheng said proudly.

The attendant leant on the railing and viewed the river scene. On hearing the sounds of drums and musical instruments he went inside, calling, "The lantern boat is coming."

Chen Dingsheng and Wu Ciwei emerged, leant on the railing and looked out. Accompanied by melodious music a small boat came towards them. Dimly they discerned four people. Chen Dingsheng stared at them and suddenly turned to Wu Ciwei. "Look, on the lantern boat, it looks like Hou Chaozong."

"It is Hou Chaozong. He is a member, let him join us."

"The lady must be Li Xiangjun. Can we invite her as well?"

Wu Ciwei said without hesitation, "It is well known in Nanjing that Li Xiangjun refused Ruan Dacheng's dowries. She acted as a friend of our society and should be invited."

Chen Dingsheng agreed. He pointed to the others in the boat and said, "That's Liu Jingting and Su Kunsheng playing the musical instruments. They refused to be Ruan Dacheng's hangers-on, and that also makes them friends of our society. It would be more interesting if we invited them too."

"I'll call them," Wu Ciwei said and without waiting for a reply shouted, "Brother Hou! Brother Hou!"

Hearing his name, Hou Chaozong raised his head and spotted Chen Dingsheng and Wu Ciwei. He placed his hands together and bowed. Chen Dingsheng invited them over saying, "We're on Ding Jizhi's waterside pavilion. Wine and dishes are prepared. Brother Hou, Xiangjun, Jingting and Kunsheng come and enjoy the lanterns with us."

"That is a welcome invitation," Hou Chaozong said, supporting Xiangjun as they climbed onto the pavilion. Liu Jingting and Su Kunsheng followed.

It was early summer, breezes blew from the river and laughter came from the pavilion as the occupants chattered cheerfully. The boy attendant, still leaning on the railing, saw dragon boats in the distance. He shouted to the people inside, "Lantern boats are coming!" As they came out he pointed and said, "The boats are magnificent! And there are hundreds of people."

The visitors peered out. The large boats belonging to the nobility were decorated with five-color corner lanterns, and equipped with large drums and trumpets. Rich merchants' boats had five-pointed gauze lanterns and carried a large number of musicians. The others with only a few musicians belonged to the literati from the National Academy.

Wu Ciwei sighed and said what the others were thinking. "Compared to the merchants and nobility, we scholars are a miserable and shabby lot." They started to make fun of each other, but Hou Chaozong changed the subject.

"It is about midnight, the dragon boats have passed by. Let's celebrate the festival by composing poems."

The three scholars talked among themselves, and then each improvised a four line verse. They drank a cup of wine. Liu Jingting beat his drum, Su Kunsheng played his *yueqin* [a four-stringed plucked instrument with a full-moon-shaped sound box], and Xiangjun linked the poems, singing them gracefully. Chen Dingsheng was so impressed that he said he would have them printed the next day.

In low spirits, Wu Ciwei, said to himself, "We sing about our feelings and they make sad music. Only a few people on the river can really understand how we feel."

Su Kunsheng tried to create a happy atmosphere and said to Liu Jingting, "An enjoyable event does not last. We should make the best use of the time and enjoy ourselves. Brother Liu, let's sing a song together. Master Chen and Master Wu propose a toast to Master Hou and Xiangjun congratulating them on becoming a couple. What do you all think?"

The others supported him and Liu Jingting said that it was a good idea.

On behalf of Wu Ciwei, Chen Dingsheng said, "Brother Wu and I have wanted to invite the new couple to a dinner to congratulate them. Today is as good a day as any." Everyone sat down.

Hou Chaozong was very pleased. Xiangjun was still indignant over the dowries so he wished to use the opportunity to appease her. He smiled and thanked his friends, and then turned to Li Xiangjun and said, "Let us drink wine from one cup again." Xiangjun nodded her head gracefully.

Master Chen and Master Wu kept urging the couple to drink while Liu Jingting and Su Kunsheng sang and enjoyed themselves.

It was midnight, the lantern boats had gone. Suddenly, one boat appeared, accompanied by songs and music played by professional musicians. The five people in Ding Jizhi's pavilion pricked up their ears and listened.

The boat was Ruan Dacheng's and it was his theatrical troupe who was playing music and singing; Ruan could not resist joining in the fun, or taking his boat out for the festival. But he had been afraid to meet the members from the Restoration Society and had waited until after midnight when all pleasure boats had gone. He had not expected to accidentally encounter them at Ding Jizhi's pavilion. When he saw the brightly lit waterside pavilion, he sent a servant ahead to see who was there.

The servant told him about the words on the lantern. Afraid that he would meet his enemies in the narrow stretch, Ruan Dacheng exclaimed, "This is terrible!" and made his followers put out the lights and stop playing. The boat turned and they moved away quietly.

On the pavilion Chen Dingsheng was very surprised at the change and Wu Ciwei asked the attendant to take a closer look.

Liu Jingting stopped him and said, "There's no need for that. Even with my blurred vision, I see it clearly. It is Ruan Dacheng's boat."

"No wonder the music was professional," Sun Kunsheng said.

Chen Dingsheng flew into rage. "How dare that old reprobate turn up in front of the Examination Office to do his sightseeing!"

"Let me pull his beard!" Wu Ciwei tried to stand up but Hou Chaozong put out his hand to stop him.

"Let it pass. We should not push too hard; he is trying to avoid meeting us."

Liu Jingting said that his boat was already far away.

Realizing that the boat had disappeared, Wu Ciwei muttered with feeling, "This time we have let him off lightly."

Xiangjun, who thought that it was very late, stood up and took her leave. They all left the pavilion together.

CHAPTER ELEVEN

Zuo Liangyu Talks of Occupying Nanjing

HOU CHAOZONG AND Li Xiangjun were still intoxicated with each other, months after their betrothal, and remained unaware of the great changes in the external world. Marshal Zuo Liangyu, the military commander of Wuchang, had caused much unrest by threatening to occupy Nanjing.

Zuo Liangyu, a native of Liaoyang in Liaoning Province, had joined the army as a young man and achieved rapid promotion but had been recently dismissed for his mistakes. He sought and received refuge with Hou Xun, the Provincial Military Commander in Changping County, Hebei Province. Hou Xun thought highly of his talents and promoted him to officer in charge of the province's military affairs. Zuo Liangyu was only 32.

At the time Zuo Liangyu was the military commander of Wuchang, a prosperous city with a large population and a place of great strategic importance in Hunan and Hubei. Through it ran the roads to nine provinces.

As commander of 300,000 troops, Zuo Liangyu was very

headstrong and only heeded Hou Xun, his benefactor. But the court had dismissed Hou Xun from his post as commander of the army and there was no one to offer him advice. He had reaffirmed his loyalty to the court, but stayed in Wuchang while others fought, claiming that treacherous court officials stopped him from fighting.

The court, however, could not provide rations for the troops or forage for the animals. Zuo Liangyu had no choice but to support the troops himself. His officers and men soon became restive.

As a born general, Zuo Liangyu was aware of the importance of discipline and training. He would gather his officers and men, and train rigorously. But on one occasion, during a roll-call, the men used this opportunity to ask for rations. Zuo Liangyu was sitting in his office he heard a disturbance outside. "Who is making such a noise?" he asked angrily.

"The soldiers are hungry and are asking for their rations," a deputy general replied.

"What? We borrowed 30 boats of grain from Hunan not long ago. Has it all gone in a month?"

The two deputy generals replied in unison, "Sir, we have 300,000 officers and men. Thirty boats of grain do not go far."

When Zuo Liangyu heard, he rubbed the table and murmured to himself, "What can I do?" He turned to the deputy generals and said, "Look, this war has left central China in a state of chaos. Jackals, wolves, tigers and leopards rise one after another, no one is willing to serve the court. Officials are incompetent, officers and men are in a state of disorder, unable to fight, we are short of provisions and the soldiers are stirring up trouble. What can I do?" Zuo Liangyu demonstrated his anger but the noise from the men outside continued. He had to find a way to alleviate the situation. He turned to his two deputy generals. "Don't blame me. We all work for the court. Over the past 300 years, the court has treated the army well. Soldiers should not make trouble. There is no grain in the depot and no money in the official warehouse. We sent people to fetch grain from Jiangxi again. Please tell them that we shall supply provisions and grain as soon as they arrive from there."

Holding an arrow-shaped token of authority, the deputy generals walked out and spoke to the soldiers. "This is an order from the marshal. Because this is a large army, it is difficult to pay for your provisions. We are in a difficult situation, but we should not forget the court's kindness, and we must obey the marshal's orders. In a few days grain from Jiangxi will arrive and we shall pay you in full. Please be patient and accept this calmly."

However, the promise came too late, and the soldiers had suffered from hunger for too long; mere talk would not calm them. They continued shouting loudly, "Pay us our provisions and give us grain!" Instead of retreating, they moved towards the office.

As a marshal, Zuo Liangyu might have disobeyed a higher authority, but he could not quell the attack of thousands of restless soldiers. To prevent them from rebelling, he allowed the deputy generals to announce an emergency measure.

"This is an order from the marshal. As soon as Jiangxi's grain boats arrive, we shall provide provisions. However, as Jiangxi is a long way away and all of you are hungry, the marshal has sent an urgent letter to Nanjing. The military department of Nanjing will convey a request to the emperor that troops from the three towns in Wuhan be moved to a location near Nanjing. There we could get food from the city. If allowed, we will go to Nanjing, the land of rice and fish. All will have enough to eat. I hope all officers and men will heed the marshal and stop the disturbances."

The soldiers although hungry accepted this. They shouted, "Good! Good!" and "Let's prepare to go to Nanjing." Then they left.

Zuo Liangyu had dispersed the soldiers but he sent no letter to Nanjing. Without an imperial decree, he dared not take his army there. The emperor had always been kind; he would not be sentenced to death during a time of turmoil, but he would be denounced by people all over the country. He racked his brains, but there was no easy answer. He could not stay and it was unwise to go. Fortunately the hungry soldiers had withdrawn and there was time to think it over.

Though they had made no preparations, everyone now knew of the plan and soldiers expressed different opinions. One petty officer said to a group, "We should discuss this. Wuhan now has the strongest force in the country. Tomorrow when we go east along the Yangtze River, no one would dare stop us. We'd better support Marshal Zuo, capture Nanjing, and holding a yellow banner, move towards Beijing. It will certainly work."

Another soldier waved his hand. "No, that's not a good idea. Marshal Zuo is loyal to the court. Don't talk nonsense, we can't do it. In my view we should just move to Nanjing to get enough to eat."

Another veteran said, "As soon as we leave Hankou for Nanjing, the country will be panic stricken. Even if we didn't attack Beijing, they will say our force threatened the court."

The provisions and funds for the army were so important that both Zuo Liangyu and his soldiers were worried about them. There was chaos brewing inside and outside of the court, and the people in central China would suffer a disaster.

CHAPTER TWELVE

Hou Writes to Convince Zuo

HOU CHAOZONG WAS still intoxicated by his happy life in The House of Enchanting Fragrance. He enjoyed the days with his lover, and spent his time visiting scenic and historical sites in Nanjing or drinking wine and composing poems with his friends. Autumn came and one day he wanted to return to hear the stories of Liu Jingting, the best storyteller in Nanjing.

Liu Jingting's talents were well known throughout southeast China. He had been an orphan and although far from home and destitute, remained an exceptional person. Some high-ranking officials and noble lords had tried to engage him as a retainer, but he was very fussy about his master. If an official or a lord was an evildoer, he would rather tell stories on the street than be attached to their household. That what why he left Ruan Dacheng.

Liu Jingting used storytelling to sing the praises of national heroes and denounce arch careerists and evil cliques. He had experienced ups and downs himself and seen the inconstancy of human relationships. His stories gave dutiful sons and loyal officials a proud and dignified end; evil people met an ignominious fate.

Most scholars in Nanjing loved to listen to him and showed great respect.

Hou Chaozong had made a reservation the day before by sending his servant boy to Liu Jingting with a deposit. After taking a nap, he walked leisurely to Liu Jingting's home but when he arrived, overheard the sound of drums and clappers. Hou Chaozong was well acquainted with Liu and, thinking someone had arrived before him, walked directly into the sitting room. To his surprise he found Liu Jingting telling a story to himself and beating the drums and clappers.

"There is no audience here. Why are you telling yourself a story?" Hou Chaozong asked.

"Telling stories is my job. I practice it whenever I can, just as you sit in your study playing *qin* and composing poems. Do you have an audience then?"

"That sounds reasonable," Hou Chaozong said.

"Young Master Hou, what story do you want to listen to today?"

"Anything that is exciting and straightforward."

"Unfortunately, Master Hou, you don't realize," Liu Jingting said with meaning, "An exciting situation begets indifference and a straightforward one always has two sides. I'd better tell you a story about a conquered nation, homeless people, patriotic generals and traitors. That will make you shed tears."

Hou Chaozong remarked with admiration, "I did not expect you, Brother Liu, to see through the current situation. It worries us all."

While they were chatting they heard footsteps. Yang Longyou rushed in. "Brother Yang, you have come at the right time. Let's listen to Brother Liu tell a story," Hou Chaozong said.

"Don't you know what's happening? How can you calmly listen to storytelling?"

Hou Chaozong was astonished. "Why are you so frightened?"

"Alas! Don't you know? Zuo Liangyu is bringing his army to Nanjing. He will wait here for a decision from Beijing. The Minister of War, Xiong Mingyu, has no idea what to do. He asked me to ask you for a plan of action." Hou Chaozong saw that the situation was critical. Yang Longyou continued, "The people, officials, gentry and merchants are panic-stricken. Minister Xiong expects you to come up with an answer." The minister had not thought of Hou Chaozong but Yang Longyou knew that Zuo Liangyu once took refuge with Hou Chaozong's father, Hou Xun, when he had been dismissed. It had been Hou Xun who had promoted Zuo Liangyu to officer in charge of the province's military affairs and served as his mentor.

Yang Longyou added, "I've known for a long time that your father is Zuo Liangyu's benefactor. If you wrote a letter to Marshal Zuo, I am certain he would give up his plan for attacking Nanjing. What do you think?"

Hou Chaozong said that it seemed a good idea but his father had resigned from his official post and has been at home for a long time. He had no power and he didn't think Zuo Liangyu would take his advice. "Moreover he lives in Guide, my hometown, over 3,000 *li* away from Wuchang. Distant water won't put out a fire close at hand."

Yang Longyou had already thought this out. "Brother Hou, you are a gallant man. Our country is in danger. How can you sit back and do nothing? Why not write a letter on behalf of your father? It is a matter of extreme urgency. You can report it to your father later. I'm sure he'll not blame you."

Hou Chaozong could not refuse and said, "All right. I'll go home and draft a copy which I'll submit to you for advice."

"It cannot be delayed. You should write and deliver it now. Otherwise it will be too late. There's no time for discussion." Yang Longyou feared that the situation could change very suddenly.

"All right, I'll write the letter here." Hou Chaozong went to a desk, picked up a brush, wrote the letter and gave it to Yang Longyou.

Yang Longyou read it with great care. Hou said that Nanjing, the former capital of China, contained the Taizu Mausoleum, and should not be wantonly trampled. Unless Marshal Zuo had good reason he should not move east but find another way of solving the problem of pay and provisions. He was known for his loyalty to the court and should reconsider twice before acting.

"It's an excellent and reasonable letter. I'm sure it will convince

Zuo Liangyu. This letter shows how capable you are."

"It should be submitted to Minister Xiong for correction before being delivered," Hou Chaozong suggested. He looked worried.

"That's unnecessary. I'll tell him later," Yang Longyou said firmly. "There's something else...," Yang Longyou mentioned.

"What is it?" Hou Chaozong and Liu Jingting asked in unison.

"We need someone to deliver the letter to Zuo Liangyu," Yang Longyou said. "The letter is confidential. We need a proper person for the task."

CHAPTER THIRTEEN

Liu Volunteers to Deliver
the Letter

LIU JINGTING, WHO had stood by and listened quietly, stepped forward and said, "Don't worry. Let me deliver it."

Yang Longyou was unsure. "It would be good if you could go but there are many passes on the way to Wuchang. It's not an easy route."

Liu Jingting pressed his case. "I not only have extraordinary physical strength but I am very resourceful in an emergency."

Hou Chaozong was also worried. "I know that Zuo Liangyu maintains tight discipline. It's not easy for an outsider to enter his camp. You're old and it will be difficult for you to get access to him."

"Master, trust me. As a storyteller, I am very familiar with the method of rousing somebody to action. Though I'm old, I can do the job. You're good at writing a letter and I can deliver it as well as I can portray a battle with words or describe how to get pearls from the sea. I swear I'll deliver it into the hands of Zuo Liangyu."

Yang Longyou could not help admiring Liu Jingting's confidence. "Wonderful! But only if you can explain the contents of the letter clearly, can you do the job."

"I understand the letter pretty well. I could even fulfill the mission without it. I'll chide Zuo until he feels ashamed!"

"How would you chide him?" Hou Chaozong asked.

"I'll ask him how an army empowered by the court to stop thievery could be allowed to engage in it." Jingting replied with assurance.

Hou Chaozong felt great respect for Liu Jingting. "Wonderful! What you say is clearer than my letter. That is quite penetrating."

Yang Longyou felt relieved. "Pack up. I'll send you some silver. You must leave Nanjing tonight." Liu Jingting nodded, bowed and went to his inner room.

"I didn't realize that Liu Jingting was such a versatile person," Yang Longyou said.

"I always thought he belonged to our group. Story-telling is just one of his many skills," Hou Chaozong replied.

Liu Jingting set out that very night. Braving the wind and snow, he walked along the side of the Yangtze River. At Wuchang, instead of staying at an inn for the night, he found an empty place to change his clothes, and there he put on his boots and hat. He was ready to deliver the letter.

At the beginning, he could not find the military camp and had to ask several people. He realized the importance of the letter; he knew he could afford no mistakes, so instead of going directly to the camp, he walked around inspecting it. Two soldiers passed and Liu quickened his steps to draw near and hear what they were saying.

The shorter soldier was singing: "Those who executed thieves got the thieves' wallets; And those who saved the people occupied the people's houses. An official is in charge of the granary; And one soldier gets the grain for three."

The taller soldier said, "That's wrong. It's out of date."

"Sing the right one for me then."

"The situation has changed. It should be like this: Thieves are fierce, leaving no wallets; The people run away leaving empty houses;

the official is poor without grain to supply; thousands of soldiers have no food to eat."

The shorter one agreed and sighed deeply. "It seems that poor soldiers like us will go hungry."

"It looks like that."

"When we appealed to the marshal for food, he said that we could go to Nanjing to get it. Nothing has been said about that in the past few days; maybe he has changed his mind."

"There's nothing to worry about. If he changes his mind, we shall go back and appeal," the taller one said.

Just then Liu Jingting came over and bowed by placing his hands together in front of his chest. "Excuse me, could you tell me where the marshal's office is, please?"

The shorter soldier whispered to the taller, "His accent is from the north of the Yangtze River. He must be a deserter or a rebel."

The taller had an idea. "Let's steal his money to buy a meal."

They agreed and went over to tie Liu Jingting up with rope. Liu Jingting had not expected this and shouted, "Alas! Why are you arresting me?"

"We're patrolling officers of the Wuchang military camp. Who else is there to catch besides you?"

Before they had finished, Liu Jingting shot out first with one hand, then with the other, throwing the two soldiers on the ground. He said with a smile, "You're two blind beggars, both famished."

"How did you know that we are hungry?"

Liu Jingting saw that the topic could be used as a way to see the marshal in person and replied, "I would not have come here if you weren't."

"Have you transported the grain from Jiangxi for us?"

"Of course. What else?"

"Alas! We are blind. We'll carry your luggage and send you to the marshal."

They arrived at the headquarters and the soldiers pointed to the mansion. One said, "That is the marshal's residence. You wait here and I'll beat the drum to announce you."

As soon as it was done, an officer walked out and asked if they had any military information. The soldier who had beaten the drum said, "We have a suspect. He said that he had escorted grain here but we're not sure that he's telling the truth. We escorted him here to let you deal with him."

The officer turned to Liu Jingting and asked, "You escorted grain here? Do you have an official document?"

"No, but I do have a letter," Liu Jingting answered calmly.

"That makes it suspicious. Without the document there can be no grain. You could be a deserter or a thief."

Undaunted Liu Jingting replied, "You are wrong. Would I dare come here if I were a deserter or a thief?"

The officer found this reasonable. "I'll present the letter to the marshal."

"It is confidential. I must present it in person," Liu Jingting replied. Given no option the officer reported to the marshal.

Zuo Liangyu sat lost in thought. The disturbance over food had occurred the day before. He knew that he could not lead his men to Nanjing and that he should wait for the grain to arrive from Jiujiang in Jiangxi. Just then he heard that the man who had escorted grain from Jiangxi had arrived. Happy with this news, Zuo asked, "Which local government's document does the grain escort hold?" On hearing that the escort had only a letter, he thought that something was wrong. Officers and men were prepared and the visitor was allowed to enter.

Liu Jingting walked in to see two rows of guards holding weapons. Calmly and fearlessly he walked past the spears and battle axes. He bowed instead of kneeling to the marshal.

"Please forgive me. I am not familiar with the military code. I have a letter for you and hope that you will read it carefully."

Zuo Liangyu, surprised at the man's equanimity, asked, "Who is it from?"

"It's a letter from Mr. Hou of Shangqiu."

Zuo Liangyu said, "Mr. Hou is my benefactor. How do you know him?"

"I work at Mr. Hou's residence."

"I'm sorry I didn't recognize you. Where is the letter?"

Liu Jingting handed the letter to the marshal with both hands. When he saw the envelope, Zuo Liangyu invited Liu Jingting to sit and the gate of the mansion was closed. After reading it, Zuo Liangyu sighed. "I, Zuo Liangyu, am loyal to the court. I would never betray the court or let my benefactor down."

He explained the circumstances. "You would not have known that, after roving rebel bands swept through and set fire to it, Wuchang became an empty city. My army is stationed here but hungry soldiers cause disturbances day and night. I have great difficulty keeping them under control."

Liu Jingting stood up. "That is quite unreasonable. Since ancient times the soldiers have always followed the general. How can a general be controlled by soldiers? Who else makes a decision if you are not in a position to decide?" Liu Jingting threw down his teacup, which made Zuo Liangyu angry.

"How dare you throw the teacup on the ground!"

Liu Jingting smiled. "I dare not be impolite. I threw it on the ground without thinking."

"Without thinking? Does your heart make decisions?" Zuo Liangyu was still angry.

"If my heart could make a decision, I would not allow my hand to do it."

Liu Jingting looked at Zuo Liangyu thoughtfully. Zuo Liangyu understood the point and said with a smile, "What you say is reasonable but my soldiers are so hungry that they have to forage for food themselves."

"It was a long way here and I'm hungry myself. Why does Your Highness have to discuss it now?"

"Alas! I'd forgotten!" Zuo Liangyu asked his subordinates to set the table.

Liu Jingting kept touching his stomach saying, "I'm hungry! I'm hungry!"

Zuo Liangyu told his men to hurry up but Liu Jingting rushed towards the inner room.

"I can't wait any longer. Let me go inside to eat."

Zuo Liangyu was very angry. "How can you go to my inner room?"

"I'm starving," Liu Jingting replied.

"You're starving. But who allows you to enter my inner room?"

Liu Jingting burst out laughing. "The marshal also knows that even if I'm starving, I should not go to your inner room."

Zuo Liangyu saw the parallel. "Ha, ha. You make fun of me. What a silver tongue! I really need a man who dares to criticize my faults frankly."

From that day on Zuo Liangyu let Liu Jingting stay in the camp and they discussed ancient and current affairs together. The question of going to Nanjing was put aside for the time being.

CHAPTER FOURTEEN

Ruan Dacheng Frames
Hou Chaozong

AFTER SENDING THE letter to Zuo Liangyu, the authorities in Nanjing adopted other measures. The government submitted a petition to the emperor asking him to promote Zuo Liangyu and to appease him by offering official posts to his descendants. Also the governors and governors-general of nearby provinces and all of Nanjing's officials gathered at the Qingyi Hall to find a way to gather sufficient food to feed the hungry soldiers at Wuchang.

Yang Longyou had been dismissed from office but was invited to attend because he had contributed by persuading Hou Chaozong to write a letter. Ruan Dacheng, who was skilled at ingratiating himself with those in authority, came also and they arrived at the Qingyi Hall earlier than the others.

Carrying his official notice, Ruan Dacheng was tremendously proud of himself and when he saw Yang Longyou he said excitedly, "Brother Yang we have been invited to discuss military affairs and we should have a say."

Yang Longyou said with indifference, "It is an important matter and we don't have official titles. We'd better listen to the discussion."

Ruan Dacheng appeared annoyed and raised his voice. "How can you say that? We must take state affairs most seriously. Emperor Taizu made Nanjing the country's capital. Now it is in great danger. We should look at the likelihood of hidden traitors when considering the troops of Wuchang."

Yang Longyou was astonished. "You should not make irresponsible claims."

Ruan Dacheng became more indignant. "I've heard about it. Why can't I mention it?"

Just then the Governor-General of Huai'an, Shi Kefa, and the Governor-General of Fengyang, Ma Shiying, arrived. The Minister of War, Xiong Mingyu, was absent because he had gone to the Yangtze River to call the roll of officers and to assign tasks according to an imperial decree. Ma Shiying was worried and said, "The military situation is critical but we can't discuss it without the minister. What shall we do?"

Shi Kefa was anxious also. He said that although old, weak and feeble he would defend Nanjing at any cost. Yang Longyou went over to comfort him.

"Mr. Shi, don't worry too much. Zuo Liangyu used to be a subordinate of General Hou Xun. A few days ago, General Hou wrote a letter to Zuo Liangyu to persuade him to give up the plan. I think Zuo Liangyu will accept his advice."

"I heard about that. Though it was Minister Xiong's idea, it originally came from you," Shi Kefa said.

Ruan Dacheng interrupted, "I haven't heard about it, but I have heard that there is a person in Nanjing who colludes with Zuo Liangyu."

Shi Kefa asked who it was and Ruan Dacheng replied that it was none other than Hou Chaozong, the son of Hou Xun. Shi Kefa did not believe him. He knew that Hou Chaozong, a distinguished scholar, belonged to the Restoration Society and would never do such a thing.

Ruan Dacheng tried to further implicate Hou Chaozong, "Your

Highness would not have known that Hou Chaozong corresponded with Zuo Liangyu. If we don't do something soon, he will surely become an agent."

Ma Shiying, who was sitting nearby, agreed with him. "That sounds reasonable. We should not let him endanger the people of Nanjing."

Shi Kefa rejected the idea. "Mr. Ruan has been dismissed from his post and should not make irresponsible remarks. This story has been fabricated." He ignored them and went off in a huff.

Rebuffed, Ruan Dacheng, said to Ma Shiying, "I have a conclusive evidence. I heard that the person who delivered the letter for Hou Chaozong is Liu Jingting."

At this, Yang Longyou stood up and said, "Please don't wrong an innocent person. It was I who invited Liu Jingting to deliver the letter. I stood by while Hou Chaozong wrote it. He wrote it with great sincerity. How can you suspect him?"

Ruan Dacheng knew that this was true, but he persisted. "You don't understand, Brother Yang. Hou Chaozong used a code in the letter."

Ma Shiying believed him. He nodded his head and said, "You're right. Hou Chaozong should be executed. As soon as I return to my office, I'll have him arrested." He beckoned Yang Longyou, "Brother-in-law, let's go together."

Yang Longyou declined, "You go first. I'll follow."

Ruan Dacheng, who wished to ingratiate himself with Ma Shiying, bowed at the waist and said, "I'm a good friend of your brother-in-law. I've heard much about your great political achievements and I'm fortunate to have met you. Could you please spare me a few minutes? I have much to tell you."

Ma Shiying, who shared some of his interests, said happily, "I've admired you for a long time. I need your help." The pair went off together.

After they had left, Yang Longyou said to himself, "Ruan Dacheng makes a false charge against an innocent man." He remembered that Li Xiangjun had refused Ruan Dacheng's dowries. That was why he persisted; he was trying to destroy him. Yang Longyou decided to inform them immediately.

It was dusk and the shadows had lengthened when he arrived at The House of Enchanting Fragrance. From the yard came the sound of traditional stringed and woodwind instruments. With all his strength he knocked on the door shouting, "Open up quickly!"

Su Kunsheng came to the door and was pleased to see him. "It is Master Yang. Why do you come so late to indulge in pleasures?"

Without replying Yang Longyou asked for Brother Hou.

"Xiangjun has learned a new *qu* [a type of verse for singing] and Mr. Hou is listening to her singing it upstairs."

"Tell them to come down immediately."

Yang Longyou was flustered and looked irritable. Su Kunsheng ran upstairs to ask Xiangjun and Chaozong to come down.

Chaozong walked down smiling broadly. "Brother Yang, you're in such a good mood that you seek entertainment at midnight."

"Brother Hou, you haven't heard. You're in great danger."

On hearing this, the couple became alarmed. "What's the danger?"

Yang Longyou told them about the meeting.

Hou Chaozong was frightened. "I've never had anything to do with Ruan Dacheng. Why does he do this?"

"You shamed him by refusing his dowries. He is angry."

Afraid that she may be incriminated, Li Zhenli urged him to go to somewhere far away. Hou Chaozong understood right away and said that it was a reasonable request, but he looked at Xiangjun and sighed. "How can I part with Xiangjun?"

Unlike her adopted mother, Xiangjun was not afraid. Her thoughts were of Chaozong's safety and she agreed that it would be best if he were to leave Nanjing. Earnestly, she said that it was not the time to think of love.

"You're right," he said. She had earned his respect by refusing Ruan Dacheng's dowries and at this critical moment she calmly advised him to go away. Chaozong admired her even more. However, his hometown was far away, the flames of battle raged everywhere, and he said, "Where shall I go?"

Yang Longyou had thought about it and said that he had an idea. "The Governor-General of Huai'an Shi Kefa tried to defend you at the meeting and said that he had a good relationship with your father. Why don't you go to his residence to wait for the letter from home?"

Chaozong was most grateful and thanked him.

Xiangjun went upstairs to pack for him then returned. Chaozong tried to comfort her, "It is only a temporary parting. You must take care of yourself, we'll meet again."

Xiangjun wiped away her tears and said, "The flames of war are everywhere. We may never meet again."

Li Zhenli saw their reluctance to part and urged Chaozong to leave: "The soldiers could arrive at any time." Su Kunsheng knew where Shi Kefa lived and volunteered to escort Chaozong to his home at Yinyuan Garden in the city proper.

After they had gone, Li Zhenli held Yang Longyou's sleeve. She was deeply worried and asked what would happen if the soldiers came to arrest Chaozong the next day.

Yang Longyou comforted her, "Don't worry. Hou Chaozong has gone and it has nothing to do with you."

CHAPTER FIFTEEN

Zuo Is Shocked at
the Changed Situation

ZUO LIANGYU STAYED in Wuchang for two reasons. The first was that the emperor sent an imperial envoy, Huang Shu, to make him a grand mentor and his son, Zuo Menggeng, a regional commander. The second was that the Governor-General of Jiujiang, Yuan Jixian, had personally escorted 30 boats of grain to Wuchang and the troops remained peaceful.

He was very pleased to see Huang Shu and Yuan Jixian and immediately arranged a banquet for them at the Yellow Crane Tower. As the host, he went there early, surrounded by his subordinates. Huang Shu and Yuan Jixian had not arrived yet, and Zuo Liangyu leant on the railing, enjoying the scenery. Dongting Lake stretched out wide ahead of him and the Mount Yunmeng towered majestically in the distance. The three towns of Wuhan were the doors to southwest China and he felt proud of being charged with defending such an important place. He wanted to speak to someone and said to a soldier, "It's dull having to wait for them here! Please ask Master Liu to come to the tower for a chat."

315

Liu Jingting was waiting below. When he heard Zuo Liangyu call him, he immediately climbed up the tower. Zuo Liangyu asked an attendant to serve the storyteller a cup of good tea. Liu Jingting began to beating his drum and took up his clappers to continue a story that he had started the day before. When Liu Jingting told the story about Qin Qiong, a hero of the Tang Dynasty, Zuo Liangyu sighed with emotion.

"I, Zuo Liangyu, rendered meritorious service in the border areas. I was very brave--the equal of 10,000 men. Now I am getting old and grey, but the roving bandits have not been wiped out. The thought of it makes me uneasy."

Just then a soldier called out, "Marshal, the two lords have arrived!"

Liu Jingting withdrew quietly as Huang Shu and Yuan Jixian climbed up the tower. Zuo Liangyu met them at the entrance. They bowed to each other and Zuo Liangyu said, "We are greatly honored to have you here. Food and wine have been prepared and I invite you to enjoy the river scenery."

Huang Shu and Yuan Jixian said together, "I've long been looking forward to meeting you. I'm very happy to meet you now."

After the exchange of conventional greetings, they sat down. They were about to raise their wine glasses when a man delivering a report on state affairs ran in.

"A report for the marshal, an imminent disaster!"

The three immediately put down their wine and stood up.

"What's the matter?"

"A report for the marshal. For three days a large group of roving bandits surrounded the capital. There were no relief troops and they broke through the city gate. They set fire to the palace and the emperor hanged himself on Coal Hill."

They were shocked, "When did it happen?"

"On the 19th day of the third lunar month."

When they heard the report, the attendants in the tower knelt facing the north and wailed bitterly. Zuo Liangyu, who had just found favor with the emperor, was devastated. He stood up, wringing his hands, then walked back and forth shouting, "Your Majesty, my master! I, Zuo Liangyu, am far away. I should have lead my troops to save you. I am guilty of a crime for which I deserve to die 10,000 deaths!" All his subordinates shed tears.

At this moment Yuan Jixian, who had kept calm, waved his hand and said, "Stop this behavior! There are important things to be discussed."

Zuo Liangyu did not understand the sudden change and Yuan Jixian said forcefully, "Beijing is lost. The country has no emperor. If Marshal Zuo had not kept the flag flying, the country would be in chaos. How can we regain control of the nation?"

The gravity of the situation dawned on Huang Shu, who nodded his head and pointed to the area stretching out beyond the front of the tower. "Jiujiang, Wuchang, Jingzhou and Xiangyang make up half of the country. If roving bandits capture them, they will be very hard to recover."

Yuan Jixian and Huang Shu convinced Zuo Liangyu who said that it would be his responsibility to appease the local people. He said, "As a marshal I am duty-bound, but I hope you will help me defend the country's territory."

They both agreed to follow him.

A memorial ceremony for Emperor Chongzhen was then held on the orders of Zuo Liangyu. The three formed an alliance in front of the emperor's memorial tablet. Marshal Zuo announced, "Today an alliance is formed and we become sworn brothers. Lord Yuan will be my military counselor, and Lord Huang will be the army supervisor. I, Zuo Liangyu, will work hard, train my troops and defend the territory with my life. Once the crown prince, or another prince, is restored at the imperial court, I will go north to support him." The others backed him and agreed that they would go to Wuchang, if required, at any time to discuss state affairs. Then Yuan Jixian left for Jiujiang and Huang Shu for Xiangyang.

CHAPTER SIXTEEN

Ma Supports Prince Fu
as Emperor

AFTER HOU CHAOZONG had sought refuge with Shi Kefa the two of them left Nanjing for Huai'an. Time flew! Six months passed since Hou Chaozong had arrived. Shi Kefa, a townsman of Hou Chaozong and a former student of his father, was very kind to him.

Shi Kefa had been a successful candidate in the highest imperial examination in the last year of the reign of Emperor Chongzhen when there was much unrest in the country. He had once served as provincial superintendent. Finally he had been promoted to governor-general of Huai'an. A month earlier he was appointed Minister of War for Nanjing to replace Xiong Mingyu who had been summoned to Beijing. After the promotion, Beijing fell to the "roving bandits". Fortunately the Yangtze River to the north of Nanjing acted as a natural moat and was safe for the meanwhile. However, with no emperor installed, the country was in utter confusion. Some supported one prince and others would have welcomed another. Shi Kefa drilled his troops by the river then returned to his residence where he was chatting to Hou Chaozong. "Brother Hou, today I heard what could be good news. Though Beijing has fallen, the emperor is safe. He went south by sea and the crown prince traveled south by back roads. Whether it true or not I do not know."

Chaozong was not convinced. "If it is true, it is fortunate for the country."

Just then a soldier reported that a letter had arrived from Ma Shiying and a messenger waited for a reply. Shi Kefa took the letter, opened it and began to read. He frowned and said to Hou Chaozong, "Ma Shiying wishes to support Prince Fu, Zhu Yousong, as emperor." He sighed and continued, "He says that it was true that the emperor hanged himself. No one knows where the crown prince is. Even if I don't support him, he will encourage Prince Fu to ascend the throne." He thought for a moment and said, "Allowing him to be emperor would accord with the imperial family's rules of seniority. I'll write saying that I agree to the proposal."

Hou Chaozong stood up, stepped forward and said firmly, "What you say is not right. Prince Fu's fief is my homeland. I know him well and he is not the right person."

When Shi Kefa asked him why, he said that Prince Fu had committed three major crimes: "For a start, he once plotted to murder the crown prince, which would have allowed him to succeed to the throne himself. He would have usurped it if high-ranking officials had not stopped him. Secondly, he extorted a large amount of gold and silver but when the 'roving bandits' were approaching Henan, he gave nothing to help the army and thus, the country was conquered. He has also seized the palace property and treasures to feather his own nest. Thirdly, Prince Fu took refuge in Huaiqing when his father Changxun was killed. During the chaos, he forced a girl to marry him. How could such a person ascend to the throne?"

Shi Kefa nodded. Hou Chaozong gave an analysis of the situation: "First, it is not known whether the emperor is alive or dead; second, even if the emperor had died, the crown prince may be alive; thirdly, if the imperial family's rules of seniority are not adhered to in selecting an emperor we must choose a person of extraordinary ability; fourth, any of the warlords may declare himself emperor while the country is in a state of confusion and fifth, evil officials could manipulate the new emperor because of their support. Therefore, we should not decide rashly."

Shi Kefa was convinced. "Brother Hou, your opinions make sense. Could you please write a reply to Ma Shiying giving the three major crimes and the five reasons?"

Hou Chaozong took little time writing the reply, which was quickly handed to Ma Shiying's messenger.

At this moment a servant walked in to announce the arrival of Ruan Dacheng. It had been Ruan Dacheng's idea that Prince Fu should be the candidate. He had sneaked out of Nanjing during the chaos to see Prince Fu in Jiangpu. Then he crossed the Yangtze River to return to Nanjing the same night and had lost no time in promoting the advantages of Prince Fu becoming the emperor to Ma Shiying. What worried him was that the Minister of War, Shi Kefa, would not agree. He allowed Ma Shiying to write the letter and came himself at midnight to convince him.

He had tried many times to get the doorkeeper to report his arrival and finally the doorkeeper had given in.

"Master. Ruan Dacheng has come to see you."

"Why does he come so late at night?" Shi Kefa wondered.

"He must be here to discuss the new emperor." Hou Chaozong said.

Shi Kefa resolutely refused to meet him. "He is the man who accused you of spying last year in the Qingyi Hall. He is a former member of the eunuch party and a real villain. Let him go."

A soldier drove Ruan Dacheng away. This upset him and he said to himself, "Shi Kefa holds the seal of the Ministry of War. He is so stubborn. What on earth can I do to convince him?" Suddenly he recollected with a smile, "Hah, no one knows where the emperor's jade seal is. What use can the seal of the Ministry of War be?" He looked at Shi Kefa's residence and shouted, "Old Shi, I came to send you a plate of buns stuffed with meat, but you refused them. You'll regret it some day!" He burst out laughing and left.

Ruan Dacheng reported to Ma Shiying as soon as he returned. Ma Shiying was very concerned that his backing of Prince Fu as emperor would not succeed. He knew that Shi Kefa had military power and could cause difficulties. He decided to act on his insecurities, and with Ruan Dacheng's agreement, contacted generals Liu Zeqing, Huang Degong, Liu Liangzuo and Gao Jie. The four were so eager to take the credit that they agreed to gather their military troops at Jiangpu on the 28th day of the fourth lunar month. Ruan Dacheng also convinced officials such as Duke Wei, Xu Hongji, Director of Ceremonies, Han Zanzhou, and the Supervisor of the Ministry of Personnel, Li Zhan, and Chief Investigating Censor, Zhu Guochang. They appointed Ma Shiying as their leader and misrepresented certain officials and officers by adding their names to the list of those who supported Prince Fu. On the day that Prince Fu ascended the throne Ma Shiying wore court costume and Ruan Dacheng served as temporary master of ceremonies. They had ridden their horses directly to Jiangpu to welcome Prince Fu to Nanjing.

On the first day of the fifth lunar month in the 17th year of the Chongzhen reign, Prince Fu went to pay homage at the mausoleum of Zhu Yuanzhang, the first emperor of the Ming Dynasty. As soon as he returned to the palace, he found officials and officers in court costume, led by Ma Shiying, Huang Degong and Liu Zeqing, who held a petition and advised him to ascend the throne. Supported by Ma Shiying and his followers, Prince Fu, Zhu Yousong, became the regent emperor.

As it was a fait accompli, Shi Kefa fell into line with other court officials. Prince Fu was very pleased; he would supervise the court and handle all state affairs.

Ma Shiying and his followers did not care whether Prince Fu called himself regent emperor or the new emperor. Their only concerns were their own interests and so they all conveyed the same message to him. "A long life to Your Majesty! Now that you are emperor we will faithfully follow your orders. However, we are faced by a formidable foe and should recover the lost land as soon as possible. There is much to do and Your Majesty must appoint all officials and officers without delay."

Prince Fu knew perfectly well what they were after and said, "Your concerns over the recovery of land indicate your loyalty to the court. As to filling official posts, I have already made arrangements.

There will be an imperial decree announced later." The officers and officials left the palace.

Soon an eunuch came and read the decree in a loud voice: "Ma Shiying, Governor-General of Fengyang, who proposed the new emperor's accession to the throne, has rendered outstanding services. He is promoted to Grand Secretary of the Grand Secretariat and Minister of War. He will enter the Grand Secretariat to handle these affairs. Minister of Personnel, Gao Hongtu, Minister of Rites, Jiang Yueguang, and Minister of War, Shi Kefa are all promoted to members of the Grand Secretariat, and still hold their own posts. Gao Hongtu and Jiang Yueguang will enter the Grand Secretariat to handle state affairs, and Shi Kefa will go to the north of the Yangtze River to serve as the chief military commander. Other officials and officers will be promoted by three classes. The regional commanders of the four towns Huang Degong, Gao Jie, Liu Zeqing and Liu Liangzuo will be promoted from counts to marquises, and go back to their respective posts. All those who contributed to the emperor's coming to the throne may be enrolled in different ministries."

The promotions made the officials and officers very happy. Shi Kefa, who thought he could contribute by recovering lost land, spoke to Huang Degong and Liu Zeqing.

"As Minister of War I am ashamed that we cannot recover the Central Plains. Now that the emperor has put me in charge of troops north of the Yangtze River, I will use the opportunity to render services to the court. I wish to see both of you. Let's get together at Yangzhou on the 10th day of the fifth lunar month to discuss relevant affairs. We cannot delay it and we should work hard." The new marquises happily agreed. Shi Kefa headed for his new post.

As Huang Degong and Liu Zeqing were about to leave, Ma Shiying called them back. He walked up to them and holding their hands said, "The emperor was kind enough to offer us high official posts. As senior officials and officers, we should be in contact with each other often to exchange information. Only by doing this can we guarantee our wealth and rank."

The two generals understood him and promised to do what he told them.

After the officials and officers had gone Ma Shiying started laughing. "I'm the prime minister. What a happy event!" Though he had driven Shi Kefa out of Nanjing, he knew that Gao Hongtu and Jiang Yueguang would be in the Grand Secretariat and he would have to make sure that they could not seize power. He decided to go to the Grand Secretariat rather than return home.

He was still happily reflecting on his success when he heard, "My congratulations to you on becoming prime minister." He looked up and saw that it was Ruan Dacheng.

"Where have you been?" he asked.

"I stayed in the court to hear the news."

Since his wish had come true, Ma Shiying saw no further use for Ruan Dacheng and said, "Ordinary people are not allowed here. Today is the most important day for the new emperor and you should not stay. You'd better go."

Ruan Dacheng was cunning and said that he had only a few words to say. He walked up and whispered, "You were promoted to prime minister because of your contribution in the emperor's accession to the throne. I also rendered services. Why didn't the emperor promote me?"

Ma Shiying had no choice but to say, "An imperial decree was announced. Those who rendered services in welcoming the new emperor may be enrolled by different ministers."

Ruan Dacheng was happy to hear it. "Wonderful, I hope Your Highness will recommend me."

"Don't worry. I'll take care of you." Ma Shiying made a few casual remarks and prepared to leave but Ruan Dacheng said, "It should not be delayed. I'll come with you to the Grand Secretariat to see if I have a chance."

Ma Shiying found that he could not get rid of him and said, "As a new member of the Grand Secretariat, I am not familiar with my work. You could give me a hand, but you must be careful."

Ruan Dacheng was eager to start his official career again and was pleased. Acting like Ma Shiying's footman, he wormed his way into the Grand Secretariat; soon, power would make him arrogant again.

CHAPTER SEVENTEEN

Four Defender-Generals Vie
for Positions

AFTER THE 10TH day of the fifth month of the lunar
year, Shi Kefa sent for Hou Chaozong to get his opinions and
suggestions on the reorganization of his forces for a plan to restore
the state. Hou Chaozong naturally went along with Shi's plan,
but warned that Gao Jie, the general garrisoned at Yangzhou and
Zhengjiang, worried him. Gao was arrogant and his men conceited.
The other generals Huang Degong, Liu Zeqing and Liu Liangzuo
resented him deeply. If they were at odds it would be to the enemy's
advantage. Shi Kefa knew of the friction and was ready to mediate.

While Shi Kefa was exchanging opinions with Hou Chaozong,
the four defender-generals came to pay their respects to him.
Shi saluted each in turn and said to them, "I have been asked to
command the forces in the area. You are marquises, not ordinary
soldiers." After saying this, he gestured for them to take their seats.

Gao Jie who was very self satisfied took the first seat so that
Huang Degong, Liu Zeqing and Liu Liangzuo had to sit down one
by one. Huang scowled at Gao. Shi saw the incident, but continued

persuading them to make a joint effort.

Huang became enraged as he listened to Shi. "With the marshal here, I should not quarrel…" He pointed his finger at Gao and rebuked him. "You are a soldier who has surrendered to the imperial court. Why did you take the first seat today?"

Gao took umbrage at his words and said, "I was the earliest to come over to the imperial court and am the oldest. Why should I sit after you?"

Liu Zeqing joined in the fray saying to Gao, "We are guests in your land. If you don't know how to treat guests how can you command your forces?"

Liu Liangzuo said bluntly that Gao had enjoyed the fruits of his high position in Yangzhou; it was their turn today.

Gao roared that he would give more than he received, if they dared take him on.

Huang immediately stood up. "Who wouldn't dare." He gestured to Liu Zeqing and Liu Liangzuo. "Come on, let's fight with him and see who is the better." He stepped forward angrily.

Shi Kefa attempted to defuse the argument and said to Gao, "They are right. You ought to humor them a little."

Gao refused, saying, "I would rather die than make a concession."

Shi Kefa felt angry and discouraged. "You are wrong. I am depending on you to recover the land but you wish to compete among yourselves. It is ridiculous to engage in an internal struggle when there are bigger battles at stake. I find this very discouraging." Shi ordered the three governors to return to their stations and wait for further commands. He said to Gao, "You are garrisoned in this station and will act as my vanguard. In these circumstances they would not dare return for a further quarrel." Gao Jie had no option but to comply.

Before this had been announced there was a disturbance outside. Huang Degong had taken the lead and backed by Liu Zeqing and Liu Liangzuo called for Gao Jie to come out.

Without a word to Shi, Gao Jie went out and strongly rebuked them, "You come in daylight with swords, you rebels."

Huang answered, "Why are we rebels? We've just come to kill

you, a discourteous man."

"You dare take liberties in front of the residence of our marshal. You are the discourteous ones." Gao refused to back down but the swords of the three generals convinced him and he retreated inside the inner gate crying for help. "Help me, Master Shi. The three have entered your residence to kill me."

The generals came to the outer gate and stopped. Shi Kefa heard the cry and knew that the generals were at each other's throats. He felt it would be easier to eliminate the Manchu Army than to unite his generals. He asked Hou Chaozong to read an official proclamation and Hou went read at the outer gate:"Your attention, I am an advisor to the marshal and have been commanded by him to warn the three generals. There have been changes at the imperial court, but enemy forces have not been eliminated. We should work for the benefit of the imperial court. If you do not keep this in mind, it will destroy the overall plan. After the central plains are recovered, you will be rewarded. Today the situation is urgent and you must keep the overall plan in mind. You should understand this and unite with each other. General Gao Jie was originally stationed in Yangzhou and Tongzhou. Today he will stay here to be the vanguard of the marshal. General Huang Degong goes back to Luzhou and Hezhou, General Liu Zeqing goes back to Huaiyin and Xuzhou and Liu Liangzuo goes back to Fengyang and Sizhou. You will wait there for further commands. This is an order and you will obey it, or be punished according to military law."

When he had finished, Huang declared, "We just came to kill a discourteous man; we did not intend to break any of the marshal's military laws."

"Your action in coming to the outer gate with swords today cannot be tolerated by military law," Hou Chaozong answered.

Liu Zeqing said that that was how it was. They would have to be off, but Liu Liangzuo was angry and said, "We will kill Gao Jie in his own house tomorrow." The three left.

Hou Chaozong returned to the hall and reported that although they had left, it was not over.

Shi Kefa wrung his hands, "What can I do?" He turned and saw Gao Jie who was in low spirits and standing nearby. "General

Gao, you are too full of your own importance and the cause of these quarrels. How can we recover the central plain in our current condition?"

"Don't worry, marshal. Tomorrow I will fight them and win their forces over. Then I will assist you to recover the central plain. It is not difficult."

Shi stopped him. "Invaders are coming from the north and will soon cross the Yellow River. The regional commander, Xu Dingguo, has already declared an emergency. He cannot stop them. I called the men here to discuss a solution to help him. And instead, you fought each other and ruined the plan. I am extremely worried about this situation."

"The three generals came to take the prosperous and bustling city of Yangzhou. I refused to give it up." Gao Jie still refused to admit that any blame lay with him.

"Your words are ridiculous," Shi said and sighed. He had no choice but to defend the imperial court, but it was difficult to get these arrogant generals to give way.

Hou said, "Marshal Shi, let's wait. Perhaps we can discuss it again." They went to the inner room leaving Gao alone.

The next morning Gao took his forces to the Golden Dam. The forces of Generals Huang Degong, Liu Liangzuo and Liu Zeqing went there too and then the two sides fell on one another. Accompanied by several soldiers, Hou mounted a platform where he held high the marshal's arrow-shaped token of authority. He cried out: "An edict from Marshal Shi. The revolt of the four generals results from my weak leadership. Please come to kill me in my residence and then occupy the imperial court in Nanjing. It is not necessary to fight here or cause difficulties for the local people."

Liu Zeqing immediately replied, "We are not rebels. We fight because Gao is discourteous, self-important and occupied the first seat. We want to make that clear and then see the marshal."

Gao Jie argued saying, "I'm the marshal's vanguard. Would I dare rebel? They came first and tried to kill me. I had to defend myself!"

Hou Chaozong ignored their arguments. "When you fight, you are breaking an order from the marshal, which makes you rebels.

Tomorrow I will report it to the imperial court and you will go there to explain yourselves."

Liu Zeqing's anger evaporated and he said, "The marshal was appointed by the imperial court which was established with our approval. If we disobey a military order, we rebel against the imperial court. We cannot do this. I would rather admit that we were wrong and allow our marshal to cool his anger."

"General Gao, what about you?" Hou asked.

"I am a general under the command of the marshal. I have violated military law and will submit to the punishment of the marshal."

"As you agree, go to the outer gate of the marshal's residence and ask for his forgiveness." Because Huang Degong and Liu Liangzuo had returned to their defense sectors after they were defeated, Liu Zeqing and Gao Jie went to the marshal to be punished by him.

Hou Chaozong asked the two generals to stay outside the outer gate while he went to report to the marshal. He returned and said, "All four generals used their forces without permission from a higher authority and should be punished according to military law. But Gao holds the main responsibility because he was discourteous. He should apologize to the other three generals. The punishment will be announced after the four generals are reconciled."

Gao Jie became angry. He had thought that as he was the marshal's vanguard he would have been protected. Instead he had been asked to apologize which made him feel ashamed. He felt that he did not have the marshal's trust, so in anger, he decided to leave and carve out his own territory. Without letting the others know, he took his forces across the Yangtze.

Liu Zeqing saw him and knew that he would join forces on the southern bank to fight against them. He left the marshal as soon as possible and joined Huang Degong and Liu Liangzuo to confront him.

Hou was shocked by the turn of events. He could not stop it and reported to the marshal.

After crossing the Yangtze, Gao planned to occupy Suzhou and Hangzhou, but the provincial governor Zheng Xuan defended the river with boats and guns. They stopped him, forcing him to retreat to Yangzhou. During the withdrawal he learned that Huang Degong, Liu Zeqing and Liu Liangzuo had arrived at Gaoyou to fight his force. Gao was shocked and could neither advance nor retreat. He had to request help from Marshal Shi Kefa.

Shi told him sternly that in the past he had been a mutinous soldier. "Later you surrendered and were granted a title and territories. The imperial court treated you generously. Why did you rebel just because of a few words? When you found that you could not cross the river, you came to me to ask for help. You rebel, then surrender as if you were playing a game. You should be punished according to military law. As it's not too late for you to repent, I will forgive you once again." Gao kowtowed and the marshal told him to apologize to the three generals as a way of defusing the situation. The generals, persuaded by Shi, ended the quarrel and finally left Huaiyin and Yangzhou.

Shi ordered Gao to defend the river but he was still anxious. He said to Hou, "The fate of the state rests on these defenses. General Gao is brave but not astute and we cannot afford to make a mistake. Once you often visited your home in Henan, why not go with the forces? You could supervise the river defenses and please your parents."

The arrangement suited Hou and he agreed. Shi Kefa emphasized the conditions. "You will be on your own and the situation could change; you will have to be careful. I will wait for news from you." Hou understood what Shi meant and after thanking him for his help, left with General Gao and his force for the home that he had left three years earlier. He went first to Huai'an where he inspected the river defenses and visited his parents on the way.

CHAPTER EIGHTEEN

Staying at Home Yearning for Hou

XIANGJUN WAS STILL living at The House of Enchanting Fragrance, but no longer wore her dancing costume, played the flute or sang. She remained upstairs waiting for Hou Chaozong.

She did not care what people thought of her or what happened. But people remembered her. After Zhu Yousong became emperor, he granted titles to those who pleased the imperial court. Those who received them still enjoyed liquor and the company of beautiful women. Yang Longyou was promoted to director of the Ministry of Rites for his services. Ruan Dacheng resumed his position as the chief minister of the Court of Imperial Entertainments.

Tian Yang, a townsman of Yang Longyou, was promoted to grand coordinator of the Transport Office and intended leaving the imperial court for this position. Before he left, he sent 300 taels of silver to Yang Longyou asking him to find a beautiful courtesan along the Qinhuai River to accompany him.

Although Yang was the director of the Ministry of Rites, he continued serving the rich through literary work. Tian Yang was a townsman and a powerful official who he could not refuse.

He thought of all the courtesans along the Qinhuai River and believed none compared with Li Xiangjun for beauty or singing. He decided to go to the old brothel by himself but realized that it was not a good idea. He had recommended Xiangjun to Chaozong not long ago. How could he recommend Xiangjun to another man? He thought of asking for help from his literary friends Ding Jizhi and Bian Yujing. He called in his head servant.

"What can I do for you?"

"Ask my friends Ding Jizhi and Bian Yujing to come to my study. We have important things to discuss."

The head servant hated his employer having anything to do with these literary friends and refused. "Master, I am your special servant and know famous officials. I do not know any courtesans. Where could I find them?"

Yang Longyou was not embarrassed and said, "Around the Qinhuai River." The head servant left to look for them but as he approached the door he heard a knock.

There were men and women at the door and when he asked who they were and what they wanted, an old man answered, "I am Ding Jizhi. These are my friends, Shen Gongxian and Zhang Yanzhu. We would like to see your master."

A woman standing by them said, "I am Bian Yujing and accompanying me are Kou Baimen and Zheng Tuoniang."

The servant was glad. They were the people he had been sent to fetch. He went inside to report to his master who was very pleased.

"We wouldn't have bothered you, but we come to ask for help." They all knelt down.

Yang rose from his seat to help them up. "Be seated, please. What can I do for you?"

"Is Master Ruan Dacheng of the Court of Imperial Entertainments a close friend of yours?" Ding Jizhi asked.

"Yes."

Ding Jizhi saw that Yang was candid. "We heard that when the new emperor ascended the throne, Master Ruan presented four operas to him. The emperor was very pleased and planned to choose some of us to give a performance inside the imperial court. Is that true?"

"It is true." Yang Longyou thought it a great event and there was no reason to keep it secret.

Zhang Yanzhu continued, "You know that we earn a living by singing. If we are chosen to sing inside the imperial court, who will support our families?"

Yang Longyou understood why they had come. He smiled and said, "Don't worry. Dancing for officials and urging them to drink are the business of those in the Music Office. You are famous and nobody would dare ask you to do such a thing."

They expressed their thanks together and asked to be put under his protection.

"That's all right. Tomorrow I will send your names to Ruan Dacheng and ask him to free you from the event."

"Thank you for your help and sympathy. You are a person of great worth."

"But, you can return a favor."

"What can we do for you?" Ding Jizhi was surprised.

"My friend Tian Yang will take up his position as the grand coordinator of the Transport Office soon. Recently, he sent 300 taels of silver for another wife."

Ding Jizhi asked, "Have you someone special in mind?"

"I have thought of one but I need your help."

Bian Yujing asked who and Yang Longyou said that it was Li Xiangjun.

Ding Jizhi shook his head and said, "No. I couldn't do it."

"Why?" Yang Longyou could not understand.

"She is Hou's lover. How could you ask her to marry someone else?" said Ding, incensed.

Yang Longyou persisted, saying, "Hou is not serious about Xiangjun. He has gone and left her behind, he doesn't miss her. Go ahead, it's all right."

Bian Yujing demurred. "Since Hou left Xiangjun has refused to go downstairs. There is no reason for her to marry someone else. It is pointless talking to her."

"That is true, but if the man were a better person than Hou, she would, wouldn't she?"

Ding Jizhi still had reservations. "You get along with her mother. It would be better if you talked directly to her."

Yang was embarrassed and said, "You know that it was me who introduced Hou to Xiangjun. How could I suggest another person to her mother? It would be far better for you to do it, and you'll be paid."

Ding Jizhi and Bian Yujing thought for a while and finally agreed; they bade their farewell and left for The House of Enchanting Fragrance. On the way they recalled that when Hou Chaozong and Xiangjun were engaged, they had sung and played musical instruments at the banquet. Today they were going to ask her to marry someone else, and felt shameful.

"We should not go," Bian Yujing said but Ding Jizhi was older and saw that it was more complex.

"If we did not, Lord Yang as director of the Ministry of Rites could make us servants in the imperial court. We would be asking for trouble."

Bian Yujing asked what they could do.

Ding Jizhi had a plan and said that they should discuss it with Xiangjun. They walked and talked until they came to the outside gate of The House of Enchanting Fragrance. Zhang Yanzhu, Shen Gongxian, Zheng Tuoniang and Kou Baimen, who had come another way, had arrived before them. They had come to make sure that Ding and Bian shared the fee and followed them in.

There was no one in the courtyard and Ding Jizhi raised his head and called out, "Zhenniang, please come out."

Xiangjun was sitting alone in her room lost in thought. When she heard somebody calling her stepmother, she walked out and leaned over the railing. "Who's downstairs?"

Bian Yujing answered, "Official Ding."

"Aunt Bian and Uncle Ding, here? Please come up."

"Where is your mother?"

"She has gone to dinner with her friends. Please be seated." Xiangjun gave them a cup of tea.

Bian Yujing asked, "Who were you chatting and playing with in the room?"

"Aunt, don't you know? Myself, I remain alone."

"Why don't you find yourself a husband?"

Xiangjun was amazed, "Official Hou and I are engaged. Can I change my mind?"

Ding Jizhi could not refrain from saying, "We all know your mind. Today Lord Yang entrusted us to ask you if you will agree to marry Tian Yang, a grand coordinator, who will pay you 300 taels of silver."

After hearing this, Xiangjun said sternly, "The love poem written by Hou should be valued at 10,000 taels of silver."

Bian Yujing knew that Xiangjun would not change her mind and said that she should forget it. She turned to Ding Jizhi and said, "Since it is so, let's go to tell Lord Yang."

Ding Jizhi felt uneasy and said to Xiangjun, "I hope your mother won't be bribed."

Xiangjun replied with confidence, "My mother loves me and would not force me to do what I don't want to do."

Ding Jizhi said, "That is good and worthy of respect."

Bian stood up to go.

But Shen Gongxian and the others were worried over their failure to persuade Xiangjun. Shen said abruptly, "How could you refuse Lord Yang's kindness?"

Xiangjun was resolute. "I don't care if the suitor is poor or rich. It is for me to make up my mind."

The unexpected rejection infuriated Zhang Yanzhu, Kou Baimen and Zheng Tuoniang who threatened Xiangjun but she stood firm. Ding Jizhi saw that they were unreasonable and said, "She has made up her mind. Let's go."

Bian Yujing said, "Although she is young, she has high principles." They had come on a shameful task and left feeling unworthy.

Ding and Bian turned to comfort Xiangjun. "Set your mind at rest. We will refuse Lord Yang and we will not do this again."

"My thanks to both of you," Xiangjun said and Ding and Bian left.

CHAPTER NINETEEN

Fawning on the Higher
and Oppressing the Lower

ZHU YOUSONG HAD been excessively fond of leisure before he became emperor but once he ascended to the throne, he spent far more time with courtesans and other diversions. Ma Shiying was happy that the emperor took little interest in imperial court administration; it allowed him to do what he wanted. He placed his own trusted subordinates in important civil and military posts and enjoyed power. Others looked upon him with fear.

Although the rebels were moving continuously southward, Ma Shiying believed the small imperial court south of the Yangtze River was stable and that they could live in peace. When the plum in the Wanyu Garden was in blossom, he ordered his servants to prepare a family banquet and invited friends so that they could admire the flowers. The banquet kept them together and gave him the opportunity to flaunt his power and accept their flattery.

Ma Shiying went into the sitting room and asked his head servant who had been invited that day.

"The guests are your townsmen: the director of Ministry of Rites, Yang Longyou; Capital Censor, Yue Qijie; the newly appointed grand coordinator of the Transport Office, Tian Yang and chief minister of the Court of Imperial Entertainments, Ruan Dacheng."

"Ruan Dacheng is not my townsman," Ma Shiying said.

"He always says that he is a close relative of yours."

"We get along quite well. All right, I'll make him a relative. It's already noon, bring them in."

"They are waiting in the sitting-room, all you need to do is ask them in," the servant said.

Yang Longyou and Ruan Dacheng entered the Plum Study and Ma Shiying said, "Brother-in-law Yang, you are a relative. Why didn't you come straight in?"

"Today a relative is the same as a friend in need," Yang said sadly.

Ma Shiying knew what he meant, but asked him what he was talking about. Then he turned to Ruan Dacheng, "You are close to me. Why were you waiting for my invitation?"

"It is a custom of your family. Who am I to break it?" Ruan said obsequiously.

"Don't regard yourselves as outsiders. Please be seated."

Yue Qijie and Tian Yang were not there. A servant said that Master Yue was sick and Master Tian was leaving for his new position tomorrow. After Master Tian had helped his family board the boat, he would come to say farewell in the evening.

Ma ordered the banquet to be set out and sat at the head of the table. Yang and Ruan sat in the guests' chairs.

Feigning modesty, Ruan Dacheng said to Ma, "You have had several family banquets. Who were invited?"

Ma answered ambiguously, "Some of my generation, but no more elegant than you."

Yang Longyou understood the purpose of Ruan's question and pressed Ma Shiying. "Who were they?"

Ma sent his servant for guest list and Ruan read it carefully. It included Zhang Zhensun, Yuan Hongxun, Huang Ding, Zhang Jie, Yang Weiyuan and others. Yang Longyou intentionally flattered Ma by remarking, "They are talented people who have experienced great events in the world and done good things for the people."

"I promoted all of them to higher positions," said Ma.

Ruan Dacheng immediately stood up and bowed to Ma. "We are younger and look forward to promotion. You have chosen talented people for the imperial court."

Ma was very proud. "You are different from the others. Tomorrow I will tell the Ministry of Rites to promote you."

Yang Longyou immediately stood up and thanked him. Ruan Dacheng knelt down and did the same.

Ma Shiying stretched out his hands to help him up. After a few cups of liquor, he was very happy to receive their flattery. The servants cleaned away the dishes and they talked freely, more like close friends.

After dinner there was to be a performance. Yang and Ruan, overwhelmed by the unexpected favor, signaled their boy servants. The servants immediately realized what was meant and took out money wrapped in red paper to hand to Ma's servant. Ma said that it was unnecessary, "The artists are not from the Palace Theatre so formal rules don't apply."

Ruan Dacheng was pleased and said, "My group of artists have nothing to do, why not ask them to perform here?"

Ma answered, "Forget it today. Next time when I treat guests I will borrow your group for a performance."

Yang Longyou joined in saying, "Today the plum is in blossom. Since ancient days men have appreciated flowers and beautiful girls. If the performance is not to be by artists from the Palace Theatre, we require a beautiful girl to sing for us."

Ma could not refuse this time. His servant would have to fetch a singer courtesan. The servant asked who and Ma turned to Yang and said, "Brother-in-law Yang, it is your choice."

Yang Longyou said unhurriedly that there was no absolute best but added that Li Xiangjun had recently learned extracts from *The Peony Pavilion* and they were good.

Ma sent his servant to fetch Li Xiangjun and Ruan Dacheng asked if it was true that she had turned down the newly appointed grand coordinator of Transport Office, Tian Yang, who had offered 300 taels of silver for her.

Yang Longyou reluctantly admitted that it was.

Ma Shiying was interested. "Why did she refuse?"

Yang Longyou remembered how he had acted as matchmaker, failed, and lost face to Master Tian Yang. He said angrily, "She is a silly girl. She will not marry because of Hou Chaozong. I went to see her several times and she even refused to come down the stairs. I was most disappointed."

"Is she that audacious?" Ma Shiying asked angrily.

Ruan Dacheng remembered that she had refused the gifts he sent her on her engagement and had shown little respect for his feelings. He said, "It is Hou Chaozong's fault."

Hou Chaozong's name reminded Ma of Shi Kefa's opposition to the new emperor through the "three crimes" and "five no's"; Hou's objections could well have damaged his career. He cried, "That is impossible. The newly appointed grand coordinator is unable to buy a courtesan with 300 taels of silver. It is ridiculous."

Ruan Dacheng added, "Tian Yang is a townsman of yours. It is well known that a courtesan humiliated him."

"When she arrives, I will do something," Ma said, but a servant came in and reported, "Master, I have been to The House of Enchanting Fragrance and told Li Xiangjun that you asked her to come. She said she was sick and refused."

Ma was angry but thought of his position; it was not seemly for a prime minister to be angry with a singing courtesan. He calmed down and said, "If she will not come to sing for us, you will go with some clothes and gifts to marry her."

The Ma family servants liked to stir up trouble and hurried away to prepare clothes and gifts; they wanted revenge for Xiangjun's refusal. Ruan grinned broadly. "Good, good. Your decision is most gratifying to all."

Li Xiangjun had nettled Yang Longyou but he disliked the idea. He stood up and told them that it was late and he would have to leave. Ruan wanted to stay and see what would happen, but he had to follow Yang. Ma Shiying did not ask them to stay and stood up to send them off. Yang Longyou and Ruan Dacheng made three bows with their hands clasped in front of them, then left for home.

After they had left, Ruan Dacheng said to Yang Longyou, "It was difficult for Ma to take such strong action. You'd better help him."

Yang Longyou asked him how, and Ruan, who could not see Yang's face said, "You are familiar with The House of Enchanting Fragrance. You could go there right away, pull her down the stairs and tell her to come."

"We can't put too much pressure on her."

"Longyou, from what you say, you would let her off lightly. I hated her because she refused my gifts and I need revenge."

Yang Longyou said nothing. They bade each other goodbye and went home.

CHAPTER TWENTY

Zhenli Stands in for Xiangjun

ALTHOUGH YANG LONG you was annoyed with Li Xiangjun, he was ever more angry with Ruan Dacheng's and Ma Shiying's high handed attitude. What Ma Shiying proposed was unreasonable and unfair to Xiangjun. He had introduced her to Chaozong and now it appeared that he would be responsible for their separation. He turned and walked towards The House of Enchanting Fragrance.

On the way, he met two servants who came out of the Ma mansion, one carrying gifts and clothes, the other holding a candle lantern. One said, "Both mother and daughter are alike. How will we know which is Li Xiangjun?"

"You can follow me," Yang Longyou said.

The servants were pleased and followed him. When they arrived one stepped forward and knocked. The door was opened by Li Zhenli who was shocked to see them. She asked, "Where have you been, Lord Yang?"

Yang Longyou replied, "At my brother-in-law Ma's place. I have come to congratulate you."

"Congratulate me? For what?"

"An official wishes to marry your daughter." He pointed to the servants and said quietly, "You see, there are 300 taels of silver and an embroidered suit…"

As he was speaking, Li Zhenli, who also kept her voice down, asked, "Who wants to marry her and why have the family not mentioned it earlier?"

Yang Longyou pointed at the writing on the lanterns and said, "Can you see the lanterns? They are from the Ma family."

Li Zhenli saw the two lanterns outside the gate and asked, "Does Master Ma himself want to marry my daughter?"

"No, it is Tian Yang, grand coordinator of the Transport Office and a townsman of Master Ma. Today he left for his post. Master Ma wants to choose a beautiful girl for him."

"A marriage to the Tian family has been turned down. Why do you come again?" Li Zhenli was surprised.

The servants saw that Li Zhenli was beautiful and thought that she was Li Xiangjun. They handed her the silver. "You are Li Xiangjun, aren't you? Please accept the money and gifts."

Li Zhenli was crafty and said, "Let me think inside."

The servants still thought that she was Li Xiangjun and said, "The Ma family does not give you time to think. Accept the silver, come out and get into the bridal sedan chair."

Yang Longyou realized that the servants believed that she was Li Xiangjun but did not disabuse them. He said, "She would not dare refuse. Wait outside the gate and I'll take the presents upstairs and persuade her to hurry up." The servants were glad to let him take over and dawdled outside.

Yang Longyou followed Li Zhenli into The House of Enchanting Fragrance. Li Xiangjun did not know what was happening and when Li Zhenli told her, she was quite frightened. Li Zhenli was angry and said, "Lord Yang, I thought you loved both me and my daughter. Why have you helped the others?"

"You are mistaken. It has nothing with me. After Ma Shiying heard that you had turned down Tian Yang, he flew into a rage and sent servants here to force your daughter to comply. I was afraid that you would be bullied and came to protect you."

Li Zhenli was immediately thankful. "That's so and I should thank you. Please help and protect us."

Yang Longyou, who had no idea what to do, tried persuasion. "To me, 300 taels of silver is not a bad price and it wouldn't be too bad if Xiangjun married the grand coordinator of the Transport Office. You're not strong enough to resist Tian and Ma, are you?"

He made it seem sensible. Li Zhenli thought for a while and said that he was right. She turned to Li Xiangjun. "Look at the situation. You cannot make them change their minds. It would be better if you packed your things and went downstairs."

Li Xiangjun had waited for Li Zhenli's response and became very angry. "What are you saying? Lord Yang acted as matchmaker and you held a ceremony betrothing me to Master Hou. Friends were present and know of the marriage. The gift that marks my betrothal is here…" She took the paper fan from the inner room and showed the poem on it to Yang Longyou. "This poem was written to mark the event. Lord Yang, you read it, didn't you? Have you forgotten?"

Yang deflected the question. "Master Hou has fled and you do not know where he is. If he does not come back in three years, will you wait for him?"

"I will wait three years, even 10 or 100. I will not marry Tian Yang."

Yang Longyou respected her and said, "How strong you are! You still have the same resolution as when you rejected jewelry and wedding clothes and so severely scolded Ruan Dacheng that year."

The name of Ruan Dacheng made Li Xiangjun angry again. "Ruan Dacheng and Tian Yang are followers of Wei Zhongxian. I refused to accept a dowry from Ruan but today I am expected to marry Tian Yang."

As they talked the two servants resumed their call for the bride to go downstairs. Li Zhenli had to persuade Xiangjun to go and moved forward to help her make up her mind. Xiangjun kept her mother away with the fan, but she was a thin girl and the man-servant, Bao'er, held her so that she could not move. She banged her head against the floor; blood spurted out spotting the paper fan. Then she fainted and Zhenli, shocked, asked Bao'er to prop her up and take her to the inner room to lie down.

The servants again urged them to hurry up. After trying to assure them, Yang Longyou said to Zhenli, "You know how powerful Master Ma is. If you made him angry, how would you and your daughter survive?"

"Please help us," Li Zhenli was flustered.

"We have to think of a compromise."

"Please tell us what you think," Li Zhenli pleaded.

Yang Longyou spoke slowly, "It is good for a courtesan to have a family. After marrying into the Tian family, you would have no more worries. Xiangjun has refused. Why should you not go instead?"

"Would that be all right?" Li Zhenli had not expected this.

"The servants are waiting, what can you do?"

There was no other way out and Li Zhenli agreed, but thinking again she cried out, "No, no. It won't work. I'm afraid I will be recognized."

Yang thought otherwise. He patted his chest and said, "I told them you are Xiangjun. Who knows any better?"

He was right. Only Hou Chaozong and Yang Longyou were allowed access to The House of Enchanting Fragrance. No one else could tell the two apart. Li Zhenli agreed. She prepared herself and went downstairs. The servants said, "Good, you are here. Please get into the bridal sedan chair."

"Lord Yang, we have to say good-bye." Li Zhenli was very sad and bowed her body to express her thanks.

Yang Longyou felt depressed and said, "Take care of yourself. We will meet again."

"Lord Yang, please stay here for the night and take care of my daughter." Li Zhenli still cared for Xiangjun.

"Certainly. Don't worry." Yang Longyou was a sentimental man. Assured, Li Zhenli stepped slowly out of the gate.

CHAPTER TWENTY-ONE

Painting a Fan
and Sending It Away

A MONTH AFTER Li Zhenli married Tian Yang, winter arrived. Leaves fell, a cold wind blew and travelers stayed away. Li Xiangjun had cut up her dancing shoes and ripped her dancing dress apart. The House of Enchanting Fragrance was cold, quiet, and bleak, only a white cat slept on a pillow.

Upstairs Li Xiangjun waited hopelessly for her fiancé. She was forever thinking of her time with Chaozong and was depressed. She had no idea where he was. Her mother had left and she did not know when she would come back. Grief overwhelmed her and tears rolled down her face. She had no sisters to confide in and the only sound she heard was the sound of the wind. She took out the fan that Master Hou had given her and folded it, determined to wait for his return.

One afternoon after looking at the fan with its bloodspots, she felt depressed and tired. Leaning over her dressing table she fell into a deep sleep with the fan spread nearby.

Su Kunsheng, an old artist who taught Xiangjun to sing local operas, was very fond of this female student. After Li Zhenli married, he was worried about Xiangjun and, as he approached The House of Enchanting Fragrance, he saw a young man walking in front of him. He recognized him as Yang Longyou and caught up with him. He said, "You're Lord Yang, aren't you?"

Yang Longyou turned his head and said, "Su Kunsheng, you're here too. I have been busy with my work at *yamen* and have been away for several days. Today I was with a friend in East City and came to call in on my way back."

They entered The House of Enchanting Fragrance and Su Kunsheng said that they should go up as Xiangjun refused to come downstairs. The pair made their way up quietly and saw Xiangjun sleeping at her dressing table. They tried not to wake her and sat on nearby chairs.

Su Kunsheng saw the fan and asked Yang Longyou why it had blood spots. Yang told him that it had been a gift from Brother Hou and told him how the spots had got there.

Yang picked it up, looked at it carefully and said, "The spots can be made into a picture by adding branches and leaves. But I have no green color."

Su Kunsheng said, "I'll pick leaves from potted plants and squeeze the juice. It can be used as a substitute."

Yang Longyou said, "Wonderful! That's a good idea."

Su Kunsheng went downstairs and returned a few minutes later with a wine cup of leaf juice. Yang Longyou took up the brush thoughtfully, added branches and leaves around the spots and in minutes a beautiful fan picture emerged. Su praised it saying, "Excellent! Excellent! It is a perfect picture of peach blossom."

Yang Longyou was excited by the result and cried out, "It is really a peach blossom fan."

Their laughter woke up Li Xiangjun who opened her eyes and called out in alarm, "Oh, I am so sorry. I did not know that you were here." She stood up and asked them to be seated.

Yang Longyou did not sit, but looked closely at Xiangjun. "I have been too busy to see you. The wound on your forehead has healed." He said that he had a picture fan for her and handed over his work. Xiangjun put it into her sleeve saying that it was an old fan that had been spoiled by blood spots.

Su Kunsheng smiled and said, "Without looking, you folded it. There is a picture on it that you have not seen."

"How did it get there?" Xiangjun was confused.

Pleased with himself, Yang Longyou said, "I am so sorry for altering it."

Xiangjun opened the fan and saw a peach blossom branch on it. It depressed her and she said, "The peach blossom has a short life. Thank you Lord Yang for a portrait of my life."

Yang tried to comfort her. "With this peach blossom fan in your hand, you will be sought after by a handsome young man. Unlike Chang'e [the goddess of the moon who in a legend, swallowed elixir stolen from her husband and flew to the moon] you will not wait years for a husband."

His words were well intentioned but they saddened Xiangjun. "You are wrong. Few courtesans live to marry their lover."

Su Kunsheng knew what she was thinking and asked if she would still refuse to go downstairs if Hou came back the next day.

The question cheered Xiangjun who raised her voice and said, "Then I would have a happy and comfortable life. I would go anywhere, including downstairs."

Yang Longyou praised Xiangjun's loyalty and asked Su Kunsheng if he could do him a great favor: find out where Hou was so that the lovers could be reunited.

Su Kunsheng had thought about it before. "I have tried to find Hou. I know he left for Yangzhou with Shi Kefa. Today he was sent to supervise the river defenses with Gao Jie. I'm going home in a few days and will look for him on the way. When I discover where he is, I'll let Xiangjun decide what to do." He asked Xiangjun if she would write a letter; it would make the task easier.

Li Xiangjun said that she was a poor writer and asked Yang to write one for her. Yang was not keen and Xiangjun did not insist. "This fan explains what I am thinking. Please take it to him."

Su Kunsheng thought it an excellent substitute for a letter and helped Xiangjun put it in a box. Su packed it carefully and said that he would do his best to get it to Hou.

Xiangjun was eager for him to start and Su said that he would leave as soon as possible. The two bade farewell to Xiangjun. Yang asked Xiangjun to look after herself and said that if Hou knew how faithful she had been, he would certainly come to marry her. After seeing them off, Xiangjun felt sad. She refused to go down stairs and remained by herself.

CHAPTER TWENTY-TWO

Xiangjun Speaks Her Mind
at the Banquet

R UAN DACHENG'S FAWNING behavior earned him a promotion from Ma Shiying and he became a palace provisioner. Some poets also secured important positions and to stay in favor, they composed whatever the new emperor wanted.

Ruan Dacheng knew much about opera and selected four to be performed for the emperor. Emperor Zhu Yousong was very pleased and asked the Ministry of Rites to select singers to rehearse *The Swallow's Love Note*. Ruan Dacheng thought that they might not be good enough and suggested that they invite singers, who had already performed the opera, from outside the palace. The emperor agreed and asked him to find literary men and singers from the old brothels along the Qinhuai River. With the emperor's backing, Ruan Dacheng selected courtesans who were beautiful and sang well. Yang Longyou tried to protect the ladies, but Ruan appealed to Ma Shiying who insisted on the better singers as the emperor was eagerly anticipating the new operas.

Ruan Dacheng selected whomever he wanted and as result, well-known courtesans and literary men were recruited by force.

On the seventh day of the first lunar month in 1646, Ruan Dacheng and Yang Longyou invited Ma Shiying for a drink in the Shangxin Pavilion where they could appreciate the freshly snow-covered scene.

There, they asked Ma for a final decision about the singers. Literary men and talented courtesans were being forced to sing, against their will. The well-known courtesan, Bian Yujing, did not wish to take part and said good-bye to her friends. That evening, she changed into Taoist clothes and left the old brothel to become a Taoist nun in the Dongyun Mountains.

Ding Jizhi was one of the literary men. He was about 60 years old and had not sung for a long time. How could he sing again? He had asked for Yang's help several days before and had been excused. He was wondering why he had been asked again when he was joined by Shen Gongxian and Zhang Yanzhu. When they learned of his plight they said, "We were excused too. We don't know why we are being called up."

Ding Jizhi looked at them and said, "You are young and talented and should go. I am old and in poor health. I can't expect to improve and must avoid this. I need your help."

They offered it and Ding, who knew that he would be caught if he stayed at home, changed into Taoist clothes and left for a Taoist temple.

After he had gone, Shen Gongxian and Zhang Yanzhu joined others from a brothel and went to the Ministry of Rites to be examined. While they were there, they saw Kou Baimen and Zheng Tuoniang arriving, accompanied by a magistrate. The magistrate saw three names on the summons and asked, "Why isn't Ding here?"

Shen Gongxian answered, "He has become a Taoist priest."

The magistrate checked the singing courtesans and was told that Bian Yujing had left to be a Taoist nun. He asked about Li Zhenli who should have been there and Kou Baimen said that she was married.

"That's strange. When I pulled her down the stairs, she said she was Li Zhenli. She cannot be anyone else, can she?"

Zheng Tuoniang said, "Most probably that's her daughter. She took her place by assuming her name."

The magistrate, who was just doing his job, said, "Mother or daughter, it's all the same. As long as we have the right number of people, it's all right." He hurried a woman along—it was Xiangjun, who had been pulled down the stairs. She had been told that she would be sent to learn opera singing, something she looked on as the work of courtesans.

At Shangxin Pavilion, they heard shouting and saw Ma Shiying arrive, followed by Ruan Dacheng and Yang Longyou on horseback. Their heads were held high. They dismounted and walked into the pavilion where a banquet was laid out. Ma Shiying took his seat and Yang Longyou asked for wine. Ruan Dacheng asked the singing courtesans to step forward, but Ma Shiying did not want their presence. "They are out of place at such a banquet. Let the Ministry of Rites do the work of selecting them."

Ruan Dacheng said, "They are only here for your pleasure."

Ma Shiying didn't want to disappoint Ruan and said, "Please ask the youngest to stay."

Li Xiangjun, who had come in her mother's name, was the youngest. Ruan, who couldn't tell her apart from her mother, shouted, "Come here, pour wine and sing." Xiangjun shook her head and refused.

Ma Shiying had not expected this and said, "You know no songs and yet, you are reputed to be a well-known courtesan?"

"I am not a well-known courtesan," she said and cried.

"Say whatever is on your mind, you are allowed to speak out," Ma said, feigning magnanimity.

"I am nervous and wanted to tell you several times. I have been forced to leave my husband and my mother."

"Oh, that's what you think."

Yang Longyou was afraid of the possible repercussions and said, "Today the masters wish to enjoy themselves. It's not appropriate for you to tell us about your woes."

Xiangjun continued and said frankly, "Lord Yang, you know of injustices, but it is pointless to talk about them here. You are all government officials and are expected to administer the southern areas. And instead, you neglect these duties and seek pleasure. You want me do your bidding in the cold wind and sing a song for you while you drink."

Her words touched a raw nerve and Ma shouted angrily, "Get out of here. You talk nonsense and deserve to be punished."

Ruan Dacheng added fuel to the flames. "I heard that Li Zhenli was a famous courtesan much appreciated by members of the Restoration Society. Naturally, she is unrestrained and should be punished."

Yang Longyou interceded, "She is so young and she is not the Li Zhenli you talk about."

Li Xiangjun ignored him and said angrily, "I am Li Zhenli. Do what you can with me. Members of the Donglin Party and the Restoration Society are scholars and we singing courtesans respect them. If you have taken up office, you are followers of the eunuch Wei Zhongxian."

Ruan Dacheng flared up first. "How dare you speak to us like that." He ordered the magistrates to push her onto the snow and shouted at her, "You bitch, you show no restraint in front of Grand Secretariat. You are detestable." He left the table, walked down from the pavilion and kicked Xiangjun.

Yang Longyou stood up and moved to help her up. Ma Shiying said, "Such a bitch. It would not be hard to have her put the death, but it would damage my reputation."

Yang took the opportunity to speak out. "Your reputation counts for far more than this lowly prostitute."

Ruan Dacheng was not satisfied and suggested to Ma that they keep her in the palace to perform an unpleasant role. Still angry, Ma Shiying, agreed. Yang Longyou was afraid that Xiangjun would suffer again and asked somebody to take her away.

Ma Shiying said, "She has destroyed good banquet. How detestable she is."

Ruan Dacheng bowed and apologized. "Please forgive me. I will host another banquet for you another day." And paying each other respect, the three men left.

On his way home, Yang Longyou thought that without his help, Xiangjun would suffer more. Today, she had been selected to perform in the palace and was safe for the moment. But no one was taking care of The House of Enchanting Fragrance. He remembered that his friend, the painter Lan Ying, had asked him to find a place for him to live. He could live in The House of Enchanting Fragrance and wait for Xiangjun to return.

CHAPTER TWENTY-THREE

Absurd King and Happy Officials

RUAN DACHENG KNEW of the emperor's liking
for spectacles and courtesans. He looked on his group
of literary men and singing courtesans as "capital" with which,
with Ma's approval, he could curry favor from the emperor. Shen
Gongxian, Zhang Yanzhu, Kou Baimen and Zheng Tuoniang were
not allowed to go home so that they could be summoned to sing for
the emperor.

Two days later Ruan Dacheng sat in the Xunfeng Hall, where
the imperial music was performed, and asked the singers to come
in. They entered one by one but Li Zhenli was not there. He asked
curtly, "Is everybody here? Where is Li Zhenli?"

Kou Baimen replied, "She couldn't move after falling down in
the snow. She is lying in the corridor and finds it too painful to get
up."

Ruan Dacheng intended to punish Li Zhenli and thought that
she was malingering. It angered him and he shouted, "The emperor
is coming to select roles for an opera. Can she be that stupid?"

Those who were there saw how angry he was and said that they
would bring her in.

Ruan Dacheng's hatred persisted and he said to himself, "What a detestable woman. Today, I will ask her to play an unpleasant and heavy role."

Two eunuchs with dragon fans in their hands came in. They were followed by two more eunuchs with a kettle and a box in their hands. Zhu Yousong was coming to court.

Ruan Dacheng knelt to welcome him. He hoped that the emperor had had a good day and wished him a long life. From the corner of his eye he saw the emperor frown and realized that he was unhappy. He said, "Your Majesty, there is peace and you should be enjoying pleasure. Why are you worried?"

"There is something on my mind and I think you know what it is."

Ruan Dacheng pretended not to and asked, "Are you afraid of invaders from north?"

"No, the invaders are far north of the Yangtze River, even the Yellow River."

"Are you worried about a shortage of soldiers or grain?"

"No, that is all taken care of. There are four battalions from northern Jiangsu stationed in Huaiyin, supplied by the Jiangling grain fleet."

"As you are not worried by military affairs I thought that you may be unhappy because you have no wife and there is no woman in your house."

"I have no concerns there. The Minister of Rites, Qian Qianyi, is busy selecting concubines for me. I will have them within days."

Ruan Dacheng took a step forward, knelt down and asked in a low voice, "Is it because the traitors Zhou Biao and Lei Yanzuo are scheming to make King Lu the emperor?"

"You are wrong. They have been arrested."

"Then please say what is the matter."

"You are Palace Provisioner and one of my trusted subordinates. Don't you know what is on my mind?" Zhu Yousong said.

"Excuse me, I am ignorant and wait for Your Majesty to tell me. Let me share your burden."

Zhu Yousong said, "Your opera *The Swallow's Love Note* is good. To perform it in the palace would be the most important thing that has happened since I came to power. Today is the ninth day of the first lunar month and the roles have not yet been decided. I am worried that it won't be ready before the Lantern Festival of the 15th day of the first lunar month."

"Oh, that's what is troubling Your Majesty. The opera is a minor composition. It was my fault recommending it to you." Ruan Dacheng knelt down, saying, "I will do my very best to show my gratitude to you." He moved forward and added, "But I need to know what roles the palace has not been able to fill."

"Most are filled, but we need satisfactory male and female leads as well as the clowns."

Ruan replied, "That's easy. The Ministry of Rites sent in a team of literary men and singing courtesans. They are waiting outside for you to choose." Zhu Yousong nodded his approval and Ruan asked them to come in. The literary men and singing courtesans knelt in a row waiting to be selected. Zhu Yousong said to Shen Gongxian and Zhang Yanzhu who were in front, "You are literary men, aren't you?"

"I'm afraid not, we earn a living by performing."

"You are opera performers. Have you performed roles in the new operas?"

Shen and Zhang replied carefully, "We have played roles in *The Peony Pavilion, The Swallow's Love Note* and *The Story of West Building*."

Zhu Yousong was pleased and said that they could teach the roles to those in the palace. Shen and Zhang kowtowed several times to express their thanks.

Then Zhu asked the three singing courtesans whether they could sing *The Swallow's Love Note*. Kou Baimen and Zheng Tuoniang said that they had once learned it. This pleased Zhu Yousong. He turned and said to Xiangjun, "You are young, why don't you answer my question?"

Xiangjun was unhappy but knew that she would have to reply and said honestly that she did not know the opera.

Ruan Dacheng used the opportunity to suggest that those who had learned the opera should play male and female leads. "She hasn't learned the opera so she can play the clown as it is traditionally done.

Zhu Yousong felt sorry for her, but agreed with Ruan. He asked the performers to rehearse the opera.

Ruan Dacheng picked an act from the opera and told them to try it while he directed it. The performance elated the emperor, who showed his approval by asking the eunuch to fill his wine cup many times.

When the performance was over, Zhu Yousong was still elated and stood up. He walked towards the group and said, "We will all share the pleasure together. Let's have a musical performance. What do you think?"

Ruan Dacheng, fearful that he had not tried hard enough to please the emperor, agreed. Ten types of musical instruments joined in. Zhu Yousong had the eunuch fill his wine cup three times and danced, exulting in the performance. "Girls from Suzhou, courtesans from Yangzhou, music performers from Kunshan and singers from Wuxi gathered in my beautiful hall, all for my enjoyment. I have not a worry in the world. It is, indeed, a most happy event."

He stepped forward to look at the singing courtesans, then pointed to Xiangjun and said to Ruan Dacheng, "This young courtesan is very beautiful. It is wrong to make her the clown." Without waiting for a reply, he spoke directly to Xiangjun, "You are young and do not know this opera but have you learned others?"

"I know *The Peony Pavilion*."

"That's good. Can you sing it?"

Xiangjun paused. Although Zhu Yousong had a poor grasp of government affairs, he was skilled at seeking pleasure from courtesans. He said to an nearby eunuch, "She is shy. Give her a peach fan. She can cover her face with it."

Xiangjun could not remain silent. She accepted the fan and started singing conscientiously. She had learned the opera under the guidance of famous singers and her singing was excellent. It delighted Zhu Yousong who praised her. He took several cups of wine and pointed at her saying, "This singing courtesan has a good voice and body. Her talent is wasted as a clown. She should take the female lead."

Ruan dared not disagree. He had planned to cause trouble for her and was thwarted; this increased his dislike for her.

Emperor Zhu Yousong, who was not sensitive to the feelings of others, said, "The courtesan with the dark skin, Zheng Tuoniang, can be the clown. Take her and Kou Baimen to the dramatic troupe and put them under the guidance of two literary men. You should give them some instructions too." Ruan Dacheng dared not disobey and left immediately with the literary men and singing courtesans.

Only Xiangjun remained and Zhu Yousong said to her, "You stay in Xunfeng Hall for three days and learn the opera thoroughly. Then you can join the dramatic troupe." The emperor went back to his living quarters and Xiangjun was left with tears in her eyes. When could she leave the palace? She had no alternative but to recite the script. How could she meet her fiancé again?

CHAPTER TWENTY-FOUR

Meeting in a Boat

AFTER SU KUNSHENG left Nanjing, he went to Henan to look for Hou Chaozong. At Henan, he came to the banks of the Yellow River where he saw retreating soldiers everywhere. A donkey driver told him to move away but he did not listen and soon, both of them were encircled by soldiers. The donkey was driven off and Su, an old man, was pushed and pulled by soldiers. Finally he fell into the river, which fortunately was not deep, and he held up the package with the fan crying for help.

People on a boat heard his cries and asked the boat's owner to help him. At some risk, the owner pulled the boat towards Su Kunsheng, "Hurry up and climb in."

He extended a pole and Su climbed up, cold and wet. The owner found him dry clothes and Su, very grateful, kowtowed to him. The owner said, "This woman asked me to help you, you owe her your life."

Su Kunsheng looked up and received a shock. "You are Li Zhenli, aren't you? What are you doing on a boat?"

It was a surprise for Li Zhenli. "It's Master Su. Where have you been?"

"It is a long story," Su Kunsheng heaved a deep sigh.

"Please sit down and tell me what has happened."

The owner saw they knew each other and left them chatting while he pulled to the shore to fetch wine.

Su Kunsheng sat down and told Li Zhenli about Xiangjun and his search for Hou Chaozong. When he had finished he heaved a deep sigh and said, "Aunt Li, if you are married to Tian Yang, what are you doing here?"

Li Zhenli cried and said, "Fate has been unkind. I have left the Tian family."

"Why? What happened?"

"After I arrived at the Tian family, I became the pet of Tian Yang. But his first wife was cruel and pulled me out of the bride chamber and beat me severely." Tears trickled down her face.

"Why did Tian Yang not stand up for you?"

"He was too frightened to say anything and gave me to an old soldier," Li Zhenli said angrily.

"What are you doing on a boat?"

"The old soldier is in charge of boats for delivering messages. He was sending a message when I saw you."

As they spoke to each other, they became unaware of their surroundings. A small boat approached the dock and pulled in beside them.

On it was Hou Chaozong. He was asleep in the cabin and heard voices in the night. He took no notice initially, but soon, his ears perked up when realized that the man's voice sounded like Su Kunsheng. The woman's voice was familiar too. He shouted Su Kunsheng's name.

There was an immediate response. Su Kunsheng was most surprised and asked Hou Chaozong to come over. Chaozong stepped aboard carefully. Before he sat down, Su Kunsheng said, "There is another person here that you know."

Hou Chaozong looked up with excitement.

"It's Aunt Li, isn't it? How did you get here? This is marvelous. Where is Xiangjun?"

Li Zhenli told him how Ma Shiying tried to force her to become Tian Yang's concubine. Hou Chaozong was shocked when he heard how Xiangjun had hit her head against the floor but was reassured when Li Zhenli said that she was still alive. Li Zhenli then gave an account of her own experiences. Hou Chaozong expressed sympathy and turned to Su Kunsheng.

"Why are you here?"

Su Kunsheng told him about the letter.

"Where is it?" Hou was impatient.

Su Kunsheng took out the fan and told him the whole story. Hou Chaozong wept.

Su Kunsheng then asked him why he was there. Hou Chaozong sighed deeply. Recalling the events made him angry, but he recounted them nonetheless.

Last autumn he had gone to supervise the river defenses with Gao Jie. Gao Jie had turned out to be a despot who treated people badly. He had insulted Xu Dingguo, the regional commander, by cursing him. To take revenge, Xu and his wife had hatched a plot to kill him. They invited Gao Jie to a banquet in Suizhou City and killed him. Hou Chaozong had known that they had a scheme and tried to persuade Gao Jie not to go, but he would not listen. Xu later surrendered to the Qing Dynasty in the north and moved his forces to the southern bank of the Yellow River. Hou Chaozong had left for his hometown before Gao Jie was killed.

Hou Chaozong felt deeply sad and pointed to the soldiers on the road. "Look at them. They are defeated and are looking for a way out. How can I face Marshal Shi Kefa?"

"Where are you going now?"

"I cannot stay at Henan. I have to go eastward and I don't know where I will end up."

"So that's it. Why you don't go to Nanjing and see Xiangjun? Then we can talk about where to go."

Hou Chaozong thought about it and decided to go back. He told the owner of the boat that they would leave and said good-bye to Li Zhenli. Li Zhenli was sad to leave the two men. She said, "It would be wonderful if we could live together again in the old brothel. Xiangjun is the only person absent here. When will we meet again?" Tears coursed down her face.

Hou missed Xiangjun but he had other things to think of. He and Su Kunsheng, said good-bye to Li Zhenli and went back to the boat.

CHAPTER TWENTY-FIVE

Arrested While Visiting Old Friends

AS HE APPROACHED Nanjing, Hou Chaozong felt a sense of urgency. He and Su Kunsheng had traveled day and night. Once they found a hotel, Hou Chaozong left to search for Xiangjun at the crack of dawn while Su Kunsheng looked after their luggage.

Hou Chaozong walked to her former dwelling and saw the old courtyard covered with moss. Birds sang noisily and the window coverings were partly rolled up. No one was around and he walked straight into The House of Enchanting Fragrance. As he climbed up the steps, he saw that the balustrade had been damaged and the staircase leaned to one side. Dust had gathered everywhere and cobwebs abound. When he entered a room he was surprised to find paintings hanging where rouge boxes had once stood.

A man walked up the stairs and asked him who he was and what he was doing there.

"This is my Xiangjun's dressing room. Why are you living here?"

"I am Lan Ying, a painter," Lan Ying said. "My friend Yang

Longyou asked that I live here."

Lan Ying was well known and Hou Chaozong said, "So you are Master Lan. I have heard of you. I'm pleased to meet you."

"May I know who you are?"

"I am Hou Chaozong from Henan Province. I am also an old friend of Yang Longyou."

"Oh, I have heard of you. It's a pleasure to meet you. Please take a seat and have a cup of tea with me."

Hou Chaozong was worried and upset about Xiangjun and unable to drink tea. Lan Ying told him that he heard that she had been picked to serve in the imperial court but he could not give any details.

While they were talking Yang Longyou arrived. He was surprised to see Hou Chaozong and could only add that it was not known when Xiangjun would be allowed to leave.

The news grieved Hou Chaozong who wept and sighed. He stood up and saw the broken window papers and torn curtains. The dressing table was empty--no silk handkerchief or ornaments.

The flute that hung on the wall was missing; the red silk bed roll was rolled up to one side and the water chestnut shaped mirror had fallen on the rack. The place had gone to rack and ruin and he felt saddened. He remembered that when they made their vows, the peaches were in full bloom and the building had been new. Now although the peaches were blooming, the place was dilapidated and Xiangjun was not there. Unable to suppress his feelings, Hou Chaozong wept. He said to Yang Longyou, "I will stay here and wait for Xiangjun."

Yang Longyou knew how complex the situation was and said, "Brother Hou, there is nothing to wait here for. It would be better to seek a beautiful woman somewhere else."

"How could I betray my vow? I shall not rest till I find her."

Yang Longyou saw that he could not persuade him and changed the subject. "Don't worry. Let's first look at the works of Lan Ying."

Lan Ying's painting had been commissioned by a veteran imperial guard official, Zhang Yaoxing, and was called *The Picture of a Peach Orchard*. He intended to hang it in his newly built pavilion, The Pavilion of Pines in the Wind.

Hou Chaozong looked at it for a while. He liked it and said that it was a unique and great piece of work.

Lan Ying said modestly, "I hope an expert like you won't laugh at my poor effort." He asked Hou to write an inscription to make the picture complete.

"If you are not afraid that my writing will spoil it, I will. But don't laugh at my poor performance." Hou Chaozong took up the pen and wrote:

One who originally was a man in the cave,
Finds a labyrinth that puzzles him when he
returns.
The fisherman points to an empty mountain path,
He lingers in the peach cave to avoid the Qin.

He signed his name as Hou Chaozong.

Yang Longyou studied it carefully and said, "An excellent piece. An excellent piece. The inference, however, is that I am to blame." He then described how Xiangjun had been rebuked at the banquet and how he had tried to defend her. He said that her life was spared as long as she served in the inner court. "Ma Shiying and Ruan Dacheng are in power. Although I am a friend and a relative, I cannot influence them. You are a friend of Xiangjun so it would be inadvisable for you to stay here."

Hou Chaozong knew of Ma Shiying's and Ruan Dacheng's cruelty and thanked Yang Longyou for his advice. They left together after saying goodbye to Lan Ying.

Back at the hotel, Hou Chaozong told Su Kunsheng of Xiangjun's fate and they moved through fear of being tracked down. Su Kunsheng gave a thoughtful account of their situation. "Society has changed. Court politics have become more corrupt and those in power exert a malignant influence. They seek revenge by maliciously inflicting harm. It would be better to stay away for the meanwhile and receive news about Xiangjun later."

Hou Chaozong agreed saying, "We have no relatives or friends in the prefectures or counties near Nanjing. Chen Dingsheng, an old friend of mine, lives in Yixing and Wu Ciwei is at Guichi. We could pay them a visit and avoid those who seek us out." Su Kunsheng agreed and they left at once.

Crossing the city, they approached Sanshan Street, a densely populated place. Su Kunsheng urged Hou Chaozong to hurry but Hou pointed to a signboard, Cai Yisuo Study, and said, "Dingsheng and Ciwei always stay there when they come to Nanjing. Let's ask the proprietor about them."

The study's manager told them that Chen Dingsheng and Wu Ciwei were living in a room at the back of the study. He went inside to tell them and after greeting each other, they sat down to talk and drink tea.

Ruan Dacheng, the newly appointed minister of the Board of War, arrived in Sanshan Street at about the same time. He rode in a big sedan chair and his official robe, bestowed by the emperor, was decorated with a jade python. Haughty and vain, he rolled up the curtain of his sedan chair so that the people could see him; it gave him great satisfaction. Looking around, he saw the posters in the Cai Yisuo Study and asked his subordinates to bring them.

When he also saw that intellectuals of the Restoration Society were choosing books there, he was outraged. "The Restoration Society is a remnant of the Donglin Party. The imperial government wants to arrest them. How audacious they are!" He got down from the sedan chair, walked into the study and asked his subordinate to summon the prison guard to search it and arrest anyone there. The official walked into the back apartment and dragged out Cai Yisuo. Ruan Dacheng yelled at him, "I am here to arrest rebels. How dare you give them shelter to the rebels and allow them to choose books? Confess your crime."

"Its none of my business. They came themselves. They are in the back room," Cai Yisuo said.

Ruan Dacheng had trouble suppressing his glee when he learned that Chen Dingsheng and Wu Ciwei were in his hands. They had once humiliated him and now he could reap revenge.

Chen Dingsheng, Wu Ciwei and Hou Chaozong were dragged before him shouting, "We are innocent, we've committed no crime."

Ruan Dacheng received them angrily. "You had better first realize who I am." He spoke to Wu Ciwei, "Have you forgotten that when we offered sacrifices to Confucius you chased after me and struck me?" He turned to Chen Dingsheng. "Why did you insult me on the day of theatrical performance?" Lastly he said to Hou Chaozong, "I provided money for Li Xiangjun to buy a dowry. Why did you let her throw away the ornaments?"

Hou Chaozong realized that it was Ruan Dacheng and shouted at the top of his voice, "So you are Ruan Dacheng. Today you wish to get revenge."

Chen Dingsheng and Wu Ciwei suggested that they take him outside to let others know about his embarrassing past. However, circumstances had changed, and four prison guards immediately arrested them. The three scholars were sent under escort to the *yamen*.

Cai Yisuo could not do anything and Su Kunsheng suggested that they should follow the three men to see what happened.

CHAPTER TWENTY-SIX

A Trial and an Official
Gives Up His Post

AFTER THEIR ARREST a report was compiled for
the Imperial Bodyguard, the *yamen*, The head of the *yamen*
was Zhang Wei (styled Yaoxing). He had served with the unit in
Beijing and after Zhu Yousong ascended the throne he retained his
post. The new court was corrupt and dishonest officials held power
there. One by one, honest people were ousted from positions.
Ma Shiying and Ruan Dacheng had people with dissenting views
promptly executed. Zhang Yaoxing, felt that he could not stay
in office any longer. He knew that men, such as Zhou Biao and
Lei Yanzuo, were innocent. In their case it was simply a case of a
personal vendetta, but he could not save them. This was why he
wanted to retire to his pavilion, The Pavilion of Pines in the Wind,
where he intended to live.

Four guards brought in Hou Chaozong, Chen Dingsheng and Wu
Ciwei. Zhang Yaoxing held a court hearing. He had read the official
report and said, "According to this you formed a society that planned
insurrection. You intended to bribe officials and free Zhou Biao and

Lei Yanzuo. You have been caught and unless you confess you will be flogged. If you tell the truth, you will be spared much pain."

Chen Dingsheng and Wu Ciwei said, "We are guilty of nothing. We were originally members of the Restoration Society and were only looking at manuscripts. There is no such insurrection."

Hou Chaozong said that he had come to see a friend and had just sat down when he was arrested.

Zhang Yaoxing did not know the men and their denial angered him. He hit the table with a gavel saying, "According to your pleas, you have done nothing wrong. Does this mean that I am guilty of making false charges of insurrection?" He told his men to get the instruments of torture ready. "This will make them confess," he said.

Chen Dingsheng prostrated himself saying, "Please do not be angry with us. I am Chen Dingsheng, a native of Yixing. I should not have chosen books in the Cai Yisuo Study. Apart from that I have done nothing wrong."

Wu Ciwei also kowtowed and made the same plea.

After studying the case carefully, Zhang Yaoxing saw that there was very little evidence against them. He spoke to the prison guards, "If these men intended to bribe bureaucratic officials, or planned an insurrection and formed a society for that purpose in the Cai Yisuo Study, Cai would know about it. Why did you not summon Cai Yisuo to the court?" The guards went off to fetch him.

Hou Chaozong used the opportunity and kowtowed to Zhang Yaoxing. He said, "I am Hou Chaozong of Shangqiu, Henan Province, and have come to the capital to study. I am an intellectual friend of Chen and Wu and had come to see them when I was arrested. I have done nothing wrong."

Zhang Yaoxing remembered the inscription on Lan Ying's painting, *Picture of a Peach Orchard*. He recalled the name and asked, "Are you Hou Chaozong?"

"Yes, I am."

"Sorry. I did not recognize you. You wrote an inscription on *Picture of a Peach Orchard*, and the verse showed much depth. I am obliged to you for it." He bowed slightly saying, "You are not involved. Take a seat and wait."

Hou Chaozong sat down and thanked him.

The prison guards returned and reported to Zhang that they could not find Cai Yisuo. He was at large and the door of his study was locked.

Zhang Yaoxing berated them. "You say that they plot an insurrection but offer no proof. How can I pass judgment on that?" He was thinking about it when his domestic servant came with letters from Wang Juesi, a cabinet minister, and Qian Muzhai of the Ministry of Rites.

The letters asked him to treat Chen Dingsheng and Wu Ciwei, leaders of the Restoration Society, with leniency. Zhang Yaoxing did not wish to harm the prisoners and said in a gentle voice, "I have been discourteous to you, brothers Chen and Wu. Are you a good friends of Wang Juesi and Qian Muzhai?"

"We don't know the ministers."

Zhang was surprised and asked, "If you don't know them, then why do they commend you and asked me to set you free?"

Chen Dingsheng and Wu Ciwei said in one voice: "They must be doing this for the sake of justice."

Zhang understood and said, "Yes. Yes. Although I am a military official, I read poetry and history. How could I sentence innocent men to death just to please others?" Then he turned to the prisoners and asked them to wait. To the guards, he said, "I shall ask the prison guards to release them at once."

But it was not so easy. As he was writing his conclusions, he received a court bulletin, an urgent imperial edict. He knew that it would have something to do with the case and read it quickly. Ma Shiying, the Grand Academician, had submitted a report to the crown, claiming that Zhou Biao and Lei Yanzuo had maintained illicit relations with Prince Lu. The evidence against them was clear. Ma urged the crown to execute the men at once. The bulletin likened the Donglin Party to a swarm of locusts that should be dealt with before they caused disaster. The bulletin gave the names of members of the Restoration Society, asking the emperor's permission to arrest them. The emperor had agreed and asked all *yamen* or government officials to implement the order.

Alarmed and surprised, Zhang Yaoxing sighed. Ma and Ruan had given a false report to the crown to back up their claim. From then on, any honest person could be executed.

He paused for a while then said to the prisoners, "You have my sympathy. I was going to release you but have received this edict. Not only will Zhou Biao and Lei Yanzuo be given death sentences but no one in the Donglin Party and the Restoration Society will escape punishment."

"We beg Your Excellency to save our lives," the three pleaded.

Ma's and Ruan's perversity galled Zhang Yaoxing. After some thought he said, "If you are released now, you will be arrested by another official and will certainly die. But don't worry. I have an idea." He wrote a report saying that since the charges had not been substantiated, the prisoners should be held in custody until Cai Yisuo was arrested. Then he said to the three, "The prison guard, Feng Kezong, is ambitious and wants to climb the ladder of officialdom. But he has a conscience. I shall write to him asking him not to be harsh." His letter advised the prison guard to use his common sense and not be too rigid. Zhang Yaoxing placed his hands together before his chest and said to the prisoners, "I am sorry but you will have to stay in prison for a while. I hope that your names will be cleared some day." He then withdrew and the three were sent to the cells.

When he thought about the corrupt politicians, Zhang Yaoxing felt that he could no longer stay in office; he would be ridiculed for supporting autocratic officials. He left the *yamen* and retired to his pavilion, The Pavilion of Pines in the Wind.

The colors there were a luxuriant green; when he opened the windows, pines were everywhere; it was a haven away from the workaday world. He took off his official robe, put on clothes of a Taoist and said good-bye to feudal bureaucracy.

His guards arrived a few hours later. They had arrested Cai Yisuo and he was with them. The turn of events surprised Zhang Yaoxing. He realized that once Cai had been arrested, the other three could not escape punishment. He sent the guards and his personal attendant on another mission and then privately told Cai Yisuo what had happened. Cai asked for his help. Zhang suggested that he became a priest in the Taoist faith with him. Cai agreed and they decided to hide in the mountains.

CHAPTER TWENTY-SEVEN

Seeking Help in Wuchang

SU KUNSHENG WAS one of the people who worried about Hou Chaozong's safety and wanted to help. Although a resident of Nanjing, he came from the same hometown and was an *kunqu* opera singer, like Liu Jingting the storyteller. He was over 50 years old and had a generous nature. He decided to seek help from Marshal Zuo Liangyu at Wuchang and arrived there after a long and arduous journey.

At Wuchang, he stayed in a small hotel in the main street but was unable to gain admittance to the marshal's headquarters. At the time, Zuo Liangyu was on a mission to train 300,000 troops with Yuan Jixian, the governor-general, and Huang Shu, the imperial envoy. When he returned to his barracks he would pass the hotel, so Su Kunsheng ordered a cup of wine and waited for his arrival.

As he drank, he became anxious and sang to an improvised *kunqu*. The hotel manager feared that the marshal might hear him and asked him not to sing which gave Su Kunsheng an idea. He ignored the manager's advice and sang louder.

Marshal Zuo Liangyu heard him as he rode back to the barracks and Yuan Jixian, the governor-general, asked, "Do you allow song and dance to be taught here?"

"The military code is strict. Who dares sing here?" roared Zuo.

The voice went higher just as Huang Shu pointed him out.

The marshal said angrily, "The curfew is in force. Anybody who sings in the night should be arrested." Su Kunsheng was dragged before the marshal by guards who had traced his voice to the hotel.

"Was that you singing?" Zuo Liangyu asked.

"Yes."

"The military code is strict. How dare you sing in such a high voice?" Marshal Zuo was very angry.

Su Kunsheng was not afraid and was rather pleased to be standing before the marshal. He said, "There was no other way. I risked death to sing that song. I beg your pardon, will your lordship please forgive me?"

Yuan Jixian was puzzled. "He must be drunk."

Huang Shu thought that he had sung beautifully. Marshal Zuo did not know what to do and ordered Su to be brought to the headquarters for interrogation.

Su Kunsheng was overjoyed. He willingly followed the supreme commander back to the army barracks where they decided to interrogate him straight away.

Zuo Liangyu ordered the soldiers to bring him in and when Su was asked why he sang, he said calmly, "I came from Nanjing to see the supreme commander. I had no choice but to sing loudly."

This angered Zuo Liangyu, but Yuan Jixian tried to calm him and allow the singer to tell his story; they soon realized that Su Kunsheng had come to seek help for Hou Chaozong.

Zuo Liangyu, however, was not fully convinced. "Hou Chaozong is a member of a family closely related to mine for generations. Why hasn't he written to me?"

Su Kunsheng went down on his knees and said, "Ruan Dacheng led the arrest himself. There was simply no time to write a letter."

Yuan Jixian was also unsure. "Why should we just take your word for it?"

Zuo Liangyu realized the need for urgent action and said, "I have a man here who is an old friend of Hou Chaozong. I'll ask him if he recognizes you."

The man was none other than Liu Jingting, who recognized Su Kunsheng at once; they were glad to see each other and Liu Jingting told Zuo Liangyu that Su, was a star of the *kunqu* opera and known by all.

When they heard who he was, they all nodded their approval. Zuo Liangyu thought it worthy that a singer should be so brave for a righteous cause. He told Su Kunsheng to sit down and relate in detail what had happened to Hou Chaozong.

Su's story outraged him and Zuo said to Yuan and Huang, "Should we not be angry when we hear how corrupt the imperial government has become?"

Yuan Jixian said that other people were being persecuted besides members of the Donglin Party and the Restoration Society. Ma Shiying and Ruan Dacheng had prevented Concubine Tong from becoming a queen. They intended installing another concubine. Huang added that Emperor Chongzhen's son was now in prison although the emperor had chosen him to be the crown prince, and he was acknowledged by all the ministers. Ma and Ruan treated him as an impostor.

These events made Zuo Liangyu even more irate and he cried out, "We have fought on battlefields to safeguard the state, but the crown itself will ruin the country. Only Marshal Shi Kefa is honest. He is hampered by Ma Shiying and Ruan Dacheng, and is unable to do anything about it. How can I alone beat off the Qing Army and restore Chinese rule in the central plains?" He stamped his feet and said, "I am at the end of my tether and now I shall have to offend the crown."

He asked Yuan Jixian to write a report to the crown denouncing Ma and Ruan for misgovernment. Yuan Jixian wrote it immediately and after reading it Zuo said to Huang, "This must be made an official document if we are to get rid of Ma and Ruan who are too close to the emperor."

Liu Jingting too voiced his support, which surprised Zuo Liangyu. He said, "You asked me not to use the army a few days back. Why do you agree with its use now?"

"Zhu Yousong is now the emperor. The times are different."

Zuo Liangyu signed the completed document and Yuan Jixian said, "This is a very important matter. It would be better if He Tengjiao, the newly appointed Huguang governor, signed it as well."

Zuo Liangyu knew what sort of man He was and said, "He is an obstinate character. There is no need to tell him in advance. Just put his name down, that's all." Yuan followed Zuo's instructions and signed his own name. Huang also signed. Zuo Liangyu told him to write the document that night. He would sent it to the crown by special mail and launch a punitive expedition. Yuan thought this unwise.

"The post may be delayed and Ma and Ruan are searching the capital for documents. If it falls into their hands they will destroy it and no one will read it."

"In that case we will have to get someone to carry it," Zuo Liangyu said.

"It's a bad situation. I have heard that Ma and Ruan secretly ordered General Du Hongyu to build defenses in Anqing to stop our army coming down by the east. If the document falls into their hands, the messenger will definitely be killed," Huang Shu Said.

"What can we do, then?" asked Zuo.

Liu Jingting spoke up, "I can act as the messenger. I will go."

Yuan Jixian and Huang Shu respected Liu Jingting's offer. "He acts like Jing Ke who made an attempt on the life of Emperor Qin Shihuang. We shall bid farewell to you."

Liu Jingting said, "My life is really worth nothing. As long as I can help the Marshal Zuo to achieve great deeds, I shall be happy."

Zuo Liangyu was very pleased and said, "I bow down to such a righteous man." He ordered a bottle of wine to be brought in and knelt down saying, "Please drink this!"

Liu Jingting also knelt and in a ceremony, similar to that accorded to a departed soul, they bade farewell to each other. They all wept; Liu Jingting said good-bye and left without looking back.

Zuo Liangyu said loudly, "A righteous man. A chivalrous man who upholds justice."

CHAPTER TWENTY-EIGHT

The Army of Zuo on
an Easterly Expedition

THE PUNITIVE EXPEDITIONARY force led by Zuo Liangyu drove eastward but the government of the young emperor, Zhu Yousong knew nothing of it. The emperor and the bureaucracy in Nanjing City were obsessed by power, wealth and their own existence.

The year was 1646. It was the first anniversary of the death of Emperor Chongzhen of the Ming Dynasty (who hung himself when Beijing fell on March 19). The new emperor was required to mark the occasion and an order had been given for an altar on a raised platform to be set up on the outskirts of the city. For the ritual ceremony, offerings—joss sticks, flowers, candles and wine—were laid on the long table.

Ma Shiying and Yang Longyou arrived in mourning clothes. As grand academician, Ma virtually held all the reins of power and he was obliged to attend the ceremony, but he was there to enjoy a spring outing rather than to pay respects to the late emperor.

Marshal Shi Kefa, who was also in mourning and stricken with grief, asked the old ceremonial official whether all the civilian and military officials were present. Although there were only a few minor officials besides Ma and Yang he was told that everyone was there.

Ma Shiying, who wanted the ceremony over and done with, said, "Since everybody is here, let's start." The old ceremonial official began and the only sound heard was that of people going down on their knees to prostrate themselves before the late emperor. The ceremony ended quickly and Shi Kefa felt sad and wept bitterly. The old ceremonial official also wept.

Ruan Dacheng arrived when the ceremony had ended and pretended to weep. He said, "On the anniversary of the death of the late emperor, Ruan Dacheng is here in tears to kowtow to the emperor." As there was no response from the others, he quickly regained his composure, and asked Ma Shiying whether he had performed the ceremony.

Ma said that he had, and Ruan Dacheng walked to the altar and kowtowed four times, crying loudly, "The late emperor left the country in ruins like a family split up. The people responsible are members of the Donglin Party. We are the few surviving loyal officials. The others have scattered. I weep for you, emperor. Why did you realize the fact so late in your life?"

Ma Shiying thought that Ruan was making a spectacle of himself and displaying hypocrisy. He dragged him to one side saying, "Do not overdo it. It would be better if you stood up and took a bow."

Shi Kefa saw this, sighed, and shook his head in disapproval. He said in a low voice, "This is a farce." He bade his farewells and left the scene.

After the ceremony Ma Shiying said to Yang Longyou and Ruan Dacheng, "We are all going to the city the same way, why no go together?" They swapped their mourning clothes for official robes, then slowly rode back to town, enjoying the spring scenery and praising each other's achievements.

When they arrived at Ji'e Lane, Ma Shiying invited them into his house to look at the peonies.

Yang Longyou realized just how close the other two were and did not want to be with them; he left saying that he had an appointment. Ruan Dacheng, on the other hand, seized the opportunity and said that he would be honored.

The pair went straight into the garden and Ruan Dacheng gushed that the peonies were truly beautiful. Pleased, Ma called his attendants to lay the table and prepare a feast.

As they drank and talked, they became boastful. Ma Shiying laughed as he said, "We bid farewell to Emperor Chongzhen today. Tomorrow we shall ask the new emperor to sit on the throne. This accords with the saying: 'When a new king is crowned, he brings to the court his own favorites and expels those of his predecessor.'"

Keen on gathering information, Ruan Dacheng asked if the court had taken any new measures; he had been busy making an inspection along the river.

"We have been considering the case of the crown prince. What do you think about it?"

"The case is obvious. It should be easy to handle," said Ruan Dacheng who liked to think that he was astute.

"Why is it so easy?"

Ruan Dacheng mumbled, "Why is it that as veteran chief minister, your power is so great that you can subvert the kingdom from within and without? Doesn't this stem from flattery and patronage?"

Although Ma Shiying did not understand what he said, he nodded and replied, "That is true. That is true."

"Acclaim and approval are important. If the crown prince is acknowledged as the real son of the later emperor, what will become of the new king whom we have supported?"

Ma Shiying understood. "Yes. yes. The crown prince should be kept locked up so that he won't have a chance to mislead the masses. What about Concubine Tong? She is mounting an appeal and demanding to be made queen."

"She was the Emperor's concubine. Her appeals must be rejected."

"Yes. Yes. I have already selected another beauty for the court. Concubine Tong must not be allowed access." Ma Shiying asked Ruan about members of the Donglin Party and the Restoration Society who had been arrested but not questioned.

Ruan Dacheng showed his true nature by arguing that they were natural opponents who could not be tolerated. They should be weeded out and killed.

Ma Shiying agreed that this seemed a sensible solution and turned to an attendant. "Get extra large cups. We shall drink to our heart's content."

A guard appeared and said that Zuo Liangyu had sent a petition to Zhu Yousong. Ma Shiying read it carefully. He read with anger: the petition declared the two, Ruan and Ma, should be impeached. Zuo had listed seven crimes and demanded that the new emperor order their execution. Another guard came in with the request to launch a punitive expedition against them. Ma Shiying managed to calm down, but the second message frightened him and he turned to Ruan Dacheng. "The eastward drive of Zuo's troops is dangerous. We will not be able to resist them." He rubbed his hands and said, "Must we stretch out our necks so that Zuo can cut off our heads?"

Ruan Dacheng thought and said, "We have no choice but to ask the three generals, Huang Degong, Liu Liangzuo and Liu Zeqing to dispatch their troops to the riverside. There they can block the Zuo's advancing army."

"But if the Qing army crosses the river, who is to resist them then?" Ma was puzzled.

Ruan Dacheng quietly asked, "If the Qing army comes, do you still wish to make a stand against them?"

"What else can I do but resist?"

"You have two options."

"What are they?"

Ruan stepped forward and said "run", and then knelt down saying "surrender".

Ma Shiying understood and agreed. "You are right. I would rather kneel down before the Qing army than to be killed by Zuo." He added that he would send the three generals to the riverside to resist Zuo, but it occurred to him that he needed a plausible reason for this.

As usual Ruan Dacheng had a ready answer. "The three generals are loyal to Prince Zhu Yousong. Tell them that Zuo comes to support Prince Lu. This should alarm them enough to send troops to fight him."

"Yes, we are all in this together. You must urge the three generals to resist Zuo or our fate will be sealed."

Ruan Dacheng agreed to go at once but Ma Shiying said in a low voice, "Wait. The cabinet ministers, Gao Xintu and Jiang Yueguang, have colluded with the insurgents. They have been removed from office. Zhou Biao and Lei Yanzuo are in prison but we must not allow them to become agents. Otherwise, they can be helped by outside forces. Should we kill them at once?"

"Yes. Yes."

Ma Shiying excused himself after seeing Ruan off quickly, and returned to his study.

The guard asked Ruan Dacheng what should they do with the messenger.

"Send him to the ministry to be executed." After saying that, Ruan Dacheng was about to mount his horse when it occurred to him that this would not look good if the three generals failed in their stand against Zuo. If the messenger were killed it would close the way to negotiations. He told the guard to ask Feng, the prison guard, to lock him up, then he left the city.

Liu Jingting, the messenger, was dragged to the cells. He was a brave man, but it was the first time that he had been behind bars. Shackled hand and foot, he found it unbearable, but in the night he heard Hou Chaozong's voice in the next cell. "Is it really you, Mr. Hou?"

"Is it you Liu Jingting?"

Hou Chaozong had been imprisoned for two weeks and as there was no evidence against him, no verdict had been given. He was anxious, and each day had seemed like a year, but seeing Liu Jingting was like meeting an old friend in a strange place. They spoke about what had happened before they were imprisoned. Hou was grateful when he heard of the efforts made on his behalf but he also felt that he was the cause of much trouble.

When Hou Chaozong, Chen Dingsheng and Wu Ciwei learned of Zuo Liangyu's advance, they were worried. Chen pointed out that if the army arrived the three of them would have less chance of survival. Wu Ciwei thought that a military officer such as Zuo Liangyu could not really help them.

While talking, they heard footsteps and voices. The prison guard was rounding up men for execution. Zhou Biao and Lei Yanzuo were to be executed that night. The three actually felt a sense of security when they realized it was not their turn. They pumped Liu Jingting for news but he only knew that officials were rounding up men everywhere. Chen Dingsheng and Wu Ciwei were surprised.

"Who are they rounding up?"

"I've heard they were arresting Huang Shu, the imperial envoy, Yuan Jixian, the governor-general, and Zhang Yaoxing, veteran imperial guard official. Many scholars have been arrested, but I can remember only a few names."

Hou Chaozong was concerned. "Why don't you try?"

"There were so many. I can recall only those with familiar names, Mao Xiang, Fang Yizhi, Liu Cheng, Shen Shoumin, Shen Shizhu and Yang Tingshu."

"So many!" Chen Dingsheng was shocked.

Wu Ciwei remarked that the prison would become the new gathering place for intellectuals.

Zuo Liangyu met with Huang Shu and He Tengjiao to urge them to join with him in the drive eastward. Yuan Jixian had already arrived at Hukou and they were discussing how to take Nanjing. They did not know that Ma Shiying and Ruan Dacheng had sent Huang Degong to block their advance at Banji. He Tengjiao, who was a fellow townsman of Ma Shiying, advanced half way and then returned to where he came from. Zuo Liangyu's son, Zuo Menggeng, intended to seize cities and townships to take more territories, but disobeyed orders for troop deployment.

As a result Huang Degong defeated the army's vanguard and retreat followed. A large fire broke out in Jiujiang, which Zuo Menggeng occupied, cutting off the retreat of Yuan Jixian.

Zuo Liangyu could neither advance nor retreat and had no explanation for the harm done to Yuan Jixian. He pulled out his sword and wanted to take his life, but Huang Shu successfully stopped him. However, immediately afterwards, Zuo suffered a heart attack, spat blood and died. News of his death spread and the army dispersed. Yuan Jixian did not know what to do and Huang Shu, aware that they would be sought by the court in Nanjing, said that they stood no chance of survival if arrested. Their best chance lay in returning to Wuchang with He Tengjiao. Yuan Jixian agreed and they went there together.

Su Kunsheng was the only person left in the army barracks. He stood by the dead commander, Zuo Liangyu, weeping over the body and burning candles and joss stick, and waited patiently for Zuo's son to come and mourn over his father.

CHAPTER TWENTY-NINE

The Southern Capital in Great
Confusion and Disorder

THE ARMY COMMANDED by Huang Degong, Liu Liangzuo and Liu Zeqing abandoned their defensive positions along the Yellow River. It had been deployed to block the advance of Zuo Liangyu, but the Qing army took advantage of the situation and crossed the Yellow River on April 21, 1645 and marched on to Huaiyang. Marshal Shi Kefa defended Yangzhou with fewer than 3,000 men. Their morale was low and many thought of deserting. Shi, a great patriot, wept. Blood flowed from his eyes and stained his armor. Deeply moved by his patriotism, his troops resolved to make a stand and defend Yangzhou.

Panic and confusion reigned in Nanjing even before the Qing army crossed the Yellow River. Rumor had it that the Qing army had surrounded Yangzhou and army intelligence revealed that the river side of the city had no defenses. With the collapse of Nanjing imminent, Emperor Zhu Yousong expected to see Ma Shiying and Ruan Dacheng, but they were not to be found. The emperor knew that he could no longer retain the throne. He gathered the royal treasure, his favorite concubines and prepared to flee. The city gates were opened to allow him passage to a safe haven. He had not told his officials that he was leaving.

At night the streets were quiet. Ma Shiying was still in the capital, hiding in his backyard. He asked his favorite concubines to pack and entered the palace when he learnt that the emperor had already gone. He later tried to flee the city with ten cartloads of possessions.

Many of those who had suffered persecution or exploitation under his corrupt rule waited for him, some with clubs in hand. He had not gone far before the hostile crowd confronted him and accused him of causing poverty and looting the national treasury. There were cries of "stop him" and he was beaten with the clubs. He fell to the ground unable to move. Young people stripped him of his robes while others plundered his possessions.

Ruan Dacheng wished to know what Ma Shiying planned. He was more cunning than Ma and had already packed his possessions and prepared his womenfolk. He had planned much earlier to flee from the invading Qing army, but wanted to know whether Ma had chosen to surrender or leave.

Passing the Ji'e Lane he tripped over Ma who was lying on the ground. They spoke to each other and when Ruan Dacheng learned that Ma had lost his money and position, he deserted his mentor and hurried back to his valuables and family.

To his dismay he found that a crowd armed with clubs had already dragged away the women and plundered his wealth. They were shouting that the spoil should be divided equally when Ruan shouted, "How dare you steal my personal possessions!"

The crowd then realized that he was Ruan Dacheng and beat and stripped him. They spared his life but decided to burn down his house. Ma Shiying and Ruan Dacheng were left where they lay.

At the time, Yang Longyou, wearing simple clothes, rode a horse into the street. It was May 10th, a good day for him to start an inspection as the newly appointed governor of Suzhou and Songjiang. He had left his books, paintings and curios at the painter Lan Ying's place, The House of Enchanting Fragrance; Lan Ying had been instructed to bring them to him later. He was feeling pleased with himself when a servant told him about the rumors. The military situation in the north was critical and the emperor and prime minister had fled in the night. He deplored the situation and decided that he would have to leave the city.

But his horse was held by two men in the street. They were groaning and the servants pointed out that it was Ma Shiying and Ruan Dacheng. Yang Longyou looked at them and dismounted. "What happened to you?"

Ma Shiying managed to say that he had been robbed and beaten. Ruan Dacheng claimed that he had come to his rescue and met the same fate.

"Your servants should have looked after your property and wives. What happened to them?"

Ma Shiying said, "They scattered. They were no help at all."

Ma and Ruan were naked and Yang ordered the servants to unpack clothes for them. Then he gave them a horse to share and they left the city.

The servants told Yang not to go with them as they had too many enemies. Yang took their advice, tightened the reins and galloped quickly away. Ma and Ruan were left to their own devices. On his way, Yang Longyou saw Kou Baimen, Zheng Tuoniang, Shen Gongxian and Zhang Yanzhu, who were also fleeing from the palace. They told him that Li Xiangjun had gone to The House of Enchanting Fragrance. Yang Longyou gave up any thought of taking up his new post and made his way to The House of Enchanting Fragrance. He intended to collect his pictures and books and flee to his hometown, Guiyang.

When he arrived, he banged on the door, crying, "Open up, Open up."

Lan Ying opened the door and was surprised to see him. "Why have you returned, your lordship?"

"The situation in the north is critical. The emperor and his officials have fled. I no longer have a job and am collecting my things to return to my hometown in plain dress."

"Li Xiangjun has just returned and told me of her experiences." He turned his head and said, "Xiangjun, look who is here."

Li Xiangjun was surprised to see Yang and asked him how he

was. Yang Longyou had no wish to speak to her and said that he was there to say good-bye; he would be away for a long time.

Xiangjun was astonished. "Where are you going?"

"Guiyang, my hometown."

Li Xiangjun's face fell, tears trickled down her cheeks and she sighed. "Hou Chaozong is still in prison and you are going home. I am alone and there is no one to help me."

Yang felt no sympathy and said, "It is a time of confusion and disorder. Even father and son are not able to look after one another. It is dangerous and you will have to make your own decisions. No one can help you."

At this moment Su Kunsheng arrived at the courtyard and pushed open the door. He saw Yang Longyou and Li Xiangjun and asked Yang if he knew where Hou Chaozong was.

Yang, who was in a hurry to leave, said, "Brother Hou is still in prison."

Li Xiangjun asked Su Kunsheng where he had been. Su told her about his trip to Wuchang. He had returned the night before and after hearing about the unrest went to the prison. The gates were open and it was empty. He was worried that Hou Chaozong might have been executed.

Li Xiangjun wept bitterly, tugged at his clothes and said, "Please help me to find him." Su did not know what to say.

Yang Longyou was about to leave and said, "Xiangjun, your old teacher is here, everything will be all right. I am leaving now." He turned to Lan Ying. "Do you want to come?"

"My home is in Hangzhou. Why should I go to Guiyang with you?"

"In that case, good-bye." Yang mounted his horse and left.

CHAPTER THIRTY

The Collapse of
the Hongguang Regime

AFTER THE EMPEROR left Nanjing, his attendants disappeared one by one and he was left with the eunuch Han Zanzhou. They traveled to the Duke of Wei's residence but were not recognized and thrown out. They went on to the army barracks of Huang Degong in Wuhu.

In the Battle of Banji, Huang had defeated Zuo Liangyu. He was now defending Wuhu, aided by his trusted lieutenant, Tian Xiong. When a soldier announced the emperor's arrival, Huang had to go and see for himself. He went out of the barrack gate and was greeted straight away by the emperor who asked, "How are you, General Huang?" Huang lifted his head and saw that it really was the emperor. He knelt down at once and said, "Long live Your Majesty! Please come inside. Allow me kowtow to you."

The eunuch, Han Zanzhou, saw that the emperor would not be rejected and escorted him into the camp where he sat him on a chair. Huang Degong kowtowed nine times and knelt three times in accordance with the proper ceremony. He asked the emperor why had he been traveling incognito and the emperor told him about the dangerous situation in Nanjing. "Things have come to such a sad state that my only hope is that you will protect me."

Huang Degong found this difficult to accept. He wept bitterly and said, "If you were in the palace, I could fight for you in the name of the crown. As you have left, you have given up power. I am not equipped to wage a war and I cannot retreat. When you left the palace, the reasons for the empire went out the door with you."

Emperor Zhu Yousong, however, was not really concerned about the empire, said, "It is my own wish to abdicate the throne."

Huang was astounded. "How could you abandon the throne? The empire belongs to all ancestral emperors."

Emperor Zhu Yousong attempted to shift the responsibility to him. "Whether I abandon it or not depends on you entirely."

Huang Degong was left with no choice. He felt obliged to protect the emperor. He arranged for the emperor to stay in the back camp and sat in the barracks thinking about his responsibility. To protect 15 provinces and the 300-year-old Ming empire was no small task. How could he live up to it?

The entire army was put on alert and a messenger went round the camp with a bell and wooden stick to warn of an emergency. Huang Degong consulted his trusted lieutenant, Tian Xiong, who, on this occasion, disagreed. He said to Huang, "I think this emperor is unlucky. If the Qing army crosses the river, everyone will surrender. You must see how the wind blows, so to speak, and hoist your sail accordingly." Huang would not accept this and Tian said nothing further.

A soldier announced the arrival of Liu Liangzuo and Liu Zeqing and their army. Huang greeted them. As the two Lius dismounted they said, "Big brother, you have a treasure, but you are keeping it a secret."

"What treasure?" Huang did not know what they were talking about.

Liu Zeqing said openly, "Emperor Zhu Yousong."

Lowering his voice Liu Liangzuo asked, "When will you present it? And why not today?"

"If we sent the emperor to the Qing army, we would be given

dukedoms, wouldn't that be marvelous?"

Huang Degong realized their intentions and beat them soundly with his double whip shouting, "Traitor! Renegade!"

Liu Liangzuo tried to calm him. "We are all brothers, don't rebuke us."

Huang Degong cried, "You don't even recognize the monarch. How can I recognize you as a brother?" He held his whip high.

Tian Xiong who was standing behind Huang ridiculed him in a low voice saying that he was a stupid ass who did not know when and how to act. He took a bow and shot Huang in the lower leg saying that he had come to end the argument. Huang had not expected this and fell to the ground. Tian Xiong returned to the back camp and personally carried out the emperor who protested and beat him with his fists. He threw the monarch on the ground before the two generals, saying, "I present to you the emperor."

The generals thanked him and took the emperor away. Tian, ignoring Huang's abuse, followed, taking a bag of personal belongings. Huang Degong, who knew that the cause was lost and that he was unable to do anything, killed himself with his own sword.

After Huang Degong's death, Marshal Shi Kefa committed suicide by jumping into the river. Earlier he had resisted the Qing assaults but the city fell after they ran out of provisions. Shi had intended to commit suicide then, but decided against, for he knew he was use to the Ming Dynasty dead. He decided to go to Nanjing to help prop up the regime. He escaped from Yangzhou by lowering himself down the city wall on a rope and crossed the river on a small boat. At Longtan, he met the old ceremonial official, who had fled from Nanjing. He told Shi of the confusion and disorder in Nanjing, and said that the emperor had already fled.

Shi Kefa had come to the end of his tether. He did not know where the emperor was and wept bitterly. He took off his cap and gown and ended his life by jumping into the river.

The old ceremonial official wept as he stood watching. Several men appeared. They were Liu Jingting, Hou Chaozong, Chen Dingsheng and Wu Ciwei; these men had just escaped from jail after the collapse of the Hongguang regime. Liu Jingting and Hou

Chaozong decided to return to their hometown in Henan on the central plains, and Chen Dingsheng and Wu Ciwei were sending them off.

When the old ceremonial official told the four what had happened, grief overtook them and they paid homage to Marshal Shi Kefa. Chen Dingsheng went down on his knees to pay his last respects while Hou Chaozong thought of the good services Shi had rendered. He wept bitterly and after some time Liu Jingting persuaded him to go.

Hou Chaozong looked at the currents in the river and asked where they could go. In the north there were columns of smoke; there was no point in setting out that way.

"As you are not going north, why not come with us to south China?" Chen Dingsheng suggested.

Hou Chaozong saw the situation clearly. "This is a time of turmoil. We cannot depend on one another forever. It would be far better if each of us went his own way, for there is no peace in the country."

"What are your plans?" Wu Ciwei asked.

"I have discussed it with Liu Jingting. We shall seek an ancient temple deep in the mountains somewhere and from there see what happens, then return home later."

The old ceremonial official said that he was going to Qixia Mountain, a secluded place, and suggested that they went with him.

Hou Chaozong decided to try it and when Chen Dingsheng and Wu Ciwei saw that they had settled on a plan, they made their farewells.

The old ceremonial official intended taking Marshal Shi Kefa's clothes to Meihua Hill where Shi used to inspect his troops. They would bury the clothes and erect a memorial later. Hou Chaozong thought that he was a worthy person and asked him why he was going to Qixia Mountain.

"Officials held a funeral service in memory of the late emperor a few days ago. It was done in a perfunctory manner so I asked the city fathers for donations of money and food for a proper service; the confusion stopped us holding it. I am taking the food and money to the high priests in Qixia Mountain to perform the service there."

His good intentions won the respect and admiration of Hou Chaozong and Liu Jingting. The three started their journey to Qixia Mountain.

CHAPTER THIRTY-ONE

Entering the Priesthood

AFTER YANG LONG you left, Li Xiangjun begged and implored Su Kunsheng to take her with him on his search for Hou Chaozong.

Su Kunsheng thought about it and said, "It is difficult. Hou Chaozong did not go to The House of Enchanting Fragrance after he left jail. This means that he fled; he could be anywhere in the country."

Xiangjun said firmly, "I shall go to the four corners of the earth to find him."

Lan Ying interrupted them. "The army is in the northeast. Hou would not go there. He could only go to the southeast which is mountainous."

"I will travel across mountains and along unknown paths to find him."

Moved by her determination, Su Kunsheng said that he would take her along. He was looking for somewhere to go himself but he had no idea where they would end up.

Just then Lan Ying walked to the balustrade, pointed to the east and said, "Qixia Mountain is a secluded place where we can all avoid the army. I am going there to study Taoism under Zhang Yaoxing, the veteran imperial guard who abandoned his career to enter the Taoist priesthood. We could go together and perhaps we might find Hou Chaozong."

Su Kunsheng thought that it was a good idea and asked Xiangjun to pack. She followed them out of the town.

When they came to Baiyun Temple, Lan Ying found Zhang Yaoxing. He stayed there and Su and Xiangjun traveled on asking about Hou Chaozong at all the temples.

At dusk they came to the Baozhen Nunnery and Su Kunsheng knocked on the door. He was surprised and delighted to meet Bian Yujing, the head of the nunnery and an old friend. The happy encounter was like a miracle. Bian Yujing asked them both to stay and as they had nowhere else to go; they were pleased.

Dressed in a straw hat, coat and sandals, Su helped out by gathering firewood. Xiangjun saw him take on the menial task and asked Bian if she could sew or mend.

Bian Yujing did not have anything for her but said that on July 15th they were holding Zhong Yuan Festival and the people of the village wanted to hold a ceremony in honor of Empress Zhou. She could help them make the banners.

Li Xiangjun was eager to help. After she had washed her hands and burnt incense, she began sewing the banners.

There was a knock on the door and someone asked who it was.

Outside were the old ceremonial official, Liu Jingting and Hou Chaozong, who had gone to the nunnery to ask for accommodation.

Naturally, the nuns were cautious about receiving guests at such an hour and, when the old ceremonial official asked permission to stay, they told him that a nunnery could not allow male travelers to stay overnight.

Liu Jingting pointed out that they were not priests, but the nuns were adamant; the rules laid down by ancestral nuns did not allow travelers to stay in the nunnery.

They were unyielding and Hou Chaozong, without realizing that he had missed his chance of seeing Li Xiangjun, said that they should look elsewhere.

They went their way and came upon a Taoist priest, who the

official greeted. "We are on Qixia Mountain to hold a sacrificial funeral offering. Can we leave our bags in your temple for the night?"

The priest looked hard at Hou Chaozong and recognized a familiar face. He called out, "Are you Hou Chaozong of Henan?"

"If he is not Hou Chaozong, who else could he be?" Liu Jingting replied.

The priest heard Liu's voice and said, "Could that be Liu Jingting?"

"Yes."

Hou Chaozong recognized Ding Jizhi. "Why have you become a Taoist priest?"

Ding Jizhi explained why he had left the court and gone to the nearby Caizhen Temple, which was close to the place where he would enter the priesthood. He invited them to stay at the temple and they accepted. They bade farewell to the old ceremonial official who went on to arrange the ritual service for the Zhong Yuan Festival on July 15th in the White Cloud Temple. In the meanwhile, Hou and Liu followed Ding Jizhi to the Caizhen Temple.

At the festival, Zhang Yaoxing, head of the White Cloud Temple, wanted to erect a large alter for the service in honor of the late Emperor Chongzhen.

On the day, he told Cai Yishou and Lan Ying to be ready and the old ceremonial official came as well. Villagers, men and women, young and old brought joss sticks, incense, sacrificial wine, sacrificial paper money and embroidered banners for the occasion. They filled the square. Cai and Lan had asked Zhang to supervise the service. Dressed in a Taoist robe, Zhang climbed to the alter on which there was a wooden tablet with the name of the late emperor. On the left were tablets with the names of civilian officials who had died during the fall of Beijing. Tablets on the right bore the names of military officials. To the sound of music, Zhang Yaoxing read the funeral oration and villagers burst into tears. The old ceremonial official remarked that the people were showing their true feelings unlike the officials outside the Taiping City Gate. The service ended; villagers ate the funeral meal and then dispersed.

Bian Yujing had brought Li Xiangjun and a few nuns to decorate banners in honor of the Empress Zhou. They greeted Zhang Yaoxing in the lecture hall.

Hou Chaozong came to the service with Ding Jizhi and spotted a familiar figure in the corridor. There were many people there but he looked more closely and realized that it was Xiangjun. He pushed through the crowd and pulled her out.

"Brother Hou, it's you. I have longed for you."

Hou Chaozong pointed to the fan and said, "Look at the peach blossom on the fan. You wrote it in blood, how can I ever repay you?"

The couple spoke of their yearning for each other, but Ding Jizhi tugged at Hou's arms. Bian Yujing warned Xiangjun, "You must not show your feelings in this way. The supervising priest is at the altar."

But the couple would not be parted and ignored her. Zhang Yaoxing saw what was going on and became very angry. Banging the table with a wooden gavel he said, "How dare you flirt here?" He walked down from the altar, took the peach blossom fan, tore it apart, and threw it away.

"The altar is a sacred place. How dare you express your love to each other here?"

Cai Yisuo, who was standing behind Zhang Yaoxing, recognized Hou and Li. He said to Zhang, "It is Hou Chaozong. You know him."

"Who is this woman?"

Lan Ying identified Li Xiangjun and described how the couple had been living apart. Hou Chaozong recognized Zhang and thanked him sincerely for his help.

"So you are Mr. Hou. I am pleased that you have escaped from jail. I became a priest on your account, I hope you realize that."

"I knew nothing of this."

"I had a similar experience," Cai Yishou said, "But I'll tell you about it at a better time."

Lan Ying told Hou Chaozong how he and Li Xiangjun had searched for him. Hou Chaozong said that he and Xiangjun were deeply grateful and he again thanked Su Kunsheng and Liu Jingting.

"After we return home to Henan, we shall surely pay back our debt."

When Zhang Yaoxing heard this, he said loudly, "Why are you talking in this manner? This is a time of supreme crisis and you talk of love, it is ridiculous."

Hou Chaozong refuted him, "The bond between a man and a woman is a most important human relationship. Separations and reunions are critical moments in life. To be sad or happy on such occasions is natural to all people."

Zhang Yaoxing accused him of being stupid. "At this time of crisis where is our nation? Where is our home? Where is the emperor? Where is our father? Why do you only think of the flesh or the petty short life of man and wife?"

Zhang's concerns struck a chord with Hou and he thanked him for enlightening him. His views changed and he decided to follow Zhang's teaching and forgo earthly pursuits. He became an ascetic and entered priesthood as the pupil of Ding Jizhi while Li Xiangjun became a daughter of the Taoist faith and the pupil of Bian Yujing. Their romance ended.

CHAPTER THIRTY-TWO

Search for the Hermits
in Deep Mountain

THREE YEARS AFTER these events, Su Kunsheng earned a living as a firewood man, and Liu Jingting worked as a fisherman. The old ceremonial official lived near Yanziji where he acted as a ritual master of ceremonies. This involved drinking and dining at sacrificial offerings.

One day he went to the mountain where he met Su and Liu and gave them the wine and food obtained from one of these ceremonies. They drank three cups of wine and became merry, each singing a song to the accompaniment of a stringed instrument.

They were being sentimental, applauding their own performances and talking non-stop when a policeman from the Shangyuan County magistrate arrived. The policeman, Xu Qingjun, was the son of the Duke of the State of Wei, Ming Dynasty. Born into an aristocratic family, he had not fared well after the collapse of the Ming regime. He became a local policeman and had been ordered to search out and call on hermits, who were formerly officials of the Ming Dynasty.

395

When he saw the revelers, one dressed as a fisherman and another as firewood cutter, he realized from their stance and dignity that they were not ordinary laborers. He was sure they must have been men of high caliber, who were now living as hermits. He asked them if this was the case. The three denied it and asked Xu Qingjun why he was looking for hermits.

"Don't you know that the Ministry of Rites have filed a report to the crown to look for hermits, men who were formerly officials of the Ming Dynasty. A proclamation have been issued. No hermits have reported so far and we have been sent to take them to a government office. I think you are hermits and I would like you to accompany me."

The old ceremonial official said, "Only literary men live on the mountain and they will not leave it."

Su Kunsheng and Liu Jingting added that they were singers of *kunqu* opera who had become fishermen and firewood cutters. They would be of no use to the government.

Xu Qingjun said, "Literary men have talents and have to submit to circumstances. Some left the mountain three years back to become officials. Now I am looking for people like you."

The old ceremonial official was outraged. "Looking for hermits for the benefit of the court! They should be invited to work for the court instead of being hunted down. You are merely an underling engaged in an unworthy task."

"This is not my doing. Here is a warrant." Xu Qingjun took out the warrant and after reading it Su Kunsheng said that it looked genuine. Liu Jingting thought that they should leave and ignored the policeman's request. They walked rapidly away in different directions. Xu Qingjun did not know whom to follow and could not catch either of them. He left the mountain, but did not give up hope. He went to the woods and streams again to look for them.

Here, the story ends, with the policeman still looking for the hermits unsuccessfully. His search goes on still.